Rivals
OF
Sea AND Sky

RIVALS
OF
SEA AND SKY

MARIANNE MOREA

CITY OWL
PRESS

RIVALS OF SEA AND SKY
The Avalon Courts, Book One

CITY OWL PRESS
www.cityowlpress.com

Cover Design by MiblArt. All stock photos licensed appropriately.

Edited by Tina Moss.

For information on subsidiary rights, please contact the publisher at info@cityowlpress.com.

Deluxe Hardback Edition ISBN: 978-1-64898-488-4

Paperback Edition ISBN: 978-1-64898-339-9

Digital Edition ISBN: 978-1-64898-338-2

CITY OWL PRESS
Escape Your World ♦ Get Lost in Ours

For the ones who look at fireflies and wonder what if...

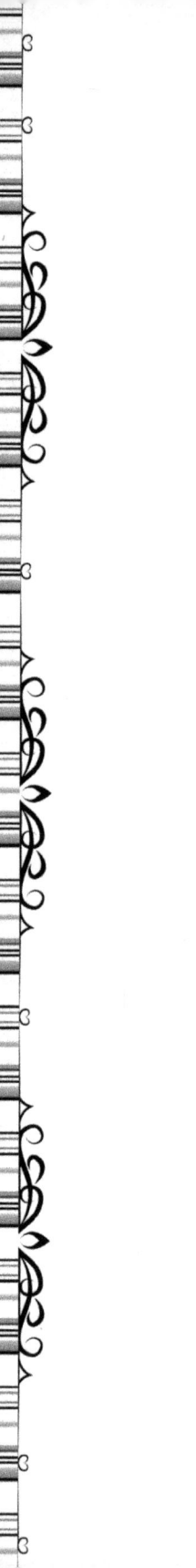

Come Fairies, take me out of this dull world, for I would ride with you upon the wind and dance upon the mountains like a flame!

WILLIAM BUTLER YEATS

CHAPTER

One

"LOITERING in the corridor won't make the hours pass, little dove. Best you come in and have your say."

I hesitated before climbing the last few stone steps to Merlin's chambers. He was the only one who called me *little dove*. Part endearment —part reminder of my duty—and a burden I felt more now than ever. "Eden Aossi, heir to the Seelie throne and future ruler of the Summer Court," I mumbled the words I'd heard far too often under my breath. "In other words, a royal dove in a gilded cage."

The heavy door was ajar, and it opened the rest of the way on its own. I grudgingly stepped over the threshold. "Why do you always assume I have an ulterior motive? Can't I pay a visit to my favorite tutor?"

The grizzled old wizard stood at his brazier. He turned from his latest potion with his waist-length beard tucked safely away from the low flame. Still, his eyes shone clear and as bright blue as the summer sky in the Seelie realm.

"You've been sneaking into my quarters since you could barely see over my worktable," he chuckled. "I can still hear your thin, reedy voice, asking question after question." His voice turned higher pitched, light-heartedly mimicking my childhood voice. "Where does the sun go at night? Why do the waves never stay on shore? Could I turn day into night and then back again?" His forehead wrinkled. "Your relentless curiosity gave your mother no choice. It was either make me your tutor—or jail us both."

I lifted a clear vessel from his worktable, holding it so its bright yellow contents caught the firelight. "We both know my mother doesn't deal in 'no choice'. Tianna's decisions are always calculated to her benefit. She knew exactly what she was doing."

Merlin didn't reply. He simply took the clear flagon from my hand and put it back in its holder. Still, the old druid wasn't wrong. Like everyone in the Summer Court, Merlin served at the pleasure of the queen. Yet, as much as he served at her pleasure, my mother understood Merlin served at his own as well. Lucky for me, he did.

Watching the man putter in his drafty space, it was no wonder his tower was on the farthest side of my mother's palace, in a keep all to its own. Merlin's simmerings were best kept as far away from the main court as possible. Both his potions, and his lack of appreciation for protocol.

"I know you as well as I know myself." He paused, and his eyes took on a faraway look. "Sometimes I wish my knowing wasn't as long or as far-reaching. Prophecy, and the weight it bears, is exhausting." His tired gaze lifted toward me. "Then again, what else can be expected of one so long in the tooth?"

Merlin wasn't Fae. He was a sorcerer, wizard, mage. The timeless druid was all the above, but even that did not explain his origins or his abilities. To be honest, I doubted even he recalled what he was and from where he hailed. His powers spanned both the human and Fae realms and were coveted by both the Seelie and Unseelie. For now, he aligned himself with the Summer Court. Or he had for as long as I remembered.

Blinking, I let my eyes adjust to the dim light. A soft screech caught my attention, and I turned toward the high beamed ceiling. Altair, Merlin's owl, sat in the highest joist, while Lyrae, his raven sister, warmed herself in the stained glass at the top of the tower.

The raven was black as night, yet her feathers held a hue of blue that gleamed in the sun. The owl was the color of wet sand, but it wasn't the beauty of his soft feathers that held me. It was the bird's eyes. Large, fathomless, and as riveting as his beak was sharp.

"My feathered friends know I'm often lost while working and have taken it upon themselves to act sentinel. Lyrae especially. Your mother likes to send spies in scholars' clothing."

"Sounds like her."

He touched a finger to the side of his nose. "What your mother's spies have yet to discover is the birds help my sight. Lyrae allows me the use of her eyes to see past the Seelie realm into Avalon whole, whereas Altair allows me to peer into the human realm. Of course, they are one means to an end. I still have my scrying bowls, or in a pinch, a good fire will do the trick."

He chuckled, closing his book of notes beside the brazier. "Now, my little dove. You're not here to discuss what the queen knows, or doesn't know, about me. Still, something tells me, she's the reason for this visit."

"Am I that obvious?"

"Only to me." Merlin headed for the hearth. The Summer Court was perpetually warm, but tower nights were cold this high up.

A cauldron hung from a metal swing, hooked to the side of the crackling flames. Leaning in, the wizard stirred its contents. "Double, double toil and trouble, fire burn and cauldron bubble." Merlin flashed a soft grin over his shoulder before touching the wooden spoon to his lips.

"Shakespeare," I replied, watching the old man. "I remember."

"The greatest of humanity's bards, at least in my opinion." He nodded, seemingly satisfied with his dinner, and tapped the spoon on the side of the black pot. "I'd ask you to share my supper, but as it was cooked in cast iron, I'd advise against it."

He was right, of course. Iron was a bane to all Fae. Toxic, if not deadly. I sat on a low couch beside the hearth, warming my hands. Merlin flourished two fingers, and a tufted chair slid to the hearth opposite me.

"You're a woman, Eden. By human calculations, you achieved your twenty-first year on your last birthday. The time for childhood escapes inside these walls is over, yet here you sit. What has your mother done for you to seek refuge with an old seer once again?"

"An old seer, but still an old friend."

He inclined his head but didn't reply. The fire crackled, and Merlin spooned his dinner into a hammered metal plate in silence. Then he placed the plate on a small wooden table to the side of the chair. Breaking off two hunks from a crusty loaf, he handed one to me. "There's cheese on the table, if you want, and small ale in the jug."

I got up for the cheese, taking the flask and two pewter mugs from the table as well. "I know you won't press, so suffice it to say I needed a place where I could think."

"Little dove, I'm too old to mince words. Has your mother arranged a husband for you?"

"Not yet, thank Danú."

"Is she boasting about something she wants from me? Last time, she demanded I do for her, what I did for Uther Pendragon."

Confused, I looked past my shoulder at him. "I don't understand."

The old man didn't reply. He didn't have to. He simply raised an eyebrow, and my jaw dropped. I couldn't fathom it. Then again, maybe I didn't want to, since I knew the Arthurian story well.

"You're saying she wanted you to transform her into the Unseelie Queen to seduce the King?"

He eyed me, neither confirming nor denying. But I knew. I shook my head in disbelief. "But she despises King Lachlan."

"She despises Queen Beira more."

With an irked exhale, I finished filling Merlin's cup. "Now that makes sense. Magically seducing the Unseelie king just to get under Beira's skin is definitely my mother's style."

"Tianna banished me to the badlands for a century because I refused. Still, it was better than the alternative."

"Death?"

He laughed, and the sound was potent and knowing. "Your mother can't kill me, child. If she could, she would have ordered my death centuries ago." He took the mug from my hand and winked. "The alternative, had I done what Tianna demanded, was a millennium of nightmare-riddled sleep. A sleep with no rest and no reprieve. Exile was a vacation."

"So now you understand why I ran here every chance I got. I love my mother, but being her daughter is too much at times. Court is..." I shrugged. "Well, you know what court is like. If not for Sorcha, I'd have asked you to help me escape."

"And where do you think you could go that your mother couldn't find you?"

I sat back on the couch. "The human world. There are plenty of Fae there, walking around unnoticed."

"Ah, but none of them are royal, and very few full *Sidhe*." He paused, watching me reach for a piece of bread and cheese. "If you're not here to escape court duties, and you're not here to warn me of another exhausting request from your mother, then why did you come tonight?"

I picked at my food. "Do you know where my sister is at this very moment?"

"Are you asking me to scry for her?"

I shook my head. "I know where she is. I meant, do you know what Sorcha's *doing* right now?"

The old druid's mouth twitched in humor. "Again, do you need me to look into the glass?"

"For the love of Danú! Sorcha is getting ready for a ball. She's preening in the mirror as we speak."

"And?"

"Merlin!" I put the pewter plate down with a bang. "Don't you think I know how petulant I sound? How ridiculous I am to complain like this at my age? Running to this place of learning, of magic and divination, to grouse about my love life, or *lack* thereof, is laughable! My mother would be disgusted if she paid me an ounce of attention."

With a grumble, I leaned on the sofa's arm with my chin in my hand. "It's not like there's anything you can do, except listen to my whining."

"Why can't you attend this ball? I'm sure your mother would insist as her heir apparent."

"The ball isn't here."

Merlin's eyebrow hiked again, but this time, his eyes were wary. "The gala is not at your mother's court?"

"It's an Unseelie ball. Sorcha got wind of it, but don't ask me how. My mother's network of spies could learn a lot from my sister and her whispering friends."

"I have no doubt."

"Anyway, they all plan to sneak out tonight and attend. As usual, she wants me to cover for her, but I'm tired of being left behind. Of always doing what's right." I sat up straight, throwing a hand in the air. "Of being the heir apparent."

"You sound like Arthur. He didn't want his destiny either. It took some persuasion."

An unladylike snort left my mouth.

"Your focus is too much on one path, Eden. Your destiny is a journey, not a destination. There are many paths. Some parallel, and at times, some in opposing directions. Whichever you choose, they all circle back to what will be."

"Me on my mother's throne." I sighed deeply. "If I'm not assassinated first."

"You Fae are so fickle. You love war, even if it makes you your own worst enemy." Food still untouched, Merlin paused, nursing his ale. "What if I told you there was a divergent path? One that didn't circle back to the throne. But instead gave you a choice."

My gaze riveted on the old sorcerer. "A choice?"

"The signs are hazy yet, but yes." He nodded. "Nothing more than a ripple in what I see when I journey with the sight. A ripple that leaves me unsettled."

"Unsettled. Why?"

His eyes met mine. "Because this ripple will cause you pain if it comes to pass."

I recoiled a bit, and he raised a staying hand. "Not physical pain, Eden. Pain of choices made, and of the consequences that follow."

"You talk as though you already know." I inhaled, considering his far away stare. "Should I be worried?"

"I have to study my tomes, charts, and the position of the stars." He drained his ale, wiping the drips from his beard. "I have to breathe in the dragon's breath and seek clarity before I can answer."

"And me?"

He smiled, getting up from his soft chair. "You, my little dove, must go to this party and forget what's expected of you. If only for a short time. You need to let destiny happen."

"What about Sorcha?" I chewed on my lip. "How will I convince her?"

"Do what the rest of the Sidhe race does when they want something."

"Cheat?"

His eyes crinkled with a laugh. "I was thinking strategize. Find out what Sorcha wants most, what she refuses to part with, and work from there."

"Well, I'm not my mother's daughter for nothing."

Merlin bent over the hearth and from the embers plucked a round stone, glowing red with heat.

"Take this but keep it hidden. If Sorcha refuses you, show her the stone. She'll know what it is, and she'll know where you got it."

I held out my hand, wincing in anticipation, but the stone was cool and smooth to the touch. "What magic is this?" I asked, rolling the stone over in my palm.

"Insurance and protection."

I raised my gaze to his. "Insurance for whom and protection from what?"

"Always questioning." He grinned, stoking the dwindling fire. "Perhaps that's why—" He shook his head, leaving the rest of his thought unspoken.

"Why, what?"

He looked at me over the fire iron in his grip. "Why the fates are still considering."

Merlin didn't explain further. Instead, he pointed to the stone in my palm. "If you are heading into the Unseelie court, you will need to get past their wards, and if discovered, you will need a swift escape. Protection and insurance."

Nodding slowly, I closed my fingers over the stone. "I'm guessing Sorcha will know what this is and where I got it because she has one of her own."

"Yes." He straightened from the fire, leaning the iron poker on the hearth.

I let a tiny smile curl around the corner of my mouth. "Such a devious old magician. You knew all along why I came."

"Blame my evasion on an old man's tender heart. I had to weigh the risks." Merlin touched my cheek. "After all, you're still my little dove."

All the earlier questions disappeared as I rolled the stone between my fingers. "How does the magic work?"

"You must keep the stone on your person. While the stone is hard to the touch, you will stay disguised. Once it softens, it's time to crush it in your palm and come home."

"Like Cinderella and her pumpkin at midnight."

The Old Druid raised an appreciative brow. "Somewhat. Only this won't leave you walking home. It will teleport you to your chambers. Unseen and unheard."

"What if Sorcha and I are discovered before the stone softens?"

"The stone will know. If you are in any danger, my magic will transport you immediately." He paused for a moment. "The fates are even more fickle than the Sidhe. Be aware and be advised. I saw a choice for you, little dove, but that doesn't mean it is a choice you'll want. It may mean sadness and loss, so guard yourself well. Especially tonight."

Certain I'd squeal giddily if I tried to speak, I pressed a kiss to his wrinkled cheek. I was going to a party, not a court summit. What could happen to set me on an unstable path tonight?

"Eden..." Merlin stepped back, but he held my shoulders. "If you find yourself at a crossroads, promise you'll come here. No hesitation. Don't make an old dragon worry. The consequences can be ghastly."

I searched his crinkled gaze. The seer knew more than he let on, but I didn't question him. If I was in true danger, he'd have never given me the stone, right?

"Eden, there is what I see, and what comes to pass. Free will isn't just a human concern. The Sidhe possess it as well, more than any other Fae. So, promise me, you'll come here."

I didn't know what crossroads he saw ahead, but I couldn't tell him no. So I nodded. "I promise. If needs be, I'll come to you."

Merlin's eyes were on my back as I left, and the weight of his gaze made me uneasy. I squelched the apprehensive feeling. Tonight, I'd taste freedom. Tonight, I would simply be Eden, and not the Seelie realm's heir apparent—and hang the consequences.

CHAPTER
Two

I CAUGHT my reflection in the floor-to-ceiling windows. It was pitch black in the gardens, but the light from the ballroom made the window more like a looking glass.

My gown was off-the-shoulder with a plunging bodice that seemed to defy gravity and an emerald satin corset-waist that cinched mine within a breath of life. Still, it was worth it for the effect. Decadent. Wicked even. And at an Unseelie ball, that was a good thing.

I'd worn beautiful gowns before, but this one dared the fates. Risk taking was Sorcha's deal, not mine. A fact that was plain as day when I showed up with my sister for her gate-crashing rendezvous. To say I was met with stunned surprise was an understatement. It was also priceless.

"You clean up well, Eden," Rylan Fullore commented, giving my reflection a quick smile.

I met the handsome Sidhe's grin in the window. The weighty swish of fabric, luxurious against my legs, was better than any dream. Yet, I wasn't dreaming. The ball was here and now, and I stood smack in the middle of the splendor.

"I still don't know how you managed to get out of the palace with Sorcha tonight," Rylan continued, "but I'm glad you did. It's not often the royal twins are out at the same time, other than on formal occasions."

My hand felt for Merlin's stone in my gown's secret pocket. Insurance and protection.

"Probably because they don't want to chance an abduction—or worse." I watched my sister on the dance floor. "Not that risk ever stopped Sorcha. Still, there's a magnificence to her rule breaking, but I never got why."

"And now?"

I chuckled, nodding. "Crystal clear."

The swell of music faded, and couples moved from the dance floor back to their cliques. Sorcha rushed over with her latest fling, Cian, both flushed and laughing.

"Eden!" Sorcha's eyes flashed. "Do you plan on standing alone the entire night or are you going to dance?"

There must have been something in my answering look as Cian coughed. "C'mon, gorgeous. There's a bottle of champagne waiting somewhere with our names on it." He tugged Sorcha in the opposite direction, saving me from a public argument.

"I could go for another drink as well," Rylan said, watching them glide toward the bar. "You?"

He turned with a hopeful smile, but I shook my head. "My mind is fuzzy enough." I put my empty glass on a tray by the window. "You go. Tell Sorcha I went for a breath of air. I'll catch up with you all in a bit."

"But—"

I gave him the same look my mother gave courtiers when she was done with them. He took the hint, nodding once, before heading to meet the others.

Typical courtier. Rylan didn't need encouragement when it came to opportunistic seduction. The calculating smile that replaced his initial shock when I showed up with Sorcha spoke volumes. He was always looking for angles.

Court gossip whispered Rylan was a contender for my hand. I snorted to myself. Not if I had anything to say about it. Rylan was full Sidhe, and he had the right bloodline to advance his position in court, but the man was as deep as a puddle. Besides his pedigree, we had nothing in common. Not a single spark. And sparks were exactly what I wanted these days.

"That was managed well," a deep voice said from the shadows. "Have you had practice dismissing sly nobles?"

The low, husky voice came from just inside the French doors to the gardens. I reached for Merlin's stone, regret biting into my stomach for not going with the others.

He stepped into the light, and my hand tightened around the stone, ready to crush it if necessary. Instead, my breath locked in my chest.

Daire Dannean.

As in the heir apparent to the Unseelie throne. Prince of the Winter Court.

I checked the stone again. Still hard to the touch. Confounding the overall Winter Court was one thing. One-on-one was another story. Especially if that one was a fellow royal. My exact counterpart in the Winter Court.

Daire was tall and broad-shouldered, with dark shoulder-length hair worn back in a low ponytail. He was as striking as I'd heard, but I never expected easy humor.

A slash of resentment bit at how carefree he seemed, but I kept a placid expression on my face. Regardless of how good-looking, Daire was an opposing royal and rival of the Summer Court.

Amused eyes, the color of a stormy blue sea, waited for me to respond. "I don't usually stun people into silence, though there's always a first time."

A nervous giggle bubbled up and my hand flew to my mouth at the breach in protocol. He leaned in with a full-on gorgeous grin and a finger to his lips. "I won't tell anyone, if you won't."

This was not good. I wanted one frivolous night of fun. Not to risk a diplomatic breach by trespassing on a rival court. Hopefully, Merlin's enchantment would hold until I could get my sister and get out of this mess.

Butterflies dive-bombed my stomach. Half from fear of discovery, half because Daire's eyes seemed to notice everything about me.

"I wouldn't say I had practice. More like a very insistent mother." I inclined my head courtier-style, hoping my voice didn't squeak. "You'll have to forgive my surprise, Your Highness. No one expected to see you here tonight."

His gorgeous crooked grin widened. "A surprise hit is the best way to catch everyone unawares. Especially when I know each one has an agenda."

"I'm sure that's not true."

He cocked his head as if studying me closer, and my stomach tightened. "For someone who gave a polished brushoff to an obviously interested courtier, you don't sound like you know much about court life. In fact, I don't remember seeing you here before."

Butterflies morphed into a knot. This was it. He knew. Time to turn the tables like any good royal. "Well, *you* make your surprise appearances sound like a drive-by."

Daire's mouth dropped, but then he laughed out loud. Full-bellied and genuine. "A fan of the human realm, huh?" Leaning in, his grin widened. "Me, too. I love everything about their world. Especially movies and music. Books, too. But don't say anything. Lachlan hates it."

Score one for the Seelie princess.

Wait. He called his father by his first name?

"Forgive my rudeness," he said, taking a step closer. "I haven't even asked your name."

I hesitate. If I told him the truth, he'd absolutely put two and two together. Unlike Sorcha, *Eden* was a Seelie name. Still, lying didn't feel right.

"I'm Edie. It's a pleasure to make your acquaintance, Your Highness."

I did a quick curtsey, but he gripped my hand, keeping me eye level— or as eye level as I could be with someone head and shoulders taller.

"Please. So many courtiers fawn and flatter. Talking to you is a breath of fresh air." He nodded. "Call me Daire. And speaking of fresh air, how about it?"

"How about what?" I knew what he meant, but this was getting fun.

"Making me work, huh? Like a romantic comedy."

I shrugged. "You may be a prince, but you're still just a guy, standing in front..." I waited, letting the human movie paraphrase sink in. Except Daire blinked. At first, I thought he missed the film reference, but then it dawned on me. Daire was speechless, not from my ingenuity, but because I overstepped the line. I was a princess as much as he was a prince, but he didn't know that, and I relaxed so much I forgot to play courtier.

"I'm sorry, Your Highness. I shouldn't have—"

His expression changed instantly. It wasn't peeved or smugly amused. He was genuinely impressed. "Walk with me, Edie. I've never met anyone like you before."

Was he flirting or just being polite?

"It's quiet outside." Daire gestured to the French doors. "You can actually hear yourself think. Something you can't always do at court."

"I know! Courtiots, right?" I blurted, completely throwing diplomatic protocol out the door.

"Courtiots?" he repeated.

I nodded, feeling heat bloom in my cheeks. "As in court idiots."

His eyes shined with laughter, and for a heartbeat, there was no one else around. "C'mon. I have something I want to show you. Something I think you'll appreciate."

Daire took my hand and lifted my fingers to his mouth. Butterflies that had fluttered earlier now zoomed with electric wings, zapping my insides with all kinds of sparks. Real, I-want-to-kiss-this-man-right-now kind of sparks.

I followed him onto the veranda, and then down the stairs into the immense gardens. He walked at a fast clip, but I didn't care. This was what I'd told Merlin I wanted. A chance to be free of duty and restraint.

Trailing behind him, I studied Daire in the bright, full moon light. There were no physical differences between the Unseelie and the Seelie when it came to the Sidhe. Summer and Winter Courts were opposite sides of the same coin.

All were beautiful, ethereal, and captivating. The Seelie tended to be fair-haired, but that wasn't the rule. Particularly for full-blooded Sidhe. It was the same for the Unseelie. Some were dark, and some were light, but all were fair of face with high cheekbones and mesmerizing eyes.

Eye color was the main difference. Unseelie had slate-gray eyes, except for the royal heir apparent. Like Daire, all heirs apparent had dark blue eyes, as stormy and fathomless as the sea that beat against the shores of the Winter Court. Some even said it was the sea that gave them their power. It was as such for the Seelie. Seelie had olive green eyes, while their heirs apparent all had glittering, emerald. Our powers came from light, from the sun and the moon. Therefore, the Seelie, or so they claimed, ruled the sky. Of course, Daire had no idea my eyes were emerald, green. Not with Merlin's confounding spell. To the Unseelie heir, my eyes appeared gray, like every other courtier at the gala tonight.

Besides eye color, there was one stark difference. All heirs to the Unseelie throne were male, following the line through their king. While females ruled the Seelie throne in a matriarchal line through the queen.

Both lines took consorts from the lesser courts: Autumn and Spring. The Seelie queen took her consort from the Spring court, and the Unseelie king took his queen from the Autumn.

I smiled to myself, watching Daire as he walked with me through the gardens. He moved with the grace of an athlete. Hardened muscles rippled effortlessly under his court attire.

Funny, I never appreciated the formal medieval style for how snugly it fit the male body. Then again, ogling was Sorcha's deal, not mine. I never had a reason to look. Well, before now. Daire's mother was a dark beauty, and he clearly got his dark good looks from her line through the Autumn court.

The breeze picked up, blowing my long red hair back from my face. The salt tang told me we were close to the edge of the palace grounds, near the beach.

Daire slowed his pace, stopping at the edge of the high cliff overlooking the sea. He pointed to the shadow of an island off the beach. "Like Avalon, it's not always visible."

I smiled at the Arthurian reference. The Unseelie didn't place much stock in keeping the legend alive, mostly because of Merlin. Still, the legend, and its twelfth century ballads, got it wrong. Avalon wasn't a lost isle. Once upon a time it was the Fae realm as a whole.

"What kind of island vanishes like that?" I asked, playing along.

"One that chooses who sees it and when." He turned, taking my hands. "Let me show it to you."

"You are."

"No, I mean truly show it to you. Obviously, the isle approves, or it wouldn't be visible from the bluff."

"How?"

With a grin, he slipped his hand around my waist. "Hold tight!" Before I could argue, we were airborne and skimming the water.

My hair billowed in the salt spray, stinging my face. My gown clung, damp and salt-stained, but I didn't dare move, so I buried my face in Daire's neck.

The mists cleared on the horizon, and the island grew in size and scope as Daire slowed our pace. He glided to the cliffs, setting me down on tufted grass.

"Flying is the only way to travel." He grinned, smoothing his hair back into its low ponytail.

I wiped the back of my hand across my mouth. "If you like being a salted nut in ruined satin."

"Sorry." He flashed a sheepish grin and then waved a hand over my dress. The salt stains disappeared, leaving the satin shiny and untouched.

I raked my fingers through damp, crunchy hair. My hands itched to use my own power to fix the mess, but Merlin's warnings clanged in my head.

"Allow me." He skimmed his palms over my hair, smoothing it to soft, silken curls. "Though with these tangles you're more salted pretzel than salted nut."

"Nutty, exactly. That's what I am for letting you nearly drown me."

The moon emerged from a cloud to illuminate a clearing ahead. At first, it looked like a monument at the center of the space. "What's that? Through the woods, over there?"

"That's what I wanted you to see." He took my hand. "C'mon, there's a path just through those trees."

I wasn't about to stand on the bluff alone, so I trudged behind him, glad I wore low-heeled slippers tonight.

The clearing opened ahead of them, and it was much larger than expected. The structure was white marble, but it had seen better days. Vines crawled the outer walls, circling the pillars at the top of their cracked steps.

Besides the strange pantheon feel of the place, the shape of the temple itself was odd. It was a linear triangle. It had a regular, wide-columned entrance, but instead of opening to a rectangular interior, it narrowed into a triangular shape. Three interior angles, instead of four.

"Talk about an archaeological find," I mumbled, looking up at the imposing edifice.

"I found this spot long before archeology was a science, but you're right. The place has a mysterious and beautiful aura."

I squinted, cocking my head to look past the stairs to the interior. Enough moonlight entered through gaps in the roof to highlight the inside walls.

"What is this place?" I asked, letting go of Daire's hand. "Does all that writing mean anything?" I pointed to the interior walls.

"You can see that?" Daire moved to my side.

"It's too dark to read any of it, but yeah, I can see the inscriptions. Are they carvings? It's hard to tell from here."

He walked to the base of the cracked steps. "I'm surprised, that's all. I warded this area against prying eyes."

"Why? Is it a secret?"

He climbed the first few steps, before motioning for me to follow. "Not exactly a secret, but a place I like to keep for myself. The temple is eons old. When I was younger, I'd come here to get away from the palace. Away from court. It's funny, really. The island is fickle with everyone else, but I always find it." He chuckled. "Or maybe it finds me."

"I understand. You'd be surprised at the lengths I've gone for peace enough to hear myself think." He looked at me surprised, and I shrugged. "My family can be overwhelming sometimes."

He took my hand and lifted it to his lips again. "Maybe that's why the isle revealed itself tonight. If you can see through my wards, then I was meant to share this with you."

He placed my hand palm down on the trunk of a large oak practically growing into the edifice itself. He covered my hand with his, whispering words I could barely hear.

"What are you doing?" I asked as a tingle formed against my palm.

"The oak is my sentinel. Touching your hand to its trunk with mine lets the guardian know you're welcome in my sanctuary."

An acknowledging breeze swayed the tree's branches as Daire climbed the stairs, leading us inside the temple.

"Legend has it, Merlin planted that oak when he envisioned this temple. It was to honor Danú."

At Merlin's name, I turned at once. My eyes searched Daire's face in the dim light.

It couldn't be.

Could it?

"Stories say Merlin was a Druid, which makes sense since the oak is sacred to the sect. Of course, that was before the sorcerer was beholden to the Seelie queen."

My eyes widened. "Merlin is *beholden* to my..." I caught myself in time with a cough. "I mean, he's beholden... how? Why?"

"I don't know." Daire shrugged. "Maybe that part is court gossip, but the rest? It has to be true. Look at the design of this place. It's unusual, until you look at the mosaic floor."

Thousands of tiny tiles formed a mosaic triquetra. The symbol for the triple goddess and mother to all Fae—Danú.

"The mosaic is beautiful, but it doesn't mean Merlin conjured this place. Anyone could have built this temple. An acolyte to Danú, or even an ancient king looking to curry favor with the goddess."

Daire waved a hand, and part of the cornice illuminated, showing a faded frieze. "Then explain why there are references to Arthur and Camelot in an abandoned temple on the outskirts of the Winter Court. Why there's a mural depicting the story of Excalibur, if it wasn't conjured by the sorcerer who lived the tale?"

My mouth dropped as a thousand questions whirled in my head. Merlin would answer every one of them as soon as I got back to the Summer Court.

"If that's not enough, then look at the columns. Three points on the triquetra, and each a portal."

My gaze jerked from the painted frieze to where Daire pointed. I moved to the center of the tiled floor, afraid to breathe.

"Portals. To where?" My hand went to Merlin's stone again, if only to ground me.

The questions in my head drew lines from one to another, connecting dots. I didn't know what was happening, but I suspected it had something to do with Merlin and his vision about choice.

CHAPTER
Three

"EDIE? ARE YOU OKAY?" Concern etched Daire's voice. "You look as though you've seen the future."

Ding-ding, Handsome.

Not the future, but it was related.

I wiped the querying doubt from my face and plastered a court smile in its place. Like I'd been taught. When royals fright, keep it light.

"So, no one else knows about this place?" I scanned the temple's interior, committing it to memory. "Why? It's not as if the human realm is forbidden. Plenty of Fae view it as their own personal playground. Not to be vulgar, but the Fae have been screwing with humanity, both figuratively and literally, for eons."

"I warded the perimeter because of my father. The human realm isn't forbidden, but it is unforgivingly frowned upon. Especially for me." His forehead puckered, and his eyes darkened for a moment. "You have no idea the pressure I'm under as crown prince."

I didn't answer. Without warning, I threw my arms around Daire's neck and planted a wet kiss on his cheek. Finally, someone who got it.

"What was that for?" He was taken aback, but that didn't stop him from slipping his arms around my waist.

"You looked sad, that's all."

He kept me close for a moment more before stepping back. "I'm not, really. It's like the saying goes. Heavy is the head who wears the crown. Still, Lachlan would destroy this place without batting an eye if he had an inkling the portals exist."

"Have you used them all?"

"No. Only the one that opens to the Middle Course."

"I get you not wanting to incur your father's wrath, but why risk it to travel to a subterranean in-between? Are you telling me you hang with trolls and goblins?" I chuckled, but Daire's expression didn't find it funny.

"The Middle Course is rich in its own history. Trolls and goblins follow the Sluagh and the Wild Hunt, and yes, they terrorize the human realm and the lesser Fae. Most are nasty creatures, but they aren't the only Fae that inhabit the in-between. Some are actually pretty friendly. Especially the half-breeds."

I regretted being so flippant, especially since it smacked of my mother's condescension.

"You should come with me, and see for yourself," Daire continued. "Still, the main reason I travel to the Middle Course is to get to the human realm. The in-between is full of hidden portals. Portals neither court knows exist. Winter or Summer."

I pivoted at the center of the floor, slowly taking in the position of each column, and imagining where they led. "You said there were three portals. Do they all go to the in-between?"

"No. Just that one. The one that faces north." Daire pointed to the column at the temple's linear apex. "The one that faces west is a portal to some forbidden realm. I tried it once, and the inner vortex flung me back so hard I couldn't breathe."

Daire walked to the portal that faced east. "Usually, the portals warm to my touch." He ran a hand over the lined marble but then shrugged. "This gateway stays cold. I'm pretty sure it goes to the Seelie realm. To the Summer Court. I don't know for certain, but it's an educated guess."

"How so?"

"Honeysuckle." He grinned sheepishly. "Every once in a while, I catch the scent of honeysuckle near this particular column. Honeysuckle doesn't grow in Unseelie, but it grows in abundance around the Summer Court. I haven't explored this one, yet. For obvious reasons."

I lifted my chin, cocking one hip. "Afraid of what you might find on the other side?" I wiggled my fingers like claws.

"So, you've heard the rumor."

"What rumor?"

"The one where Queen Tianna gave the scalped beards of three discarded lovers to Merlin, and he conjured a Cerberus from their remains to guard the entrance to the Summer Court."

I burst out laughing. "And you believe that?"

"Hey, the woman is a known tyrant." He shrugged again. "I hear she keeps the princesses locked in a tower for fear they'll outshine her and raise a coup."

"How very Snow White. The idea is ridiculous," I snapped. "Her daughters are fine, and free to do as they please. The only dog, three-headed or otherwise, is the Queen's Captain of the Guard. Though he's more three-headed pig—"

I froze mid-rant, swallowing hard, especially when Daire's eyebrows hiked to his hairline.

The prince took a few steps closer, suspicion all over his face. "And you know all this, how?"

I forced myself to meet his steady, probing gaze, and lifted my chin. "Maybe you're hesitant to try different portals, but I'm not."

His eyes tightened, but with interest rather than suspicion. "Are you telling me you've risked a portal to an opposing court?"

I nodded but didn't voice a reply. He said opposing realm, not Unseelie realm, so technically my answer wasn't a lie. There were other Fae courts besides the high courts. Autumn and Spring, particularly, not to mention the Sluagh, and then the Shadow Courts no one knew much about.

"I'd love to know where you found an unmanned portal. Lachlan has guards posted at every gateway in the realm, save these."

He had me on that point, so I pulled a maneuver from my mother's playbook. Be vague. If pressed, lie.

"I was with friends. One of them managed to bribe a guard. I don't know how or what with, so don't ask. It was a while ago, so I don't recall."

Hmph. "Whoever the guard, he should quit while he still has the chance. Lachlan will show no quarter if he's caught."

This was too close for comfort. I had to do something to deflect the conversation, other than heading back to the palace. I didn't want to waste this chance at being alone with Daire. It wasn't just his good looks. My butterflies had butterflies when he took my hand, and my knees went weak at his full-on gorgeous grin, but it was more than that.

Of course, he was charming and funny. Princes were trained to be so, but he was also sweet, and honestly vulnerable at times, yet strong enough to carry me when we flew over the water. As the humans said, he was the perfect package.

"So, all this writing." I swung an arm toward the scribbled paragraphs, quotes, and random thoughts covering the smooth stone across the interior wall and cornices. "I was right. They're not etchings. To be honest, it looks a lot like graffiti. You know, the kind you see in human movies and on their television."

The deft redirect wasn't just to get Daire off portals and guards. I wanted to know. "Did you write all this yourself?"

He nodded.

"If you warded this place so no one else could read what you wrote, then it must mean something, right?"

Daire was at my side in two steps. "I call this place the Omnibus," he said, tugging my hand. "It's my own private collection of favorite song lyrics, movie quotes, and passages from books and poetry."

He waved his hand like he did with the frieze, and the writing glowed. The handwriting was masculine and sure, and the look on his face told me every word meant something special.

A strange expression shadowed Daire's face as we glanced at the writing. "We should go."

A slash of disappointment hit me, but I wasn't in any position to argue. "Of course. My sister probably thinks I got lost in the gardens maze."

"I meant we should go to the human realm. An adventure. Just you and me." He stepped closer, meeting me toe-to-toe.

"Daire—"

Sliding his hand behind my head, he dipped his mouth to hover close. "You're not like anyone, Edie. You're a complete stranger, yet I'm drawn to you like no one else. It's not just your beauty. There's so much more to what I feel, and I can't explain it."

"You're a very tempting devil, you know that?" I relaxed into his hand, angling my head for a kiss.

Sparks. Definitely sparks.

He grinned, leaving a hair's breadth between our lips.

The relaxed joy in his genuine laugh warmed me to my core, while the feel of his hard body against mine made my head swim.

"Did you ever wish the rest of the world would just fall away so you could freeze time?" he asked.

"We're Sidhe. Winnowing time comes with the territory."

He ran his tongue over my bottom lip. "Not sifting time. Freezing it. Just to savor one moment over and over. A moment like this."

If he didn't kiss me soon, I'd go up on tiptoe and do it myself. "Daire—"

My words clipped as he took my mouth with a thirsty kiss. He slid his hand to my throat, teasing the curve of my neck to my collarbone as his lips devoured more. A soft moan left my mouth in a breathless gasp, but a jagged alarm pierced the air, jolting us apart.

"What the hell?" I winced, covering my ears at the shrill sound.

"Palace alarms." He let go of me and rushed to the temple doorway. "The wards have been tripped."

The stone in my pocket hadn't changed form or temperature, so it wasn't me or Sorcha. Who then? Was the Winter Court under attack?

I moved to his side. Across the water the palace was flooded with light. "Who? How?"

"I'm not sure, but the last time this happened it was the Sluagh." He looked between the palace and me, and then back again. "They're supposed to be our allies, but they have their own ideas about loyalty, as well as their own agenda."

"Everyone knows the Sluagh are destructive and malicious, but I thought that was part of their deal with your father as his enforcers."

Daire's mouth was a thin slash. "That's the problem. Lachlan gave them too much leash, and now they want their own court. My father dismissed their rumblings as meritless." He shot a hand toward the chaos across the water. "Now we know they weren't."

"We need to get back to the palace, Daire. My sister is in the middle of this mess."

"No. You need to stay here. It's safer. I'll get your sister."

I wasn't taking no for an answer. "I'm not waiting here while my sister is in trouble. She's probably frantic by now, wondering where I am. I'm going with you."

"Okay." He glanced over his shoulder toward the panic. "We'll have to go in low, and that means getting very wet."

"Who cares? It's water. Not iron ore."

"I won't have time to save your dress, no matter how cute a salted pretzel you become."

"No worries. It's a glamoured dress, anyway."

"Okay, then, Cinderella. Hold on even tighter this time." He slipped both arms around my waist, brushing Merlin's stone in my pocket. "What's that?"

"My good luck charm."

"It must be pretty powerful, then. Meeting you has been the luckiest thing that's happened to me in a long while."

Daire launched off the temple steps, clearing the trees before diving for the water. The blue-black sea crashed against our bodies with a power that forced breath from my lungs.

White knuckled, I held onto Merlin's stone. If it was lost to the sea, the Sluagh weren't the only ones who'd set off a breach.

Chills bit into my legs from the frigid water, and the weight of my sodden gown threatened to pull me and Daire below the depths.

If I tapped into my powers to help speed us across, it might trigger the stone, or worse, reverse Merlin's magic altogether. We approached the shore, and Daire barely made it onto the beach without stumbling.

He knelt in the cold, wet sand. His fingers splayed while he caught his breath.

"Are you all right? In our rush, I didn't think to add my powers to yours." I flashed him a sheepish grin, cringing at how silly and helpless it made me sound—and I was neither.

"It's better you didn't, Eden. You wouldn't want to give yourself away totally."

Eden.

He called me, Eden.

I took a step back from him as he straightened but ended up stumbling over my soaked satin and landing on my butt. "I... I'm—"

He held out a hand to help me up from the sand. I hesitated, realizing this could be it for me as well as Sorcha. Bowing my head, I slipped my fingers into his waiting palm to let him help me to my feet.

"I'm sorry, Your Highness. I came tonight for the music and dancing." I lifted my eyes to meet his dark blue gaze. "I meant no disrespect. I just wanted—" I glanced down again, exhaling.

"You wanted what, sweetheart?"

My throat tightened at the endearment. Was it genuine, or just mocking? As if he read my mind, Daire cupped my face, dipping his lips to mine. It was a kiss filled with want and a hint of danger.

The alarms continued, the shrill noise blaring across the grounds and in the tiered gardens above the beach. All hell had broken loose with the Sluagh, yet in that moment, time stood still. Frozen. As though Danú granted our shared wish.

When he stepped back, I forced myself to meet his eyes. "When did you know who I was?"

"The moment I kissed you. Your back was to the Seelie portal. The moment our lips touched, the gateway lit up like a Christmas tree. The pull from the portal was so strong, it stole the breath from my chest."

"Pull?"

He nodded. "I tightened my hold on your waist, afraid the portal would suck you right into the jaws of the Cerberus."

"For the love of Danú, there is no three-headed dog on the other side. My mother may be a despot, but she's not a sadist."

Now it was his mouth that dropped. "Wait. You're THAT Eden? As in Princess Eden, heir to the Seelie throne?"

"Shout it a little louder, Daire, I don't think the Sluagh guard heard you." My whisper was as jagged as my nerves. "Do you know what kind of price they'd put on my head?"

"Yes, I do." He reached for something inside his doublet. "The same price they'd put on mine if they got the chance." He pulled out a small, stone pendant on a leather cord, similar to the one Merlin gave me and Sorcha.

"Is that what I think it is?"

"You're not the only one with a sorcerer who can cast a confounding spell, Princess."

I reached for the stone in my skirt pocket and then held it out in my palm. "It concealed my essence as a Seelie. From you and from your court."

"Merlin?"

I nodded. "Yes. Whom I plan to kill with questions the moment I get home."

"Questions about me?"

"Among other things. Like why I was able to see through your temple wards. Why my charm only worked until you kissed me, and why yours didn't work on me at all."

"I can answer that one, at least." He stuffed the pendant back into his shirt. "My confounding spell was aimed at those who wished me harm. You weren't a threat."

The wind blew my wet hair back from my neck, leaving my décolleté exposed. "You're beautiful, Eden. Inside and out." A small grin tugged at his mouth. "Though, I think I like Edie better."

"You're not going to charge me with trespassing and exact reparations from my mother, are you?"

"If the tables were turned, would you?"

I thought for less than an instant and then shook my head. "Like you said. You're not a threat. If anything, you're nothing like what I've been told."

He exhaled, raking a hand through his own wet hair. "I can say the same thing about you. I knew you were beautiful, but I never expected you to shine with such light from within."

"Is that a metaphor?"

"No. It's one of my talents. I can read Fae auras. In humans, I can see the reflection of their souls. The ability helps me see purpose and intent. It comes in handy more than you'd think."

"Were you able to see my aura? I mean, before Merlin's charm broke?"

Daire opened his mouth to answer, but a crash of boots on the garden's path above snatched his attention.

"Intruders on the beach! Guards! Guards!"

He pulled me toward the rocky face below the bluffs. "Those are my guards, but you need to hide. With a broken confounding spell, it's the only way I can protect you."

"EDEN!" Sorcha rushed from the base of the narrow stairs leading to the gardens.

Merlin's stone warmed in my palm, growing hotter and softer by the second. This was it. Time had unfrozen for me and Daire.

"Thank Danú! Hurry! There's no time!" Sorcha grabbed my hand, barely sparing a look for Daire.

"Wait!" Daire held my other hand, tight. "When will I see you again?"

"Eden! NOW!"

I pulled my hand from his and raced across the sand with my sister. "Day after tomorrow!" I yelled back, hoping my voice wasn't lost to the wind. "The Omnibus! Midnight!"

CHAPTER
Four

"MERLIN!" I banged on the heavy oak door. "I know you can hear me. Like it or not, I'm coming in."

I opened the door to a bare room. Everything was gone. Merlin's library of books. His papers. His braziers, iron pots, and glass bottles. Even his tufted chair. There was dust on the floor and cobwebs in the windows as though his quarters had been emptied for months.

My jaw tightened. This had my mother written all over it. If I hadn't slept half the day away dreaming about the night before, I might have been able to mitigate something. Anything. The chance was slim, but still. This was my fault, and on top of that, time was ticking on my rendezvous with Daire.

I scanned the rafters for Merlin's birds, but they had disappeared as well. "If she banished him, I swear..."

I didn't finish the thought. Even in this corner of the castle, the eaves had ears. If my mother found out Merlin's part in my Unseelie adventure, she'd do worse than banish him.

Guilt bit at the thought as I walked in a circle, my skirts kicking up dust, so it swirled in the light. My friend was gone, and I had no clue as to where he went. Or more likely, was sent.

I had to do something, but what? The only thing that remained was

Merlin's small wooden table beside the hearth. A single stone rested on the floor, half-hidden behind a scarred table leg. It wasn't the same kind of stone the wizard gave me for the ball. This one was jagged. Its color a curious blend of white and amber.

I knew Merlin well enough to know the inconspicuous stone might be more than it seemed, so I turned for the cold hearth and bent for the stone. The instant I touched the rock, the room whirled.

Everything blurred, taking my equilibrium with it. My knees buckled, and when they hit the floor, the spinning-top sensation ceased.

"Aim for the bucket if you feel sick. The foul smell lingers otherwise, difficult to remedy."

"Merlin?" My stomach was ready to heave, so I kept my eyes squeezed tight. "Have you been banished? Where is this place? What happened?"

"Give me your hand, Eden."

I grudgingly loosened the vise grip on my middle, but he didn't help me to my feet. Instead, Merlin pressed a small cup into my palm.

"Drink. It will stop your whirlies."

I opened my eyes, wincing at the smell coming from inside the cup. "Ew, no! If I haven't vomited yet, this will definitely do the trick."

"Down the hatch, little dove, or you'll be sick for days."

With a grimace, I swallowed the nasty brew. "Ack!" Gagging, I squeezed my eyes shut again but kept the contents of my stomach intact. "That was absolutely foul."

"There's a reason patience is considered a virtue. Give the concoction a moment."

No sooner did the words leave his mouth, than my internal spins stopped, and my stomach settled from my throat. I cracked one eye open, and then the other, testing my head.

"Better?"

I nodded, expecting a wave of vertigo with the effort, but I was fine.

"Good. Now eat." He took the cup from my hand, replacing it with a thick slice of crusty bread and butter. "You'll feel even more recovered once you get some food in your belly."

"Did Tianna banish you because of last night?"

He helped me to the low couch opposite his chair. "To answer the first of what I am sure will be many questions, I'm not banished. Nor have I gone anywhere. I merely tested a new spell." He tapped a finger to the side of his nose. "And you, clever girl, figured it out."

"What kind of spell? A virtual reality roller coaster without the human realm gadgetry?"

"A just-in-case spell." He glanced at me over his shoulder as he moved to his potions table. Lyrae cawed in the rafters, and between the look on Merlin's face, and the gentle warning from the elegant raven, there was more to this just-in-case spell than he let on.

"So, I was the perfect candidate for a trial run."

"Little dove, you are the perfect candidate for many trials, I think."

Merlin had never used me as a guinea pig before, and certainly not without my knowledge. "Why don't I like the sound of that?"

Maybe the just-in-case scenario was my mother's wrath, and how she might react if she found out about Daire and the Unseelie ball. Was Merlin's vortex spell an escape hatch for both me and Sorcha because mother dearest would punish my sister if I left her behind?

I pulled the doughy center from the bread, plopping it in my mouth. "Incidentally, your confounding spell worked like a charm last night."

Merlin's beard twitched at my human realm pun.

"Still, you might want to revisit your binding incantation. The spell broke the moment the Unseelie prince kissed me."

The old sorcerer didn't turn from his worktable, but his hand paused over his latest potion.

Reliving the thrill had me babbling at the speed of light, but I didn't care. I was excited to talk about it with someone, and with Sorcha giving me the silent treatment, Merlin was it.

"Daire knew I was Seelie, but he didn't know I was Eden, Princess of the Summer Court. I gave that one away by accident."

"He kissed you before he knew who you were?"

Nodding, I munched on my bread. "It's one of the reasons I wanted to see you." I gulped down my mouthful. "By the way, did you build a temple to Danú on a hidden island in the Faewyn Sea?"

Merlin's potion bottle fell from his hand, shattering on the floor. The old wizard stood without moving in the middle of the mess.

I'd never known Merlin to drop anything, let alone one of his potions, and I think I was more stunned than him. I put my bread down and rose from the couch.

"Are you all right?" My question was aimed at more than minor cuts from flying glass.

Merlin waved his hand, and the shards swirled into the trash bin. "Why are you asking about that temple?"

"Because Daire took me there last night."

He took a step toward me, his face a mix of interest and dread. "Why? Were you in danger?"

"Only of losing my ability to speak." I brushed crumbs from the couch and sat again. "Have you seen the Unseelie prince? Daire is definitely Sorcha's type, so I'm surprised he gave me a second look. It's no wonder she's giving me the cold shoulder."

"A second look for what?"

I blinked at the old seer. Was he being purposely obtuse or just teasing? "As in interested, Merlin. Interested in *me*."

I watched a scrunched line of bushy silver form above his eyes. "In what way do you mean interested."

"For the love of Danú! What other way do you think? Boy meets girl. Boy likes girl, and girl likes boy. Boy takes girl to a secret island for their first kiss. You know, interested. Like you and Nimue, a billion years ago."

The sudden pang on Merlin's face made me wince. Nimue was a sore subject. Like Morgana. The old sorcerer was lucky in magic and battle strategy, but not in love.

"I'm sorry, Merlin."

"The past is where it should be, little dove. It doesn't burden me. Unlike the prospect of *you* feeling that same kind of loss."

"Why do you assume it will be a loss? Meeting Daire was exciting. Freeing. Even after he realized who I was, it didn't matter."

When Merlin eyed me, it looked as though he'd aged. "You're sure of that?"

"I hope so." I lifted one hand before lowering it to my lap. "It was you who taught me about the birds and the bees, so I know he was attracted. As to my being adept at gauging a man's intentions?" I shrugged, admitting my sheltered shortcoming. "It's not like I can talk to my mother.

Her interactions are purely for pleasure or political gain. Love isn't exactly her area of expertise."

I returned my attention to the slice of bread in my hand, waiting for my friend and mentor to offer comment. When he didn't, I glanced up to find him still eyeing me. "Stop looking at me like you expect war to be declared. Everything's fine. Ask Sorcha. She found Daire and I on the beach before we were forced to leave the Winter Court. If I know my sister, she's scheming something to turn this her way."

"Forced to leave? I thought you said the charm worked."

"Daire's kiss broke the confounding spell, but not your escape clause. The stone didn't soften until the Sluagh breached the palace."

"Dragon's teeth!" His voice rose. "The Sluagh? I should never have sent you last night. War will be the least of our worries if Tianna gets wind of my part in this folly."

"Why? We were fine until the breach. To be honest, Sorcha was impressed at how well I handled the rush."

He went back to his potions, stirring and staring into the brew. "You give your sister too little credit. She will prove invaluable to you, mark my words. Even with her petulance, Sorcha loves you, as I do."

"There was a strange pull between us last night. One I can't explain."

He looked up from his writing, momentarily perplexed. "Between you and Sorcha?"

"No." I rolled my eyes. "Between me and Daire. At first, I thought it was just me. Unlike Sorcha, I'm not skilled at playing the coquette, and he seemed to like that I didn't play games."

Merlin pursed his lips at that.

"Political strategy is something I've yet to master, and one my mother would like to split my skull over. I can dodge and evade, when necessary, but court flirtations are not my thing."

I got up again, this time to sit at Merlin's worktable. "Between my mother's machinations and her court intrigues, it's no wonder I'm inept when it comes to matters of the heart. Maybe spending most of my time in this tower makes me lucky."

His eyes grew soft, the weight of his affection clear in his gaze. "You're not inept. You're genuine. Something all Fae courts lack. Sounds to me like the Unseelie prince is as much a Sidhe anomaly as you, my girl."

"Maybe." Leaning my elbows on the rough wood, I watched him scribble notes. "You still didn't answer my question. According to Daire, legend has it you built that temple. Did you create the portals to go back and forth between realms and the Middle Course?"

Merlin put his quill down and his eyes took on a distant gaze. "Many, many years ago."

"Why? And that third portal. The one Daire said goes to a forbidden realm. Does that go to a Shadow Court?"

"No. The Shadow Courts are something altogether different. As for that third portal, there's a reason it is not to be used."

"Daire tried to explore it." Merlin's gaze jerked to mine. "But a vortex knocked the breath from his lungs, sending him flying back through the door to the temple."

"He's lucky it didn't kill him, or worse, pull him into a void of no return." Merlin's face held an expression of both dread and caution. "Promise me you will never attempt that portal. No matter who suggests it."

I didn't reply, but a pit formed in my stomach, nonetheless.

"That portal was created in anticipation of a prophecy. A vision shown to me too many centuries ago to count, yet the memory is one I will never forget."

"What prophecy?"

He shook his head. "Eden, you are the daughter of my life. Even more so than Arthur's half-sister, Morgana. I cannot tell you what I saw all those years ago. The vision was a harbinger of war. A portend of catastrophe, destruction, and then finally, redemption."

Merlin was always one for being cryptic, so this was uncharacteristically direct. Direct and dire. I swallowed the small lump in my throat. "Is the portal an escape to another realm? Sidhe legends speaks of Avalon as a realm we escaped to eons ago. Are the Fae in danger of history repeating itself?"

"I cannot say."

"Can't or won't?"

He turned away from me. "Time, little dove, is a great thickener of things."

I chewed the corner of my mouth. He was back to being cryptic. Still, Merlin's evasions usually meant variables had yet to reveal themselves.

"Daire said you were beholden to my mother. Are you? Does it have anything to do with this secret prophecy?"

He wrinkled his nose as though the idea offended. "I am not beholden to your mother. My loyalty to the Summer Court springs from one thing, and that is my vow to keep you safe."

"So, this prophecy is about me..."

CHAPTER
Five

MERLIN SMOOTHED HIS BEARD, watching me watch him. He moved to his chair by the hearth and waved his hand toward the soot-stained bricks. A low flame ignited, growing to a steady burn.

"Sit down, Eden, if you want to know the truth."

I hurried to the couch to sit, tucking one leg underneath my bottom.

"I've told you the story of Arthur, of Excalibur. You know about Mordred and Morgana."

I nodded.

"Morgana and I were similar creatures. She wasn't born of my kind, but she had an innate kinship for magic. I taught her. Danú forgive me." He closed his eyes, and when he lifted his lids pain etched his face. "She manipulated my affections, and when she learned enough, she used my own knowledge against me. Encased me in ice for nearly a millennium."

I swallowed my shock, hoping my face didn't register my disbelief. "What happened? Obviously, you got yourself free."

He shook his head. "Tianna freed me."

"My mother?"

"Eons ago." He nodded. "At that time, the Sidhe walked freely between realms. There was no need for portals and guards. Though much changed while I slept in ice. Morgana persuaded Arthur's bastard son,

Mordred, to wage war on his father, releasing a powerful darkness into the world. A darkness that was both infectious and uncontrollable. It diseased men's souls, killing the dream of united realms existing together in peace and magic."

"Surely, you've repaid my mother for freeing you by now."

"There's more to the story, little dove." He manifested two goblets and a flask of wine. "Would you like more bread and butter? I churned it myself."

I put up my hand to refuse the food but accepted the cup of wine.

"As I said, much had changed while I slept. Morgana enjoyed her unchecked dark freedoms, such as toying with Arthur. She played her half-brother like a practiced fiddler. Whispering about Guinevere and Arthur's champion, Lancelot. Sewing doubt and jealousy. It was a game. Divisive and cruel. She worked on Mordred, as well. Promising power. Enticing him to war. Eventually, Mordred lay dead by Arthur's hand, and Arthur not far behind from his wounds."

"So, Guinevere and Lancelot never...?"

Merlin leaned over, taking my goblet. "Human-realm movies are like sweet wine. Too much, and the brain withers."

"Point taken, but you know what I meant." I picked at what was left of my first serving of bread and butter, chucking a crumb at the sorcerer.

"I do, and the answer is yes and no. Yes, they were tempted. No, they did not act on it, contrary to legend. Guinevere loved Arthur. That's why I'm beholden to your mother."

I stopped fidgeting with my bread and looked at the wizard. "My mother saved Arthur and Guinevere?"

"*I* saved Arthur. I took him from the battlefield, but Tianna allowed me to take him and Guinevere to Avalon before the borders closed between realms forever. Before Avalon itself was fractured. That is why I'm beholden to her. Every day those mortals exist in Faerie, I am beholden to the Summer queen."

"Arthur is here? In the Seelie realm?"

Merlin's eyes took on a guarded look. "He is not. He and Guinevere exist in a realm where most Fae cannot travel."

"The Forbidden Realm."

Merlin didn't answer, but I knew I was right. I'd known the old magician long enough to read him like one of his spell books. "And Morgana? Daire had a charmed stone similar to mine, though it didn't glow."

"Let me guess. He said it could only confound those who meant him harm."

"How did you know?"

He laughed, and the sound was both mischievous and sad. "Morgana absorbed whatever I taught her, but as foolish as I was to be taken by her wiles, I wasn't foolish enough to teach her everything." His eyes twinkled with a tiny spark of smug gratification. "She was drawn to magic, but we were not of the same ilk. Morgana le Fey, as she likes to call herself now that she's aligned with the Unseelie court, is no more than a witch in Fae clothing. A practitioner with no true magic. That she still lives, is only the result of her residing in the Fae realms."

"So, Morgana is Lachlan's minion?"

"Not that she would see it that way, but yes. She is under Lachlan's thumb."

"Does all this tie into the prophecy you mentioned? The one you won't talk about?"

"If I won't talk about it, little dove, then why ask me?"

We sat in silence for a bit, watching the fire crackle and pop in the hearth. "Merlin?"

"Hmmm?"

"That temple you built to Danú on Daire's island..."

"What about it?"

I hesitated another moment. "He said the isle was a fickle place. Only visible to some, but more than that, he warded the temple so no one could find it." Merlin didn't say a word at first, but the curl of his fingers tightened on the edge of the chair's arm.

"The island presents itself to those it deems worthy. I created it that way by design. That Daire found it, and was able to wield magic on its shores, speaks volumes about his aura. About his soul. No wonder there was a connection between you. He is of your ilk, I suppose."

I pondered Merlin's choice of words. *Ilk*. It was unusual even for him. "You keep using that word. Ilk. What do you mean by it? Like-minded? A kindred spirit?"

"For you and Daire, yes. Kindred spirits. But for Morgana, I meant a different connotation. She is mortal, with a kiss of magic in her blood through her mother's line, though ages past."

"You're not mortal, then?" I suspected as much, but never had the courage to ask outright, until now.

"I am immortal, but not Fae. I am ageless, Eden. Even more ancient than the Tua de Danann. Legend paints me as a Druid. I am that, as well, but my origins stem from the gods—and I'll leave it at that."

"If you come from Danú, then how can my mother hold you?"

"Ours is not to reason why, little dove. Ours is but to do and die." He winked.

"Tennyson."

"You're not the only one who can channel human entertainments. *The Charge of the Light Brigade* is one of my favorite poems." He cocked his head, looking at me. "There's something else."

"Daire loves human entertainments, as you call them, as much as I do." I told Merlin about the Omnibus and Daire's wards.

"Maybe his wards are too weak for your mind. You're as headstrong as your mother, whether you want to admit it or not."

"That's comforting." I snorted.

"A strong mind and spirit should be a comfort. How you choose to use them is where the difference lies." He regarded me. "Perhaps you saw through Daire's wards because he was meant to share his secret with you."

"That makes no sense. He barely knows me."

"Doesn't it? Look inside, Eden. He showed you the island, probably thinking you'd never spot it on the horizon. When you saw it, he chose to take you there. Each time, challenging the expectation. He brought you to the temple, and when you saw his Omnibus, he knew."

"Knew what?"

"That you weren't an average courtier. You intrigued him from the first, Eden. Not just your beautiful face, but your beautiful spirit. Because he felt something with you. A connection. A pull. You said you felt it yourself. There's something there. Something neither of you can explain."

I doubted that completely. "We're both heirs apparent to rival courts. A romance doomed before it even begins."

"Ah, but it's already begun. The strings of fate are weaving furiously, or isn't that the real reason for your visit?" Merlin got up from his chair. "Come."

Leaning over a silver bowl of water on his worktable, he beckoned me to look as well. With a single wave the water shimmered, and an image formed.

Me with Daire. Our kiss...

I gripped the bowl, but it was too late. The vision faded, leaving only a whisper on the air.

Midnight. The Omnibus...

I blinked at the still clear water before lifting my eyes to Merlin. "I promised him."

With a nod, he opened his arms, and I walked into their warmth. "I'll unlock the portal, but you have to swear you'll not abuse it. Daire cannot come into Seelie without permission.

"Fat chance." I sniffed.

Merlin's chest shook with a sad chuckle. "Fat chance, indeed." He stroked my hair. "Be warned, daughter of my heart. You cannot share this magic, or the backlash will be terrible."

I nodded. "Not even Sorcha."

Stepping back, he cupped my face. "Especially not Sorcha." With a wink, he reached into his pocket. "Wear this, and the portal will obey."

A pendant unlike any I'd seen dangled from his fingers. Two silver dragons twisted into the shape of a triquetra, one with eyes the color of emeralds, the other blue as a storm-raged sea.

I reached out to touch the shining silver, but Merlin pulled the pendant back. "Not yet."

He walked to the hearth, taking a sword from the wall. Hanging the pendant on the sword's pointed end, he thrust it into the fire. Smoke billowed, aqua, and the dragons' eyes sparkled gemlike.

"Put your hands together, Eden. Palms touching," he instructed, before pulling the smoldering sword from the flames.

The pendant slid from the sword's end to Merlin's waiting hands. He wrapped the chain around my fingers before slipping the pendant between my joined palms. The silver glowed hot, but like the confounding stone, it didn't burn.

"*Cuimhnigh*," he whispered. "Remember."

I hissed, jerking my hands back from the searing pain from his single-word spell, but Merlin held my palms together. "Cuimhnigh!" he yelled this time, and thunder clapped above the tower keep, rattling the slate rooftop.

I bit the side of my cheek not to cry, but tears stung my eyes. Merlin let go, and I opened my hands expecting to see charred flesh, but there wasn't a mark on my skin. No pain, either.

"What did you do?"

He looked at me, his crinkled eyes twinkling as ever. "Insurance and protection. Now I don't have to worry if you accidentally lose the pendant or tell someone about the portals. Keep it with you, Eden. It's a symbol of what the fates may allow, but you no longer need it as a portal-opening talisman. *You* are now the talisman."

I gaped at him. "Me? I can open the portal to meet Daire?"

"Yes."

"From anywhere in the Summer Court?"

He chuckled. "I'm ambitious, girl. I don't have a death wish. No. Seek your portal in the druidic ruins and the giant oaks that reign there."

"The Eventide Forest."

He nodded but then lifted a warning finger. "The Eventide belongs to many Fae, not just the Sidhe. You would do well to remember that when ambling there or suffer the consequences."

"Is it dangerous?"

Merlin didn't blink. "Yes."

CHAPTER
Six

I CLOSED my bedroom door and leaned on the painted wood. "Is it dangerous? Why yes, Eden, it is." I mimicked Merlin's voice.

That was it. Don't call us, we'll call you. The one who waxed euphoric about Arthur and his brat half-sister, Morgana, couldn't spare two words about what lurked in the Eventide.

"Great." I chewed my lip.

I wasn't set to meet Daire until the following night. That gave me thirty-six hours, give or take, to find out what Merlin meant by dangerous, and to do a dry run. At least my mother was at her pavilion with her latest paramour. One less obstacle to dodge.

I was an adult. Or at least I was by human measure. Twenty-one years old. An adolescent by Sidhe standards, but still. Old enough to know I wanted Daire. And not just for conversation. Hells bells, Sorcha had a dozen lovers to date. And the queen? The court stopped counting.

There was still the Captain of the Queen's Guard to deal with, and Caxton was nothing short of a bull when it came to me and Sorcha. Considering my sister outsmarted him every time, it spoke volumes about the man being all brawn and no brains. Then again, beefy but brainless was how the queen liked them.

"Three-headed pig." I tugged my blouse over my head, snorting at the description I used for the odious man, before stepping out of my heavy skirts.

"Who's a pig?" Sorcha peeked in from the doorway.

"Caxton." I shrugged into a soft, cotton tee before pulling on a pair of leggings. "And don't you knock?"

Sorcha rolled her eyes, closing my bedroom door. "Please. The walls between our chambers are wafer thin by design. I think the queen expected we'd be like her and Aunt Ysaryl, ratting on each other for sport. Newsflash, mommy dearest, we're not."

"Surprise, surprise."

"Why are you letting Caxton bother you?" Flopping onto my bed, Sorcha made a face. "The man makes me cringe."

"I know. Him and his creepy Cheshire Cat smile."

Sorcha took one of the decorative pillows from against the headboard and plopped it on her lap.

"What do you want, Cha Cha?" I asked, knowing my sister hated the nickname. "I thought you were giving me the silent treatment."

"I told you, don't call me that."

I picked up a brush from my vanity and gestured with it her way. "You can thank the queen for your nickname. Not me."

My sister toyed with the fringed edge of the throw pillow. "Well?"

"Well, what?" I sat on the vanity's round tufted chair. I knew what Sorcha meant, but for once, I had the juicy story. Not the other way around.

"Don't be such a brat. You and the Winter Court's most eligible bachelor?"

"And?"

"For Danú's sake! Tell me already!" Sorcha knocked the pillow from her lap in frustration. "I've been dying to ask since we got back last night."

I brushed the underside of my hair, the carved handle tingling my palms where Merlin burned the portal charm into my essence.

Not a word. Especially not to Sorcha.

"We walked through the gardens, talking. Then we ended up on the beach. The sirens went off. End of story."

Sorcha got up from the bed and stalked to stand behind me at the vanity. She put her hands on my shoulders, eyeing me in the mirror with a probing stare that rivaled our mother's.

"Cut it out, Sorcha." I shrugged her off, but she didn't give an inch. "Not a chance. You've had your nose in books, squirreled away in that musty tower with Merlin since you learned to read. One night of coloring outside the lines, and you nail the crown prince."

"I didn't nail anyone. We talked."

Sorcha's reflection raised an eyebrow, and I replied by pushing my chair back, nearly knocking her over. "Maybe it's unfathomable to you, but real conversation is actually a good thing." I got up from the tufted seat and brushed past her. "Some would even call it an aphrodisiac."

"Yeah." Sorcha snorted. "If you're a book nerd."

"Then Daire must be a nerd too, since he kissed me. Twice. If the damn Sluagh hadn't showed up, who knows?" I stared Sorcha down. "After all, like goes to like, or isn't that what you said when you tried to fix me up with Donwyn Bartlo."

Sorcha stifled a snicker. "Stinky, ol' Downwind Fartlo. Poor thing has the flatulence of a bull seal."

"Don't be a mean girl. Donwyn is a nice guy, even with his parents' unfortunate choice of name. He can't help being half-Selkie/half-Phooka. A pairing that's—"

"Revolting?" Sorcha interrupted.

"I was going to say unusual."

My sister sat on the end of my bed again. "That's half your problem, Eden. You're too nice. Mother isn't going to relax until you toughen up. Though once she hears you nabbed, 'Don't you DAIRE,' she'll bust! You'll be the golden child."

I put my hands on my sister's shoulders where she sat, leaning in so she had no choice but to look at me. "You can't say a word. Sorcha, I mean it. Not a peep. To anyone."

"Why?" Sorcha blinked, clearly not understanding. "Did he threaten you?"

"Just the opposite," I replied, straightening. "You heard him on the beach. He wants to see me again."

"Yeah, until he finds out who you really are."

I met my sister's skepticism. "He already knows."

"Eden!" Sorcha's eyes bugged with a blink. "Are you really that naïve?"

"Naïve? How many times have I covered for you? Adventure after dubious adventure. Lover after questionable lover."

"That's different."

"How?" I shot back. "Your lovers weren't all Sidhe, and they weren't all Seelie. Or have you forgotten that Greyrym you met on the parapets last month? A raunchy cross between an octopus and a bat, and I'm being nice.

Sorcha shrugged. "They have tentacles. Suckers make things... interesting." She actually giggled.

"Mother might find it interesting, as well." I examined my red hair for nonexistent split ends, letting the unspoken threat sink in. "Hell, a play-by-play on what those suction cups can do might make *you* the golden child."

"You wouldn't dare!"

I glanced at her for a moment, before smoothing my hair and then the front of my dress. "Of course not. I gave you my word, but you have to do this for me, Sorcha. Any one of your less than savory lovers could've had ulterior motives. They could have harmed you or taken you for ransom."

"I always have backup. So, they know better."

"And you think I'd be any less cautious? Sorcha, I wrote the book on caution. Trust me. I've got it covered."

"You mean Merlin."

I didn't answer, but then again, I didn't have to.

"Eden, you're the heir apparent. If anything happened —"

Now it was my turn to cut her off. "Then your eye color would change from olive-gray to emerald-green, and you'd be in like a flash." I clicked the inside of my cheek, sliding beside her on the bed. "Instant Queen."

"I'm not *that* mercenary." Sorcha gripped the footboard on either side of her skirt before meeting my eyes. "You're my sister, Edie. What would I do without you? I know I don't say it, and Danú knows I don't show it, either... but I love you, flame-head."

Merlin's words came back at that. *You give your sister too little credit.* I covered Sorcha's hand with mine. "Ditto, Cha Cha."

She bumped my shoulder with hers. "I said don't call me that."

"We're good, then?" I asked, drawing a line under the question. "You'll cover for me?"

Sorcha nodded, and we sat in silence for a moment before she got up from her spot.

"Just so you know, Mother is back from the pavilion, and she expects us both at dinner. So, whatever you and Merlin cooked up for your Winter Court rendezvous will have to wait."

I got to my feet. "Dinner, now? Great. I'm a mess!" I raked a hand through my hair before exhaling. "One more reason for her to frown at me."

"Not on my watch." Sorcha picked up my hairbrush and then pointed to the vanity chair. "Time for *my* kind of magic..."

I spared a look for Sorcha as we waited for our mother at the table. "I thought she was supposed to join us."

"She is," my sister whispered back. "You know what she's like."

The double doors to the royal dining room opened, and Tianna breezed through. Tall and ethereally beautiful, the queen's buttery blonde hair was cut to a chic, chin-length bob. The angle as straight and sharp as her temper. Fitted white slacks and matching tank top molded her lithe body, and a sheer duster trimmed in white silk billowed as she walked.

She raised an eyebrow at us both as she approached. Neither of us got up from our seats.

"Nice of you to join us, Mother," I said, reaching for a crusty roll.

The queen's eyebrow hiked even higher as her footman pulled out her chair, and I put the roll back in the breadbasket. "Sorry," I mumbled.

Mollified, Tianna laced her fingers under her chin, her nails perfectly manicured and as bright red as her lips. "You need to cultivate patience, Eden. Though I'm glad to see you tried with your appearance tonight. The peridot necklace I gave you is a nice touch with that russet gown." She spared a glance at Sorcha before giving me another assessing look. "I hope you thanked your sister."

"It was nothing, Mother," Sorcha added quickly. "I was happy to help."

I kicked Sorcha under the table.

"Ow! What was that for?"

"Girls. Just because dinner is family only doesn't mean etiquette gets left at the door. Decorum. Always."

"Even at the Pavilion?" Sorcha coughed at my subtle dig, watching me reach for a crusty roll.

Tianna's eyes narrowed. "I see I've left you girls to your own devices too long. Especially *you*, Eden."

I froze with my butter knife in hand.

"It's high time you took on more of a role at court. Accompany me on court business. In fact, I should pick your ladies-in-waiting. That way Sorcha isn't burdened with keeping you looking the way a princess, and my heir apparent, should."

I felt the color drain from my cheeks, which explained my mother's satisfied grin. The queen was nothing if not Machiavellian.

"After all, your sister is as much a royal as *you*," she continued. "Why should Sorcha be tasked with your upkeep, simply because you refuse to follow protocol, or learn the ways of court?"

With my butter knife still poised over the dinner roll, I blinked at my mother. "Accompany you?"

"Mmmm."

"Where?" I asked, afraid to hear the answer.

The queen spread her hands, leaning back to allow her steward to fill her wine glass. "Let's start with the Privy Council meeting tomorrow morning. It's time you made a formal appearance." She lifted her goblet, studying me across its silver edge. "It's also time I hosted a ball. You and Sorcha are young yet, but when it comes to strategic marriages, you can't leave things to chance."

"Marriage?" The butter knife clattered to my bread dish. "You can't be serious."

Tianna put her wine glass down. "Eden, I honestly don't understand this impertinence. I need to have a word with Merlin, so he can explain why my daughter chooses to defy me at every turn. Perhaps the sorcerer has outlived his usefulness."

Panic gripped my belly. If the queen willed it, Merlin would be gone from their realm before I could warn him. He would be banished for real. No experiment necessary.

I opened my mouth to argue, but Sorcha pinched me under the table. "A ball sounds wonderful, Mother. May we have new gowns? Maybe even peek at the crown jewels for tiaras?"

Tianna smiled at the younger twin. "See? There's the enthusiasm I expect." She inclined her head. "Yes, to both requests, provided you can stir a fraction of your eagerness in your sister and future queen."

Sorcha pinched me again.

I took the hint but didn't dare look at my sister. I kept my gaze on my mother, while trying to seem contrite. "I'm sorry if my reaction disappointed you, Mother. I meant no disrespect. You never mentioned the M word before, and the idea of a suitors' ball threw me. You know how I am in mixed company."

I held my breath. Pointing out my own flaws always seemed to mollify the queen. Perhaps self-deprecation gave my mother something to consider, or maybe she simply enjoyed the groveling. Probably both. The Seelie queen wasn't exactly maternal, falling just short of eating her young.

The footman served their dinner. "Yes, your inhibitions are a problem. So, perhaps we should go about this another way." The queen turned her gaze to Sorcha, and I felt my sister stiffen.

"Why don't you take Eden with you the next time you sneak out of the palace?"

Sorcha choked on her wine. "Mother, I—" she croaked.

"You aren't as clever as you think, dear. Though, with the conquests you've had, you're rivaling me at your age." The queen smiled, cutting her food. "Eden could use your help when it comes to the art of seduction. You're both Sidhe royalty, and that can prove a bit of a problem when looking for horizontal titillation. Particularly in Faerie."

Both my sister and I were slack-jawed.

"Good." My mother nodded. "That said, I'm granting you both passage to the human realm. Three days and three nights. You can use them all at once, or one visit at a time. Either way, I don't care. It's time you had this rite of passage. I did at your age with your Aunt Ysaryl, and I found the experience invaluable. Both for titillation, and for knowledge.

The human realm is easily conquered by any member of the Fae. Many call the place home. As Sidhe royalty, it's important to understand the lure and use it to your advantage."

"What does that mean?" I lifted my chin.

"This boon isn't to be spent in a dusty library or a museum unless that museum happens to be about sex. If that's the case, have at it. This boon is for hands-on experiences. She eyed me purposefully.

I played with the food on my plate but didn't dare contradict my mother. Maybe I could get word to Daire and have him meet me in the human realm. If my mother demanded hands-on experiences, I'd be more than happy to explore whatever with him.

"Eden, I know you're not comfortable with the idea, but it is necessary. The art of seduction and flirtation is a vital play in gathering intelligence. How else would I know the Sluagh crashed a party at the Winter Court last night, and the prince injured in the fray?"

My head jerked up. "Injured? Injured how?"

My mother's knowing grin unnerved me, but I didn't dare look away.

"My informants say he took a blow to the chest from an ogre's club. He suffered broken ribs and a punctured lung. In that respect, Merlin is worth his seer's weight in gold for an ounce of forewarned protection. His runt protégé, Morgana, is useless with all her feigned magic. Which brings me to another skill set you both need to work on." She put down her fork, but kept her knife in her hand, delicately trailing its sharp edge with her thumb. "Defense. Both of self, as well as realm. You are both sorely lacking in the art of war."

That wasn't exactly true, but who was I to question my mother? I wasn't the best at sword play, but I could hold my own *and* I had my own weapon. A longsword gifted to me by Merlin.

I didn't dare ask about the Winter prince, despite questions rushing from my head to my tongue, only to be swallowed along with my dread. At least Merlin was safe. My mother could posture all she wanted, but the old druid was a jewel in her tiara.

"Are they planning a counterattack against the Sluagh?" Sorcha asked. Despite her nonchalance, I knew my sister worried about her parapet rendezvous with the Greyrym.

Our mother shrugged, wiping her mouth on a cloth napkin. "If I were

Lachlan, I would impale Taltos upside-down, leaving the birds to peck at his balls. First, for what that ugly Sluagh did to Bain, and second for having the cheek to crown himself King of the Dusk Court!"

"Bain?" Sorcha asked, drawing the queen's attention away from my marked exhale. The injured prince wasn't Daire.

"The spare was hurt, while the heir was nowhere to be found. Funny how my spies have nothing to report on Daire."

"Maybe he wasn't there when they attacked." I didn't make eye contact with my mother, concentrating on my plate instead.

"My birds say otherwise," the queen contradicted. "Though they report he spent most of the evening with a pretty little thing no one seems to know."

Sorcha spared a careful glance my way. "How very Cinderella. Did she leave behind a shoe?" She played it off.

"Not funny, Sorcha," the queen admonished. "An unknown in any court is a risk. For all anyone knows, this girl could have let the Sluagh into the palace."

"That you managed spies at a Winter Court gala is a pretty coup," I deflected. "Then again, they probably sneak into our parties as well."

"We don't sneak. I bribe Winter Court courtiers to do my spying for me, something you need to learn. What you tease from allies and adversaries alike will define your rule."

"Sex as a weapon," I paraphrased.

The queen nodded. "A weapon, a promise, a punishment, a pleasure, a reward. All of the above and more." She lifted her cup. "You'll see. And you will do."

I pushed my chair back from the table, and my cutlery clattered to the floor.

"Where are you going?" A flash of angry green followed my mother's haughty tone. "You have not been dismissed."

That flinty gaze used to make me cringe, but not tonight. Not after the possibilities awakened in me. "I'm going to the library. It's that large room lined with books on the opposite side of the palace." I stormed away, ripping my mother's peridot from my neck so the gems clattered to the floor.

CHAPTER
Seven

I WANDERED THE LIBRARY. The scent of leather and parchment filled my nose, and the comforting aromas replaced annoyance with peace. This was as much my sanctuary as Merlin's keep. Not that my mother would follow me here. Tianna didn't actively parent unless it was punishment. On that front, I'd have to wait and see what my outburst held in store.

Craning my neck, I scanned the shelves that ran from floor to vaulted ceiling. I had the room pretty much to myself most of the time. Time spent reading was an anathema in the Summer Court. Not when there were easier, more tactile diversions to be had.

Those diversions found their way onto the wide library couches from time to time. I learned to sit conspicuously or risk an eyeful. Plus, the library's acoustics rivaled that of an amphitheater, echoing those diversions like a porn flick in high def surround sound.

Still, the clandestine hookups gave the maids a reason to clean. Otherwise, the library would rival Merlin's keep in dust and my heart in desolation.

Thousands of books lined the walls and upper galleries. Finding what I needed to navigate the Eventide would be impossible, except for a secret Merlin taught me when I was a child.

The moon was in perfect position over the library's glass ceiling. The spell didn't require a fully round orb, just enough silvery light to invoke its magic. Daire's talent was reading auras, and this was mine. I lifted my hands to the sky and inhaled.

Danú's wonder, Danú's night
Grant me now a seer's sight
Cast a glow on leather and spine
The writings sought, the knowledge mine.

The books I needed shimmered in purple light on the shelf nearest the ceiling. I smiled to myself. The last time I used this spell, it was to play a prank on Sorcha for talking trash. Funny, what you'd find in books when you looked.

I chewed my lip. I could climb for them, but even from this distance one of the books appeared huge and ancient. If I fell, it was game over. No Daire, and no trip through the portals. The Sidhe healed quickly, but not overnight.

There was one more thing to try. I lifted my hands and concentrated. Merlin taught me just enough magic to make things interesting, but after Morgana, he was more than a little hesitant to take it further. Instead, he urged me to tap into my inborn Fae abilities and combine them with what he'd taught.

The Sidhe could manipulate energy from Fae elements, but that was more for defensive purposes. Summer and Winter Courts had mages and sorcerers for most other magic, and even the lesser courts had witches to do their bidding.

I tightened my focus, and the books wobbled on the shelf. Closing my eyes, I dismissed all other distractions.

Concentrating on the glowing books, I harnessed my Sidhe power and twined it with the moonlight streaming in from the window. Energy to energy. Magic to magic.

The pull was extraordinary. Strands of light, weaving and twisting, until the bond was solid and palpable. I opened my eyes.

"Hello there." I watched the books suspended in open space.

Ethereal threads tightened in my fingers. I drew the volumes down, moving them closer, until I grasped them with outstretched hands.

The light winked out, releasing the silvery threads. I exhaled, a little lightheaded. Still, I had what I wanted.

Whispering my thanks to the universe and its mysteries, I then placed the books on the closest table. "Okay," I muttered. "Let's see what you've got to say on the Eventide."

Sliding into a chair, the hairs on my bare arms stood on end as residual magic sizzled purple sparks across the cover and spine of both books.

One volume was more tome than reference book. It was heavy and ancient in appearance with a cracked leather face and faded spine. The other was clearly more recent.

"You first, I guess." I lifted the cover on the newer book, and the pages flew open to a glowing passage. "That was easy enough."

I scanned the entire page, not just the glowing passage. If I'd learned anything working with Merlin, it was context changed everything.

"The Nocturna," I murmured, reading, "live in shadow and gloom. They slip from hidden places in the Eventide at night, only to slither back at dawn. They include remnants of the Sluagh and their allies, abandoned at the time of the Western Rim War. They draw evil and malevolence to their number."

If I remembered our history correctly, the Western Rim War was a millennium before my mother took the throne. The Seelie refused to bend, defeating the Sluagh horde. We took the Eventide back, driving the horde from the Summer Court borders forever.

"So, the Nocturna are ancient Sluagh and their ilk," I muttered, repeating what I read. "Slithering into hidden places makes them sound a little slimy, but maybe being cut off for so long they're—"

The tome abruptly slammed shut, making me jump. "Hey!" I jerked back even further, when the ancient tome skidded forward, knocking the newer one off the table. The cover hummed, glowing even brighter as if asking to be opened.

I reached for the cover's edge, only to yank my fingers back. "Ow! Damn!" The large, cracked leather cover stung my fingertips. "What the hell? Open up, or I swear you'll feed the fire in the great hall tonight."

A yellow glow shimmered over the faded cover and spine, illuminating the almost negligible title. *Conradh Cúirte Gemhridh leis an Sluagh.* The words were ancient, but clear. A chronicle of the Unseelie's contract with the Sluagh and the Wild Hunt.

My breath locked. The book was forbidden. Only the most revered Sidhe scholars and strategists knew what its pages held. "Danú help me," I whispered.

Reaching for the cover once more, the aged leather opened of its own volition. Yellowed pages fluttered lightly, almost as if hesitant in revealing their secrets.

"Please," I murmured, gripping the edge of the table. An invisible gust answered my plea, whipping at the pages. Tiny bits of ancient parchment churned in the mini torrent, finally fluttering to the table surface when it calmed.

The pages stopped at an ornate spread trimmed in gold. Painted panels on the outer margins depicted the history of the Winter Court on one side and the birth of the Wild Hunt on the other.

I mouthed the words as written, struggling to understand the ancient tongue as it spoke of battles long fought and the emergence of the Sluagh.

"Neither welcome in heaven nor hell, the great horde rose, troublesome and destructive in Avalon. Spanning the frigid sky, they flew at night like furies from the west.

The most dread of the faeries, their great, leathery wings beat the dark sky, hunting for souls. The far-thinking Winter Court struck a bargain with the strengthening horde. Offering its leader, Taltos, a contract and protection as a faction of the Royal Court."

The words were too faded to read more, but it was there in ink and blood. The Sluagh belonged to the Unseelie and had been under their command for a millennium.

So why did Taltos attack the Winter palace the other night? And why was the book showing this to me now? What had this to do with the Nocturna of the Eventide Forest?

No sooner had I thought about the question than the pages flipped again.

The Nocturna wait in shadow. The sleeping horde. They bide undisturbed until trespass awakens vengeance. No light of foot, no light at all, illuminate the darkened ruins. The clash of swords echoes still, until blade touches blade once more.

I swallowed hard. "So how do I get through this forest of doom and find Merlin's ruins?"

The aged paper fluttered one last time, but not for more history or veiled threats. This time it was something useful.

Under cover of night, the dryads dance.
Bring honey, mead, and frankincense.
An offering make, to Druitia's heart,
her temple ruins, to make a start.
Your journey there, your passage earned,
only silver pure, ensures return.

I read the poem over and over, barely committing it to memory before the book slammed closed. Scrounging for paper and pen, I transcribed the poetic instructions word for word.

Merlin. I had to tell him. For no other reason than to make sure the forbidden book wasn't playing me for a fool. One thing was clear, though. I wasn't entering that forest tomorrow unarmed.

The book may have given me a way in and a way out, but it was an Unseelie tome created in conjunction with the Sluagh. Anything could go wrong, and with Merlin's penchant for cryptic, I wasn't taking a chance.

Until blade touches blade...

More like an iron blade dipped in salt.

That would kill a Sluagh dead for sure. Problem was, it would kill me dead too.

CHAPTER
Eight

MORNING WINKED along the floor of my bedroom. I rolled over, taking the covers with me. A dull ache behind one eye, coupled with pain in my jaw, told me what I already knew. My anxiety had gotten the better of me, even in my sleep.

I could handle a case of *pre-date-with-Daire* jitters, but this was much more. The weight of my mother's current machinations pressed on me, and that, coupled with what I might find waiting in the Eventide, made things worse. Meeting Daire was the easy part. Getting there? That was another story.

The glowing texts from the library only amplified my anxiety. That meant two things took precedence over everything else on my plate today —swords and sorcerers. Practicing my defensive skills, and then convincing Merlin to can his cryptic and tell me everything I needed to know about what lurked in the Eventide—like the Nocturna, for one—or for many, in fact, was paramount. According to the tomes, there were plenty of lesser Fae calling the gloom-filled wood as home. Fae that weren't exactly friendly to the Summer Court—or my bloodline.

After my dramatic departure from dinner, I doubted my mother meant for me to keep my appointment with her and her Privy Council. Still, I was already in the three-headed doghouse for disrespect and impertinence. I didn't need her locking me in one of her towers because I pushed the issue.

Throwing my covers back, I sat up with a wince. Sidhe didn't often suffer headaches, but stress was a great equalizer. Humankind had Tylenol. I had Merlin. Years ago, he'd whipped up a concoction for me, but as I got older and my pesky nerves had made themselves at home behind my right eye, he'd made sure I always had his remedy on hand.

I padded barefoot toward the covered windows across from my bed, the sunlight crisscrossing the floor like a laser trap from a human realm movie. Folding the shutters back, I breathed in, tasting the soft blend of sea salt and honeysuckle. The Summer Court palace was on a fragrant bluff overlooking a horseshoe cove of aquamarine water. It rested on a protected peninsula on the southeastern shore of the Faewyn sea. The same sea we shared with the Winter Court—just from opposite sides.

Merlin once said our fertile green shores and white cliffs reminded him of where he'd met Arthur. I once thought that romantic, considering the tragic story of the once and future king and his Camelot. Not so much now that I knew how the story truly ended, or didn't end, since the human king and his consort were what kept Merlin tethered to my mother and her whims.

I breathed in again, letting the honeysuckle aroma transport me. The scent would forever remind me of Daire and our first moonlight kiss. Of possibilities. Of anticipation. I pulled myself from my reverie and then headed for my bathroom and Merlin's tonic. If I wanted more than just reveries and anticipation, I needed to get moving.

I washed and dressed quickly, throwing on my kirtle and corset before stepping into a day gown. Struggling with my sleeves, I puffed damp hair from my forehead, wishing I could walk into court in my human realm clothes. However, if the Privy Council was still a thing this morning, I had to look the part.

Fiddling with the combs holding my curls, I glanced at the silver clock beside my bed. If I hurried, I might catch the queen as she left breakfast, or at least run into someone who'd happily tell me she was displeased—and looking for me.

The main staircase curved past three floors in the east wing of the palace, the uppermost floor being our private quarters. The second floor held our music room, our private dining room, my mother's private anteroom and informal throne, the Privy Council chambers, and various other offices. The main level of the east wing was the most sumptuous. It housed the great hall, as well as the queen's formal throne room, a receiving hall where courtiers waited to be granted audience, and of course, the grand entry where all things pomp began, and on the opposite side, the famed Summer Court pleasure gardens.

I pulled the heavy door open to the private dining room only to find it devoid of people and food. A frown tugged at my lips as I closed the door again.

"May I be of assistance, your Royal Highness?"

I turned toward the questioning voice to see one of the stewards watching me as I mused to myself. "Mason...yes. Where is everyone?"

Glancing toward the stairs, he shifted the weight of the linens he carried to his hip. "Breakfast is alfresco this morning, on the south terrace."

"That's...unusual, but thank you." I nodded and then pivoted for the stairs. "Mason?" I stopped, glancing at him across my shoulder. "Have you seen the queen this morning?"

He shook his head. "I'm sorry, princess. I have not." He dipped his chin to his chest once and then continued into the empty dining room.

I rushed down the stairs, making a sharp turn for the corridor that led to the south terrace. It was a chilly place to set an alfresco meal, let alone breakfast. The sea spray was rather aggressive on that side of the peninsula, and it made everything damp even on the brightest of days.

Sorcha was coming in from outside as I arrived. "Well, well. For someone who slept in, you don't look it. Are you okay?" My sister eyed what I'm sure was my haphazard hair and puffy eyes.

"Headache," I replied. I didn't have to say anything else. Sorcha knew exactly what I meant.

"Relax. Mother left for her pavilion at dawn. She canceled all her meetings, including the one with the Privy Council. Niall stormed out afterward. He was a pretty shade of purple when she dismissed him like a serf. She did leave instructions for you, though."

The Lord Chancellor was well acquainted with the queen's whim, however annoying. As much as I disliked the man, I understood his frustration. I exhaled, already tensing. "Let me guess. I'm to muck out the stables wearing my favorite ballgown and slippers. I'm sure last night's outburst is the reason everyone has a wet ass with their eggs this morning."

"No, to ball-gowned mucking, and yes, to our collective wet asses, but that's not it." Sorcha's arms crossed loosely over her chest. "You are to spend the day with Rylan. What you do is your choice, but Mother was very specific. He is to escort you. Everywhere."

I closed my eyes, my head sinking between my shoulders with a groan. I needed to speak with Merlin, and I was not about to invite Rylan into the sorcerer's keep.

"It's not a punishment, Eden. Mother was serious last night, and if you hadn't stalked off like a baby, you wouldn't be so shocked now." Sorcha touched my arm. "On paper Rylan is an eligible suitor for you, and you know it."

With an exhale, I opened my eyes and straightened my shoulders with an audible crack. "Trouble is, Rylan knows he ticks all the royal boxes, which makes him insufferable." I glanced at the carved wood and glass door at the tables set along the slate terrace. "Well, I suppose I could score brownie points with Mother and ask him to give me a few lessons in defensive sword play. It was a sore point with her last night, and Rylan is skilled in that arena."

The words came out of my mouth resigned, but the more I thought about it, I couldn't have asked for a better excuse to clash steel. This was a win-win. Of course, I'd have to ditch Rylan before I headed to Merlin's tower, but one of the benefits of having an ageless druid as your only friend, was learning every secret passage in the castle that led to his lair. Merlin had made a game of it when I was a child, and now, that game would pay off.

"You've got that look again, Eden." Sorcha's eyes narrowed at me.

"What look? I have to spend the day with a courtier whose idea of meaningful conversation is discussing who would win in a troll versus ogre wrestling match."

"You know what I mean. You've got the same look as Mother whenever she finds a loophole to get what she wants."

I hugged my sister before she could press. "Stop worrying. You'll get wrinkles."

Kissing her cheek, I didn't give her a chance to say anything else, though if Sorcha wanted, she would've followed me out on the terrace to push the issue. Now I needed to channel my mother and plaster a welcoming smile on my face.

The doors to the terrace closed behind me, and I stood for a moment deciding how to approach. I had dismissed Rylan at the Winter Court gala and hadn't even feigned an apology. Not even after our forced scurry.

If I sought him directly now, how would that look? Not that I cared, really. He was a means to an end. A beguiling, heart-racing end. Namely, Daire. Courtiers understood two things well. Opportunity and advantage. Just as the queen confused kindness for weakness, most courtiers confused enthusiasm with desperation, and desperation was not a look I wanted.

I hated to admit it, but in this instance, it was pot, kettle, black. An ice-cold eye was an unforgiving thing, and I was just as guilty as the most cunning courtier. Rylan was opportunity and my mother's edict, my advantage. Sometimes a princess needed to do what a princess needed to do.

My feet left damp splotch marked along the slate as I walked to a small café table across the courtyard from Rylan. A tray with fresh baked scones and melt-in-your-mouth croissants arrived before I took my seat along with a pot of lemon green tea. I helped myself to a blueberry scone, slathering butter and jam on one half.

"I didn't expect to see you this morning, Eden." Rylan pulled out a chair and sat before I could protest. Not that I planned to, but I had a part to play.

"Scones." I gestured with the crusty, jam-covered half. "I can't resist when cook bakes a fresh batch. These are still warm from the oven."

"Hmmm."

Eyeing him, I picked a sugared blueberry from the pastry's edge and plopped it in my mouth. "Not a fan of sweets?"

"No, I love bakery for breakfast. I meant I figured you'd opt for a trip to the Badlands rather than risk crossing paths with me, especially today."

I feigned ignorance. "What reason would I have to avoid you, today or any other day? You're more of Sorcha's friend, it's true, but I have no issue with you, Rylan. Yet."

"So, you don't know, then." He reached to pluck a juicy berry from the other half of my scone.

"If you mean my mother's request, of course I know. I'm the heir apparent. If it concerns me, I know about it." I nearly winced at the tone of my voice. I sounded almost imperious. Like I had an army of little birds spying for me like my mother. Still, a role to play was a role to play.

Rylan seemed genuinely surprised. "Well, good. I admit, I expected you to bolt."

"Why? Because I didn't fall for your practiced courtier routine at the Winter Court gala?"

Rylan's eyes darted to the few courtiers still on the terrace. "I wouldn't advertise that too loudly."

"Which? That I gave you the royal brush, or where it happened?"

Rylan's face darkened, and his posture changed from brash nonchalance to defensive and stiff. He would bolt and then blame me as defiant, and knowing the queen, she'd see the lie as too plausible not to believe. I needed Rylan's swordsmanship help, so reining in my overall dislike was a pill I had to swallow. He wasn't a bad person, really. Just shallow in his role as courtier.

"I'm sorry, Rylan. That was rude. I've spent so much time alone, I guess I still have a lot to learn when it comes to people." I pulled the last fat sugared blueberry from my scone and held it out as a peace offering. "Friends?"

He took the blueberry from my hand, but he didn't eat it. Instead, he placed it on a napkin. "What is it you want, Eden? We've been thrown together today, whether we like it or not. I can no more refuse the queen than you, so I suggest we call a truce. I'll forget I'm a courtier, and you can leave the princess bit behind, and let's see how the day goes. We might actually surprise each other."

Either Rylan was surprisingly optimistic, or he played the odds. Either way, I appreciated the unexpected camaraderie, even if I only half bought into the idea. I watched him for a fraction longer before extending my hand across the café table. "Deal."

"Okay, then." He smiled, taking my hand.

Rylan was handsome. Even more so when he smiled and his eyes flashed, yet there was no skitter of flesh when his hand gripped mine. No spark, like with Daire. Thank the fates.

"There are a lot of hours between now and sunset." He angled his head, still holding my hand. "How do you suggest we spend our time?"

Oh no, he didn't.

Had I imagined the innuendo in his ask? If he hadn't kept my hand longer than required, I wouldn't have questioned it. But imagined or not, the minor red flag left me second guessing my plan. Had I inadvertently sent wrong signals, or had Rylan assumed there was more for the taking because my mother deemed him suitable? I needed to nip this now.

Turning my hand palm up in his grip, I changed his hold so I could slip free. It was a classic move I learned from the queen. It left the courtier off balance, allowing him to think the move was an opening instead of a practiced disentanglement. Rylan got the point.

Pulling my hand back, I kept his gaze. "How does a clash of steel sound?"

"I'm sorry?"

"You're not as thick as you like people to think, Rylan. You know what I mean. Your swordsmanship is well known among courtiers our age. The queen thinks I need to learn to defend myself, and while I can hold my own, I never paid much attention when Caxton tried to teach me more. It's become a problem."

"Ah. I see." He nodded, even if his eyes were calculating what I shared with how it could be used. Once a courtier, always a courtier.

"So?"

He pushed his chair back, scraping the metal against the slate before holding his hand out to me. "I think you'd better change, first. Skirts and swords don't mix."

I humphed, getting up from my chair. I had to get my sword anyway. "If I didn't know better," I replied, "I'd think that was a tad woman-hatey."

He shook his head, but I caught the ghost of a smirk teasing the corner of his mouth. "Simple logistics, milady. As opposed to *misogynistics*."

"Clever," I granted. "Even if that's *not* an actual word. Still, I get what you mean."

He inclined his head. "I'll be in the armory courtyard when you're ready."

CHAPTER
Nine

SWEAT DIDN'T TRICKLE. It ran in rivulets from my scalp down either side of my face. The linen shirt beneath my leather armor was drenched as well, and my arms were leaden and ached. We'd been training most of the afternoon, and either Rylan was a ruthless blade master, or he was making me pay for yet another brush off—however stealth and politic.

I'd need to soak in a hot bath with Merlin's salts for a week after this workout. The old druid had to have something in his store of magic to help, or my date with Daire and destiny was doomed. I'd never be ready for the Nocturna this way. I could barely lift my sword another moment.

"Concentrate, Eden. Push through the pain. It's the only way you'll get stronger." Rylan's sword clashed with mine again, and I stumbled back. "Tighten your stance and keep your blade up. Stop forecasting your next move."

"I'm not!" I swung again only to have Rylan block and turn me completely around, the sole of his boot hard and fast against my bottom, adding insult to injury.

"Then how did I know you'd come at me from the left with a front edge diagonal strike? Half the battle is keeping your strategy to yourself while anticipating your opponent's attack."

This was supposed to be a refresher lesson, but Rylan barked as if lives depended on my blade. Maybe he was proving something. Or maybe he was just an arsehole.

"Think, Eden," he continued. "Sword play requires both deception and calm. Traits second nature to our kind. Tap into that. Remember, physical strength is only one part. Keen awareness coupled with composure, as well as a quick wit to turn the tables on an opponent, are as necessary as confidence, rhythm, and intimidation."

Caxton had said the same thing. The only difference was he threw his sword at me in frustration and stormed off mumbling something about women and weapons. He'd been lucky that one of my mother's little birds hadn't whispered about his temper tantrum, or he'd have felt her steel— and I didn't mean her sword.

"There's definitely no *play* in sword play." Breathing hard, I lowered my sword to the packed ground. "It's a sick misnomer for sadomasochists."

"This isn't a game, Eden. There's art in the discipline, but the operative word is discipline. Until you take this seriously, you'll always be on the receiving end of someone else's blade. If it helps, think of your training as a necessary evil. Tricking your opponent can give you an edge leading to their defeat."

"I'm not wired that way, Rylan." Wetting my lips, I steadied my breathing. I wanted a lesson, but what I thought was a resourceful idea had backfired. I expected a review of the basics. Maybe a few tricks to get me out of a tight squeeze. Not this thank-you-sir-may-I-have-another paramilitary thing.

Clearly, Rylan took his role as blade master seriously, but I never thought he'd prove me so inept. The hopeless feeling made having a conversation with Merlin about the Eventide's waiting dangers all the more imperative.

Nothing was going to keep me from my rendezvous with Daire. Had he gone through a similar kind of rigor? Was he trained to mislead to attain an end? The answer was as plain as the glint off my blade in the afternoon sun. He most certainly had. The question was had he used that training to mislead me. Was I a means to an end, and just too naïve and thirsty to see it?

My gut said no.

Merlin had taught me to follow the signs of my body. That my gut would never deceive me, whereas my head and my heart might. They were governed by want, rather than truth, and want was something a person's gut didn't take into account. When it mattered, one's sympathetic nervous system never lied.

Rylan was still talking. I forced myself to pay attention. Again, he was right. If I was to pass through the Eventide unscathed, I needed to focus and find my control. I wondered what the courtier would say if he knew why I suggested we clash steel.

"You're full Sidhe, Eden. And of royal blood. Whether you want to admit it or not, you have every one of the attributes I described. How you choose to use them is up to you, but the fact remains, you have the power in you to wield steel. We're all taught as children how to tap into our borne elements. This goes deeper than that. You need to trust your instincts and your magic. You can't count on raw adrenaline to raise that kind of power. You have to cultivate the ability to raise it at will. It might save your life one day."

He advanced again, swinging his blade with fierce blows, pushing me back. Jolts shuddered my bones straight to my spine, clash after clash. I gripped the hilt of my sword, white-knuckled, with each counter and parry. Tears pricked, but I steeled my jaw, refusing to give in to weakness. Rylan was right, and he was not about to let up.

Metering my breath, I concentrated on each inhale and exhale. Each heartbeat, and the feel of sweat on my skin in the cool air. My senses were alive and tingling, and I kept my chin low and my eyes on Rylan as he circled again.

Every sense fired, engulfing me, and a strange awareness sparked. The sharkskin-covered hilt in my hand pulsed with energy, an echo of the sea beast and its fight to survive before giving up the ghost. In that moment, the term *alive* took on a different meaning. Everything coalesced. Aching with life. The taste of the air. The scent of dampness on the stone walls surrounding the armory courtyard. The hum of insects, and the feel of the ground beneath my feet.

Sunlight crackled, beckoning me to make it my own before centering in my core and exploding out into my limbs. I no longer needed a spell to command the light. It was part of me. Power. Pure and flowing.

Merlin's pendant warmed beneath my leather tunic, reassuring me, even as energy-charged synapses conducted newfound strength. I was one with my blade. My arms were like steel, and my feet moved in deliberate maneuvers as though guided by an unseen force.

Rylan advanced, wielding a crushing blow that I met with equal intensity. Now it was his turn to stumble back, and the look on his face was stunned surprise. Even more when I advanced farther, my steel met his retreat, stopping short of pinning him to the cobbled walls.

"Well done, Eden," he replied, gingerly moving the point of my blade away from his chest. "It seems someone found their inner Sidhe."

Exhaling a satisfied breath, I took a step back to let him off the wall. "Like they say, a student is only as good as their teacher."

"Keep that attitude and you might make a decent sword fighter one day." Rylan inclined his head, and the show of respect tasted even better than my quick win.

"Maybe, but right now I want a shower and a change of clothes." I plunged the point of my sword into the dirt, relishing the reverberations up my arm.

"I could do with the same." He wiped sweat and dirt from his face with his forearm. "Why don't we meet at the entrance to the pleasure gardens after we clean up? We could go for a walk, then maybe have dinner together. It might be nice to talk without the threat of possible bloodshed."

I tilted my head to better read his expression. Was he being a friend, or was he still posturing for more?

With no warning, he closed the distance between us and bent to kiss me, and my hand shot up, palming his face like a basketball. Shoving him back, I didn't care if I insulted him or not.

"Are you insane, or just stupid?"

"I'm sorry!" he sputtered. "You angled your head, and I thought—"

"No, Rylan." I cut him off, gaping at his stunned look and my finger marks on his cheeks and forehead. "That's the point! You didn't think. You assumed."

He opened his mouth to speak, but I shut him down again. "Not another word. I'm going to chalk this up to crossed wires, but I swear, if you ever try it with me again, I'll split you from throat to balls."

I didn't need him to reply. I pulled my sword from the ground, keeping my sharp gaze pointed at him, punctuating my promise. Was he that obtuse? I offered friendship. Albeit, with an ulterior motive, but friendship, nonetheless, and Rylan confused that with verbal foreplay. Like I'd said. Once a courtier, always a courtier.

Stalking back to the main palace, I trudged up to my chambers muttering to myself and feeling even more stupid than Rylan's lapse. I needed to get to Merlin's while I had the time. If I was lucky, I could bathe and get to the old druid's keep before nightfall. My mother would never deem Rylan's move an affront. In fact, I was positive she planned his overstep, giving him leave to find an opening and run through center with it. What she didn't count on was me, or how I'd feel about it.

By the time I left the armory courtyard, I had already compiled a list of questions for Merlin in my head. Time was ticking. I washed quickly, doing a fast rinse and repeat before dressing in a pair of lined leggings and a thick, hooded, close-knit sweater that fell to mid-thigh. I braided my long, red hair, happy with how it fell across my shoulder. Maybe I'd leave it that way for the night.

For now, I was going for warmth and ease of movement. A pair of thick-soled boots with a hidden blade completed the outfit. All I needed was my sword at my hip, but between now and moonrise, I didn't need raised eyebrows alerting the queen. I could glamour something sexy and fun once I made it through Druitia's portal in the Eventide.

A sound turned my attention toward my bedroom door. I thought it might be Sorcha, but she had been uncharacteristically absent since I'd seen her in the morning. More than likely for plausible deniability in case things didn't go as planned tonight. Not that I blamed her. Why should we both have to suffer the queen's wrath if things went south? She didn't know exactly what I had planned, but she had an inkling, I was sure.

It was only when I went to turn back to my vanity mirror, I noticed a note on the floor. It was an apology from Rylan, slipped under my door. Again, was he truly that obtuse?

Eden,

Forgive my unseemly assumptions and have dinner with me.

I know you'd rather eat iron nails, but I hope you'll meet me anyway.

If only to satisfy your obligation and your mother's orders...

I crumpled the note without reading the rest. "When the Rugged Mountains grow teeth," I mumbled, tossing the balled paper into the trash beneath my vanity.

Dismissing Rylan and his affected mea culpa, I gave myself a last once over in the glass and then left for Merlin's tower without looking back. From there, I'd wait for moonrise in the library and head for the Eventide.

Moving quickly, I slipped into the anteroom outside my mother's informal throne room. When the queen was in residence, the room was abuzz with voices. Tonight, it was as empty and quiet as a tomb, which wasn't surprising. Not with my mother off on another whim.

I took advantage of the solitude and headed into the throne room and straight toward the tapestried wall behind the carved wooden dais. A shadow caught my peripheral eye, and I stopped, turning slowly to scan the area. If there was anyone there, I missed it. Had my mother had me watched today? It was possible, but I hadn't given her a reason. Yet.

Stepping behind the throne, I waited for footsteps or some other telltale sign of my mother's little birds. I was hidden from every angle facing the throne head-on and to the side. I knew, because as children, Sorcha and I hid behind the queen's throne during her informal audiences, trying not to giggle at her silly sycophants. It worked...until it didn't, which is why our mother posted guards behind her throne whenever she occupied the dais.

I wasn't the only one who knew about the castle's secret passages, but I was pretty certain I was the only one of my generation to know about this one. Well, me and Sorcha. Still, what we discovered during that innocent time was invaluable. A hidden escape route built into our mother's throne. What meant so much was the hidden tunnel led straight to an outer keep near Merlin's tower. One of the ways I spent so much time with the old seer as a child. I couldn't be sure, but it was probably the way Sorcha snuck out to meet her Greyrym as well.

It had been years since I used the secret passage, but the release mechanism snicked open as though it was yesterday, and I squeezed into the neck of the escape hatch before the panel closed behind me. It was much narrower than I remembered, but I ignored my claustrophobia and climbed down the ladder to the tunnel.

"Good Goddess..." I whispered, scrubbing a hand over my face, clearing gossamer spider strands, and then reached for the knife in my boot.

Spiderwebs hung thick and curtain-like along the inside of the tunnel, and I was sure things I didn't want to know had made themselves at home in the unused space. Considering the creepy factor, there was no way my sister used this passageway, regardless of how hot her rendezvous.

I didn't recall the tunnel being this haunted when Sorcha and I explored as children. Maybe the queen gave a damn after all and had the place swept for us. Although, it was more likely to keep the heir and the spare safe than anything like maternal concern.

Tapping into my newfound power, I conjured a light ball and started into the tunnel. The crackling energy must've scared whatever lurked because I made my way to the other side without so much as a scuttle or a hiss in my wake.

If memory served, the exit was a square stone set into the floor of the icehouse outside Merlin's keep. Moss grew at the tunnel's end along the upper walls and along the tunnel ceiling from the ever-present moisture.

The thick carpet obscured any hint of the exit, and I had to ferret around, digging my fingers into the cold, damp growth until I found the stone's telltale edge. Pushing my full weight into its center, I shifted the mossy stone up and over and then climbed out of the tunnel and into the icehouse vault.

The ice pit was empty. Not a single ice block remained, but leftover meltwater puddled in spots and along the floor's edge, making the air dank and the mucky ground stink of mold and unmentionables.

Not seeing an ice chute, or the ladder workers used to enter and exit the subterranean storage, I exhaled, annoyed. I'd purposely come this way to avoid alerting people to my plans, and now I'd have to head back the way I came.

Scanning the damp mess, I caught the edge of a ladder hidden under old hay along a side wall. I was already a filthy mess, so what was a little more dirt? I cleared the debris, hoping the tall wooden form was still in one piece and functional. It must've been placed against the wall for eventual repair, but it would serve for now.

I struggled to lean the heavy ladder against the carved indent below the ground level door. Once secured, I climbed slowly, taking care not to overburden the tenuous rungs. The door at the top was locked, and rightly so. One false step, and splat! Headfirst into a stone pit.

Working my knife out of my boot again, I slipped the blades tip into the lock. A few twists and the mechanism gave way, allowing me to steal out into the twilight.

"Hey! You!" a booming voice echoed off the stone building. "Get away from there or I'll call the guard!"

With my hood up, I'd pass as anyone but the heir apparent, something I usually relished. Just not when it came with the threat of being manhandled. My emerald eyes would eventually register my identity with whomever, but not everyone was quick to make the connection. I didn't have the time or the inclination to play games, so I spared a quick glance toward the deep voice and then took off at a run for Merlin's tower. It was question-and-answer time for the old druid.

CHAPTER
Ten

"LITTLE DOVE?" Merlin's voice drifted from the worktable, but he didn't turn to greet me. Then again, that wasn't unusual. "Am I correct in assuming you are responsible for the commotion outside my keep tonight?"

I wiped a stray cobweb from my face, listening to the sound of guards looking for an errant boy skulking around the outer buildings. "Guilty."

Merlin glanced at me over his shoulder, one brow hiking in an arched query at my disheveled appearance.

"Don't ask," I replied to the silent question.

He returned to his scribblings, but his posture told me he wasn't about to leave it alone. "You look as though you've crawled through a fetid crypt, which means you used your mother's priest hole escape to visit me this evening. Since you haven't used that passageway in nigh over twelve years, the question begs...why?"

I didn't answer. Instead, I reached for Merlin's ever-present stash of ale and poured myself a large draught.

"Your body is tense and practically vibrating. Is there something you wish to tell me, Eden?"

I wiped my mouth with the back of my sleeve, smearing dirt across the knit. "Not me... You."

"I'm not in the mood for games, Eden. If you have something you wish to know, just ask. I'm old and tire easily these days."

"Sounds like someone's nose is growing."

The old wizard turned, genuinely puzzled, and I couldn't help a small grin when answering his silent query. "*Pinocchio*? The children's story from the human realm?"

"Ah."

"You may be old, but I've never seen you tire of anything besides suffering fools. You're right, though. I do have questions, and I need you to be brutally honest with me."

"Brutally, eh?" I watched him turn the fire down on his latest bubbling brew, his long white hair tied with a leather cord at the nape of his hunched shoulders.

"Merlin, please."

He faced me at this point. "Again, just ask me whatever it is you feel you need to know. I've always been honest with you, little dove, albeit never brutally so."

"I don't *feel* I need to know. I *know*, I need to know."

His face wore a look as familiar and soothing as an old pair of slippers. Reassuring, yet tacit. "And what is it you think you need to know."

"What am I facing in the Eventide? I know what you told me, but you were so cryptic. I found sources in the palace library that spoke of the Nocturna..." I explained the rest, telling him what I discovered in the tomes, while watching his expression. "If I don't know what I'm up against, then I'm not sure I should go, and if I don't, I'll never forgive myself... or you."

"I see."

The reassuring and somewhat amused look on his face sobered, prompting me to take a step toward the old sorcerer. "Do you, Merlin? You pointed me in the direction of the portal near the old oaks and made me the key. I know it was at my behest, and you warned me it was dangerous, but now I need to know *how* dangerous. Will I come out of this unharmed?"

He stared at me with a wizened gaze, and the shadow that passed his eyes scared me. "I won't, will I?"

"Eden, what is it you want to hear?"

"I don't want to hear anything but the truth and not couched in cryptic or one of your blasted riddles. I need to know what I'm up against."

"Yes."

"Merlin, for Goddess's sake! Yes what?"

"Yes, you might not come out of the journey unscathed. In fact, you might not survive. Then again, you might. You might even more than survive. You might learn something about yourself and your future and maybe find an ally. I can already see you've tapped deeper into your power. Your aura is shimmering around you in a golden glow because of it."

"You're being cryptic again."

"And you're looking for guarantees." He paused, moving slower than usual toward his chair by the fire. "Life, whether it be Fae or human, or anything in between or otherwise, does not come with guarantees. The only guarantee in life, is death, at some point. Even for those of us deemed immortal. Immortality is as cruel a misnomer as it is a cruel state."

Was Merlin trying to tell me something? He said he was tired, but I dismissed his claim as a ploy to get me to make my point. Observing him in the firelight, he suddenly seemed older, even more so than his usual state. "Merlin, are you ill?"

He smiled and his eyes twinkled inside crinkled flesh. "I'm fine, little dove. Perhaps a little taxed trying to read the portends."

"You mean *my* portends."

He tapped the side of his nose. "I told you, free will is not just for the human-realm. If you choose to go into the Eventide tonight, you set certain paths in motion. What waits for you there will also be a choice. Theirs. The Nocturna, as you learned. How you interact there will also be a choice. Many variables, and many outcomes, depending on those variables."

"So, you're saying what happens in the Eventide tonight is dependent on me and the choices I make."

"Just so. Which is why I suggested caution and prudence."

I blinked at him for a moment. "I only remember you suggesting insurance and protection, and that had to do with the Winter Court gala."

"Then your infatuation with the Unseelie heir has given you selective hearing. How am I to help if you only hear what you want? I advise and counsel, Eden, but it does both of us ill if you choose not to listen." With a wave of his hand, Merlin showed me the conversation like human-realm instant replay: *The Eventide belongs to many Fae, not just the Sidhe. You would do well to remember that when ambling there or suffer the consequences.*

It wasn't as straightforward as insurance and protection, but I couldn't argue with that.

"Little dove," he continued, "whether you venture forth tonight isn't the question. It's already written, even if the ink isn't yet dry. The question is what you make of it going forward."

More cryptic. Like his talk of prophecy.

My lips parted, my mind trying to make heads or tails of his words. In that moment, my gaze jerked to the old druid, and his eyes said it all. Everything was connected. My choices. Merlin's hazy visions. My future. I had to go tonight, regardless of what or whom I faced.

Merlin's earlier words came back in a rush, and this time they resonated: What if there was a divergent path? A choice that didn't circle back to the throne. ...nothing more than a ripple in what I see... a ripple that leaves me unsettled...

I opened my mouth to question more, but Lyrae screeched a shrill warning, stopping me cold. The strident sound rattled the windows, and the raven swooped from the rafters, talons bared. Altair, her brother owl, matched her at her flank.

I whirled on my feet, knocking over a high-backed chair. The old wizard cast an arm toward the tower door, flinging it open. *Nocht tú féin!* The gruff command granted his birds leave to intercept the uninvited guest.

Their screech was pitiless as they swooped, talons first. "Call them off!" Rylan covered his face, protecting his eyes. "For pity's sake! Please!" He scrambled for his blade, but the dagger and its scabbard clattered across the room with a flick of Merlin's hand.

"Seas síos ach fan gar!"

The birds retreated, circling overhead before flanking Merlin on either shoulder. "You can lower your defenses, boy. The birds are calm. For now."

Rylan lowered his bloodied arm from his face. "Those birds are a menace!"

"Says the trespasser!" I shot back. Annoyance overtook my disbelief, and I stalked between him and Merlin. "What are you doing here, Rylan?"

Merlin dismissed the birds and then pulled a curious cloth from his robe and handed it to Rylan. "Use this on your wounds. It will stem the blood and speed your healing."

"Hmph. No doubt soaked in one of your poisoned potions." Rylan's derisive snort more show than stay.

"As a courtier of the realm, you know better than to lurk in stairwells near private quarters." The old druid's face was more curious than annoyed. "Which begs so many questions."

"Begs?" I retorted. "Try demands."

Rylan took the cloth with a suspicious sniff, but the moment he wiped the blood from his forearms, the wounds closed, leaving no trace. "Count yourself lucky your magic worked, sorcerer. I could have you pilloried for this."

"Give it a rest, Rylan," I replied, disgusted at his entitled tone. "Considering Merlin's value to my mother, I doubt she'd give a flying fig about your complaint. Especially since you're the guilty party. An apology as well as a thank you is in order, if for no other reason than Merlin and his keep are protected."

Eyeing him, I caught his daggered glance toward the rafters. I didn't need Merlin's second sight to know Rylan's mind. "I'm warning you. If harm comes to either of those birds, I will personally see you and your family banished to the Badlands. Like Merlin, those birds are under my mother's protection, as they serve her well. Now, why are you following me?"

For a split second, I wondered if he was the shadow that caught my eye in my mother's throne room, but I quickly dismissed the idea. Rylan was many things, but the only time he was stealth was when he had a sword in his hand.

"I have better things to do with my time than follow you, Your Highness. I came to see if this is where you ran after you ditched me." He sniffed, giving my dirty appearance a quick once over, but was smart enough not to comment.

"Ditched you?" I shook my head. "You overstepped the boundaries of friendship, Rylan, and you know it. Everyone, including the queen, knows I'm either here with Merlin, or in the palace library when I'm not required elsewhere." I paused, waiting for him to say something, but when he didn't, I asked once more. "Again, what are you doing here?"

Both of us stood in defensive postures, arms crossed and scowling. Merlin moved from his place by the fire. "If I may," the old sorcerer interjected, "I think it might hasten an end to this standoff if we each took a dram of something calming."

Rylan didn't reply, but his eyes darted to the bottle that appeared on Merlin's worktable along with three crystal tumblers. "Whiskey?" he asked.

"A blend from the age of men when dragons filled the skies." Merlin winked.

"Guaranteed to warm the innards and cool fiery tempers." He poured three glasses, two fingers each, before lifting his glass to ours. "To those who venture where curiosity beckons. Slainte."

Rylan shot back his drink as though it was elderberry water. The boy coughed and sputtered, and I had to stifle a laugh. "Smooth," he croaked, coughing again.

I cradled my glass, knowing better than to down the dragon's brew in one go. "So, it's true, then. Curiosity is what had you loitering outside Merlin's door."

"Eden." Merlin gave me a nearly imperceptible head shake. My instinct was to argue the point, but why bother? Rylan wasn't about to be placated by anything I said.

A practiced courtier's mask fell into place across Rylan's face. "No...Eden is right. I forgot myself and my place, and I apologize for my ill-mannered idling."

"I believe skulking is more the word you're looking for."

Rylan's mask faltered as I watched him weigh the truth against a more politic answer. "Fine. Since you're clearly hellbent on flaying my pride today."

"Your pride is just fine, Rylan, or you wouldn't be here right now. Like most courtiers, you've simply forgotten how to be real. If you're curious about me, then just ask. Whether I share anything with you is another story. Stop playing games. I'm not one of your lot, something your backhanded compliments drove home at the Winter Court gala."

His eyes darted to Merlin, but he didn't pursue the accusation I knew sat on the tip of his tongue. "Well?" I prompted.

"Fine." He pressed his lips a bit. "Since we were children, you were always sequestered up here. At first, I thought it was part of your training as the heir apparent. Then I thought it must be some sort of punishment, but Sorcha said it was neither. I suppose I wanted to see for myself what held your interest all these years."

"Knowledge, Rylan. That's what holds my interest. Merlin and I both share a thirst for truth and exploration. And that is part and parcel of my training as heir apparent. Nothing more, nothing less." I shrugged. "It suits me."

His gaze dropped for a moment, and I swear his shoulders drooped. "Unlike me, I guess."

Rylan's posture was the perfect picture of regret, but I caught the glint in his eyes when he looked up. Another mask. He was fishing. If not for me, then for something. Ulterior motives, as always.

I didn't take the bait. Instead, I stared at him until it was uncomfortable enough for him to put his glass on the table and then turn for the door. I followed him out, trailing him as he headed down the stone steps to the keep. I watched from the door as he stalked halfway through the courtyard before turning to point his finger at me.

"You're right about one thing, Eden. You're thirsty, but not for what's inside that tower. You gave me the brush off the other night, and then again, this afternoon, but you sought me this morning. Remember that."

His claim was ridiculous, considering he was the one who interrupted my breakfast, and he had conveniently forgotten my mother's orders.

"You weren't sought, Rylan. You were there, and it suited my needs." I put as much disdain in my reply as I could muster, rivaling the queen. "If Cian had been stuffing his face with bread and jam instead of you, he would have sufficed, and I doubt my mother would've cared that I made a substitution. You were a means to an end. That's all."

He nodded a little too knowingly, and I cursed myself for handing him the wrong impression. The means was a training lesson, and the end was my entering the Eventide forearmed, but how could Rylan know that? I couldn't blame him for reading sexual innuendo into what I said. In his world, everything revolved around exploits and their usefulness.

"An itch that needed to be scratched... *hmmm*," he replied. "If that was the case, then why threaten me with bodily harm when I tried to kiss you? If you wanted another kind of sword to practice with, I'd have gladly obliged."

He grabbed his crotch before I could explain or deny, and the vulgar things that came out of his mouth dissolved any guilt I felt. "You're gross and you've got it all wrong." I shook my head, but he wasn't listening.

"C'mon, Eden." He closed the distance between us, overconfident. "Tell me the real reason you refused my kiss."

I didn't hesitate.

"Your breath."

The courtier gaped at me, his hand involuntarily shooting to his mouth. He blinked for a moment and then turned on his heel to leave without a word. I lifted my hand, about to call after him, but I didn't. The hurtful retort wasn't my finest moment, and fresh guilt slashed knowing I'd sunk to his level. Even with his vulgarities, Rylan wasn't completely repugnant, even if he was a jerk a little too often for my taste. He proved his covert amiability in the way he trained with me this afternoon. Still, I needed him to go away. Even if it meant going away mad. Otherwise, he'd bloodhound me for the rest of the evening.

Sprinting up the stairs, I found Merlin where I left him nursing his whiskey, only now he gazed into the fire. He didn't acknowledge me when I came in, nor did he look away from the flames when I sat beside him at the hearth.

His blue eyes were fixed and staring, and I knew then he was caught in his second sight. Was his vision about me, and what would transpire tonight? Or was it more far-reaching? With Merlin, I never knew, though I didn't dare disturb whatever vision held him held rapt. Most times he wasn't aware of my presence at all, so I moved to rest my hand on his knee to say goodbye.

The vision hit hard and fast the moment my hand touched his robe. Ground fog swirled over a path broken by gnarled roots and spindly scrub. Thin branches whipped in the wind as I raced through the overgrowth. Voices echoed behind me, gaining ground. Closer. Closer. Daire beckoned. His hand out, waiting. I had to get to him, but my steps grew heavy. My body thick. Warm and wet spilled to my thighs. Blood red. I screamed, reaching for Daire...

The vision broke with the sound of a choked cry, except the cry came from me in the here and now. Merlin gripped my wrist. Hard. "Eden! Have you learned nothing? I taught you better!" He shoved my hand from his knee, his eyes flashing with anger.

"I... I... only wanted to say goodbye. I didn't mean to... I didn't think..." I couldn't stop my stuttering. "Was th...th...that real?"

He closed his eyes for a moment, and when he opened them again, there was no anger. Only sad concern. "I don't know, little dove. It's as I've said. The visions are too disjointed. Too hazy. It's only one possibility out of thousands."

"But..."

He shook his head, reaching for my hand again. When I recoiled from his grip, the hurt in his eyes broke my heart. "This is the reason I'm cryptic with you. These visions float through unconscious minds like specters, haunting dreams and even waking moments. They make us doubt what we know to be true and have the power to paralyze life."

"But..."

"No buts." He got up, moving quickly as if years shed from him in that moment. He bent over the trunk at the end of his bed, and from it, he took a small, jeweled box. Inside was a blue vial the size of my hand.

Merlin poured three drops from the vial into a cup and then filled the rest with wine. "Drink," he said, handing me the concoction.

"What is it?" I sniffed the rim, remembering the last foul brew he bid me drink.

"Just do as I ask, Eden."

I nearly put the cup down to force the issue, but the expression on Merlin's face brooked no argument. He was adamant, and I trusted him with my whole self, so I downed the mixture in one go. It didn't taste like anything strange. Just Merlin's usual mulled wine.

"Was that for my nerves?" I asked.

He didn't answer.

"Merlin...was that to help calm my worries about the Eventide or was that for—" I shook my head a bit, my train of thought suddenly lost. I knew I wanted to ask him something, but I couldn't remember.

"You were saying, little dove?"

I tried to recapture what was in my mind to ask, but the thought was gone. Like a leaf falling into a running stream. I shrugged, chuckling. "I guess it wasn't that important."

Merlin's clock struck the first bell for seven in the evening. I had much to prepare, and I needed to talk to Sorcha. She could head off Rylan and the palace rumor mill before it beelined.

"I'd better go." I put the cup down on the small table by the hearth, and in that instance, an overwhelming urge crashed over me. I hugged my old friend around the waist.

"What's all this about?" he asked, letting his hand settle on my hair.

"I'm not sure, but I didn't have a choice."

His answering chuckle vibrated against my cheek. "Godspeed tonight, daughter of my heart. Whatever your path, have faith in yourself and your choices."

There was something about the word path that rang a bell, but I couldn't put my finger on it. I pulled back from the sorcerer and then tapped my nose with a wink and a smile, same as he often did. "I'll tell Daire you said hello."

He didn't reply, so I left with him watching after me as I headed for the stairs with my rendezvous on my mind.

CHAPTER
Eleven

I'D MADE it back to my chambers without raising much notice. One of the perks of being the nerdy twin, even if I was the heir apparent. My quiet nature all but made me invisible when it came to members of the court, and to be honest, I preferred it that way.

I showered quickly after dumping my tunnel-soiled clothes into a bag in my wardrobe. Luckily, I had more human-realm clothing than I'd ever need, courtesy of my sister, so I dug out a similar outfit. I opted for another pair of thick, black leggings, only this time I paired them with a forest green thermal top and matching goose down vest. Maneuverability and warmth. Not to mention camouflage.

My thick-soled boots were another story. Stinking of mold and droppings from the tunnel floor, I swapped them for a pair of knee-high riding boots: black leather with a green cuff at the top. The green bit matched my vest and thermal and was perfect for hiding my blade, so win-win.

I decided to keep my hair down, instead of in a braid. I liked my thick, corkscrew curls, and I knew Daire did as well. Going light on makeup by Sorcha's standards, I still did enough to make my sister proud. All in all, she'd be happy with my look, if not happy with my choice tonight. Not that she knew much.

I hadn't seen nor heard from Sorcha since breakfast, and she wasn't in her chambers. We were polar opposites, but we were still in each other's pockets most days, which explained why we bickered. Still, not hearing from her, or about her, all day was worrying.

Chewing on my lip, I moved to my bedroom window to peer at the lower terrace and its sprawling marble leading down to the pleasure gardens. Beyond that was the Faewyn Sea, lapping against the peninsula that housed the Summer Court.

Seelie lands were vast, spreading out from the coast to the western edge of the Badlands, and north to the border of Unseelie. That Daire's home and mine shared a common border left me with a sense the fates were on our side—and our connection was meant to be. I wondered if Daire felt as I did.

Even with all its intrigues and annoying pomp and courtiers, I loved my home. The beauty of the land. How the sea met the mountains with lush valleys in between where our people lived and worked. The Seelie and the Unseelie weren't that different. The Western Rim War caused the schism, and the sad reality was that no one from either main court, or even the lesser courts, remembered why.

Glancing down, I spotted what looked like a small bonfire on the beach below the south terrace. Sorcha loved a good bonfire. Dancing under the moon with abandon, you'd think she was part witch. If I'd find her anywhere in the palace, it'd be there.

I rushed over the steps off the same southern terrace that started my day, taking care on the wet stone not to slip. The smell of burning wood and smoke met me the moment I stepped onto the terrace, the scent growing stronger the closer I got to the beach.

The wind was surprisingly calm, as was the surf. High tide had receded, leaving the shore in dusky shades forming sand waves in the moonlight. There were a few couples around the fire, but I only recognized them by sight. Eventually, they paired off, busying themselves in the romance of the dunes.

I sat on one of the logs ringing the fire, watching lofted sparks rise toward the dark sky. The way they swirled and climbed made me think of wishes Sorcha and I made at bonfires as children.

"Little dove..."

I looked around for the odd murmur, but there was no one. "Merlin?" I whispered back, not wanting to call attention to myself.

"Look to the flames."

I peered into the crackling embers and the fire consuming the stacked boughs. Merlin's face wavered in the flames, coming in and out of focus.

"What the...?" I leaned in, close enough to feel the full heat on my face. This had to be some strange, reverse scrying technique. Either way, it was remarkable. "How did you know I'd be here?" I whispered into the fire's crackle.

Merlin didn't have to answer. I knew. The double dragon pendant. Leave it to the old sorcerer to give me something multi-purposed.

"Your courtier friend interrupted our conversation, and there are some things you need to know before you venture out tonight. We discussed choices and the inherent danger, but I agree my advice was too cryptic in nature to be truly useful."

Hmmm. What I wanted to say was 'I told you so,' but I opted for a simple thank you, instead. If Merlin was about to impart actionable steps, I didn't want my cheek sending the old druid off on a tangent.

A column of red sparks spewed toward the sky, and Merlin's face wavered almost to obscurity. "I haven't much time, so listen well. There are signs on rocks and woven into low branches and scrub. Rune signs. Remember your lessons, and how to decipher their meaning if the runes are inverted or not. They will help your choices along your way and even warn you what to avoid and where to turn."

The fire hissed as if protesting Merlin's presence. "I left you something under your pillow you'll need as well. Heed me, Eden, and take care."

"Merlin?" I knelt in the sand, peering so close to the fire I nearly burned my hair. He was gone, leaving nothing but the crackle of wood meeting fire and air.

"Who are you talking to?"

I turned at my sister's voice, watching her approach. "Myself, I guess." I got to my feet to wipe sand from my hands and knees. "I wasn't talking though, I was muttering. There's a difference."

"So, you're still pissy."

I didn't reply. So much had happened I couldn't remember if we'd bickered or why.

"And here I am trying to be nice and bring you something to eat."

Now I remembered. I wasn't allowed dinner after my stunt with my mother's peridot necklace. As if being shackled to Rylan for a day wasn't punishment enough.

"Aren't you afraid Mother will know? You know how she considers kindness a sign of weakness. To be honest, I think she may have had me followed today."

Sorcha handed me the plate and then sat beside me on the log. "Too bad. I'm not going to watch her starve you just for showing initiative and enthusiasm, something she says you lack."

"I'm pretty sure she didn't mean my brand of those characteristics." I bit into the sandwich Sorcha brought, relishing the taste. She managed most of my favorites, and I appreciated the thought.

"True," she replied, "but tough tea bags."

"Thank you, Sissy," I said chewing slowly. "For both the sentiment and the food. I didn't realize I was even hungry."

She smiled. "Sissy. Now, that's a nickname I will definitely do."

"Good."

She picked up a stray piece of driftwood from the sand and poked at the fire. "So... I saw Rylan this evening, and *ooof*... Something has really gotten under his skin." Tossing the beach branch aside, she deliberately kept her eyes on the flames, waiting, but I didn't bite.

Everyone knew Rylan and I spent most of the day together, and I'm sure they knew it was at my mother's behest. If he was that publicly upset, then the rumor mill already churned out speculation.

"For the love of all things human, Edie! Tell me." Sorcha wiped her hands and then took a handful of grapes from my plate, plopping two in her mouth at once.

I didn't want to stir the pot and make things worse, but Sorcha could sniff gossip at ten paces, and she wasn't about to let it go. We had just gotten past our latest tiff, and I didn't want to head into the Eventide with my sister angry with me, so I told her everything that happened.

She stopped chewing.

"I just wanted a sword lesson, Sorcha. It's not my fault it wasn't the kind he expected to give." I shrugged. "Suffice it to say, Rylan doesn't understand no means *no*."

"Did you really blame it on bad breath?" She whistled low. "I don't know whether to cringe or applaud. That burn took guts, Edie. To be honest, I didn't think you could be mean for sport."

"I'm *not* mean for sport." I exhaled, unhappy. If my own sister felt that way, then the rest of the palace did as well. "I feel awful, Sorcha. I just wanted him to leave me alone. I'm not Mother. I can't lead someone on simply because it might prove useful later. Rylan just wouldn't listen."

Sorcha snorted a laugh. "Beefy, beautiful, and brainless. That's the norm when it comes to courtiers, and coming from me, that's saying a lot. If their antics are getting old for me, then woof! Maybe you and you-know-who are a good thing for our gene pool."

"I guess I'll find out soon enough. Even if Merlin did call my attraction an infatuation."

She took my hand and squeezed it. "Look. I heard you two on the beach at the gala the other night, so I know you've got something planned. Just promise you'll be careful."

"Does that mean you decided you don't want to be the Summer Queen after all?"

Sorcha knocked my plate off my lap, sending most of the food into the sand.

"Hey!"

"That's what you get when you say stupid things. Now promise me, whatever you have planned you'll be careful."

Her eyes held mine, and I felt her fear. Should I tell her everything? No. Plausible deniability was the way to go, even if the most likely person to face my mother's wrath was mixing potions high in a far tower. Sorcha would be fine with just an inkling. I'd give her a play-by-play when I got back.

"If something happens, don't panic." I took her hand. "Go see Merlin. He'll know what to do."

Sorcha's face was not happy. "You've spent too much time with that old wizard that you're talking in riddles like him."

"I'm not saying anything other than if you're worried, or if I'm not back by morning, go see Merlin."

I got up to kick the sand-ruined food into what was left of the bonfire and then gave my sister the same kind of bear hug I gave Merlin. It was the first time I stopped hugging first, and for me, that meant the world. Merlin was right. I didn't give Sorcha enough credit.

The moon had crested the horizon, which meant it was time to go. I needed to get my sword from my closet and whatever Merlin left for me under my pillow.

Sorcha's friends arrived at the beach, ready for a party at that point, giving me the perfect excuse to take my leave. I glanced back at her from the stairs, and though she threw her arms in the air, carefree and wild, there was something in her posture that told me she wouldn't relax until I sat on the end of her bed with all my juicy details.

Turning at the head of the steps, I caught her looking up at me from the beach. Human-realm twins weren't the only ones who shared uncanny connections, and Sorcha's voice was clear in my head. "You are irreplaceable to me, so take care, or I'll kick your ass..."

I had to laugh. "Back atcha, Sissy..." The breeze carried my whisper to the beach along with a soft kiss.

Feeling confident, I wound my way up to the terrace and then to the east wing of the palace. I couldn't be sure, but everything in my gut told me this was the beginning, not the end, and an adventure that would determine my life would soon unfold. How so? I had no idea, but the fates were about to show me, and I was ready and willing.

CHAPTER
Twelve

SNEAKING out of the palace was easier than I'd thought. Maybe because Caxton had traveled with the queen to the pavilion, thus leaving a gap in his usually tight web. Whether as a strongman to remove a tedious lover, or even pinch hit as a third in a ménage à trois, the Captain of the Queen's Guard was as loyal as he was versatile in his service, and he never refused.

Lucky for me.

The Eventide was cold, but that didn't surprise me. Not when it sat at the top of the westernmost corner of the Seelie realm. The forest bordered the Badlands along the Duiryn River, or *Abhainn uisce sioc* in the old tongue, meaning Frost Water, at the base of the *Beanna Garbh*, or Rugged Peaks. The same mountain range that separated the Seelie realm from the Unseelie.

My head spun from transformational magic. Merlin's magic. Otherwise, my journey would have required a horse and a three-hour hard ride from the coast.

The old druid left fifty ducats of silver and two stones in a pouch under my pillow. At first, I didn't understand, until I remembered the last line from the poem in the Unseelie tome.

...only silver pure, ensures your return.

The twin stones were another story. One touch told me they were like the stones Merlin gave me the night I met Daire, minus the confounding part. Crushed under foot, the first would transport me to the Eventide. The second was a way to return, if things didn't turn out as planned.

I didn't need the reminder that anything could happen once I stepped foot into the forest. From being taken political prisoner by the Unseelie to getting lost in the Eventide, Merlin's stone was my insurance policy and way home. Now I stood front and center in the damp gloom, and the rest was up to me.

Seelie children were raised with stories about the Eventide. The forest was stuff of bonfire tales told to both scare and delight. Only now, I knew those childhood stories were real, and they had a name. All that remained was for the Nocturna to show their face.

I was somewhere near the Druidic temple. That much I knew. But where to turn next? That was the question. Would it have been easier for Merlin to transport me to the portal entrance? Of course. Then again, when it came to the old sorcerer, things were never that simple.

A soft tinkling, like a kiss of laughter, drew my attention and I squinted into the gloom. I'd know that telltale sound anywhere. Unlike Sorcha, I'd seen Will-o'-the-wisps since I was a small child, when they'd called to me from the edge of the woods around the palace. They were said to lead the way to one's destiny but were known to be as mischievous as a pooka or a boggle. Had they known this night would come, or were they here sowing trouble?

The wisps winked, like a flicker from a lantern in the distance urging me ahead. The forest path wasn't a path as much as a narrow line of flattened leaves, a damp carpet through brush and between trees.

"Merlin, seriously. Did this have to be so confounding and far?" A flutter of ground birds startled my complaint into silence.

When it came to me, the old druid never let a teaching opportunity pass. Did I think he would let this one slide? I should've known better. He had the ability to make this rendezvous with Daire easy, but why would he do that when with one breath he hinted my connection to the Unseelie heir was multi-layered, and in the next he called my interest mere infatuation. Seers were historically vague, mostly so they could keep their heads attached to their shoulders, but Merlin's opacity wasn't borne of self-preservation. He was an immortal being with unfathomable power. He didn't need the practice or the protection. His reluctance to tell all was a safeguard.

I sighed. At least my old friend never said, "I told you so," or "You'll thank me for this when you're older." Clearly, Merlin thought I was ready for whatever I'd face in these woods, or he'd never have let me leave. At least I hoped not.

The leaves under my feet muffled my steps as I followed the wisps. The gloom gave the Nocturna an edge. I had an inkling the dark was more than just cover. Merlin told me to always trust my gut, and right now, it told me the darkness gave them power.

If I was correct, then let there be light. I twined dappled strands of moonlight as I walked, infusing the borrowed light with my own power to cast a wide silver-white swath around me.

"Look for the signs, little dove..."

Merlin's whisper startled me in the quiet. I should've known he'd keep an eye out from a distance. I took comfort knowing he kept tabs. For now. Although once I got through the portal and met Daire? Nope. Nope. Nope.

The idea of Merlin as a voyeur made me laugh out loud, puffing breathy clouds into the chilled air at the thought. He would never cross that line. He valued privacy as much as he valued my safety. Both his and mine. The seer would leave Daire and I alone, trusting me to use my return option if necessary.

Ahead, I caught a hint of a pulsing blue from inside a bramble thicket. The shimmer was faint, and it could've been anything from where I stood. The hair on the back of my neck tingled, so I moved closer, keeping my hand on the hilt of my sword just in case.

The rune's distinctive contours took shape before my eyes. *Kenaz.* The sign of the torch. Of purpose. And it seemed to point ahead.

If there was one rune sign, then there had to be more. I scanned the brambles and scrub, attuned to the color and feel of the embedded magic. The sharp R-shape of a familiar rune sat woven into a twine of thin branches, hidden in plain sight. *Raido.* The rune usually meant progress, but the sign was inverted, foretelling a blocked path.

I chewed the corner of my lip. Which was it then? A clear path ahead or a block? Maybe I didn't remember my lessons as well as I thought.

The gloom thickened, and my borrowed swath of light seemed to dull. Wisps danced ahead, bouncing in impatience while I scanned for more signs. The tiny glimmers were fickle creatures. There one moment, and then gone the next, leaving wayfarers wondering if they'd seen anything at all. Tonight, they beckoned and hovered, forming a luminous line pointing northeast. The same direction as the Winter Court. Was it a ruse, or a true path to the druidic temple that housed the portal?

Nothing ventured, nothing gained. So, I followed the flickering wisps, finding another set of runes in the overgrowth. One, a sign meaning, misdirection. The other, showing survival and necessity. The contradictions brought me to a full stop.

"Okay, Merlin. Care to weigh in?"

Crickets.

Literally. Chirping in the ground cover.

"Okay, then."

The forest fell silent except for my footfalls, and a skim of gooseflesh under my thermal told me I wasn't alone. The Eventide had its own eyes and ears, and it watched. I picked up my pace, keeping my senses high for the slightest movement.

The path widened, spilling out into a half-moon clearing. Nine great oaks stood sentinel, their thick roots reaching through the earth in a protective embrace, and at their center was the Druidic ruin.

Gooseflesh became an excited shiver, climbing over my skin. This was the precipice of everything I planned. Everything I wanted. The silver ducats and my return stone were in my boot, and the offerings for Druitia and my passage through the portal were tucked into a small bag at my belt. Honey. Mead. Frankincense.

Check. Check. Check.

The wind fluttered the oaks' leaves in a welcoming ripple, beckoning me through the opening in their protective ring. I moved to enter the sacred space, but stopped, my excited shiver puckering to a distinct prickle of fear.

A smudge of red in the shadows chilled my blood. Unsheathing my sword, I raised the blade hip height. If my gut was correct, that momentary blur of crimson meant an evil, murderous goblin with an insatiable bloodlust and a penchant for ruins. A Redcap.

Sharp teeth. Taloned fingers. Red eyes.

Tightening the grip on my sword, I ignored the fresh wash of adrenaline in my blood. My power. My will. The biddable energy coursed through my limbs, imbuing my blade as it did when I circled Rylan at the armory. Except this wasn't practice. This was life or death.

"Show yourself, you little shite." I knew the Redcap watched, waiting for a misstep or for my guard to drop.

Redcaps were fast, but I had underestimated *how* fast. In the time it took to blink, the small creature buzzed me on the left. I pivoted just in time to dodge the sharp edge of its pike. The close call threw me, slicking my palms and my grip on my sword. My power faltered, and my racing pulse throbbed in both temples where dread threatened to narrow my vision.

Focus, Eden. Don't forecast.

Rylan's words came back, and I slowed my breathing, despite the feel of panicked sweat between my breasts. I shifted my stance, ready. I wouldn't make the same mistake.

"Crimson red, it's time you bled!" The goblin's laughter taunted in another blur of motion. "Your gut to plunge! My cap's the sponge!"

Redcaps were nearly impossible to catch, which meant I had to outwit the little bugger, or... I refused to finish the thought. There was no alternative. Stealth, speed, and strike. Lucky for me Redcaps were solitary creatures.

"You call that sad nursery rhyme a threat?" I tracked another red streak, tearing from broken cobbles to the cover of brambles.

A second blurred strike caught my upper arm, gouging my shirt and the flesh beneath. Raw pain flashed, paralyzing my arm. I stumbled back, forcing a deep breath to stop the instant nausea.

"Your flesh bleeds 'cos you can't catch me! Death be nigh, so don't even try!"

The Redcap's sing-song voice grated, making my teeth hurt. I didn't dare let my defenses down another notch. Not even to look at my wound.

Think, Eden.

Knowledge is power, same as your sword.

Redcaps kill regularly. Why?

Adrenaline flowed, muting the agony in my arm, and helping me focus. Its cap! That was the answer. The horrid goblins soaked their caps in the blood of their victims, and the macabre drench was tied to the Redcap's life force. As their caps dried up, so did the creatures' lives. The fresher the blood, the stronger the Redcap, and *this* little shite had a crusty cap.

I ignored the wet feel of my blood-soaked sleeve, focusing instead on movement in the shadows. "You call that scratch a strike? You're going to have to do better than that, or you're done for. Even I can see your cap is in sad shape."

The goblin hissed, only this time I was ready. I scooped a handful of loose dirt on my pivot, keeping it tight in my fist. My senses homed in on the bloodthirsty cretin, and the subtle changes in the air as it scuttled.

"Come out, come out wherever you are..."

With a battle cry, the Redcap launched itself from the brush using its tall pike as a pole vault. Power, fluid and flowing, crackled over me, and I lobbed the loose dirt into the goblin's face before its feet hit the ground. The creature sputtered and spit, and that's all it took.

My blade connected in a backhanded blow, severing the goblin's head from its shoulders. With a whoosh, it juddered my arm from my wrist to my collarbone.

The goblin's head arced in a macabre *loop-di-loop* before rolling to a stop in the dirt, its body slumping to the ground where it stood. The creature was dead. That much I knew, but there was no time to survey the scene more.

Breathing hard, I circled slowly, keeping my eyes on the shadows. Redcaps were solitary creatures, but that didn't mean this one didn't have friends. Damn. I gripped my sword tighter. The weight of a dozen pairs of eyes or more glowed from the gloom, and I braced for the worst.

CHAPTER
Thirteen

NOT KNOWING WHAT I FACED, I kept my mouth closed and the grip on my sword tight. One by one, a small band of dryads and sprites crept from the shadows. My senses were still wound tight, but my gut told me they weren't a threat.

Dryads were shy and reclusive creatures who acted as guardians of the woodlands. They were usually bound to specific trees, so it made sense the copse of giant oaks was their home, but the sprites worried me.

Sprites were *biotáille laochra*. Trooping warriors. Protectors of the forest. It was said they sat judge and jury over those who trespassed with harmful intent and could smell a creature's true nature. I had just killed a forest dweller. An evil, tried-to-kill-me-first, forest dweller, but an inhabitant of the Eventide, nonetheless. And I had spilled its blood at the mouth of their most sacred space.

"I had no choice." My admission was more blurt than explanation as I gestured to the Redcap's body. I kept my stance neutral. Too defiant, and they might deem me a threat. Too complacent, and they might think I killed the Redcap for sport.

Two sprites ventured closer, bold, and unintimidated, but a shimmering at the entrance to the ring of oaks stopped them in their tracks. They didn't seem to halt out of fear. Just the opposite. They seemed to stop out of deference.

A beautiful woman materialized inside the soft golden glow. I didn't know her, yet she was somehow familiar. As though her presence called to something deep inside me. The sprites knelt on the loamy ground, and the dryads gathered to her light as though dancing around a maypole.

This was someone of importance to those outside the grip of the Nocturna, unlike the unfortunate Redcap. Perhaps a woodland Goddess or a queen from a Shadow Court.

"Eden Aossi, heir to the Summer Court." The woman addressed me as though she knew me. "The Sidhe are not welcome here without cause. Especially those belonging to the Seelie realm. Your presence has reawakened the darkness in the Eventide. State your business."

The woman's voice was a melodious double-timbre, siren-like, making my thoughts disjointed and floaty. I tried to speak, but I couldn't. Almost as if drugged.

"Let her answer, milady. We will know by her words, yes or no."

The second voice was deep and woodsy. Who was he? What did he mean, yes or no? A soft breeze wafted the coppery scent of blood-tinged earth, and that was enough to clear the floaty feeling from my head.

"I beg your indulgence," I replied, still a little befuddled. "I meant no disrespect." Blinking, I shook my head. "To whom do I speak? You know my name, but I've not the same pleasure."

"I am Aerith," the woman replied, evenly. "Forest Mistress and Protector of the Lesser Fae." She inclined her head, and I did the same out of proper respect.

I didn't know who she was, but at that moment, I knew *what* she was, and not because she told me. Aerith was *Leanan Sidhe*. An ancient being from a time before recorded history. Oral tradition spoke of ancient ones whose blood called to ours in times of strife and portend, but I always believed they were a myth.

Keeping my eyes lowered, I prayed my actions hadn't angered the Leanan Sidhe. Merlin hadn't prepared me for the possibility, nor had he schooled me in the proper etiquette to answer her questions. My mother taught when in doubt, redirect, but in this instance, dissembling would not serve. This was their home, and I was the trespasser. They were waiting for an answer, and they deserved the truth.

"I seek Druitia's portal for a personal quest. A quest sanctioned by my Druidic mentor." I raised my eyes slowly before sheathing my sword even more carefully. "I brought proper offerings."

Careful to avoid the Redcap's blood, I untied the pouch from my belt to place the three items on the ground. An approving murmur rose from the dryads, and even the sprites nodded.

"My mentor arranged my passage through the Eventide portal, gifting me with this..." I freed the double dragon pendant from inside my thermal shirt, holding it high enough for the Leanan Sidhe to note. I purposefully didn't mention he'd made me a living portal key. Aerith could probably smell Merlin's residual magic, but I wasn't about to volunteer the information.

"Merlin... *hmmm*." A small smile tugged at Aerith's mouth, and her expression was both wistful and indulgent. "We have shared many talks about his less than orthodox use of magic. Still, that you wear his pendant tells me he is aware of what once was, and what is to come, though my guess is his second sight dances and dodges him a pretty step."

I was not about to dish the dirt on the old sorcerer. He was as much an ancient as Aerith, but he was *my* ancient, and I didn't know this Leanan Sidhe.

A single brow arched over Aerith's eye. Had the Forest Mistress read my thoughts? I knew Merlin caught snippets from time to time, but he never trespassed in my head. If mind reading wasn't one of her gifts, then I needed a serious note to self. Stop telegraphing.

"Your loyalty to your mentor is commendable. Sentiments I know he both mirrors and values. Which begs the question, why didn't he—" Her words clipped short, and her gaze tracked past my shoulder toward the darkness beyond the clearing.

The dryads retreated from her circle of light back to the oaks. When threatened, their place was with their trees. Postures changed among the remaining lesser Fae, shifting from qualified calm to imminent alarm.

A long, straight blast from a horn had warrior sprites scrambling around the Leanan Sidhe. Most sprites were the size of an ear of corn, with a wingspan nearly equal to their height. Warrior sprites were much larger.

They were equal in height and strength to the mountain dwarves living inside the Rugged Peaks—about four feet tall—only lithe of limb, instead of stocky and squat. Warrior sprites had the ability to borrow magic to increase their size when threatened. Whatever Aerith sensed, had the sprites circling her the size of a man.

"Your presence brought this upon us, Eden of the Summer Court!" The Forest Mistress pointed a slender and graceful finger my way. "Now it is your burden to return the Eventide, and its Lightlings, to peace and safety."

What the hell had I unleashed on these poor Fae? I had never heard the lesser Fae called by another classification. Was that simply Sidhe arrogance, or had Aerith dubbed this benign group of forest folk as the equal, yet opposite, of the Nocturna? Either way, the name Lightlings suited.

Unsheathing my sword, I turned to see what sent Aerith and her entourage into such a spin. The creature thumped to the edge of the clearing. It was grotesque. A beast with a single eye in the middle of its face, and one bony hand attached to a piece of forearm protruding from the center of its chest. It had one leg, which explained the heavy, awkward gait.

"A Fachan?" My disbelief was barely a whisper. "You've got to be kidding me." I had read about hybrid Sluagh species, but I never imagined I would see or smell one this up close and personal.

A single strike of my blade to the creature's knee would fell the beast, but I was learning fast, nothing was ever that simple. The Fachan carried a heavy, iron-flail in its one skinny hand. I'd have to get past that first, not to mention the twenty or so chains hanging from the flail's spikes. If that wasn't bad enough, each chain had a bulbous orb attached at the end. Orbs with venomous secretions, more corrosive than acid. A single swing of a Fachan's club could maim or kill a dozen men.

"Careful, milady." A single sprite warrior flanked my left side in a blur of motion. "A Fachan will launch its vicious orbs without much provocation, and others grow back in their place."

"I'm sure she knows that already, York." A second sprite flanked my right in the same kind of blur. "She's a Sidhe, and a princess. Not a feckin' Brownie. Besides, Fachan are feebleminded."

"Exactly, Kip. Which makes them even more volatile. No sudden movements, either of you."

If the situation wasn't next door to sudden death, it might have been comical. The sprites flanking my sides were a cross between Elven hotties and fairy tale folk. Lithe of muscle and ethereally gorgeous, point-eared, and ready for battle, but dressed like they flew in from a human Ren Faire.

"I don't mean to be rude," I began, addressing them both. "Only, this is my fight, my doing, and I don't need sprite blood on my hands."

The one called York gave my bloodstained vest and thermal a once over. "As opposed to Redcap blood."

I opened my mouth to argue but then thought better of it. There was strength in numbers, and three swords were better than one, especially when two of those swords could supply an aerial attack.

"You need our help, Princess," York continued. "Your Sidhe blood may have stirred the Nocturna the moment you stepped foot in the Eventide, but when you spilled the Redcap's blood you drew a line in the dirt."

"How is it I drew a line in the dirt, when that Redcap drew first blood?" I lifted my blood-soaked arm, making my point. "It attacked *me*. Not the other way around."

Kip shrugged. "The Nocturna aren't known for following the rules of fair play. One of their number is no more. It doesn't matter if it was Sluagh, or any of the darker Fae. The goblin's demise is all the provocation they need. The Fachan is just next in a line of attacks awaiting you. If we fell this beast, the Nocturna might slither back to the shadows to await your return. They know you plan to use the portal."

"How? If Aerith didn't know, how would the Nocturna?" I wanted to stalk back and question the Forest Mistress, but I didn't dare. This was their realm, even if it was technically tucked into a corner of Seelie.

"Aerith knew as well," York replied. "Seelie ways spin pretty lies when asked. We needed to see if you would follow your kind or if you'd tell us the humble truth. Humble isn't a word much associated with High Fae, but you passed the test. Which is why Kip, and I, are offering you our help."

That was the yes or no, York referred to when he asked the Mistress to let me answer in my own words. Hells Bells. Another question for Merlin when I got back. Why were the Sidhe so mistrusted?

Glancing at the red tinged earth beneath what was left of the Redcap, I didn't need to guess. The Sidhe had brought war to this forest a millennium ago, and now I had spilled more blood in the Eventide, regardless of self-defense. I had awakened the sleeping Nocturna and their need for vengeance on the Sidhe. *When blade touched blade.* I took what the Unseelie tome said to be literal. Silly me. I hadn't crossed blades with another sword, yet here I stood. Had my need to see Daire set wheels in motion for another war?

"Pay no heed to York's doom and gloom, milady," Kip added. "His boldness is his charm, even if he hardly cracks a smile."

I filed away my newest worry for now. I would discuss the possible consequences with Merlin when I got back to the palace. I had bigger fish to fry, and right now, the biggest was the Fachan and its iron-flail.

"Milady?" Kip snapped his fingers twice, pulling my attention back.

"Right... Doom, gloom and boldness."

York snorted. "Boldness indeed. If being bold means I take protecting our kind seriously, then aye. Whereas Kip's charm is getting up my nose and in my way."

"Ha! I could say the same about you, Sir Sour Sprite. Except I never have time. I'm forever saving your arse from the scrapes you manage."

I should've been surprised Aerith hadn't stepped in or offered help, but I wasn't. Maybe the sprites had that covered, and she was happy to sit back with her popcorn and pointed blame, and watch. The Forest Mistress doubtless subscribed to the same school of thought as Merlin. Answering questions with questions. Again, lucky me. At least she hadn't vanished into her protected oaks with the dryads. The weight of her eyes watched from a distance. Like Merlin.

While the sprites bickered, I kept my eye on the Fachan. It hadn't attacked, though we stood no more than forty paces away. Instead, it sniffed the air, lifting its face as if trying to place us. It did so with its mouth open, showing a full complement of cracked and yellowed teeth.

"I think the answer to our problem is staring us in the face. You said Fachan are feebleminded, yet quick to anger. Still, the beast hasn't lunged.

It's lumbering in the same circle, vexed and on a hair trigger, but I don't think it sees us."

"Fachan aren't blind, milady. We sprites know that for sure."

"I don't doubt that, York. The Fachan knows we're here. It can smell us, but I'd bet you a bag of silver each, it can only track overt movement. It can't place us where we stand."

Kip nodded slowly. "She could be right, York. I read a theory from the human realm that talked of something similar when it came to dinosaurs. T-Rex especially."

"If that's true, it explains a lot." York followed my line of sight, assessing the beast himself. "Fachan are unpredictable and deadly, not only to Lightlings, but to the Eventide itself. Thank the fates the beasts can't breed."

Breed? Urgh. I cringed at the thought. Still, I understood what York meant. The Eventide was more than just its Fae inhabitants. There were spirits inherent in everything. Every plant, flower, and tree. Every brook, stream, and even the rocks. The Fachan and its venom threatened them all.

There was purpose and method to Merlin's plan in sending me to Druitia's portal. He knew my heart. He knew once faced with the truth of this place, and its people, I'd never rush through with nothing but my own wants in mind. He knew I'd have to help. Hang the consequences.

I needed to kill this beast, or make it retreat before the fallout from my presence desecrated the ground outside their sacred space any more than it had already. There was only one way to do it, but it needed a coordinated effort.

"You look like you have a plan in mind." York cocked an eyebrow at me as if he sensed my wheels turning.

"Sort of, but first we need a diversion..."

CHAPTER
Fourteen

"DIVERSION?" Kip asked. "How do you mean?"

I was out of my element and spit-balling at this point. "We need something that grabs the Fachan's attention. Something that draws the beast away from the others, away from the ring of oaks." Chewing on my lip, I looked from one sprite to the other. "Whatever we do, we decide together. Agreed? We work in tandem, so nothing rash. No hot dogging."

"Why are you giving me that pointed look, Princess?" York frowned. "I don't even know what hot dogs are?"

"Ooof, Yorkie. I believe milady has got your number, boyo."

I needed the sprites' help, but I had to make sure we were on the same page. I refused to have innocent blood on my hands, regardless of it being their choice to help or not.

The sprite's dagger-eyes should have been aimed at me, not Kip, so I drew his attention back to me with a quick explanation. "I didn't mean to get up your nose, York. It was just a turn of phrase and not directed at anyone in particular. All I meant was we need to work together...or everyone suffers."

York shot Kip another quick look before addressing me again. "I do what needs to be done, but I agree with you. Defeating the Fachan and sending a message to the Nocturna requires a unified team."

"So, a diversion, then?" I prompted.

York pursed his lips, mulling over the idea. "Aye. Kip and I can distract the Fachan away from the clearing. We'll need height enough to stay out of range of its iron-flail, yet low enough so the beast can still see us." He frowned. "It's those blasted orbs that concern me."

"The Fachan can try all it wants, but its wee bit of an arm and spindly hand won't have the range of motion to reach us airborne." Kip sounded confident, but I wasn't so sure.

"What it lacks in range of motion, it makes up for in scale, Kip. Not to mention its capacity to replenish its venom."

Kip clicked the inside of his cheek. "It seems York's worrywarting is a wee contagious. You both forget we've got the fates on our side. It's to be a wild goose chase for a wild Fachan."

"That kind of cheek will end with us claimed by the Horde and riding the skies indentured to the next Wild Hunt. Given a choice, I'd rather not." York looked as though he'd willingly face a pack of goblins rather than go up against the Sluagh.

Still, I was surprised he uttered the thought aloud. The Wild Hunt was an army of malevolent Sluagh and wicked mixed breeds whose whirlwind blighted the skies on moonless nights. Calling the Horde by name invited them to swoop in from the west to steal souls and increase their number.

"Let's not invite more trouble than we already have," I said, redirecting back to the task at hand. "How much of a running start do you need?"

The question left my mouth before I realized what I'd asked. Sprites were born with wings. They were as much a part of their working anatomy as their arms and legs.

"We're warrior sprites, milady. Not butterflies," Kip replied, losing a bit of his good humor. "We don't flit. We don't flee, and we can vault for the sky from anywhere."

Foot. Mouth. Insert again.

Way to go, Eden. Spill blood in their forest, then insult those who want to help. I exhaled a tired breath. I wasn't well acquainted with many of the lesser Fae. One of the drawbacks of being raised royal, and something painfully obvious now. I wasn't sure who dubbed any Fae other than Sidhe, *lesser*, but the denigrating term would stop with me.

"I'm sorry, Kip. I didn't mean to doubt your abilities. It won't happen again." My apology was genuine, and I supposed he knew it because he inclined his head.

"What do you need us to do?" he asked, but the beast shrieked toward us before I could answer. We were out of time.

"Keep the creature occupied." I drew my sword. "I'll do the rest."

York's blade was at the ready as well. "We'll lure the Fachan away. You do whatever's necessary but keep its acid from the oaks. Those giants stand sentinel for more than just a crumble of Druid stones. They are a sanctuary against the Nocturna, and a safe place for Lightlings who call the Eventide home."

A kiss of adrenaline fluttered through my blood. If this worked, I would send the Nocturna back to the shadows and still be through Druitia's portal—and into Daire's arms in no time. What I wouldn't give to be able to send a human-realm text. Funny, really. What the human realm lacked in magic it made up for in technology.

Before I had time to think or call my power, the sprites issued a battle cry that could curdle milk. Kip and York vaulted for the trees, and the Fachan roared in response. It pivoted on its one heel, thumping after them with its iron-flail chains swinging like a pendulum.

I crouched low and followed the beast. It shrieked in frustrated impotence, thrashing its great flail at the sprites in frenzied strikes. A hail of toxic orbs hurtled after them, but Kip and York were too fast. Acid exploded against perimeter branches, sending noxious fumes into the air. Cries rose from the dryads, and the ground seemed to quake in agony.

Nostrils flared, the Fachan roared again. Its one eye searched for me, but I had planted my feet, still as a stone. It knew I was there, and it was only a matter of time until it had me in its sight. The creature was sent to hunt me, not sprites or any other Lightlings. *I* was its quarry. I had to do something. Feebleminded or not, the Fachan had its orders and would use its venom against the sacred oaks to flush me out.

Kip buzzed the beast from behind, slicing off the top of its ear before shooting out of range again. York did the same on the opposite side, tag-teaming the beast. The Fachan screeched, twisting left and right with its flail swinging venom-loaded chains in a killing spin.

Hells bells! There was no approaching that lethal vortex at sword range. I had no other choice. I sheathed my sword, reaching instead for the dagger in my boot. I had one shot. If one of those chains deflected my blade, it was game over for more than just me.

A scream ripped from my throat, jerking the Fachan around again. Inertia from its abrupt turn swung the flail's chains to one side, leaving the beast's upper chest and throat exposed for a second. The dagger left my hand with an audible whoosh, the juddering force ripping the breath from my chest. Was my throw strong enough?

What if I missed? Then what?

The Fachan keened, emitting broken gurgles. Its flail hit the ground with a wet thump, and the beast staggered in pooling acid, scrambling for the dagger splitting its gullet. It was too late. Its leg gave out, crumpling the beast to a heap in its own caustic poison.

The sprites landed on either side of me, surveying the carnage. "Perfect aim, milady," York said, clearly impressed. "You do your kind proud."

Kip elbowed my good arm. "High praise, coming from old grumpy wings."

I didn't feel proud though. Both sprites had burns on their limbs from acid splatter, and I had reopened the gouge on my arm. Not to mention I had taken two lives. Neither were innocent, and they would've both taken my life without missing a blink, but still.

"Milady?" York prompted.

I simply nodded. "Yes. Well done, all."

"Don't you have a portal waiting, Princess?" Kip lifted his gaze to the sky. "Based on the position of the moon, I'd say the stroke of midnight is nigh." His twinkling eyes met mine with a teasing smile.

"Yes... Thank you, Kip. And you, York."

"Thanks are fine, well, and good." York pointed his finger at me, but his lips crooked in a half smile. "But I'm holding you to that bag of silver, Princess."

It hit me then. I was free. Choices had been made, and the consequences paid. I had to stop myself from squealing. The portal and Daire awaited.

"Silver. Upon my return. I swear!" I rushed for the offering that I had left on the ground before the Fachan interrupted.

"Wait!" Kip called after me. "What about your dagger?"

"Let the acid have it," I yelled back.

"Can I have it, then?"

I pivoted, walking backward and watching Kip reach for a fallen branch to dig through the melted muck that was once the Fachan.

"Leave it, you daft, droop-winged idiot!" York yanked the branch from Kip's hand, tossing it. "Milady's dagger is poxed by now. We can buy blades fit for a king!"

"Better yet...," I called to them both. "How about blades fit for a queen? Hand-wrought by my mother's own swordsmith in gratitude for your help tonight."

York's mouth split into a wide, block-toothed smile, and Kip burst out laughing. "Oh, milady. You've done it now."

"Shut your gob, Kip."

I couldn't help my own grin, and the feeling the tides had turned for the better in the Eventide. "Come to the castle tomorrow as my personal guests. You can choose whichever blade you wish."

Aerith met me with an approving nod when I turned back around. "You have proved your heart, and your true nature, Eden of the Summer Court. The Nocturna have receded, for now. The portal is yours to use. We await your return with safe passage through the Eventide if you wish."

Dryads and sprites, alike, watched me walk through the sentinel oaks with my offerings. They followed, processional-like, behind Kip and York who fell in step behind Aerith. The tomes in the palace library painted such a false picture of the forest and what lurked in its gloom. I was ashamed the Sidhe had perpetuated superstition and the idea of the Eventide as a wicked place, a home to libertines and the unwanted. Another thing I intended to change when I got back to the Summer Court. The Lightlings of the Eventide deserved better than living in the shadow of the Nocturna.

I placed the three items on the low, flat threshold and waited. Had spilling blood so close to Druitia's stones negated my entry?

"You must state where you wish to go," Aerith instructed.

I flashed Aerith a sheepish grin.

A hush fell across the Lightlings as they waited for me to say something. The words, "take me to Daire," were on my tongue, but I bit them back. What if he wasn't on the island? What if he had his own manic night of mayhem and delays and was still at the Winter Palace? The last thing I needed was to be transported to the Unseelie's Great Hall looking like I'd fought my way out of a bear pit. The truth was inconceivable enough, thank you very much.

I squared my shoulders and spoke clearly. "Take me to the temple on Daire's hidden isle." If he wasn't there, at least I could leave a message or a sign I had kept our date.

Anticipation locked my breath, waiting for the fates to answer one way or the other. The stones glowed a soft gold, beckoning me. My skin vibrated and coursed with energy. I was the key. Even with blood on my hands—and in my hair—I must've done something right, so I walked toward the gateway and its shimmering center and whatever came next.

CHAPTER

Fifteen

AERITH CALLED MY NAME, but her voice was thick and faraway. The portal's hum muffled everything behind me. Had she called after me with a caution? I couldn't be sure, but it was too late. I stepped through the shimmering membrane, smiling at its gossamer feel, but the moment my foot hit ground, a crash of vertigo upended me.

Everything whirled. My mind. My stomach. One hand lunged for an anchor, while the other wrapped around my middle, but there was nothing to grab. No cracked columns. No crumbled stones. Squeezing my eyes shut, I pressed my chin to my chest and gathered myself into a ball.

Do not vomit.

DO. NOT. VOMIT.

The words became a mantra in my head. Bloodied and mud-covered was bad enough, but bloodied, muddied, and covered in sick? Nope. Nope. Nope.

Was this the same vortex Daire met? Was I about to be hurled back to the Eventide, ricocheted, and rejected, or was this another test? I squeezed my eyes tighter, wondering if the fates were enjoying themselves at my expense.

The humming stopped, and just like that, the vertigo subsided. I lifted my chin, and when I opened my eyes, I wasn't sure what I was looking at.

Amber-colored current crackled in golden sparks, teasing the hair on my body on end. I seemed alight in a contained kind of nothingness. There was no ground beneath my feet, or anything concrete around me. I was somewhere and nowhere all at once.

The current coalesced, forming the same shimmering membrane I saw in the crumbling temple. I was a breath from Daire's sanctuary. A hundred questions raced through my head. Was this how all portals worked, or was this one curious by virtue of its age? Would my magic work in the Unseelie realm? Merlin's magic had, but then again, it was... *Merlin*.

The shimmering membrane winked as if prompting me, so I stepped through the doorway straight into a circle of stones. It took a moment for my eyes and my body to adjust. Nothing looked familiar. Then again, why would it?

Hoping the portal had taken me to the right place, I scanned the area for anything recognizable. I hadn't seen much of the island the night of the Winter gala. Then again, the Sluagh interrupted a lot of things that night.

Moonlit shadows made it hard to see, but I spotted the side of the triangular temple past the circle of stones. It sat atop the bluff, overlooking the Faewyn Sea. Its familiar shape winked through the trees, including the tall, sentinel oak Daire had touched with my hand.

A sea breeze tickled my curls, and I licked my lips. Salt. Like the first kiss I shared with Daire. Was he here? I couldn't be sure. I had assumed enough tonight and wore the dirty, blood-spattered consequences to prove it.

The gouge on my arm throbbed now that the adrenaline had cleared my system. It had clotted over twice, but it probably needed particular tending at this point. Sidhe healed quickly, but this wound was deep. The ache was raw, but normal as far as I could tell, and there was no tingling or numbness that spoke to the goblin's pike being poisoned. Besides, Redcaps were more rip and gouge. They wanted blood flow from large wounds to douse their caps, not slow death by poison.

I was a hot mess, and not the type of *hot* I wanted. Thinking I could conjure a sexy dress, slinky and clinging to every curve, was probably overoptimistic. I had done it before, but at home. Still, at least my appearance came with an adventure to tell. Whether Daire saw it that way? I could only hope.

It was time to turn theory into practice. If I wanted hot, then I needed a little cool magic. I wiped my hands on my ruined vest and then raised my palms to the silver light. "Okay, Moon Mistress. Time to help me kick it up a notch." I needed a killer spell to glamour a bit of sassy couture when a twig snap jerked me completely around.

"Eden?" Daire pushed a low branch aside and stepped just inside the ring of stones. He went from glad-to-see-me to stunned disbelief in zero to sixty. "What the —?"

"I know, but I can explain." I cut him off, but he didn't let me continue.

He gaped, giving my disheveled state a once over. "Bloody hell." Despite the harsh whisper, there was nothing but concern on his face, especially when he saw the deep gouge courtesy of the Redcap. "Gods! You're hurt!"

Rushing to my side, he took my arm for a better look, making me wince. At my sharp intake, he let go at once. "Damn! I'm so sorry! Are you okay?" He squeezed his eyes shut. "Idiot! Of course, she's not okay!"

"Daire...breathe." The prince's fingers raked his hair, and his face was as pained as my arm. "I'm okay. Relax."

He exhaled, opening his eyes. "Are you sure? It's clear you've been in a fight." He took my hand again, but this time he was careful not to tug.

"No, I'm really okay."

"Edie, I'm serious."

So was I, but I wasn't sure he'd see what happened in the Eventide as a rite of passage. Ironic. Merlin had warned me about facing the Nocturna in order to access Druitia's portal, so in essence, my ordeal was both a rite *of* passage, as well as me *earning* my passage. Leave it to the old Druid to play with semantics to instill a lesson.

"I'm here, and I'm with you," I replied. "The rest doesn't matter."

Slipping his fingers under my forearm, he kept his touch feather light. "This isn't a surface wound, Eden." He lifted my arm, turning it for closer study. "This is nasty and deep. Did this happen in Unseelie? Is there something I should know?"

His eyes searched mine, but I shook my head. It made sense, him thinking I ran afoul of Unseelie guards, but that wasn't the case. I wasn't going to lie, either. Even if letting him believe portal guards were responsible was easier than telling him the truth.

"Daire, stop." I covered his hand with mine. "This mess happened in Seelie."

"Was it the portal?" he prompted. "Did it hurl you backward like the west one did me?"

I shook my head, again. "The portal itself wasn't the problem. It was getting to the portal that proved difficult. Suffice it to say, keeping our date was harder than I expected."

I told him the whole story quickly and succinctly, half expecting him to interrupt with questions or at least baulk, but he didn't. He listened quietly, and when I finished, he sat on the base of a standing stone, his face unreadable.

"Daire—"

He didn't look up. "You shouldn't have come, then, Eden."

I blinked for a second. "I'm sorry, what?"

Daire didn't reply. Had I heard him correctly? Of all the ways he could've responded, this was the last thing I expected.

Was meeting me tonight just a casual thing? If it happened, great. If not, who cared? Had I built up this rendezvous to be more than it was because that's what I wanted? Maybe the blood I spilled changed his opinion of me. Maybe in his eyes I was a murderer. After all, the Sluagh were Unseelie allies. Perhaps that meant the Nocturna were as well, by default.

I felt for Merlin's stone in my pocket. It was safe in the zippered inner lining of my nylon vest.

"If that's how you feel, Daire, I have no problem leaving. I have the means." I waited for him to meet my gaze. To say something. To argue with me, anything, but he sat staring at his linked fingers. "Daire, please."

I waited another moment, but he still said nothing. "Fine. Be that way. Neither of us is obligated, so don't bother yourself with how I get home, but I do think you owe me an explanation. As you can see, I went through hell and back to keep our date, and for that reason I deserve an answer before you throw me out of your realm."

He stared at me with his mouth open as though stunned.

I straightened my shoulders, stiffening my bravado in self-preservation. "Save your disbelieving death glare for someone else. I'm not a courtier who crossed a line of protocol. I'm the heir apparent to the Seelie court. Equal and opposite to you." I lifted my chin, very much aware of the dirt and blood on my cheek.

My hopes for the night had been dashed with that one sentence. If he thought I was another fawning courtier, he had another thing coming. I wasn't my mother in many ways, but here and now, I was definitely the Summer Queen's daughter.

Daire got to his feet to face me, and I steeled myself. His lips were parted, but his expression was soft. Not a shadow of disdain in his eyes. "I've done nothing but count the hours until I could see you again, Eden. I've dreamed of you. Of this night." His hand motioned to my blood-caked clothing and the clotted, dirty wound on my arm. "But this? I don't understand. Why would you choose a brutal gauntlet just to keep a hastily made date? You could've died."

"But I didn't."

"But you could have. What then?"

"If you're worried about political repercussions, don't. No one but Merlin knew where I was headed tonight."

Gobsmacked, he threw up one hand. "That's not the point, Eden. How do you think I'd feel if I heard something happened to you? Especially knowing we were to meet. News of your death or serious injury would spread across every realm in Avalon."

Daire studied me from his place in front of the standing stones. They vibrated with energy, something I wasn't sure he noticed. Maybe I sensed the hum because the stones spoke to the power in me. Or maybe they hummed because Daire and I were together...and tensions ran high.

"You misunderstood my earlier meaning, Eden." He closed the distance between us, stopping short of toe-to-toe. "And that's on me. Maybe if I wasn't so alarmed and unbelievably sad that you thought you had no other choice, I might have reacted better. You have to know I'd never ask anything like that of you, nor expect it."

He paced in a small circle with one hand thrust in his hair. "Would I have been disappointed if you didn't come tonight? Of course...but I'd have understood. Or tried to. I'd have thought you couldn't get away, or that you changed your mind. We both knew the political risk, but political risk is *not* the same as having your life hang in the balance fighting a Redcap and a goddamned Fachan!"

I didn't need clairvoyance to know there was more he wanted to say, but he didn't. My ire had ebbed, and I saw the situation from his perspective. On more than just the surface, the idea of me brandishing a sword to fight my way to a portal to see him sounded insane. However, Daire didn't know Merlin, so he didn't understand the whole of it. To be honest, I wasn't sure I did either, but my gut told me it was a necessary task. The why of which remained to be seen.

"If something happened to me, it wouldn't have been your fault," I replied. "I own my choices, just like I own the consequences."

He shook his head and then looked away. "I wanted to be alone with you. To just be Daire and Edie. Not the heirs apparent to rival courts...but I never thought the girl I fancied would have to endure a baptism by fire for me to get my wish."

I took that final step, bringing us toe-to-toe. "That's exactly why I chose the Eventide, Daire. There was no other way for me to get here. I wanted us to be just *us*, too."

My heart skipped a beat with the way he drew me close. "Eden..." he began, wiping the dirt from my cheek with his thumb. His lips took mine, hungry and desperate. As if everything he couldn't say was poured into that single kiss.

I met him breath for breath and need for need until his hand slipped to my collarbone and then down my wounded arm where he tightened his grip. I stiffened, and a painful gasp broke our kiss.

"Gods, Edie! I'm sorry! I forgot myself."

He jerked his hand from my arm, but the accidental damage was done. Fresh blood sheened the underside of his fingers from the reopened gash. Cursing under his breath, he reached for my good arm. "That's it. Come with me."

"Wait! Where are we going?"

"Down to the beach." He tugged me toward a sloping path that wound from the bluff to the sand. "The surf around the island has particular healing properties. I'm not sure why, but I'm glad of it now. I'll clear the dried blood and then cleanse the wound, letting the salt surf do its magic. After that, I'll wrap your arm with crushed calendula flowers to help speed healing."

"Did Morgana teach you that?"

"No, Silvan," he replied, walking with me in tow. "The head of my father's palace guard. Lachlan charged him with teaching me to fight and then threatened the man with losing his sword hand if he didn't bloody me once a week. Teaching me about healing was Silvan's way of making it up to me."

I snorted. "Sounds like your father and my mother went to the same school of parenting."

Daire led us down the slope and onto rocky steppes at the base of the bluff before stopping to help me to the sand. The Faewyn was surprisingly calm. Its water appeared nearly black under the night sky. A soft surf lapped at the shore, and Daire stood with me in the clean, silvery-white foam. Bathed in moonlight, he was even more handsome than I remembered.

"You really are a mess," he said, pushing a few sticky strands behind my ear. "But, to me, there's no one more beautiful. Even if you are a bit—"

"Foolish?" I cut in, finishing his thought.

"I was going to say impulsive."

I nodded, loving the feel of his hands on my skin. "What about brave?"

"Definitely brave, but also honest, and true to yourself, and—"

"Willing?"

He laughed, angling his head. "Will you let me finish a sentence, please?"

"If you insist." I smiled. "But I am, you know."

"Am what?"

I went up on tip toe, letting my good arm slip around his neck. "Willing," I whispered above his lips. I kissed him, thirstier than I knew was possible. Tongues wrestled and plundered until a wave crashed, soaking my legs to my thighs, and nearly knocking me over.

Was that a cold shower courtesy of the universe? A warning to slow things down? An echo of my mother's voice intruded: *Hold the mystique, Eden. Keep them eager and you'll hold the power.*

The ghost of old princess' lessons threw metaphorical cold water all over my moment. Daire was not a conquest. He wasn't a pawn. I wanted him as much as he wanted me, so I ignored the lingering memory—and any other that might creep up and dampen things more.

"Let's clean that wound before the Faewyn face plants you in the sand." Daire moved to help me kneel in the foamy surf, but I hesitated. "It won't hurt." He chuckled. "That much I can guarantee."

I glanced over my shoulder to the open water. "It's not that. Isn't there a more sheltered part of the beach where we can do this?"

The last thing either of us needed was a visit from Lachlan's guard, in effect ending our first official date, or any others for that matter. If the Winter Court was anything like its Seelie counterpart, there were plenty of watchers who reported back to the king, especially about the heir to the throne. I had my own set of tattletales. Caxton being one of many. Little birds flew in both Winter and Summer.

"Stop worrying. The island is warded, remember?"

My gut had been right too many times tonight to ignore, so I pushed the issue. "Yes, but—"

"Better to be safe than sorry, right?" He smiled, finishing my thought this time.

"Exactly."

"C'mon. I know just the place. It's very secluded, and very," he whispered in my ear, "very intimate."

CHAPTER
Sixteen

DAIRE and I retraced our footprints through the sand back to the base of the lower steppes. "I thought this secluded place was still beachy, just not here in the open," I noted, taking his hand to help me onto the rocky path.

"It is, and it isn't." He turned to push a low-hanging branch aside. Beyond was a trail, parallel to the beach, yet concealed from prying eyes by trees and heavy brush.

Keeping my hand in his, I followed single file watching where I walked. The moon hung high enough in the inky sky to showcase flowering weeds and low scrub lining the uneven terrain. Moss-covered rocks defined the path's outer edge, acting as guideposts against a painful tumble.

"Did you forge this path yourself?" I asked, stepping carefully so as not to trip.

"Years ago. When I first found the island, I spend every free moment exploring here."

I smiled to myself, watching the lean muscles in his back and long legs as he trekked ahead. Gorgeous. Clever, and funny. Not to mention sweet. How did I get so lucky?

"You know, I asked Merlin about the island and Danú's temple when I last saw him."

Daire's steps halted for a moment, and he looked at me over his shoulder. It wasn't overt, but I caught a flash of uncertainty in his eyes. That gave me pause.

"There was no fuss and feathers. Merlin already knew. Not about you taking me here, but about the island itself. You were right about him as the architect. He admitted he built the temple to Danú when Avalon was still unified."

I didn't tell him about the significance of the western portal and the Forbidden Realm, or about Arthur and Guinevere. That was between Merlin and my mother. If Lachlan didn't know, I wasn't about to give him a sniff. The Unseelie King was Daire's father, regardless of our new friendship.

"To tell you the truth, the old seer was surprised you spotted the island, let alone stepped foot on it," I continued. "The cay only presents itself to those it deems worthy, so your guess about that was on point. Merlin went so far as to say it was the reflection of your true self that gave you leave to wield magic here."

"What about you seeing through my wards from the very first?" Daire questioned. "Did he say anything as to why?"

I opened my mouth but then closed it. Talking with Merlin about the unusual pull I felt toward Daire was one thing. Admitting it to the Winter heir was another. I'd either blush or feel foolish. Probably both.

"I know he had an opinion, Edie. Just tell me." He arched a brow. "Is it something bad?"

"No."

"What did he say, then?"

I sputtered, hoping I didn't sound ridiculous. "He said we were linked."

"Linked?"

"As in connected."

"How do you mean?"

"He said we were kindred spirits."

"As in fated?"

Gods, he was like a dog with a bone. I didn't know how to answer.

According to Merlin, strings of fate had been pulled the night Daire and I met. How could I explain that without sounding like a desperate nutter? No. It was too soon to have this conversation. What if Daire didn't feel the same pull? There was an attraction, for sure. We both felt *that* allure, but this? Merlin hinted at our connection as preordained. It sounded irrational, and I wasn't ruining this night talking presage mumbo jumbo.

"I'm not sure, Daire." When in doubt, deflect. So, I swerved like a chased chicken. "Merlin is many things, but he's not a matchmaker. He interprets the signs, just as Morgana does for you and yours. He said we were connected. I wouldn't read too much into it, though." I swallowed before adding, "I don't."

Liar, liar, pants on fire.

Average girls daydreamed about their life mates, writing prospective married names over and over again in notebooks and diaries. *Mrs. Dannean. Mrs. Eden Dannean.* Not me. I gave into my infatuation so much I dragged a sword into a forest death ring and spilled blood. Albeit, in self-defense, but still.

"Morgana does no such thing." Daire was still caught in my deflect. "She tried eons ago, but got so much wrong, Lachlan relegated her to spells and simple sorcery. She was so angry I thought she'd go mad. To be honest, I'm surprised my father didn't try to lure Merlin from Tianna's clutches."

I had to laugh. "My mother isn't the clutching type. Unless it's for ulterior motives. Besides, how do you know your father never tried to coerce Merlin to switch sides?"

"I don't." He shrugged. "Though why there has to be sides is ridiculous."

Daire was thoughtful after that, even as he continued toward our destination. But he didn't comment. Maybe I shouldn't have told him what Merlin said about us. Even in abridged terms. It was one thing not to share about Arthur and Guinevere, or that the island's portals were created in response to a hazy vision, which may or may not have something to do with us. If Fae history was doomed to repeat itself, I wanted no part. Ego and greed had already ruptured the compact between the realms. I didn't want to think what more could happen.

"You're very quiet," he asked. "A gemstone for your thoughts?"

"They're not worth that much." I smiled when he glanced back. "So, how much longer until we get to this secluded oasis?"

"The entrance is just there, at the end of the trail." He pointed ahead.

By now we had probably circled half the island's perimeter. Yet, what waited ahead looked very much like the edge of a cliff. "Daire, I know it's dark, but are you sure?"

He winked. "Don't worry. I've got this."

I stood with him looking over the edge of the drop. It wasn't a huge descent, but it wasn't small either.

"Perfect timing. The tide's just about out." Daire motioned for me to follow. "We can make our way into the cave, no problem."

Cave? My head jerked up at that. "Did you say cave?"

"Yes. Though I prefer grotto since it's so beautiful. You'll see."

I swallowed. "Daire, I don't do well with confined spaces. Especially ones that fill with water." I didn't know much about time and tides on the Faewyn Sea, but if it was anything like the caves around the summer peninsula... I didn't let myself go there.

"Trust me, Edie. This is spectacular, and no one is going to drown."

Daire helped me down to a wet, rocky ledge above the water. From there, I glanced to the top of the rock face at the cave entrance. The same moss that covered the markers lining the upper path grew there as well. As in ten feet above where we stood on the ledge.

"That looks an awful lot like a high-water mark." I pointed to the stained rock and its mossy growth.

"It's fine, Eden. The water only gets that high during a storm. Most times I can wade out from the inner grotto. Even at high tide."

Most times. Great for drowning, maybe.

The navy-colored water shimmered in the moonlight as it lapped against the rock walls on either side of the cave. This was just the entrance, and though Daire claimed the water here was only a few feet deep, it was too dark to see the bottom.

I took his hand, giving the bluff above a quick glance. Something caught my eye. A shimmer or glint, high on the clifftop not far from the standing stones. Maybe we weren't as alone as we thought. I spared a look for Daire, ready to say something, but when I searched the bluff again, whatever had been there was gone.

The moon played tricks with dappled light and shadow. I knew that. Still, my gut had tapped me on the shoulder at the beach earlier. Was I being paranoid? After the Eventide my senses were on a hair trigger, but maybe that was me being twitchy.

Unsure, I let it go. For now.

My boots scuffed behind him, the reluctant sound in staccato rhythm with dripping water from the cave ceiling. The air was damp, but surprisingly cool and fresh. So far, so good. I don't know why I expected it to be dank.

"Let there be light." Daire palmed the air, conjuring an energy ball similar to the one I summoned in the Eventide. The only difference was his was blue, and mine had been silvery white.

"I can do that as well." I pointed to the crackling energy in his hand. "Why is yours blue?"

He gestured to the lapping waves. "I pull energy from water. Its motion. Its adaptability. Its changing forms. From there, I manipulate the borrowed energy however I need. Why? Is yours very different?"

"Not much." The ledge widened enough for us to walk side-by-side. My hand was still laced with his, and my claustrophobia ebbed a bit. "I pull energy from light. Moonlight, sunlight. Even firelight. From there, I can twine light strands into whatever I need."

It made sense we'd be similar, yet different. Most Sidhe pulled power from one of the twelve natural elements: earth, water, wind, fire, thunder, ice, force, time, flower, shadow, light, and moon.

Merlin once said if the Sidhe ever gave birth to one who pulled power from all twelve, the event would herald an end and a new beginning for the Fae. The old Druid mused out loud often, but there was something in his tone about this that had marked my memory. More of his cryptic that gave me headaches.

"C'mon. This is something to see." Daire picked up his pace, hurrying with me deeper into the cave. "It's just a bit farther."

The metronome tick of dripping water increased to the sound of trickles as we made our way into the gloom. The blue swath of Daire's conjured light winked at something on the walls. I squinted for a better look, pulling Daire to a stop.

Runes, as ancient as Merlin and Aerith, had been carved into the stone on either side of the dark water. I let go of Daire's hand and moved to run my fingers over some of the carvings. "Have you seen these before?"

"Of course. They're in the old tongue, but I don't know much more than that."

"These runes tell the story of the island, Daire. Of Avalon." I hesitated, coming to a set of ancient symbols I didn't recognize. My time with Merlin had schooled me well, but these were beyond my scope. "I can't quite read this part, but the rest talks about the compact made with the realm of men, and the rise of the sabbats to keep the treaty between realms intact."

He exhaled a cynical chortle. "And we all know how that went." He pressed his fingertips together before jerking them apart, mimicking an explosion.

"I wish I could read the rest. Maybe then we'd know what happened back in the day. Gods know I searched the library at the Summer Palace for answers but came up goose eggs."

"Trust me, Eden. No one remembers. There's not a whisper of it in my father's archives, either." Daire didn't tug me away from the runes. Instead, he traced a finger over their carved edges. "Maybe you can ask Merlin. Or maybe the story died when the compact fractured, and we're not meant to know."

Pfft. "I don't believe that for a moment. It's our history, Daire. Someone has to know." Merlin was my best bet, but if he knew he was very quiet on the subject.

Daire didn't push the issue. He took my hand again, kissing my knuckles. "C'mon. my grotto awaits, and we need to get that wound cleansed."

The cave opened into a wide expanse. Stalagmites and stalactites sprouted from the floor and ceiling, and Daire expanded his light, brightening the interior. It cast an azure glow over the white moss growing on the walls, and it was then I saw the whole grotto.

"Daire, this is incredible!" I scanned the original stark beauty that ran into this lush subterranean haven.

Sea water flowed from the entrance into a deep basin of white limestone where Daire's light illuminated the water in iridescent turquoise. The ceiling rose fifty feet from where we stood with flowering plants and thick greenery, growing into the cavern from an old sink hole. Moonlight spilled from the opening, shimmering on the water below, and highlighting the vines creeping downward, giving rise to moss and succulent plants sprouting from cracks in the higher rock. Ground water flowed in trickling rivulets, making the grotto truly oasis-like.

"I suppose we could've repelled down those vines, instead of traversing half the island's perimeter," I joked.

"Not unless you want a cave-in." He kissed the side of my head. "The rim's not quite stable."

I half-laughed. "Right. Add that to my claustrophobia, and this place would be super fun to explore."

"It *is* super fun." Daire winked, pointing to a wide, flat outcrop above the water. "Perfect place for a swim, don't you think?"

"Swim?" The Summer Court was surrounded by water on three sides, but I didn't swim. Ever. I needed to get a grip. I had wielded a sword, killed a Redcap, and foiled a Fachan. I could deal.

"That's not all," he said, and I followed his gaze to a wicker hamper and blanket tucked against the rock wall. Daire had planned for us to come here all along. Probably not the way he envisioned, but still.

"I told you. I would've been disappointed if you didn't come, but that didn't mean I wasn't stacking the odds in my favor the whole time."

Who was I to thwart such a romantic gesture? I went to throw my arms around his neck, but the hasty move jarred the gouge in my arm, and I winced. "Ow!" I cradled my injured limb. "I need to remember not to do that."

Daire didn't say a word. Instead, he took my hand and led me across the ledge toward the flat, rock shelf. He arranged the thick blanket and then motioned for me to sit.

"First things first." He unfolded a small knife from his pocket. "That sleeve has to go." Cutting the seam around my shoulder, he slipped the blood-crusted fabric over my hand and then tossed it away from the blanket.

"Boots. Off." He motioned to my feet. "We are going for a healing dip before we get this picnic started." I lifted one leg for him to wiggle the knee-high boot free, except I forgot about Merlin's drawstring pouch. It slipped from the boot top to the blanket with a soft thunk.

"Huh." He picked up the bag of silver, jiggling its heft in his palm. "Planning to do a little shopping, are we?"

I sniffed, trying to ease the other boot from my foot with my toes. "It's for me to get back to Seelie. The Eventide requires certain offerings, to and from, though Aerith promised me safe passage after my ordeal tonight."

"You are *not* going back the way you came." Daire looked aghast. "Are you telling me Merlin didn't give you an alternative? He gave you an escape plan the night of the gala, so why not now? Sending you through that forest of fear is not an option. I don't care if I sound like a troglodyte. It's not safe. Better we use that coin to bribe guards on the other side of the Seelie portal here."

"Relax. Merlin has me covered." I unzipped the inside pocket of my vest and took out Merlin's stone. "Crush under foot and wham. Home sweet home."

"That needs to stay some place safe, and not in the pocket of that tatty vest."

"I know it's tatty. I didn't expect to look like an extra from a slasher flick when I arrived tonight. But I didn't pack extra clothes, and I didn't get the chance to glamour anything. What do you suggest? Skinny dip, and then stay au natural?"

"Now that's an idea."

I crossed my arms to my chest. "How about a compromise?" He could swim, and I could watch.

"I could give you my shirt."

"Not what I meant, but..."

I spoke too soon. The idea of slipping into something that smelled like him, something I could take home and sleep in was not a bad idea.

"...Uhm, on second thought, I accept your offer." I held out my hand for him to help me up from the blanket. I slipped Merlin's stone into the bag with the silver and then put the pouch on top of the wicker basket. "There's just one problem."

"What?"

"I don't swim."

CHAPTER
Seventeen

"YOU DON'T SWIM because you don't like it...or you don't know how?"

I shrugged. "I suppose both. Didn't you notice how I clung for dear life when you whisked me here the night of the gala?"

"You mean it wasn't because you found me irresistible?"

I crumpled my vest and tossed it at him. "You were...then."

Daire laughed, pulling his shirt over his head before dropping it to the blanket. Whoa. His torso was as sculpted as the statues commissioned for my mother's pavilion. I licked my lips, watching as he slipped his hikers off before unbuttoning the first button of his pants.

"Why don't you swim, and I'll watch." I said, grateful I didn't trip over my tongue hanging out of my mouth.

"Not a chance. The water is one of the reasons we came here. You're going in it with me whether you want to or not. If only to cleanse that wound and clean up what's left of Hell Night in the Eventide."

I stood in my ripped shirt and leggings. This was the moment of truth. I wasn't a coward, and it wasn't the idea of submerging myself in the water. Most people looked better with their clothes on, than off. Daire was the exception. He was breathtaking. The question was, would he think the same of me? Forget butterflies. I had pterodactyls tearing around my stomach.

"We hear all sorts of rumors about the Summer Court," he continued. "What's the protocol on dating according to the Seelie?"

"What do you mean?"

"The usual." Daire shrugged, moving so close I had to stretch my chin to look at him.

"If you mean my mother, the stories you hear are no different than the stories we hear about your father and his debauches." I didn't blink, though I hated the direction this conversation was headed.

Daire fingered what was left of the top of my thermal. "You said we should compromise."

"I did."

"Good." His fingers traced my collarbone across to the base of my throat. "We've both seen enough human-realm movies to know the kind of compromise we need."

I fidgeted with the thermal's ripped hem. "I suppose." I don't know how I managed to reply. Not when Daire's fingers slipped from my throat to the swell of my breasts beneath my shirt. "Three dates. That's the usual in movies. Three dates and then couples..."

"Exactly." He slipped his hands to my waist, letting his lips brush mine. His mouth hovered, teasing me as he lifted my thermal off my body.

I stood in a lacy camisole, the cool damp air hardening my nipples to stiff peaks beneath the thin fabric. He stepped back from me and slipped out of his pants, waiting for me to do the same.

We stood together barely clothed, and it now wasn't my arm that throbbed. My body ached, wanting Daire's touch. His mouth. His tongue.

Daire held out his hand, and it was all I could do not to squeak. In that moment, I understood what my mother meant when she warned me to keep the mystique. Imagining what was beneath that soft cotton of Daire's boxer briefs made my own panties wet.

I held my breath as we walked to the edge. He climbed into the water first and then held out his arms for me to follow. "Daire!" Gooseflesh marked my skin, sending my shoulders to my ears. "This water's freezing!"

Ripples shimmered in rings around us as I stood with him in the pool. "It only feels cold because you're so hot."

I laughed. "Right, because chattering teeth is such a turn on."

"If you want to clean that wound and the rest of the muck, you're going to have to do more than just stand there."

"Who's standing? I'm frozen in place." The joke was more for my benefit than his, considering the water was only waist deep.

With a laugh, he splashed the still dry parts of my anatomy. "Hey! Quit it!"

"Don't be such a baby. You know what needs to be done." He put his hands on my shoulders.

"Don't you dare!"

"Too late."

Careful of my wound, he pushed me under, soaking me from crown to core. I surfaced, shivering and sputtering. "Daire!"

"Again? Of course, Your Highness."

I went under a second time, only this time Daire's hands gripped my waist. He helped me find my feet, waiting for me to steady myself on the smooth limestone floor.

"Th...th...that wa...was awful!" I stuttered through chattering teeth. "C...c...can't you d...do...something about th...the c...cold?"

"If I pull power from the water to change the temperature, it will affect the healing properties. Patience." Cupping handful after handful, he cleaned the wound on my arm until every bit of crusted blood and dirt was rinsed away.

The water must've had anesthetic properties as there was no sting. No burn. The bloody debris dispersed, absorbed, and clarified in the Faewyn. Daire did the same for my hair, gently combing the strands with his fingers until the water ran clear and my curls were once again soft.

The cold dissipated. Whether my body normalized to the temperature, or Daire used his magic to manipulate the water, it didn't matter. I relaxed in his arms, leaning back against his chest.

"How do you feel?" he murmured behind my ear. His fingers traced small circles over my waist and stomach.

"Like Hell Night in the Eventide never happened." I stretched, arching my back. Pink, ridged nipples poked through my camisole, playing peek-a-boo through the lace.

"Eden, you are such a tease."

"I'm not. It's all bravado gleaned from watching my sister flirt with every courtier with a penis and pulse. I'm a flirtatious fraud. I have no hands-on experience. Or hands off, for that matter. It's a theory, no practice."

He kissed the tender spot between my shoulder and my neck. "There's Sorcha's kind of sexy, and then there's yours. Hers is like you just said. Practiced. Artificial. Purposeful. But you? You're sexy and you don't even know it. It's honest. Natural and unaffected. I'm not saying Sorcha isn't genuine when it comes to you. I'm saying she's been schooled by your mother and has taken those lessons to the next level. Her reputation precedes her, even here."

"Look, I don't know the rumors you've heard. Yes, my mother is notorious for using sex. As punishment. As reward. Sorcha is my mother's daughter, but she's also my sister and that's not an easy role to play. She's me without the responsibility of ruling. She gets to the fun without the frump. She leaves that to me.

"How is this even close to frumpy?" Daire cupped my breasts, and I gasped. "Maybe it's time we exchanged that borrowed bravado for something up close and personal."

He turned me around to face him, and every one of his hard lines molded against my softness. "See what happens when you let go?" Small curls of steam rose from the surface as if the water mirrored the heat between us. "Every choice doesn't have to be weighed until its devoid of pleasure. You're still you. With all your responsibilities. Just don't forget to live your life."

"What about our compromise?" I asked, afraid to move.

"This has nothing to do with our three-date rule. This is all about you. About teaching you to follow your want. Your need. To let your body go. To feel it tense until every nerve is ready to burst and then give in to sweet release."

I sighed.

"Let me touch you, Eden."

His words buzzed in my ears, making my breath catch. My head dropped back, giving him entrée, and he pushed the straps to my camisole away, freeing my breasts.

I'd known Daire for such a short time, but this felt right. Maybe it was hormones. Or maybe it was our connection. Either way, I didn't care. At this moment in time, if this was wrong, I didn't want to be right.

"Are you sure about this?" I could barely form the words as his one hand found my breast, while the other skimmed up my thigh.

"I'm positive. What about you? Are you sure?" he asked, pausing for me to answer.

"Yes. Please, yes..."

Daire took my mouth, hard and hungry. I plunged my fingers into his hair, deepening our kiss. Throbbing jolts pulsed in my lower belly. As if reading my mind, Daire lifted my leg over his hip. "Gods, Eden," he murmured, cupping my ass to grind his hard bar against my panty lace.

"Take them off." I panted, but he shook his head.

"This is just a taste, Eden. To whet your appetite."

My leg slipped from his hip, and he turned me again in one fluid motion. My skin vibrated with sensation. I drew breath through my teeth, leaning back against his chest.

This was real.

This was happening.

To me.

Daire splayed his hands over my belly. One hand slid to my breast again, and the other slipped beneath the lace triangle-front of my panties. I gasped at the feel of his fingers. Spreading. Plunging. His thumb. Circling. Teasing.

Electric jolts sent friction higher and higher, coiling in my belly. With a ragged gasp, I arched my back with a cry. A kaleidoscope of color exploded behind my eyes as the climax ripped through my core and down my thighs. My legs went weak. Daire held me tight, letting me ride the aftershocks until I floated boneless in the warm grotto pool.

"So, up close and personal enough?" He pulled his hand free to hug me around the waist.

I squeaked, not sure I could speak.

"No?"

"Yes," I croaked. "Just don't ask me to walk yet.

He laughed, kissing the side of my head. "Fine, but I've got a ton of food in that basket just waiting."

I arched my back again, only this time with a laugh because I knew exactly what I was doing.

"Okay, now you truly are a tease."

"Considering what you just showed me, then I'd say that's a compliment and exactly what I should be." I sighed, stretching my neck to look at the sky. It was no longer inky black, but a dark purple. "Shit."

"What?"

"Dawn's breaking. Which means I have to go."

"It can't be." He looked up as well.

Before Daire could argue the point, I caught a shadow along the upper periphery and a tumble of pebbles plinked from the rim of the sink hole.

"Did you see that?" I pointed to the edge of the crater.

"See what?"

"I saw something. Maybe someone."

Doubt angled Daire's head, but he moved to my side for a better look. "It's just island shadows, Edie. My wards are intact."

"But the pebbles..."

"I told you. The rim is unstable. It's why I avoid the ground around the sink hole. It might cause a cave in and ruin my secret oasis."

"So, no repelling down vines?" I made light, but I still wasn't sure.

"Very funny." He waded to the edge of the pool, hopping up on the ledge "Are you sure you can't stay for a bit? I pack a mean sandwich, even if I say so myself."

My gaze slipped to the sink hole rim again.

"Eden..."

I shook my head, clearing my qualms. "Right. Sandwich. Sorry."

"Forget the sandwiches. I just want you to stay a little longer." He patted the edge of the ledge for me to join him. "I want to see you again, Eden."

I hopped up beside him. "That might be tricky. I'll have to check with Aerith about the portal."

"Forget it." He shook his head. "We're done with unnecessary gauntlets."

I laughed. "Good. Because given the choice, I'd rather not."

"Don't worry. We'll think of other ways to satisfy your inner adventure junkie."

"Ha! After what you showed me tonight?" I closed my eyes. "Mmmm."

He shifted on the ledge to face me, taking my hand. "Gods, you're beautiful. Funny. Sexy...and most important of all...mine."

Mine.

The word rang in my ears making me want to squeal, but I played it cool and kissed him instead. "I feel the same way, Daire. About you, I mean. The jury's still out about the sexy bit, but I'm glad you think so. My mother doesn't agree. In fact, she thinks I need schooling in—" I froze for a moment.

"What's happening? Are you okay?"

How could I forget? I squeezed Daire's cheeks, pushing his lips together. "I'm fantastic!"

"Great. Can you let go of my face, and tell me why you're making me sound like a duck?"

This time I did squeal a little. "I know how we can see each other again. No forest. No threats."

"Now you've got my attention."

I told him about the passes to the human world, courtesy of my mother's attempt to educate me in the ways of other realms, and the pleasures they offered.

"Eden, why didn't you lead with that? I'm sure Merlin could've figured out how to get a message to me, and we could've met somewhere in the human-realm instead of you having to battle through the Eventide.

"Stop with that. As bad as it was, I learned a lot. About myself, and about the Lightlings." I told him about the lesser Fae that lived in the shadow of the Nocturna, and how I wanted to right that wrong.

"I'm not saying I wasn't scared, and I'm not saying the thought of my dying didn't cross my mind. It did. Especially with the Redcap. Still, I'd be lying if I said it wasn't exhilarating. I proved a lot to myself tonight. I proved I can survive. The quiet nerd. The one who lived adventures through the pages of books. Who watches from the sidelines, whether it's watching Sorcha or watching human movies."

"Is that how you see yourself? A quiet nerd?"

I shrugged. "Until I met you."

"How do you mean?"

"The night I met you was the first time I'd ever ventured out of the palace without a sanctioned entourage and personal guard. Sneaking out was always Sorcha's deal. She says a wild ride is a spare's rite of passage, otherwise they spend their lives in endless waiting."

"Waiting?"

"Yes. It's morbid, but true, nonetheless. Both Sorcha and your brother, Bain, spend their lives as a spare part, waiting for a tragedy to give their lives purpose."

"Purpose...as in our respective demise," he reiterated.

"Surely, you realized that? It sucks, however true. I'm not saying Sorcha wishes me dead. In fact, she said she'd kick my ass if something happened to me tonight."

"And what constitutes happening to you?" His hand slipped to my upper thigh, lingering for a moment. "Tell me."

"She meant if I was hurt or died, but if I come home in one piece, the threat takes on a different meaning."

"Like?"

"Basically, any juicy detail I refuse to share."

"So, you kiss and tell?

I brushed his lips with mine, nipping his bottom lip.

Daire went to slip his arm around my waist, but I wiggled free and got to my feet. "You promised me a picnic, and that means food."

"What about getting home before dawn?"

"I forgot about Merlin's stone. Crushed underfoot and zoom. Snug as a Seelie bug. Besides, we've got three days and three nights of freedom to plan. Like my mother says. Don't lose the mystique."

I couldn't believe I quoted my mother to my soon-to-be-full-on lover. Sorcha would roar with laughter if she knew.

"So..." I teased. "All at once, or one at a time?"

"Ladies choice...."

CHAPTER
Eighteen

I OPENED my eyes to bright sunlight. For a moment, disorientation had me blinking away the rest of my sleep. I was in my bed, but how? The last thing I recalled was my fingertips touching Daire's before I crushed Merlin's stone under my boot. We were at the standing stones. That was at least an hour past dawn. Maybe two.

So why was I in my nightgown with my hair smelling freshly washed from my favorite shampoo? Had I dreamed everything? If I did, then it would be one hell of a dream. Maybe Merlin's stone reset the clock. Still, why was everything so fuzzy?

Was my night with Daire real?

The thought nagged. Like I imbibed too much wine and couldn't trust my own senses. I'd had vivid dreams before, but not to this extent. Daire's kiss. The way his fingers plucked my body like a well-tuned instrument. The deep pleasure.

It was real. It had to be.

The window was open across my bedroom. Funny, I didn't remember opening it. A honeysuckle breeze teased the curtains, and a faint thought edged my mind. Was I supposed to do something today?

I sat up, trying to remember. The covers slipped to my lap, and the breeze from the open window sent a chill over my thin nightgown. I rubbed my arm, pausing at what I felt under the thin cotton.

Rushing from my bed, I stood in front of my dresser mirror. I pulled down my sleeve and there it was, jagged edged and an angry pink. The scar from the Redcap's pike.

It wasn't a dream.

I examined the fresh scar, letting the memory of the pain and fear flood back. I survived the Eventide. It was real, and if the events of the Eventide were real, then the rest of it was too.

Daire. The grotto. Everything.

I shrugged my nightie back into place and then stood staring at my reflection. "Who's the book nerd now?" I whispered, hugging my middle.

A frenetic kind of energy took over, and I didn't know what to do with myself. I wanted to see Merlin, to ask him about what I saw on the island, but I was also dying to tell Sorcha everything.

I hunted around for my bloodied and muddied clothes. I had to dispose of them, and I knew I hadn't come home in my camisole and panties. So where were they? Maybe Merlin's stone had a temporary amnesia element.

Oh well. I gave up looking. The clothes would turn up at some point, but right now, I needed to get dressed and find some food.

I pulled a soft maxi dress from my closet, pairing it with a pair of strappy sandals. Dressed, I piled my hair in a loosely coiled top bun, stopping to arrange a few tendrils around my face.

The stupor was wearing off, thank the gods. Besides the feel of Daire's hands and the taste of his kiss, it was how we talked and talked, I remembered most. Connected. Merlin's words came back as well, and they were spot on.

"Oh, good. You're still in one piece."

I smiled at my sister from the mirror. "I'm better than that. I'm *alive*." Of course, I didn't mean the opposite of dead. I meant exhilarated.

With a laugh, I whirled from my dressing table and grabbed Sorcha's hands, spinning with her in a circle. "Sissy, I'm so happy! I can't wait to tell you!"

"Edie..." She jerked me to a stop. "We've got trouble."

With her hands still in mine, I tried to read her face. "Why? What happened?" She couldn't mean last night. I purposely hadn't told her my plans for this very reason.

"I'm not stupid, Eden. I knew you had something up your sleeve, but sneaking out to see Daire? Without telling anyone?"

Screeching halt.

Eden, zip. Sorcha, one.

I couldn't gauge how much she knew, so I played it off with a shrug.

"It's true, then." She inhaled, shaking her head.

"Spare me your disapproval, Sorcha. You're not the only princess who has adventures now."

"Eden! This is different. And I'm not the only one who figured it out!"

If Sorcha meant our mother, then I was anxious but prepared. I'd already come up with an idea on how to spin it, so the queen saw my rendezvous as a sly plus. On the other hand, if it was Lachlan who figured it out, first? I swallowed.

My mind weighed every possibility, throwing out most. The one thought that kept creeping up was the shimmer on the bluff above the cave entrance, and then again near the edge of the sink hole. Someone was there.

I knew it.

It had to be someone with access to quiescent portals, lesser known and disused.

But who?

I stopped my mental cataloguing and faced my sister. "Tell me." It wasn't a question. It was a demand. "Who else knows?"

"Rylan."

Brows furrowed, I blinked. "Rylan. Big ego. Even bigger jerk... *that* Rylan."

"Yes, Edie. What other Rylan do we know?"

I dismissed her claim and went back to fixing my hair. The idea of Rylan accessing any portal, let alone one that could break through Daire's wards was ridiculous. Even without protective elements, the island would never reveal itself to that shallow blowhard.

"Eden, this is serious! Rylan is in the infirmary. Truth be told, he's lucky to be alive."

I glanced at Sorcha from the mirror. "This is Rylan we're talking about. He probably got drunk and fell off a parapet."

"Not with that kind of blood loss. I heard he was practically sucked dry."

My hands froze in place fixing my hair. "Sorcha, do you know *where* Rylan was hurt?"

My sister shrugged, not helping. Nothing other than what lurked in the Eventide inflicted those kinds of injuries, but how? Had the Nocturna infiltrated palace grounds searching for me?

I whirled again, but this time it wasn't to spin like a silly girl. I grabbed my sister's wrist, holding it tight. "You're not telling me anything, Sorcha. I need to know. Where was he attacked, and how did he learn where I went?"

"Quit it, Edie!" She jerked from my grasp. "I came here to help. Not to be manhandled."

My gut twisted. I needed her to confirm what I already guessed. Rylan had followed me again. Like he did when he showed up at Merlin's keep. He followed me and somehow tracked me to the Eventide.

Had the Nocturna targeted him the way they targeted me? Rylan was a High Sidhe. Not of royal blood, but a noble. It had to be that malfeasance. Lightlings didn't initiate conflict. They were peaceful, for the most part, unless forced to defend themselves.

I grabbed my sister's arm, pulling her toward the bedroom door.

"Hey! What are you doing?"

"*We* are going to see Rylan, and on the way, *you* are going to tell me everything you know and everything you've heard about what happened to him. Every whisper of gossip."

The truth was buried in the murmurs and innuendo. I knew the realities of the Eventide, so I was sure I could separate fact from fiction.

"I don't know all that much," she replied. "Just that two sprites brought him back to the palace. They said they found him unconscious in the forest."

"Yes, but *which* forest, Sorcha."

She stared at me incredulously. "Absolutely not. He wouldn't."

"He would if he thought that's where I went."

Her face paled. "And why would he think that's where you went?"

I kept my face impassive. We were on the central landing in the middle of the main staircase above the palace's formal entrance. There were too many ears around for me to tell Sorcha the truth. If she freaked out, the news would travel at the speed of light.

Two sprites. There was at least a dozen species of their winged ranks throughout Seelie. So why assume they were warrior sprites, let alone Kip and York. Aerith relied on them to help defend the Lightlings and protect the Eventide. With my actions metaphorically poking the Nocturna, she needed all hands on deck.

Still, Kip and York were the only sprites with a personal invitation to the Summer Court. I could volley back and forth all I wanted. Assuming it was Kip and York made sense. They must've been on their way to collect their reward when they ran across Rylan. The question was, did they find Rylan...or did Rylan find them?

I doubted my sprite friends were responsible for the courtier's injuries. My gut hadn't been wrong yet. Aerith said the Nocturna retreated to the shadows, but my guess was they waited and watched. Hells bells, they probably counted on my returning the way I came, but instead, they got Rylan.

Sorcha and I rushed across the main keep to the stone building attached to the castle ramparts. The infirmary shared a parapet walkway along the manned perimeter. It was constructed that way to best serve the guards in times of crisis. Not that the Summer Palace had been threatened since the compact ruptured the realms. Most attacks were political in nature. Espionage undermining the structure of rival courts.

We slipped in through the main doors, making our way to the upper floors where most nobles were nursed. No one questioned us. Not when Sorcha was smart enough to swipe a bunch of flowers from a carriage stopped outside one of the market stalls.

We hovered outside the ward, watching the nurse move around Rylan's bed. Most of his body was bandaged, and his eyes were closed. The matron's white wimple bobbed as she tucked sheets, tsking about the condition of his linen.

"Oh, gods." I chewed my lip, trying to ignore the guilt biting into my conscience at how terrible he looked. If I hadn't embarrassed him, maybe he wouldn't have gotten it into his head to follow me.

"I told you it was bad."

Sorcha's whisper was accusatory, getting my back up. "Rylan's condition is not my fault, so quit it." I ignored another pang of guilt, despite my nerve.

"Methinks you sound a wee bit culpable."

"For what?"

She raised an eyebrow. "You didn't come home last night, and you already admitted you were with you-know-who. What you haven't said is where you were, or how you got there." She looked past the doorjamb, tracking the nurse inside the ward. "I know we can't talk here, but you're not off the hook. I expect all the details."

I pressed my lips together. "Fine."

The matron noticed us loitering, her eyes moving from me to Sorcha and then to the flowers and back again. She put one finger to her lips and then beckoned us in.

"Your Highnesses." She smiled, showing dimples on each cheek. "It's nice to see you visit your friend."

"How is Rylan?" I asked, ignoring my sister.

The matron clicked her tongue. "He's very weak. We can't be sure, but with the amount of blood lost, we think he was attacked by a Dearg Due."

Aghast, I sucked in a breath.

"Aye." The nurse bobbed her head up and down. "At first, we thought he ran afoul of a Redcap. That kind of blood loss is typical for those nasty wee goblins, but with the number of bite marks on his body, the lad had to have been lured and then fed upon."

Stunned, I looked at the bandages wrapping Rylan's arms and legs. The nurse saw my reaction and nodded again. "Your friend was fair covered with bites. On every limb, and everywhere in between. That was the dead giveaway. Dead being the word. If this wasn't a Dearg Due, then whatever it was rose from the grave thirsting."

The bell to the main doors clanged, and she glanced toward the ward door. "That'll be the herb medicine I ordered. His wounds will fester without it. I'll be a moment, ladies. You can stay if you're quiet." She nodded once and then waddled out toward the steps leading down to the main keep.

"What in the actual hell," Sorcha hissed. "A vampire. That woman just said Rylan was attacked by the fae version of the undead."

I didn't know what to say. I'd know more once Rylan woke, or I spoke to the sprites that brought him back to court.

He stirred in the bed, wincing when he tried to move. Sorcha's face paled, looking from me to him and back again. "What if he wakes up and the matron's not back yet?"

Her whisper was tinged with panic, but I ignored it. After what I'd been through in the Eventide, and from the look of what Rylan had been through as well, not having a nurse to cluck over him didn't sound like a problem.

"Sorcha?" Rylan's voice was weak. His eyes fluttered for a moment and then opened. "Have you found Eden?"

"I'm right here, Rylan." I inched closer. "What did you get yourself into?"

Sorcha put the flowers on the small side table beside his bed. "Don't try to speak, Ry. Save your strength."

His eyes found me, and he winced, lifting his arm a few inches off the bed.

"Ah, I don't think you should move around. You'll reopen your wounds."

"Wounds." He exhaled a weak breath. "How is it you don't have any yourself?"

Sorcha's eyebrows jerked up at that, but she settled her face just as quickly. "Ry, I think you're confused."

"I found your dagger, Eden. Or what was left of it." Rylan winced again, trying to push himself up on his pillow. Tiny blooms of crimson dotted his bandages after that, and he swore under his breath.

"What are you talking about?" My stomach knotted even as I kept my face impassive. Damn. If Rylan had found my dagger, then he found what was left of the Fachan outside the ring of sentinel oaks, which meant he found Druitia's temple.

He pointed to the small drawer under Sorcha's flowers. "In there."

Sorcha pulled a dagger's hilt from inside. It was badly damaged. Pitted and scored, the blade had disintegrated, and the hilt mostly melted. The only thing naming it as mine was the emerald in the pommel.

My sister held the dagger up, her eyes full of questions and suspicion. "Is this yours, Edie?"

I shrugged. "It might be." I took it from her hand. "It certainly looks like mine. Except I haven't seen my dagger in ages. In fact, this looks like it could be one of yours Rylan. I saw you with a similar one last evening, if you recall."

He knew exactly what I meant. The dagger was definitely mine, but the Fachan's acid had damaged the jewel. I knew it was an emerald, but it had been scorched so badly it could've been a smokey topaz. The jewel in Rylan's family crest.

"It's yours, Eden," he insisted. "I found your tracks in the Eventide last night."

My knees wobbled, but I managed to rest my fingers on the end of his hospital cot to steady myself. "That's ridiculous."

"Is it? I wonder what your mother will say when she finds out you're sneaking into Sluagh territory. I wonder how quickly those emerald eyes will turn flat and lifeless when you're accused of treason."

CHAPTER
Nineteen

"TREASON?" I stifled a laugh. Of all the absurdity Rylan's pique could hurl at me, that was the silliest I could fathom. "You must be fevered to think something so stupid."

"You were there, Eden." He wheezed. "If I hadn't been attacked, I could prove it beyond a shadow of a doubt."

"I don't think so. The Eventide is a hard ride. Unless you had magic to transport you, it's three hours in the saddle. And where would you get that kind of magic, huh? It's one thing for our kind to sift time when we travel to the human realm, but it's quite another to move from place to place in real time here. For that, you need a sorcerer, and the only sorcerer I know works for the queen. I highly doubt Merlin would spare you a moment, let alone conjure a league jump for the likes of you. Not after you barged into his keep and threatened his familiars."

Sorcha's mouth dropped. "What are you two talking about?"

I told her what had happened before I insulted Rylan and his breath, and she frowned, giving him a hard look. "You are not painting a convincing picture, Ry. This sounds like you, slighted and doing something stupid to get even."

"Exactly," I reiterated. "And what makes you so sure I was in the forest or that the tracks you allegedly found were mine? In fact, except for the gala, when have you known me to be able to leave the palace without an entourage appointed by the queen?"

That gave him pause. "Sorcha could've helped you. She's always sneaking out."

"Don't try and pin this on me," Sorcha shot back. "If Eden wanted to traipse through the Eventide, I'd be the first to tell our mother."

"Then Merlin." Rylan raised his chin with another wince, and I caught a glimpse of ripped flesh beneath one of the loosened bandages. He had suffered at the hands of that creature.

"C'mon, Ry," Sorcha prompted. "Even you can't believe that."

"Eden has the old seer wrapped around her finger. Everyone knows that."

Sorcha put her hand up and palm out. "Now you're talking insanity. Merlin is my sister's mentor and guardian. Our mother would have his balls if he put Eden in jeopardy. Sneaking out to a ball is one thing. We were in a large group with multiple safeguards. What you're accusing Eden of is suicide."

She stalked to the side of his bed to poke his chest. "Just because you're crazy enough to traipse through a bloody deathtrap, don't put that on my sister or me. You were the one who has had a wild hair up his ass about her since the Winter Court gala. You have no one to blame but yourself for your foolishness and its fallout."

I stifled a smile. Sorcha was a spitfire when riled. Too bad all that indignance would be aimed at me once she found out Rylan was right. Did I have to tell her about the Eventide? Well, no. The juicy details she cared about had everything to do with my meeting Daire. Not how I got there. Maybe my Eventide ordeal was something I could keep between me, Daire, and Merlin.

The matron came back, and her white veil flapped behind her as she hurried toward the bedside. "Well now, look who's joined us in the land of the living. And here I thought the creature had bled you to death, poor lad."

"How long do I have to lay here?" Subtlety was not Rylan's strong suit. Neither were manners unless they promised a return on investment.

She clucked her tongue, tucking his bed sheets closer again. "You'll stay in that bed as long as necessary. Ach, look. You've opened your wounds again." Her lips pursed, and she lifted the back of her hand to his forehead. "And you've got fever plaguing you. We were worried those bites would fester, and now it seems they have. No wonder you've been talking nonsense."

"But I need to see the queen!" Rylan struggled to sit up further, but the nurse placed two firm hands on his shoulders and pushed him back to bed.

"You'll do no such thing, love. Not with the trouble I had binding your poor limbs. You've already ruined my work squirming about, and I won't have it. Besides, the queen isn't here. Not to worry, though. Her lovely daughters have come to keep you company."

Despite his dagger eyes at me, Rylan knew he wasn't winning this battle. "Fine. Could you at least tell me when the queen arrives back? I need to tell her what I found in the forest."

"You found death, my boy. Tis lucky you escaped with your life." She tsked again. "Whatever possessed you to go wandering in the *Réimse Maron* is beyond my ken."

Sorcha raised an eyebrow at me, and I mouthed 'the dead realm'. My knowledge of the old tongue was courtesy of Merlin, so I wasn't surprised Sorcha didn't know it. Not many of our generation did.

An awkward silence fell across the ward, though we were the only visitors and Rylan the only patient. "Nurse," I interjected, breaking the weirdness. "You said the healing herbs you ordered had been delivered. Are they just for fester, or are they for pain as well?"

I didn't want Rylan to suffer, regardless of how much he annoyed me. Still, if the herbs drugged him into a stupor, then he couldn't push the issue with my mother.

"Ach, yes. I have them right here." She reached into her apron, pulling out two brown bottles sealed with wax. I smiled to myself. Merlin. I'd know his private seal anywhere. He sent the medication, and if I knew my mentor, he had Rylan's claims well in hand.

If there was the smallest chance Rylan's claim could be seen as anything but fevered ranting, Merlin would handle it. I knew the old Druid could alter memory, and fingers crossed, that was the purpose of those vials.

"I was going to wait until I cleansed and changed your bandages, but the princess is correct. There's no reason for you to suffer." The matron unsealed the first bottle, giving Rylan a healthy swig, and then did the same with the second. "This will help you sleep. Gods know you need it."

The nurse helped Rylan lay back and then waited for his eyes to flutter closed. "Good. Now when I change his wraps, he'll be none-the-wiser."

Clucking, she walked around to the other side of the cot for a sick bucket. She reached out a hand to stroke Rylan's forehead, brushing back his damp hair. "If his wounds are any hint as to what he went through, he put up quite a fight."

She put her finger to her lips the same way she had when Sorcha and I arrived, only this time she shooed us out of the ward. "That's enough visiting for one morning. The lad's knackered after all he's endured, so you two go on with yourselves. I'll send word when he awakens."

I thanked the nurse, stealthily secreting the dagger into my pocket. Hurrying out, I caught up with Sorcha as she ambushed me out the door. "Edie, was any of what Rylan said true?"

Now it was my turn to put a finger to my lips. "Look," I said, pulling her to the closest corner near the stairs. "Merlin helped me get to you-know-who the same way he helped me go with you to the Winter Court that night. That's all you need to know. I promise I'll tell you all the juiciness about you-know-who once we have a minute alone."

She angled her head unsure. "But that was your dagger, Edie. I know because I have its mate in my dresser drawer."

My gut squeezed with the lie of omission I just told my sister. "Sorcha. Please. I kept you in the dark about my plans for a reason. If I tell you everything now, you won't like it."

"Just tell me one thing." She inhaled a breath, letting it out quickly. "Were you in the Eventide last night?"

I opened my mouth to answer, but a commotion down in the keep grabbed my attention. I peered through one of the stone windows and cursed. Kip and York were in the courtyard in shackles.

I clattered down the stone steps and out into the courtyard faster than I thought possible. Catching my breath, I skittered to a stop in the dirt just as one of the guards shoved Kip in the back. The warrior sprites were man-sized again, and neither had their swords.

"Hey!" I marched straight up to the handsy guard. "Is this how we treat invited guests in this palace?" The guard's lips parted, and it was clear he didn't know what to say.

Sorcha joined me at this point. From the look on her face, I knew I wasn't off the hook. I couldn't worry about that now. Not with two biotáille laochra in shackles. I had earned Kip and York's trust in the Eventide, but now the Sidhe were living up to their bad reputation.

"Milady! Thank the gods!" Kip lifted his chained hands. "A little help, perhaps?"

A guard thumped the back of Kip's head. "Shut your gob!"

"What the actual hell is wrong with you?" Sorcha yelled, shocked. "Lift your hand again and you'll answer to me! You don't strike a man already in shackles."

The guards didn't know what to do, and that was my cue to get my friends released. "These men are warrior sprites, and they're here at my personal invitation. Release them now."

"But Your Highness, we were told to hold them for questioning."

I put my hands on my hips. "By whom?"

I would've bet my teeth, it was Rylan's father, but the deep voice behind me said otherwise. "Me. I gave the order, Your Highness."

Caxton.

I turned to see the Captain of the Queen's Guard walking toward us. Sorcha flanked me in solidarity. Caxton was not going to argue with both of us. After so many years, the man's glare no longer scared me. The ever-present scowl seemed as much a part of his persona as his swagger or his uniform.

Court gossip whispered he was once as chivalrous as he was ruggedly handsome. I had seen shades of that gallantry, but not for a very long time. My guess? He made the mistake of falling in love with my mother. An emotion she mocked, if not out and out despised, and rather than suffer the humiliation, he twisted the feeling inward, corrupting it to scorn.

"Take the sprites to the cells."

Sorcha planted her feet between the guards and the sprites while I stared down the queen's three-headed pig. "Has my mother returned from her pavilion?"

The muscle in Caxton's jaw stiffened. "Not as of yet, Your Highness."

"I see." I crossed my arms over my chest. Not tight, as to be defensive, but casually so, as to let this bully know I wasn't about to be intimidated. "That means I am the highest-ranking royal in the palace, and after me, my sister. Am I correct, or do we need to summon the Privy Council to reiterate the laws of succession?"

His jaw was so tight, I thought it might shatter.

I didn't flinch. Instead, I kept an unblinking gaze on the man. Despite his history with the queen, Caxton was still devoted. So much so, he'd roast Sorcha and I on a spit if the queen asked. I didn't need to make an enemy of him any more than I already had.

"As Captain of the Queen's Guard, I understand your concerns, and that you were acting with the best interests and safety of the palace in mind. I applaud that sentiment and am grateful for your concern. However, these sprites are my friends. How I made their acquaintance is immaterial, but treating them in this fashion, however misconstrued, is not to be borne. That said, I ask you to please release my friends."

Caxton's jaw loosened a fraction, and the barely perceptible nod was all the acknowledgement I'd get. It was enough to know he was mollified. I had granted him deference, but at the same time made my point.

Diplomacy. One.

Three-headed pig. Zip.

"Release the sprites." His growl was clipped, and I knew his guards would pay the price. I felt bad, but that wasn't my concern right now.

"One more thing, would it be too much to have their weaponry returned? My friends are biotáille laochra. As you know, their swords go where they go."

I knew he understood the old tongue. Or at least as far as the formal title for warrior sprites, since they had been dubbed such by the first Seelie queens. He nodded once, and with a wave of one hand, dismissed his men.

York rubbed his wrists and had yet to say a word. Kip eyed my sister, inclining his head in respect.

"I can't apologize enough," I said, both embarrassed and relieved at the same time. "Had I known you were set to arrive so early, I would've met you at the gates properly, and none of this would've happened.

York gave me a curt nod but stayed silent.

"It's not your fault, milady. We're just glad you came when you did."

Kip jerked his chin toward the infirmary. "We brought your man back. We thought he was a goner for sure."

Sorcha snickered at that. "Rylan wishes he was my sister's man. Was it you who found him in the forest?"

"Aye. Milady Eden invited us to the palace last night, after we —" My sharp cough cut Kip off, and he nodded in understanding. "— we did her a service, and she was kind enough to invite us for a visit. We were making camp when we saw the lad crumpled at the base of a tree. He'd been savaged. We hadn't planned on arriving until this afternoon, but his injuries would've gotten the best of him if we waited."

Sorcha spared a glance for me before extending her hand to Kip. "Thank you for saving our friend, and for whatever service you did for my sister. Please, call me Sorcha."

Kip exchanged a look with York, who finally piped up. "I can see you and your sister are of the same mettle. You placed yourself between us and your own guards. That takes guts. It's nice to see both High Sidhe princesses aren't just beauty, but brains and bravery as well."

A guard exited the garrison carrying two longswords. He held them out to both sprites. He didn't say a word, but a quick incline of his head said it all. Diplomacy aside, the palace guards were quick to see the truth for truth's sake. Warrior sprites had fought shoulder to shoulder with Seelie armies since the fracture and deserved respect.

The guard turned and left, and I slipped my arm through Kip's elbow. "How about I treat you both to lunch on the south terrace. It has the best view of the Faewyn Sea, even if it can be a little damp."

"Will the Lady Sorcha join us?" York asked.

My sister shrugged. "Why not? I haven't eaten yet today, and since my sister has been so close-lipped about her adventures, I'm counting on you two not to spare the details."

"Kip and York are here to visit the swordsmith, Sorcha. They don't have time to gossip. Especially when that gossip is about *me*."

She stuck her tongue out at me. "Spoil sport."

Sorcha scooted ahead to talk to one of her friends, leaving me with the sprites. "I hope you'll both forgive me." I motioned toward the now quiet garrison. "Although, what happened was unforgivable."

"Forget that for now, milady." York lowered his voice to a warning whisper. "There was another who used the portal last night."

CHAPTER
Twenty

"SOMEONE USED THE PORTAL AFTER ME?" My gut squeezed. "How? Rylan was the only one who followed me to the forest, and we know he didn't make it to the temple."

"Begging your pardon, milady, he's the only one that you know of." Kip shared a look with York. "We know better."

My head spun. I put my hand to my forehead, and as if he sensed my discomfort, Caxton walked into the garrison doorway. He stood with a mug in his hand looking relaxed, but I knew he was there to spy. Did he know something as well? Maybe he sent someone into the forest to keep tabs on me, and they ran afoul of whatever mauled Rylan.

I dismissed the thought. Caxton was arrogant and carried himself with more authority than granted, but he'd never adopt a wait and see attitude when it came to the safety of the heir and the spare. Doing so would threaten his position with the queen, and that was a point of pride for the man. So, no.

He would've stone cold stopped me the moment I left palace grounds. Maybe even before that. He'd have dragged me back to the castle and locked me in my chamber with a guard posted to my door until the queen instructed otherwise.

Maybe Kip and York were right, and Rylan wasn't a solo act. He and

Cian were thick as thieves. All it would take was one hypothetical joke to get them thinking. After all, we were together as a group at the Winter Court gala. They knew I'd spent time with Daire.

"We can't talk here." I chewed my lip, scanning the bustling keep and its market stalls, not to mention the garrison only steps away. I didn't need a reflection to see the worry on my face. "Let's get lunch. Some place quiet, away from prying eyes and listening ears."

"Milady…" York put his hand on my arm. "There's no need to worry. We're here to help."

"That's right," Kip added. "We know your man in the infirmary came alone."

York lifted a staying hand, picking up where Kip left off. "…but we also know your man was followed."

I exhaled with my hand in my hair now. "So, you're telling me Rylan followed me, and then someone followed Rylan."

Both sprites nodded.

With a muffled curse I turned and stalked for the keep's arched gate, my body language an unspoken directive for them to keep up.

"No lunch, then?" Kip whispered.

"Is your belly what's minding you now?"

"Well…"

A mumbled expletive followed a soft whack.

"Hey! That's my head."

"Then use it for once, and keep your gob shut."

I stifled a smirk. Leave it to the Fae comedians to lighten the dourest mood.

The sprites followed me toward the main palace and the great hall, but instead of heading to the south terrace, I took them down the veranda steps and into the pleasure gardens. There were always sandwich carts in the afternoon with boxed lunches. During the day, the gardens were relatively quiet. Nights were another story.

The famed pleasure gardens were well named with wide, manicured spaces interspersed with secluded niches for more intimate trysts. Courtiers and guests wanted for nothing when it came to pleasing the senses. Illuminated with thousands of twinkle lights, the gardens were host to all manner of entertainments. Concerts, acrobats, and other curiosities in the main rotunda, while champagne fountains provided nonstop drinks, and every night ended with fireworks over the Faewyn Sea.

York cleared his voice when I stopped with them at a sandwich cart. "Uhm, milady?"

I didn't answer. Instead, I handed York the boxed lunches and then headed into the gardens' main thoroughfare.

"So, she's not answering you either, Yorkie. Maybe I should clout you in the head like you did me."

"Both of you, quit it. We're going down to the beach, just not the way I originally thought."

"Well, why didn't you just say?" Kip replied.

York rolled his eyes. "Because we weren't far enough away from earshot, you dolt."

I slipped with them into the shadows, turning for a lesser used path along a hedgerow on the outer perimeter of the sundial rockery. "I keep a key here for when I want to be alone."

Teasing my fingers along the overgrown shrubbery, I stopped at the end of the hedgerow to rummage inside the dense green.

"Careful, milady. Boggles sometimes booby-trap hedgerows for sport." Kip poked at a suspicious pair of twined twigs, only to jerk his hand back. "Ach! Those little wingless bastards!" The sprite cradled his hand.

Stifling a laugh, I pressed my lips together. "Are you okay?"

"Fecking spring-loaded thorns! You wicked, cowardly articles!" A soft snickering in the brush followed a rush of tiny twig snaps. "Aye, you better run!"

"What have I always said." York shook his head, laughing. "Never mess with the wee ones."

I found the key I hid in the brambles and then motioned for the sprites to follow. "There's a forgotten tool shed toward the back. It's practically invisible in the overgrowth."

"I thought you said we were heading to the beach." Kip sucked the side of his finger.

I nodded. "There's a set of stairs behind the shed, but we need the key I hid in the hedgerow to open the gate."

We sat with our boxed lunches on two fallen branches at the edge of the sand. "This is lovely, milady. Thank you," York said, chewing.

"Aye. It's glorious," Kip agreed. "We never get to see or hear the wild water from where we are in the forest."

"Feel free to wade in, if you want. It's warm up to your ankles, but deeper than that it gets pretty cold."

York put his palm up, shaking his head. "I appreciate the offer, but the salt will negate Aerith's spell. She gifted us some of her magic so we could walk tall at the palace."

"I understand." I wiped my mouth, placing the napkin in the empty box and then the box on the sandy ground. "Now that we've eaten, I need to know what else happened after I went through the portal. I don't believe you finding Rylan is where the story ends."

"Like we said," Kip replied, chewing the last of his sandwich. "Your friend was followed. We don't know by whom, but we found their tracks when we found your man."

I knew it was only an expression as Rylan was from the palace, but he wasn't my man, and the term grated. "Maybe Rylan wasn't followed. Maybe he was stalked by the bloodsucker that attacked him."

"I suppose it's possible." York shrugged. "Except Dearg Due don't hunt the Eventide. Not enough prey to make it worth the effort."

I stared at them both. "If they don't hunt the forest, then what was it doing there?"

"Ah, that's the point." York raised one finger. "Whoever followed your man deserted him when he found your tracks."

"How do you know?"

"Because *their* set of tracks led away from where we found him."

My brows furrowed. "Toward the temple?"

"That's the rub." York shook his head. "We found tracks in the opposite direction. Whoever followed your injured friend abandoned him, and we think we know why."

Kip eyed me at this point. "Do you know the history of the Eventide? Of its inhabitants?"

"I do, or at least I know the version in the Seelie archives."

He nodded. "The Nocturna are the Sluagh abandoned after the Western Rim War..."

I stopped him, instead telling them both about the Unseelie tome in the library and what I'd read.

"Good," York responded. "Then you know about Taltos."

Hesitating, I nodded again. "What about him?"

"Taltos considers the Eventide his land. Part of the Dusk Court, and by extension, the Horde, and its Wild Hunt," York explained. "He's not the only one to claim title to the vast forest and its various inhabitants, but because the Nocturna are former Sluagh, he has thrown down a gauntlet, staking his claim as singularly valid. Both Lachlan and your mother are aware of his claim. They've chosen to ignore it."

Kip nodded. "Taltos has been flexing his muscle. Showing the main courts he'll stop at nothing to prove his rule and annex the Eventide."

"Like attacking the Winter Court, the night of the gala." I exhaled. "While I understand all this, and it's worrying, what has this got to do with me entering the portal to meet Daire?"

"In Taltos's eyes, you had no right to use the portal," York furthered. "He was furious."

Kip whistled low. "He demanded Aerith tell him where you went. She refused, of course. Stalemated, he paced in fury, and you could fairly see him weighing and dismissing his options. You see, he has no power over Aerith, and the consequences if he hurts her or her Lightlings is unthinkable."

"What consequences?"

"Aerith is a queen. An ancient, true, but also a queen," Kip continued. "Her power is such she can gift parts of her soul to those she protects. If Taltos were to kill a Lightling in vengeance, the strike would be at Aerith as well. The cost to any ruler for killing an ancient is to have their mind severed. To wander formlessly, a vacant shell."

"But that's not the case if someone were to strike at my mother, for example. Or Daire's father, Lachlan," I argued. "Or if someone were to strike at Taltos."

"That's right, milady. Aerith is a different breed altogether, and those consequences of fate aren't just for the Lord of the Dusk Court. It's the same for all."

I nodded, understanding. "Hands off the ancients."

"Indeed."

I wondered if it was the same for Merlin. I doubted it. He wasn't Fae, so the tenets didn't apply. "Okay, so Taltos is upset, and Aerith has blown a huge razzberry at him. What does that have to do with Rylan...or me?"

"Stymied, the Sluagh leader saw your offerings. He drew his blade and sliced open his wrist, dripping his own blood over your gifts." York mimed the act.

"Why?"

"It's an old Druid law called a tribute. An offering of blood, especially one's own, earns the bestower a boon. Essentially, Taltos opened the portal on the back of your offerings and demanded he be taken through."

I didn't know how to respond.

Kip rose from the log to pick up a flat stone and skim it toward the water. "Before Aerith could stop him, the portal shimmered and Taltos leaped for the void."

"I sensed someone last night. For barely a moment. I didn't know who it was, but I sensed a presence."

York got up to gather the lunch boxes, putting them in a neat pile before the wind took them. "If Taltos saw you at all, it was unholy luck. The portal spewed him back, not once, but twice. The gateway rejected him and his tainted blood."

"I don't think so, York. It wasn't the portal that rejected Taltos. It was the destination he demanded. He asked to be taken to me, but the place I went to meet Daire is warded. Veiled. It only reveals itself to those it deems worthy."

The sprites exchanged a look. Did they know something more?

"What happened after that?" I asked.

York exhaled, lifting one shoulder in a sad shrug. "Taltos was thwarted, angry, but still calculating. It wasn't until he spotted the Redcap's head and the mucky remains of the Fachan that he lost the thread. He was a man possessed. No reason or rationale left. He willed a maelstrom to life, crumbling the very ground. From there he unleashed part of his Horde. Orcs. Rage Wraiths. Ogres, and the Dearg Due, as though he didn't care about the cost to himself or any creature they might harm. Including your friend, now in the infirmary."

York looked at me with caution in his eyes. "The Eventide is a very dark place now, milady. Kip and I were lucky to escape with your friend in tow. Aerith has taken her Lightlings to the Middle Course to keep them safe, and she's hidden Druitia's temple and the sentinel oaks. Kip and I found your friend, but we didn't journey here for any promised reward. We came to ensure you don't venture back."

"What about you?" I rubbed my arms from a sudden chill, looking between them. "How will you get to Aerith and the other trooping warriors if the Eventide is overrun?"

Kip smiled. "Aerith's old friend, and yours."

"I'll take you to him."

CHAPTER
Twenty~One

THE SPRITES HADN'T ANSWERED my question as to who followed Rylan and why he was abandoned. The human realm had a saying, you didn't have to outrun the bear, you just had to outrun the guy next to you. Was Rylan too slow, or did he think he could outfight a Fae vampire?

To be honest, I didn't think the sprites knew or cared. Not after the story they'd told. A story that left me in a precarious spot. Taltos unleashed walking, breathing, feeding evil into the Eventide. Land that bordered both the Seelie and Unseelie realms, and all four courts, as well as the Badlands. From there his Horde could multiply and spread like a disease.

Did I warn my mother? Did I admit my part in waking the Nocturna? Throw myself on the sword for the greater good? Maybe Merlin had a hypothesis. Either way, we needed a strong pot of coffee because this was setting up to be an all-nighter.

The sprites were in awe of the castle—its scope and how commerce boomed in its midst. It was obvious, not just to me, that the two hadn't been out of the forest much, especially when Kip stopped to see the wares at the leathersmith's stall.

"Oi! Greasy Fingers! If you're not buying, put that down."

Kip dropped the leather breastplate faster than he could blink.

"It's all right, Cappy. The sprites are with me, and their credit is good." The craftsman changed his tune and apologized the moment I intervened, but in the spirit of keeping everyone happy, I bought both sprites a set of leather armory, decimating Merlin's pouch of silver.

"I hope you meant what you said about not collecting your reward, because I spent most of it on those togs." Grinning, I handed them each a brown paper package with their new armor.

The way to Merlin's keep took us through the most remote parts of the castle. Not that palace grounds were dangerous, but workers liked their drink, and that led to misunderstandings. Ones where my claim to be the princess would fall on deaf ears until those ears sobered up in a cell and had to face Caxton. I suppose the man was good for some things.

Opening the tower door, I climbed with the sprites to the top of the stone steps. Merlin's door was ajar. I stood still. The old Druid never left the door to his private quarters open. Unlocked, yes. But never open.

With a staying hand halting both sprites, I put the tips of my fingers on the heavy wood before gently pushing the door open. As always, Merlin stood at his worktable.

"Merlin?" I prompted.

The old seer didn't look up, so I tried again. When he didn't reply for the second time, I put my arm out to the side to push the sprites back through the threshold.

"INCOMING!"

A blinding flash stunned us all. I staggered back with the sprites, slamming the door closed. Kip tripped down a few stairs before grabbing the edge of a stone window. York was still at the doorway with me, shaking off residual sightlessness.

"What the feckin' hell was that?" Kip said, steadying himself on the stairs.

I blinked, squeezing my eyes open and shut. "An experiment gone wrong. A spelled tripwire. Knowing Merlin, it could be anything."

"Eden?" The old sorcerer opened the door, neither beard nor hair out of place. "I see you've brought unexpected friends, which explains the tripped snare." He stepped aside, his robes swishing the top of his soft boots. "I suppose you'd better come in, then."

York rubbed his eyes, while Kip shook his head to clear the shock. "You pack quite a punch, milord."

Merlin seemed mildly disquieted, so I scanned the room for other booby traps or signs this wasn't real. There was nothing telltale, and I turned for him next. "Do you mind telling me what that blast was about?" My eyes still teared from the surge. "You of all people had to guess I'd come here today."

"I never guess, little dove. Fate has burdened me with capricious sight, forcing me to weigh everything until sure."

"Merlin, please. What was supposed to be a simple case of girl meets boy has morphed into something incomprehensible. I need your help. *We* need your help."

He touched my cheek, so familiar and grounding. "I know, child." With a soft pat, he turned for his worktable again. "I also know what happened with your courtier friend last night." He looked at me over his shoulder. "Rylan Fullore is trouble, Eden. Not just because you rejected his romantic aims, but because that rejection scotched his father's plans. Orin Fullore has far too much ambition, and when it comes to Rylan, the apple didn't fall far from the tree. Why else would I set that trap at my own door?"

"Trap?" Kip said, moving to stand at my side.

"Indeed." Merlin motioned to the fire and the bubbling contents inside the cook pot. "Please, help yourselves. I know sprites have appetites thrice the size of their stomachs, and I assure you the food is safely prepared. I traded my cast iron for an aluminum alloy from the human realm. Not as good, but I've grown weary of Eden never partaking for obvious reasons."

Kip leaned over and took the lid off the pot, inhaling the delicious scent. "Stew. Yum!" Fishing a potato from the broth, he tasted a sample. "Oh, that's lovely. Much better than that poor box flavored sandwich we ate earlier."

"Kip!" York's mouth dropped before sparing a look at me. "Don't be an ingrate!"

"Am I wrong, man? That wee bit of bread and ham wouldn't slake a pixie."

York's face went red, and I had to bite my cheek not to laugh.

Merlin smirked, as well. "There's a little bread and cheese on the table if that's more to your liking. I keep some on hand since Eden doesn't eat. She nibbles like a mouse."

""I do not nibble." I humphed. "I'm picky."

"I'm sorry you're having such a hard time today, little dove. I say with full surety, Rylan's family blames you for what happened to him, though the silly boy knew full well how foolish it was entering the Eventide without invitation. They blame you, and by extension, me. I set that trap at my door to protect myself and of course, my friends." He pointed to the rafters where Altair and Lyrae sat together in the sun. "Orin isn't one to relinquish his plan to see his son elevated, so we need to be cautious."

"Elevated?" I snorted. "If you mean Rylan as my royal consort, fat chance."

He tapped the side of his nose. "I've taught you to trust your inner compass in all things, Eden. That you're here now tells me you listened to your gut. Aerith told me what happened after you went through the portal. She told me, not only as a warning, but that I prepare you, and by extension, your mother and your sister, for what we see stirring. Both the Seelie and the Unseelie have rested too long on their laurels. Happy with the status quo. Taltos is growing in strength. Avalon is changing. Unless the realms work in concert, this world will be unrecognizable."

I'd never heard Merlin speak in such decisive terms. He usually preferred ambiguities, but not for the reasons most thought. The old seer wasn't interested in preserving what fate deemed rewritten. He was interested in truths.

"Your friends need safe passage. Correct?" He looked from me to them, and York nodded. "And where would you trooping sprites care to go?"

Kip moved with his bowl of stew to York's side. "Is there an option?"

"Yes and no. As you already know, Aerith is in the Middle Course. You need to join her there, but the situation being what it is, I'm not sure how to get you to your destination."

I went to open my mouth, to offer the portals from Danu's temple, but Merlin lifted his hand. "I can guess what you are about to say, little dove, and while you are generous to think of that, the option is not yours to grant."

I nodded. He was right, of course. Daire would never say no, especially since Kip and York helped save my life, but there was no way for me to ask him outright.

"What other option is there, then?" I asked. "All portals in Seelie require an official pass. Even Sorcha couldn't bribe her way through after what happened to Rylan."

Merlin acknowledged that. "Which is why we need to stop thinking about portals and start thinking about cross keys."

York glanced at Kip who shrugged with a mouthful of stew.

"Is it something like this?" I lifted the double dragon pendant from inside my dress.

"Very good, Eden. It is something like that, but it doesn't require spelled flesh."

Kip swallowed hard. "Spelled what?"

"A spell that burns the desired outcome into the flesh of a person. Rarely used, and for good reason. The spell can reject the flesh it's meant to imbue, but I'd rather not get into that."

My mouth dropped. Spell rejection? Merlin made me the key to the portal in the Eventide, rather than imbue the pendant for fear of my losing it or it being stolen. Is that why I had to run that gauntlet? Had my flesh rejected his spell?

"I know what you're thinking, Eden, and I would never do anything with you or your person unless I was absolutely sure it was the correct course of action. Did you hear the portal's hum? Did your skin vibrate?"

I bit my lip and nodded.

"Proof then." He looked from me to his table to the chest at the end of his bed. "What to use, what to use..." He put a finger up in an *ah ha* moment and then turned for the tiered shelf near his window.

He picked a wide, squat stone from the top. It was nondescript, gray, and completely smooth to the touch. "This will do nicely."

Merlin placed the stone in a shallow, silver bowl. Into that, he poured sea water and various herbs. He took a blue swirl jar from another shelf and emptied three spoons of black dirt into the water. The stone was surrounded by muddy liquid but not completely submerged.

"Come." He gestured to the sprites, and they moved to flank the old seer on either side.

Taking a small knife from the table, he cut a snippet of hair from each sprite and sprinkled that into the bowl as well. "It's time." Merlin's arms swooshed in a circular motion, arcing fire from the hearth into the bowl. The water caught flame, and grabbing the sprite's hands, the seer held their fingers to the blaze. "*Cruthaigh an sliocht. Cruthaigh an eochair*! Forge the passage. Forge the key!"

The flame went out, and the sprites jerked their hands back. "You said no fleshy spell thing!" Kip blew on his fingers but was stunned to see them unscathed.

"I didn't imbue your flesh, warrior sprite. If I did, you'd be writhing."

York rubbed his fingers as well. "What did you do then, if you didn't attach that spell to us?"

Merlin smoothed his long beard, untucking it from the front of his robe. "I simply told the cross key to remember you and grant you passage, that you had my permission to use it to travel to the Middle Course."

The sorcerer lifted the stone from the bowl. In Merlin's palm its gray color swirled with an iridescent light, but the moment he put it on the table, it returned to its pale, nondescript form.

"Hold the stone in your palm." Merlin gestured for York to pick up the cross key. "Its inherent power should recognize you, same as me."

York picked up the stone, and when it hit his palm, it glowed in the same way.

"Boyo! Toss it here." Kip clapped his hands.

York tossed the cross key over, flinching as Kip bobbled it from hand to hand. "Oi! Don't drop it, you fool!"

Folding my arms, I stood with Merlin watching them play hot potato with the stone.

"Ahh, sprites." The old seer's eyes twinkled. "No extra cost for the comedy." He cleared his voice, grabbing their attention. "That cross key will only go to the Middle Course, and it will only go one time. So, you both need hands on the stone when you say your destination. Is that understood? It's ready when you are, and you don't need a special place to activate the magic."

"Could we activate it here? Now?" Kip asked.

"Of course," Merlin replied. "If that is what you wish."

The sprites looked at each other and then at me, and York reached into his pocket for something before they both stepped in closer. "Milady, we've discussed it, and we want you to have this." York pressed a strange coin into my palm. "It's a *toghairm mian*. A summoning wish. If you have need of us, drop the wish into flowing water. We'll take it from there."

I closed my fingers over the coin, holding it tight. "Thank you both. For everything." Slipping my arms around their shoulders, I hugged them tight. "Take care of yourselves, and the others." Kip sniffed as he stepped back, and whether he knew I had caught it or not, I saw York wipe his eye on his cuff.

"Good. Grand." York cleared his voice. "Let's get this cross-key party started."

Merlin placed the stone on the floor between his worktable and the hearth. "You can crouch, or you can kneel. It doesn't matter as long as you both touch the stone and speak clearly."

"Can we take our parcels with us?" Kip lifted his brown paper package from the leathersmith.

"Of course. Just hold it tight, or better yet, stuff it inside your shirt. Otherwise, I have no idea, where, or to what dimension, it might spin off to."

Kip's eyes went wide at that, and I bit the side of my cheek. Merlin was messing with them and I kind of loved it.

"Ready?" I asked.

The sprites knelt on the stone floor, each with their fingers poised over the stone and their parcels tucked away.

"Wait!" York looked at Merlin. "Shouldn't we decide together what to say before we say it?"

The old Druid nodded. "I think that's very wise."

"On three, then." York gestured to the stone. "We each say Aerith."

I nodded to them one last time, privately hoping Aerith wasn't in the bathroom when they suddenly dropped in on her.

The stone glowed when they touched either side, and in a flash, they were gone. I inhaled, surprised at my sudden sense of loss. "Well, that's that."

"And what about you?" Merlin asked.

"I'm okay, I guess. Daire was wonderful last night." I lifted one shoulder, unexpectedly restless. "You know. After everything."

"Indeed."

Merlin went to sit in his favorite chair by the hearth, motioning for me to sit in mine. "Tell me. Was seeing him worth all the bother?"

I thought he'd raise an accusing brow, but he didn't. Instead, he poured us both some ale and then sat after handing me my cup.

"If you mean the Eventide, I'm not sure anymore. If you asked me last night, I would've said yes. No question. But now?" I shook my head. "After hearing about Taltos, and what he unleashed. After Aerith and the Lightlings..." I lifted one hand, at a loss.

"My ears are always willing, little dove. Speak your heart."

"They lost their home because I had to see Daire. I *was* that petulant Sidhe girl Aerith expected. I didn't throw a tantrum, or stamp my feet to get what I wanted, but I made damn sure I got my wish, come hell or Redcap." I tried to make light of it, but it didn't help.

"I think some would call that determination."

I nodded halfheartedly. "I suppose, but what about Rylan? If I wasn't so hellbent on getting my way, he wouldn't have followed me and almost die in the process."

"No, he would've cornered you somewhere in the palace and you would've been forced to defend yourself or submit. Both choices equally abhorrent, and neither of your doing. His lust, fed by his father's ambition, is a toxic mix. I'm not saying the boy is all bad, but Orin pulls his son's strings like a marionette."

The idea both sickened and saddened, but I knew Merlin was right.

"And what about Daire?" he asked. "What did he say when he learned all you did to keep your clandestine meeting?"

I told him how Daire reacted. What we discussed, and what I deliberately left out.

"I see."

"Was I wrong not to tell him everything, Merlin? About your hazy vision, and what it might portend? About being fated?"

"Prudence is always best, little dove. Last night you acted beyond your years, and beyond your skill. I'm proud of you but not surprised. The fact you feel guilt and compassion now only speaks to your growth. You've matured, Eden. And not just in body, but in mind and heart."

"Thank you, Merlin."

"Last night the fates put many things in motion, and they will move very quickly. You need to be ready for changes that will force you to make adjustments you might not want to make. Threads, eons old, are unraveling faster than the fates can reweave. You must use caution in everything you do and all you decide. The palace is safe, but the rest of Avalon…" He shook his head. "I can no longer be sure. As I said earlier, so much depends on the rulers of each realm and how they act—and with whom they ally."

Now was as good a time as any to ask what to keep close, and what to reveal, when it came to my mother. As queen, she needed to know about the Horde terrorizing the Eventide, or that terror would bleed into Seelie towns and villages. Chances were, she already knew, but if she found out I knew as well, and didn't say?

"Merlin?"

"Hmmm."

"Does my mother know what Taltos let loose in the Eventide?"

He held his mug of ale, staring into the fire. "Your mother's network of spies is the finest I've known. My guess is yes, but if she doesn't, she will very soon."

"What should I do?"

He turned his gaze from the fire to look at me. "Are you asking if you should tell Tianna what you know, and by doing so, admit your part?"

I nodded.

He inhaled, considering me. "Do you want to tell?"

"I don't want anyone hurt or worse because I kept quiet."

"I see. Are you afraid Rylan's family will get to your mother before you have the chance?"

I blinked at that. "I thought you already took care of Rylan and his time in the Eventide."

"What made you think that?"

My hands gripped my mug tighter. "The medicine the nurse had in the infirmary. It had your private seal." I took a breath. There was no reason to scramble. Yet.

The old Druid touched the side of his nose. "Very good, little dove. Sometimes the smallest detail will show you all you need to solve a dilemma."

"So, Rylan is dealt with, then?"

"He is, but that won't stop Orin from trying to implicate you. Rylan, of course, will have no memory as to why he entered the Eventide, and from what I can tell, he no longer has proof."

Merlin's gaze slipped to my pocket. I pulled out what was left of the dagger and showed it to the old sorcerer. "I still have no clue who followed Rylan. Or how they escaped the Nocturna and their Horde friends. Or how Rylan got his hands on my blade. The last time I saw this knife, it was stuck in a Fachan's chest while the beast slowly sank into a pool of acid muck."

The old seer stroked his beard, an unconscious habit while weighing something of extreme importance. Yet he said nothing. "Do you know any more about what happened?" I prompted. "Is there something I should know?"

"I will tell you this much. Do not underestimate Orin Fullore. At this point, he can't go to the queen without first revealing his scheming. While Tianna appreciates a good Machiavellian maneuver, she only does so when it's to her benefit. This doesn't qualify. Orin will try to coerce you. He will use whatever means necessary to force your hand, even if that means threatening those you love most. Me. Sorcha. Even Daire."

My brows knotted so tightly, they hurt. "Are you saying he'd threaten blackmail? Or hurt my sister...or you?"

"Orin has planned Rylan's rise since the day your mother granted the boy favor in his cradle. The man sees his son on the throne, in effect putting an end to the Seelie tradition of female rulers."

The notion was laughable. "My mother would see the entire Fullore family impaled on pikes before she let that happen."

"Your mother would no longer be around to wield that power. That responsibility would fall to you. If my conjecture is correct, Orin would let you live long enough to make his son your consort. After that?" He drew his thumb across his throat.

The thought sobered me. I was trained to believe threats came from without, not within. "Does my mother know this is happening right under her nose? Does she have an inkling?"

Merlin spread his hands. "Like I said. The realms have become complacent."

I had a hard time believing the Privy Council would follow blindly. And what about Sorcha? If I died without leaving an heir, she was next in line. Would Rylan force a marriage with my sister to keep the realm from uprising?

"All this brings me back to my original question. Do I tell the queen what happened in the Eventide and my part in it?"

He stared at me with an unfathomable expression. "No."

"Okay, why not?"

"There are too many variables yet. So many twists and turns before the paths are clear. The fates will reveal much, soon. You've already taken on more than you should at this point. Your shoulders are overburdened. My solemn advice? You need a respite to clear your mind."

A respite. Okay, then. Merlin could tell me the determinants were unclear all he wanted. I knew better. He always knew much more than he let on. "Then it's a good thing I'm planning to get away for a bit," I replied.

"Oh? And where are you planning to go? If you don't mind my asking."

"The human realm, and I won't have to sneak out. This trip is fully sanctioned."

Merlin was pensive. "I know you, little dove. So, it's not a stretch to presume you plan for the Unseelie heir to meet you."

"Yes, but—"

He put a hand up, stopping my protest. "I am not judging you, nor am I telling you it's an unwise choice. Go. Have fun. I would only caution one thing. Humans are very susceptible to Sidhe glamour. They are inherently, and sometimes uncontrollably, attracted. There are some Sidhe who use this to their advantage. They treat humans as playthings to be used and then discarded. To safeguard yourself, you must keep your Sidhe nature camouflaged. No magic. No glamour. Sorcha is well aware of this caution, and I trust you will impart my warning to...you-know-who." He winked, putting a finger to his lips.

Merlin was too cute sometimes.

"And when are you planning this momentous excursion?" He got up to spoon stew into a bowl for himself.

"This weekend. If Sorcha agrees."

The old druid's hunch about Orin Fullore had teeth, but not enough to put a halt to this trip. If it had, he'd never give me leave to go, let alone meet Daire. I tapped my fingernails on the side of my mug.

"Is there something else, little dove?"

"Just one small thing. I need to get a message to Daire."

CHAPTER
Twenty~Two

I STOOD with my suitcase in front of the portal. I hadn't slept a wink, and now I couldn't stop fidgeting with the straps on my backpack. Sorcha was late, and I was ready to scream. She knew what this trip meant to me. This was a weekend of firsts. I even had a private sit down with our mother in her chambers about what she expected of me on this trip. To be honest, I was surprised she couldn't sense I'd already had my first orgasm. Albeit not traditionally.

I hadn't had a chance to see Merlin since our talk after Kip and York left for the Middle Course. If he wasn't able to get a message to Daire —

Nope. I cut the negative thought midway. No pessimism allowed. Daire would be waiting for me at the hotel, and the two of us would take New Orleans by storm.

We were supposed to go to New York, but Sorcha nixed the Big Apple in favor of the Big Easy. She said since she was third-wheeling this trip, she got to pick the destination. I didn't care, really. I'd be happy on the moon with Daire.

This weekend was Imbolc, the sabbat celebrated in the human realm in February, which marked the halfway point between the winter solstice and the spring equinox. In the old tongue, Imbolc meant, in the belly of the mother, because the seeds of spring begin stirring in the belly of

Mother Earth. Humans didn't often connect seasonal celebrations to fertility rites that originally came from the Fae. Like Mardi Gras. Which was why we were headed to Nola. That is, if Sorcha ever showed up.

"Sorry, Edie!" My sister rushed down the path to the queen's portal. My mother was not far behind, with two ladies-in-waiting in tow.

"Are you trying to give me a panic attack?" I whispered. "What took you so long?"

"Girls... that's quite enough." My mother waved her ladies to one side while she gave us each a quick once over. "I'm glad you took pains this afternoon, Eden." She nodded, and I swore I saw the ghost of an approving smile at the corner of her mouth.

"I wanted to look my best straight out the gate. We may have to tamp our Sidhe identities, but we're still your daughters and need to represent."

Looking good for Daire. Check.

Mollifying my mother? Check. Check.

"I'm glad you're taking this seriously, Eden. While the purpose of this trip is a royal rite of passage, it's not pleasure for pleasure's sake. This is for you to learn other realms, and to familiarize yourself with the human world. Humanity often proves very useful to us, in that they are easily controlled and coerced. While you learn your body, you must also learn what you want and the art of making your partner beg to give it to you."

Heat scorched my cheeks, earning a concert of chuckles from my mother's ladies.

"Mother, perhaps that's too tall an order for Eden's first weekend away." Sorcha tried to mitigate, but I kept my eyes on the floor, hoping she hadn't shot us both in the foot.

The queen paused, and I braced myself to be sent back to the palace. "Hmmm. Perhaps Sorcha is right. We can think of this as a beginner's weekend and then follow up with more if needed."

Did I just hear what I thought I heard? Jerking my eyes up, I met my mother's cool gaze. "I...I... I think that's a wonderful idea."

She pursed her lips. "Wonderful, perhaps. Prudent at best." She snapped her fingers for her ladies to bring forward the bags they carried. "I should tell you Cian Bannerol will be meeting you when you arrive."

Sorcha's mouth dropped. "What? That's not fair!" She snapped her mouth shut on her blurt, but it was too late.

"This trip isn't about you, Sorcha." One eyebrow tweaked slightly higher, but the rest of the queen's face was unperturbed. "This weekend is about Eden."

"I know, but —"

"Isn't Cian a favorite of yours? I thought you'd appreciate the company."

I knew Sorcha wanted to cringe, but she kept her gaze steady. "He is... or was."

"Ah." The queen nodded. "Far be it for me to send a stale paramour with you. I can easily choose someone else."

Sorcha started at that. "No... please." She touched the queen's arm, stopping her from sending her attendant. "Cian is fine for this trip, and Eden is comfortable with him. New places, new faces, and such."

She didn't have to do that, but better the devil you know than the devil you don't. Mother could've sent Caxton instead.

"Very well, then." The queen nodded. "New Orleans has much to offer, even for the jaded."

I wasn't sure company for Sorcha was the only reason the queen wanted Cian with us. Unlike Rylan and his family, Cian's father, Aldric, earned his noble status through service rather than bloodline, and that service was in intelligence gathering.

"Mother, is there another reason you want Cian to accompany us?" My mother seemed fleetingly impressed. Though why she questioned I had a brain was beyond me.

"You're thinking like a queen, Eden." She angled her head, considering me. "It's about time. The answer to your astute guess is yes. There have been reports of stirrings instigated by the Shadow Courts, but nothing of serious concern."

"Like the attack on the Winter Palace gala?" I asked.

Her eyes narrowed slightly, and I swallowed at what that meant since suspicion was the queen's go to emotion.

"Eden's only asking because we discussed the attack at dinner with you the other night," Sorcha chimed in.

"Yes. Of course..." Mother waved a slender, manicured hand. "These stirrings are nothing like that. Lachlan chose to let that barely evolved ape,

Taltos, and his Horde of misfits into his bed, and now he has to lie with them."

Tianna pursed her lips, clearly pleased with her own rhetoric. "Did Merlin speak to you about the rules regarding the human realm?"

"He did."

"Good. Then you may have these." She snapped her fingers, and one of her ladies handed her two satin pouches, which she in turn gave to Sorcha and me.

"Are these in-case-of-emergency packs?" I asked, feeling the outside of the bag for one of Merlin's stones.

My mother looked surprised. "Why in the name of Avalon would you have an emergency? Do you think I'd send you both into the human realm without taking precautions?"

It was on the tip of my tongue to say, "because trouble finds me and the fates laugh", but I didn't. Instead, I replied, "How would I know? I've barely been away from the palace."

Tianna was not a tactile person, but she patted my arm, making me think I was having a brain bleed. "Things are well in hand, Eden. You're not to worry. I have people for that."

We walked to the portal entrance in awkward silence. I had no idea what to expect, but Sorcha didn't seem concerned, so I relaxed.

"Seeing you off on your first awakening trip..." My mother exhaled a soft breath. "I'm almost jealous."

Wait. Did the Queen of the Summer Court just sigh?

A wistful smile tickled the corner of her mouth, and Sorcha and I exchanged a glance. "Don't look so surprised. Seeing you poised for your first trip to the human realm makes me remember my own. It truly is a rite of passage. Of course, your grandmother didn't deign to see me off, and I barely had your Aunt Ysaryl to show me the ropes. You two need to count yourselves lucky."

The moment of softness faded, and the queen gave us a curt nod. "Be sure not to overstay your trip, or what's in the pouches won't work."

I looked at Sorcha, but she shook her head. "I'll tell you when we get there."

Tianna put a large shopping bag on the ground between us. "Coats," she said. "It's chilly where you're headed, and since you're technically not allowed to use glamour, I ordered these made for you." She gestured toward the tissue paper covered lumps inside the bag. "Your medallions are in one of the inside pockets. Wear the coats, don't wear the coats. I don't care. However, you WILL wear the medallions."

I opened my mouth to ask, but Sorcha shook her head again. The royal gateway hummed behind us, and my skin vibrated the same as it did when I approached Druitia's portal. Had Merlin's spell unintentionally made me a key to all portals? Interesting.

"Remember!" The queen called after us. "Seventy-two human hours. Not a second more!"

I walked into the shimmering center after Sorcha, bracing for a wave of vertigo. I stood with my eyes squinched, but it didn't come. I assumed the vertigo, the nausea, the amber tingling sparks, were all part and parcel of a standard portal jump, but I never asked.

We hadn't used a portal the night of the Winter gala, so I had no frame of reference. The stones Merlin provided that night had most likely been cross keys to get there and back. This, unlike Druitia's portal, was easy peasy. Like walking through a regular doorway, except a completely separate realm existed on the other side.

"C'mon, Edie. We still have a couple of things to do before the fun starts." Sorcha tugged me through the opposite membrane into what looked like an empty public restroom. The minute we cleared the threshold, the gateway door swirled, disappearing into the wide mirror above a row of porcelain sinks.

"Our portal is a public toilet?" I asked.

Sorcha laughed. "No, of course not. Just here in this hotel, and only for this part of the trip." She put the shopping bag on the tiled floor and then checked her hair and face in the mirror. "Put your coat on, or we'll look conspicuous when we walk into the hotel lobby."

I unwrapped the sleek, black peacoat, sliding my arms through the sleeves. "I'll give Mother this, she has great taste in clothes." I turned to admire the fit in the mirror.

"Here." Sorcha held out one of two identical medallions. They were small. Gold colored and cool to the touch until I slipped the chain over my head.

The medallion warmed against my skin, shimmering with an emerald hue the moment it slipped to the cleft at the top swell of my breasts.

"First Seelie princess. Check." Sorcha teased before slipping her own medallion over her head. "Second Seelie princess. Check. Check."

I glanced at the door from the mirror. "You're being very free with our identities. What if someone overhears?"

"No one's going to hear us, silly. We're not quite in the human realm, yet. We will be as soon as we walk out that door." She jerked her thumb over her shoulder.

"But this is a public restroom."

"It is, and it isn't. Trust me."

I shook my head. "I do, but you're confusing me."

"Look, remember the Room of Requirement in *Harry Potter*?"

"Of course." I blinked a moment. "No. No way." I shook my head again.

She patted her medallion. "Merlin's idea, actually. He said, and I quote, 'Insurance and protection need never be something sought,' end quote."

I was gobsmacked.

"The variable portal spell was Merlin, but the jewelry idea was all Mother. Pretty neat, huh?"

"So, portals are wherever and whenever we need them."

"All that's required is a mirror." Sorcha patted her handbag. "Even purse-sized will do the trick. Have mirror. Will travel. Literally."

"So, mommy dearest *has* considered the possibility of emergencies." I pushed my lips to one side in a gotcha smirk.

"Nope. Still all Merlin." Sorcha licked her fingers to smooth a stray hair into her sleek pony. "Though Mother liked the idea of designing the medallion herself."

"Ha! If I know Merlin, and I do, he probably played up the convenience angle rather than necessity to get her to approve the spell."

"Speaking of necessity." She opened the satin pouch Mother gave, pulling out a vial with a dropper top. "Two drops on the tongue every twelve hours. Without fail." Opening her mouth, she did hers first, then motioned for me to do mine.

"Why?" I mumbled, curling my tongue to catch both drops.

"To hide our scent."

I swallowed; happy the drops tasted like peppermint. "Hide our scent from whom? Do humans think we stink?"

"Edie, really. For someone so book smart you really are dumb. Sidhe blood is an aphrodisiac to certain supernatural species. Of all people, I figured you'd already know."

I snorted. "Nice try."

"I'm serious."

"Okay, smartie. Name one."

"Vampires, among others. They're the worst offenders. Our blood is a drug to the undead, and New Orleans is their North American playground. There have been stories of Sidhe who fetishize the undead, only to end up chained and used as a drinking fountain from dusk until dawn. Kept alive, but barely. In pain, and almost drained."

"Okay, okay. I get it." I waved a hand at her to stop.

"Good." She put her satin pouch in her purse, gesturing for me to do the same. "It's important, Edie, but not a hardship. It's why Mother warned the drops would stop working if we overstayed our welcome. Sort of a built-in deterrent for going AWOL."

I chewed my lip. There went my idea of using my super portal opening powers for spontaneous trips to the human realm with Daire.

Sorcha glanced at the restroom door. "Our seventy-two human hours start the minute we cross that threshold. Are you ready..."

CHAPTER
Twenty-Three

"CIAN SHOULD BE HERE SOMEWHERE." Sorcha scanned the hotel lobby. "Mother probably had him check-in for us and then do a sweep of the rooms and floor. Like father, like son."

Looking around, I was fascinated by the pink veined marble and lush décor. The hotel was opulence meets modern day in the best sense. The bar was set at the top of a short, wide staircase with a fluted balustrade. Octagon shaped, with wall-to-wall glass, the inner structure rose two floors above the lobby. At its center was a circular, two-story wine cellar, with cirque-du-soleil-style acrobats, ascending and descending on swaths of ribbon to fetch bottles for the bar.

"This place is unreal," I mumbled. "What's next, an infinite edge pool in each room?"

Sorcha chuckled. "That's on the roof."

"No way." I laughed as well.

"Welcome to the Hôtel Plaisir Royale."

It figured the hotel's name meant royal pleasure. I wouldn't be surprised if I found out Tianna owned the property or had a stake in it. The Privy Council didn't like the idea, but many High Sidhe owned property in the human realm. Now, I understood why.

"Hey." I tugged on Sorcha's arm. "It's dark outside. Did we lose half our day in that bathroom-in-between-thing?"

"I told you already." Sorcha exchanged a quick look with people passing and then lowered her voice. "The clock started counting down after we stepped through that door." She turned, but the gateway had been replaced by a large indoor palm. "Well, you know what I mean."

I stood watching people in the lobby. Some were elegantly dressed, while others looked like they were part of a burlesque troupe or frat party. "New Orleans certainly seems like a place for all kinds."

"It is."

I watched my sister fidget. Something she rarely did. "What's wrong with you? And don't tell me it's nothing."

She didn't answer.

"Sorcha."

She made a face and then exhaled. "Fine. If you want to know, Cian and I have been seeing a lot of each other. When he's away from Rylan and the rest of our crew, he's so sweet. I mean he's even thoughtful. It's unnerving, Edie. I don't know how to handle it."

"Is that why you didn't want him with us?"

"Yes." She fidgeted more, telling me that wasn't the entire story. "The thing is, I like him better when he's not playing the frat boy, except his new temperament holds up a mirror, and I don't like the me I see looking back."

"Why Sorcha Aossi! Vulnerable looks good on you."

"Shut up, Edie."

"Why? This is a good thing, Sissy. It means you care."

My sister's gaze dropped before meeting mine. "It doesn't make me a horrid person?"

"Of course not." If anyone was a horrid person, it was our mother. Her lack of feeling had emotionally stunted us both. "Look, if Cian can be thoughtful and tender, even funny, when he's with you—without it being premeditated or because he's scheming or setting you up—then it's not wrong or unreasonable for you to want him to be that way all the time. Regardless of what his friends think. If he's not able to do that, then you have some hard thinking to do. Just because his friends set the bar low, doesn't mean you can't raise it for what you want in a partner. Don't settle, Sorcha. You're worth too much to do that."

I never saw my sister tear up, but she did now, and she slipped her arm around my shoulders and squeezed. "That's why you're the smart twin."

"Nope. It's because I've spent a lot of time on my own. I know what I want and how I want to be treated. Plus, I've had Merlin to guide me all these years. You know, hanging out with him isn't as boring as you think."

She put up her hand. "Thank you, but no. I can deal with the likes of Rylan and his influence on Cian. You've spent years being schooled by Merlin, but the ins and outs of court life has been my school. We're suited to where we are."

"True, I guess."

She hugged me again. "I'll always have your back, Edie. Just like you have mine."

Cian walked toward us, and I turned my sister around to see him. "The boy cleans up well, when he wants to."

"He does at that." Sorcha's voice was a stunned murmur.

Cian looked sharp. He walked toward us in a pair of pale-wash fitted jeans and a white sweater, topped with a short, dove gray overcoat.

I had to smirk. She couldn't take her eyes off him.

"Do I meet with your approval, then?" Cian spread his arms as he approached.

"I'll answer yes for both of us, since Sorcha's tongue is on the floor." My sister punched me, but it was worth it to see the light in Cian's eyes.

"So, our rooms?" Sorcha asked, changing the subject.

"Yes. Of course," he replied quickly. "You're already registered. We've got two rooms on the top floor. The views are amazing, even if I say so myself."

"Wait," Sorcha questioned. "I thought we were getting suites."

"Each room is a suite. I'm in one, and you two are in the other. We can revisit the sleeping arrangements later, if you choose."

Sorcha rolled her eyes. "There's no need for feigned formalities, Cian. You and I will end up in one room, but not until Eden's friend arrives."

"What friend? I wasn't informed there was another person joining the party." Cian's eyes slid to mine. "Was this prearranged?"

"Sort of...it depends." I shrugged. "Actually, I'm not sure."

His eyebrows went up at that, and I couldn't blame him for doubting the situation. Who wouldn't when all I did was ramble about my plans. Truth was, I hadn't had word from Merlin about Daire, so I had no idea if he was able to reach him or not. All I could do was trust he had and go from there. If he hadn't? Then either I was third-wheeling Sorcha and Cian, or we all went home.

"There are a lot of moving parts to this trip, so it's better if we go with the flow." Sorcha tried to lessen Cian's wariness, but all it did was make his eyebrow hike even higher.

"Do I know this person?" Cian asked, skeptically.

Sorcha and I exchanged a look, but when she went to answer for me, I stopped her. This was my party, so it was up to me to put off any possible poopers, and that meant Cian.

"I doubt you've met him, but you know of him." Cian went to shake his head, but I shut him down. "Look, I know Rylan is a courtier and one of your closest friends, and I know he's convinced himself that he and I should be a pair. I'm telling you now, he and I are just friends, if that. Anything otherwise is not up for debate."

Cian's expression seemed to accept the cold facts. "It is what it is, Edie. Though this will be news to Rylan's father. Orin already has your mother's ear about the benefits of keeping the House of Aossi under one roof, if you know what I mean."

"That's ridiculous," I replied. "Orin knows almost all consorts come from the Spring Court. Not that I'm in the market for one."

"That's just the point. Rylan's mother, Orin's first wife, was from the Spring Court."

Sorcha poked Cian's chest. "Are you here to play matchmaker for your foolish friend, or are you here to ensure our safety and maybe a few other needs? As in *my* needs."

That got his attention.

"Well, yeah...I mean, of course." Now it was his turn to stutter.

Sorcha didn't nudge Cian's chest anymore, but she kept her finger there, trailing a teasing line. "My sister's choice is just that. Hers. As long as there's no safety breach, it doesn't matter what court her friend is from, what realm he's from, or even what species he is." She smirked. "I've had a

Greyrym, and I'm telling you, if you want this weekend to be memorable with me, you've got some catching up to do."

Cian licked his lips like he was already tasting the challenge.

"Good," she said. "Now, room keys and registered names, please."

"Names?" I questioned.

She nodded. "For security purposes we don't use our names or titles." Turning for Cian again, she pursed her lips. "Well?"

"Names...right." He pulled key card envelopes from his pocket. "The names are Daisy and Faye Buchanan. Edie, you're Daisy," he handed me my key, "and Sorcha, you're Faye."

"Daisy Buchanan." I smiled at the reference to one of my favorite books. "Did you pick *The Great Gatsby* on purpose?"

Cian looked at me funny, and Sorcha laughed. "Careful, Daisy, or you might break Cian's brain."

He rolled his eyes and then reached into the inside pocket of his jacket. "These are for you, as well. Fully functional for everything, including surfing the web."

"Burner phones!" I took mine and immediately swiped the touch screen. "This just keeps getting better and better."

"Edie, how in great Avalon do you know about burner phones if you've never been here before?" Cian asked, gesturing around us.

"Movies, Cian." Sorcha answered for me. "You'd be surprised what my sister knows."

We took the elevator up to the penthouse, and when we walked into the first suite, I was surprised to see both suites were adjoining. "Wow. This is...convenient?"

"It'll be fine, Edie. It's always this way. In case we have to scoot, it's best we're basically in the same place."

"If you say so." Sorcha wasn't listening. She had already tugged Cian into their suite.

The rooms were certainly large, with an L-shaped living space off the primary bedroom. Large comfy couches faced a wide flatscreen television and a full bar, while a dining table for six was tucked beside floor-to-ceiling windows with views of the river.

The bedroom was a whole other experience. It had a California king with enough pillows to sink a person straight into dream sleep. The large ensuite bathroom housed a free-standing tub, big enough for three people, and a separate shower with rain head and body sprays. I already pictured soaking in that tub with Daire after making full use of every inch of that spacious bed.

I walked out of the bedroom, and that's when I noticed a red blinking light on the telephone beside the couch. "Sorcha!"

She and Cian both poked their heads through the door. "What's the matter?"

"That. Is it a warning?"

"No, dummy. It means we have a message. It's probably just the front desk welcoming us." She dialed the code on the phone to retrieve the message and then hit speakerphone for the voicemail: "Hey, beautiful! Meet me in the octagon bar at eight. I can't wait to see you."

A small squeal left my mouth at Daire's recorded voice, and I stamped my feet in a happy dance. Merlin made it happen. Not that I doubted him.

"It's him, isn't it?" Sorcha grabbed my hands and squeezed. "See? I told you it would all work out."

"Hello!" Cian waved both hands in the air. "Will one of you tell me who left that voicemail?"

I glanced at him and grinned. "If I'm Daisy Buchanan, then that was Jay Gatsby."

The boy blinked, squinching his brows together. "Oh no." Sorcha laughed. "I think you actually broke Cian's brain, for real."

"Very funny, but unless you tell me the identity of Mr. Mystery Date, no one is going anywhere. It's my responsibility and my ass on the line if something happens to either of you."

Sorcha stalked toward Cian. "Where's your sense of adventure? Your devil-may-care? Did you turn in your membership card when you started training with your father, because I don't remember you being this worried when we broke into Caxton's house."

"Wait...what?" I looked between them both.

She nodded at me. "Last week. Caxton was giving me a hard time, as per usual, so we decided to leave him a little present."

"Nope. Don't tell me." I didn't want to know. With Cian's friends, that present could be anything.

Cian's arms were crossed at his chest, tight. "I'm not yielding on this Sorcha, so don't argue. You, and that means both of you, go nowhere until I give the all-clear. Is that understood?"

Sorcha and I exchanged a look. From the moment my mother said Cian was joining us, I knew contact with Daire would be tricky.

"Cian! You are being so... so... Caxton!"

My sister's accusation must've hit a nerve because he stormed toward the other suite.

"Seriously?"

"Fine." He shot Sorcha a look from the doorway. "Order room service. We'll eat and then get dressed. That way we can head down to the bar to meet this mystery man together. But I am not happy about this at all."

Cian disappeared into the other suite, and I exhaled. "Remember when I said this was getting better and better? Strike that and reverse it."

"Don't worry, Edie. He'll come around." Sorcha blew me a kiss, turning for the adjoining suite. "You'll see."

Two hours later, I held my breath walking out of the elevator. Sorcha had me dressed in a short, black skirt and a tight, black lace, cold shoulder midriff top. My boots were over the knee, but they had a flat heel. According to my sister, Bourbon Street was not a friend to high heels. I didn't care. I hated heels anyway, and my legs were long enough to make the outfit work.

"I got it!" Cian snapped his fingers. "That Gatsby thing was a movie! I remember my sister watching something or other a couple of years ago." He bobbed his head, proud of himself before looking at me. "Jay Gatsby. He was the rich guy, right? *The Great Gatsby*."

I nodded, impressed. Cian was different from the rest of his crew. "Yup, and his love interest was named Daisy Buchanan. Quite a coincidence, don't you think?"

His brows knotted at that, and Sorcha laughed. "C'mon, Cian. This is going to be fun."

"Fine." He feigned a grumble inside a grin. "Twist my arm. Laissez le bon temps rouler."

We turned the corner at the lobby and Cian's grin faded. Daire was waiting for me at the bottom of the stairs.

CHAPTER
Twenty~Four

"OH, HELL NO!" Cian grabbed my arm, and Daire was at my side in a blurred instant. "This is none of your business, Dannean. Back off!"

Daire held his ground, stepping between me and Cian. "Grabbing Eden like that makes it my business."

"According to whom?" Cian raised his chin, flexing.

"According to *kiss my ass*, that's whom. You're the one gatecrashing, so I suggest *you* back off."

The two High Sidhe stared each other down, neither giving an inch. I had fought a Redcap without any help, and it was my blade that brought down the Fachan. I didn't need or want this performative chest beating.

"Enough, both of you! Cian, I mean it. Daire is here because I invited him, and that's all there is to it. If you can't handle my choices, then you can stay in the suite and binge watch movies, or you can go home. I don't care which, but it'll waste a perfect weekend for no good reason."

"No good reason?" Cian was incredulous. "You do know who this guy is, right? I mean, I'm not imagining this set up."

My frown felt like it scrunched my whole face. "Of course, I know who he is, Cian! I'm not a fool. And yes, this is a set up. Just not the way you think."

Sorcha slipped her arm into Cian's, in effect locking him to her side.

"You're not seeing the big picture. Like me, Edie knows full well what she's doing. So, in order for us to have the good time we all want, you are going to go with the flow. It's as simple as that. With all identities kept secret. And I mean all."

"But—"

She went up on tiptoe and kissed his cheek. "You're going to have to trust Eden and me on this one. Daire is just like us, even if he is technically a rival.

Cian's eyes were still narrowed, but the set of his jaw had softened. "Fine. Far be it for me to stop royalty from playing with fire. I'm warning you both, though. I sense any threat and the weekend is over."

Daire's chin went up at that. "There's no need for a warning. I'd never hurt Eden. Or Sorcha. Eden means the world to me in ways I can't explain. I know the idea of us together is beyond belief, but here we are. I know how important Edie is to you and yours. She's just as important to me, and not for the reasons you think. Court rivalries have nothing to do with us. My feelings are personal. Not political."

Cian considered Daire for a long moment. I watched his eyes, and I knew he weighed the odds and options. He knew the consequences if things went south, but there was a glint in the courtier's eye, as well. His devil-may-care was back.

"Okay." He exhaled, skeptical, but resigned. "Fun times. If my father hears of this..." He trailed off, and Sorcha kissed his cheek again. "You girls are going to get me killed."

I laughed, lacing my hand with Daire's. "Not if we can help it, and not without a fight."

"Famous last words."

"The queen said this weekend was a rite of passage. A time for exploration and experimentation. So, let's get this party started."

Sorcha raised an eyebrow at me, and I shrugged. Our mother wasn't here, and since control and coercion were her style, not mine, I took liberties interpreting her directive.

I already saw what she meant when she said humans were unreservedly attracted to the Sidhe. I had one man follow me into the ladies' room, and another stare at me while licking his lips as I bought a bottle of water from the front desk market. He whispered how he imagined licking my toes and would gladly volunteer to lick anything else I wanted. I left the water bottle on the counter. Imagine if we didn't suppress our natural glamour?

"Is there anything I can do to prove my intentions?" Daire asked. "A test or something you could keep in your back pocket if needed?"

Cian pursed his lips and then nodded. "I was given something to detect spelled identities. It was to protect the girls from hidden threats. Its purpose is to reveal truths and anything cloaked by magic. I suppose intentions fall under that category."

"Great. Let's do it." Daire motioned toward the elevators.

"The test doesn't require anything but stealth. I can administer it right in the bar and no one would be the wiser. My father got the idea on his last visit to the human realm from products used to detect the presence of date-rape drugs. I'll show you."

The four of us walked into the bar and then up the stairs to the second level, taking a glass four top overlooking the entire lobby. "Wow. This is a people watching paradise," I said, sliding onto my seat beside Daire.

"What can I get you?" a server asked, pen and pad in hand.

Sorcha glanced at other tables. "Is there a bar menu?"

"There is, but the bartenders list the nightly cocktail specials on the mirror behind the bar." She gestured behind her. "Tonight is pitcher night."

"How about a pitcher of martinis, then?" I suggested, never having one but always hearing about them in movies.

"Sure," Sorcha agreed. "What flavor?"

I had no idea. "You pick."

She told the waitress to bring a pitcher of dirty martinis, extra dirty.

"That sounds...yummy?" I made a face, and everyone laughed.

"Ha. I know, right?" Sorcha grinned. "Dirty just means made with a splash of olive juice, so its cloudy in color and briny in taste. Extra dirty just means more olives."

"Well, I love salt and vinegar chips, so..."

"Exactly."

The server returned carrying the pitcher and four salt-rimmed martini glasses. "Enjoy."

"Shall I be Mother?" I asked, earning a snort from my sister. I stuck my tongue at her but poured the drinks anyway. "What should we toast?" I asked, holding up my glass. "How about to freedom?"

Everyone lifted their glasses at that, talking in general. The martini was good, but I wanted something sweet. "I wonder if they serve dessert. I'd love to try molten chocolate cake if they have it." Daire hadn't said anything yet, and I worried he regretted coming after the scene with Cian. "Are you okay?"

"I'm fine, Eden. Stop worrying." He lifted my hand to kiss the tops of my fingers.

"Then why so quiet?"

Sorcha kicked Cian under the table. "Ow! What was that for?"

"Do the test." Daire pushed his drink aside. "It'll settle the questions in your head once and for all. I want Eden to have a good time, but she won't if you and I remain suspicious of each other."

Cian stared him down, and the tension ratcheted up at the table. "You sure?"

"Positive. It's the only way you'll relax."

Cian pulled a tiny round box from his pocket. Inside was a blue iridescent powder, and one pinch went into Daire's martini glass. "It won't change the color or taste of your drink, but the moment your lips touch the glass, anything cloaked will be revealed and you will only speak truths."

"Wow. That has the potential to be so embarrassing." Sorcha chuckled. "Can you imagine if you tested that powder on some of our crew?"

Cian smirked.

"You didn't."

He waggled his brows.

Daire rolled his eyes at the two of them and then picked up his glass, saluting Eden. "Here goes nothing. Remember, I'm doing this for you, love." He drank half his martini in one gulp, wincing as it went down.

"That bad?" I asked.

"I'm not a big fan of olives." He smacked his lips, making a face. "They taste a little like salty dirt."

"Then why didn't you say so when we ordered?"

Sorcha chuckled. "Because now he has to tell the truth."

"Should I feel something?" Daire looked to Cian. "A tingle or anything?"

"Honestly, I'm not sure...Edie, ask Daire something."

"Like what?"

"I don't know. Something important."

"This is your test, Cian. You do it. I already trust him."

Cian looked at Daire, and it was obvious he'd rather be anywhere else than here right now. "This is going to make me sound like a jerk, but I have to ask. I don't want you to take it the wrong way."

"That's fine."

"Are you here because you're using Eden in some kind of ploy?"

"I am not."

Cian nodded. "Good. Are you using her for sex? Or for political maneuvers? Or both?"

"Cian!" Sorcha shoved his shoulder.

"I have to ask. He's from you-know-where. I may believe what he says, but if questioned, Caxton, my father, and the queen aren't going to take my word for it simply because Daire's a nice guy. They're going to want proof."

Cian asked again. "Are you using Eden?"

"No. I love her..."

Daire's eyes flew wide at the involuntary admission. He wasn't the only one stunned to hear the blatant reply. Sorcha glanced at me before tapping on the glass table. "Then riddle me this, lover boy. You just met my sister. How can you know you love her? Maybe this is just a case of wanting what you can't have. Forbidden fruit."

"Sorcha!" Cian mimicked her earlier outburst.

"You, shut up." She shot Cian a look. "You," she pointed at Daire, "answer the question."

"I don't know how, Sorcha, but I do. I'd risk everything for Eden in a heartbeat."

Sorcha and Cian couldn't have looked more stunned. Me? My heart skipped a beat, even as I cringed for Daire being put on the spot.

"Okay, Eden. Now you." Cian directed, but I shook my head.

"Edie, you have to."

"No, I don't. This isn't a game played at Daire's expense."

Daire squeezed my hand. "It's okay, Edie. Ask me. I don't mind."

I licked the briny salt from my drink off my lips. I knew what I wanted to ask. Something that worried me since the night on the island, but I didn't want to ask in front of my sister and Cian.

"I'll ask you later."

Cian shook his head. "The powder doesn't last long. If there's something you want to know, now's the time."

"Just ask, Edie. Daire already said it was fine."

"No."

"Come on!"

"I said, no!"

"Ask!"

"Fine! Do you think I'm a murderer?"

"Seriously, Edie. C'mon." Cian made a face. "Why would he think something like that?"

Daire opened his mouth to answer, but he couldn't make a sound. That got everyone's attention, me especially. "Daire? Are you okay?"

He put his hand to his throat.

"Are you choking?"

He shook his head.

Cian leaned on the table. "He can't answer because he was about to tell a falsehood. Or a half-truth. What is the real answer, Dannean?"

"Yes!" he croaked.

Stunned, I nearly swallowed my tongue.

Cian's head spun from me to him and back again. "What is he talking about. Why would he believe that's the truth of something?"

I ignored both Cian and Sorcha. "Daire is that true? You think I'm a killer?"

The words hurt him, but he forced them out. "In self-defense."

Sorcha slammed a hand on the glass table. "Someone better tell me what he's talking about right now or this weekend is over."

I couldn't tell them. If I did, then Cian would know Rylan's story wasn't just a fever dream. For all I knew he figured it out already. Sorcha knew the dagger Rylan brought back from the Eventide was mine, but I never told her the whole story. Her I could trust. Cian, not so much.

"I can't tell you. Not here. Not now. If you want to wait until we get home, I promise I will tell you, Sissy, but now..." I shook my head.

Cian went to get up, but Sorcha put a hand on his shoulder. "No, it's okay. I trust my sister to tell me the truth." He sat, and with a slow nod, agreed.

"Eden," Cian began. "Answer me one thing, then. If this was self-defense, and I have to trust it was, since the powder doesn't allow for anything but the truth, are you certain you had no other choice?"

That much I could tell them all. "It was either kill or be killed."

"Does this have anything to do with the rumors Rylan's father has been spreading?"

Damn. I knew the situation with Rylan would come back to bite me, though I didn't think it would happen this fast.

"Eden..."

Before I could answer, Daire chimed in. "We've heard rumors at the Winter Court. Our informants tell us your man, Orin, is lying. That he fabricated the story to discredit Eden and force the queen's hand for his own ends."

That was the powder talking, so it must be true. Whether the informants reported back spun meticulously circulated to protect me? I had no idea. I was grateful for it, nonetheless.

Cian's shoulders took on another level of tense. "If Orin is lying, then that means he's using what happened against you, and that's unforgivable. That you were attacked is unthinkable. That you survived is a miracle. What I don't understand, is why the court isn't abuzz with this."

"Isn't it obvious?" Sorcha interrupted Cian's external musing. "The queen doesn't know, and no one wants to be the one to tell her the heir apparent was attacked on Seelie ground."

"I don't want to talk about it, Cian. I told Daire, but only because I didn't want any secrets between us. Not with our positions being what they are."

Gods, that was a whopper. Merlin told me not to tell the queen, and now there were lies of omission on top of lies of omission. As much as I believed the old seer had his reasons, I hated the way this felt. I swore then and there I would put everything right the moment we got back to Seelie.

At least parts of what I told them were true. It *was* a case of kill or be killed, and the Eventide was technically Seelie ground, or it was when I went into the forest the other night. That Orin was trying to spin this for his own gain wasn't a lie either.

When the truth about what happened in the Eventide came out, along with the reason I was there in the first place, that would be the part that backlashed on me. Was I prepared for the consequences? No. The queen would either exile me to the Badlands, ban me from seeing Daire, and then force a marriage to someone of her choosing—or worse yet, have Caxton play huntsman and take *Red Riding Hood* back to the forest in order to bring my heart back in a box. Whatever waited for me, it felt like a thick web with me caught at the center. Were these the threads Merlin spoke of unraveling faster than the fates could reweave?

"Eden…"

I looked at Cian and Sorcha. "I think we could use another pitcher or martinis. Just not dirty, okay?"

Daire slipped his arm around my shoulders, pulling me into a side hug so he could kiss my head. "And something sweet for my sweetheart."

Sorcha rolled her eyes. "Gods. Please tell me that powder will wear off before we hit Bourbon Street, or all this cuteness will make me ill."

"Then you'll fit right in." Cian grinned, signaling for the server again. "Bourbon Street is no stranger to sick."

"Except Sorcha and I are princesses. We vomit glitter." My sister choked, nearly spitting her drink again, and I clicked my cheek. "See? I'm right."

"Can I get you something else?" she asked, walking over.

Daire lifted a finger. "Yes. Do you have molten chocolate cake?"

"We have individual lava cakes, but they take a half hour to make."

"Then bring four, please."

She raised an eyebrow but wrote it down anyway.

"And a pitcher of lemon drop martinis," Sorcha added. "We have secret olive haters at this table."

The server laughed and then headed back to the bar.

This was everything I'd imagined this weekend to be. So far. Daire and I had yet to be alone, but we were here, together, and with my sister and

Cian it felt like the Fab Four. I had one goal: cramming as much freedom and fun as possible into the sixty-eight hours.

"So?" I asked. "Where should we go next?"

CHAPTER
Twenty~Five

WALL TO WALL people spilled onto the sidewalks and pavement from every door along Bourbon Street, including the entrance to the Cat's Paw. The club was packed with Mardi Gras revelers. Music poured into the street, where partiers drank and danced like it was last days.

"This place is amazing!" I yelled over the chaos. We were crammed six people deep against the bar and lucky to have seats. The music was jumping, and I bopped to the beat, trying to connect my mouth with my straw.

"Edie!" Sorcha's hand shot out, stopping me from bopping right off my barstool.

Cian laughed. "Dude, we hit one bar and your woman is already sozzled!"

I leaned in to say something, but a loud burp left my mouth instead of words and my sister nearly spit her drink. "Sorry, guys. It's the lava cake. I'm not used to eating chocolate."

Sorcha rolled her eyes.

"Lava cake. Right." Daire slid my drink from my hand. "More like mixing martinis and daiquiris."

I hiccupped. "Hey! You're supposed to tell the truth."

"I am," he replied. "And the truth is you're drunk."

Giggling, I wiped a hand across my lower lip. "Drunk?"

"Absolutely squiffed."

I threw my arms in the air. "Hey, human world! I'm squiffed!"

"Eden!" Sorcha scrunched her forehead in secondhand embarrassment. "Daire, do something with her... please."

He took my hand, helping me stand from my barstool. "C'mon, killer."

"I object! You go up against a Redcap and see what *you* do!"

Goggle-eyed, Cian laughed. "What did she just say?"

"I have no idea." Daire tugged my elbow tighter and pivoted me away from the bar.

"Wait. Cian—"

"Nope." Daire cut me off. "Dance floor." He pushed through the crowd with me in tow, maneuvering me toward the thumping beat.

"Oooh! I love this song!"

The cover band played their rendition of "Tainted Love", and my hands went up with everyone else's on the beat. I sang at the top of my lungs.

Daire caught me around the waist with a laugh, pulling me closer. I slipped my arms around his neck, swaying with him to the rhythm, and he smirked.

"What?"

"You're cute when you're drunk."

"I'm cute all the time."

"That you are."

The feel of his body moving with mine was almost as intoxicating as the martinis. "You know, some might say this song is like us."

"Tainted? Gee, thanks."

"You know what I mean, except instead of running from each other, we have to get away from everyone else."

He angled his head, and his crooked smile made me sigh. "I thought that's what we were doing this weekend."

"Exactly." My fingers toyed with the hair at the nape of his neck. "We're here. So, let's not worry about anyone or anything but us. Especially not anything at home. No matter how bad."

"Deal."

The band segued into a ballad, and Daire twirled me around once before pulling me into his arms.

"Do you regret telling me?" I asked, hiccupping again.

"Telling you what?"

"You know."

He lifted his chin to glance at the ceiling. "Oh, that."

"Daire!"

I tugged on his neck, earning a crooked, teasing grin. "What do you think?"

"I think you're sleeping on the couch tonight if you don't tell me."

That half-grin spread to an even sexier smile.

"C'mon, tell me. Do you regret telling me you love me?"

His lips softened, and the feel of his fingers slipping up and down my back gave me tingles. "The only thing I regret, is not telling you on my own terms. That I didn't get to make the declaration special. Romantic."

"It was sort of a blurt."

"Hmmm."

"An involuntary one, but still a blurt."

"Don't rub it in."

I pressed in tighter as we danced. "Well, this sort of qualifies as romantic. Dancing together. Here...now."

"Does it?"

I waited a moment. "Well?"

Daire stepped back from me, and before I could protest, he twirled me around again. Only this time he turned me back into a full dip. His lips were a breath from mine as he held me suspended in his arms.

Time stopped around us. There was no one on the dance floor, or in the Cat's Paw, but us. Just him and me, in one perfectly romantic moment.

"I love you, Eden," he whispered. "I have from the very first. You are everything that matters. My world...my realm." His lips brushed mine in the softest kiss. "They mean nothing unless I can share them with you."

Lingering with his eyes on mine, he slowly straightened until we both stood toe-to-toe once more. I tried to attach myself to gravity again, not just from his spontaneous dip, but from his tender words. "That was certainly on your own terms," I murmured.

Daire moved to twirl me again, but I stepped back. The abrupt move clearly puzzled him as a shadow crossed his eyes. "What is it?" he asked, closing the space between us.

Our hands clasped against his chest, and his gaze held mine completely. "Nothing and everything at once...," I replied, pausing. "Because you mean the same to me. I love you, Daire."

His mouth claimed mine then and there, not caring we stood in the middle of a throng. If his lips demanded everything before, this kiss was all or nothing. Mingled breath. Mingled taste. Wants. Needs. Everything. An unspoken compact of passion and more. Dizzying and breath-stealing, I lost myself to his lips...to him.

"Get a room!" A gruff voice teased from somewhere.

The intrusion broke our private spell, and Daire broke our kiss. Heat burned in my cheeks but not from being caught out. "Wow. Even on a debauched street like Bourbon. No public displays."

He laughed. "Unless it's for beads."

"Humans, huh?"

"C'mon, pretty and pickled. We've got the whole night ahead, and this is just one club. Let's go somewhere else."

"Like where?"

He didn't answer. Instead, he finessed our way across the crowd, signaling Cian and Sorcha to meet us by the entrance.

"Hey, you two!" A petite server with dyed black hair and pierced cheeks stopped us at the edge of the dance floor. She carried an odd tray with long narrow tubes filled with brightly colored liquid atop it. "You look like you enjoy a challenge. How about a test-tube shot? They're two for ten bucks."

"Ooh, these remind me of Merlin's worktable," I replied. "What kind of potions are these?"

The server laughed at that. "I've heard them called a lot of things, but never potions. I like that." She nodded. "I've got blue raspberry tease, orange screwdriver crush, and pretty-in-pink lemonade."

"That lemonade sounds yummy. We'll take one of those."

"I don't think so, Daisy. Our friends are leaving." Daire waved Cian and Sorcha through.

"You sure?" the server asked me, dangling the bright yellow tube from her fingers. "You put the test tube in your cleavage, and your handsome prince has to take it from there and drink it, no hands."

I guffawed. "How did you know he was a prince?"

"Ha! Your girl's a hoot."

"I think you mean *hot*." I laughed. "We were just exiled for kissing on the dance floor, but now you tell me boob drinking is okay. What kind of realm is this?"

Cian and Sorcha strode up behind us. "What's going on?" Sorcha asked.

"Boob drinking."

Daire gave the server an apologetic look and then steered me out the door.

"Where to next?" Cian rubbed his hands together. "Perhaps some steamy blues or maybe an underground club?"

"You two go," Daire said. "I think Daisy here needs coffee and about a gallon of water."

Sorcha grabbed Cian's arm. "Café du Monde! C'mon. No trip to New Orleans is complete without beignets and chicory coffee."

"Beignets?" I questioned. "Aren't they some kind of hat?"

"That's berets, squiffy." Sorcha laughed. "I need to get you drunk at home. Beignets are the most delicious dough fritters you'll ever eat. Hot, crispy, and covered in sugar."

Daire nodded. "And plenty of hot coffee."

We walked down Bourbon Street, and the farther we walked, the less crowded the streets became until ours were the only footfalls along the pavement.

"Where is everyone?" I looked over my shoulder, my skin tingling as I gazed into the shadows. I rubbed my arms at an involuntary shiver. "I think the temperature is dropping."

Cian exchanged a look with Daire. "I think we need to get out of the dark for a bit." The courtier took my sister's elbow. "C'mon." Giving Daire a quick chin pop toward a close hotel lobby, the two walked me and Sorcha toward the revolving doors.

No sooner did we step into the lobby's bright light than Cian pointed to the sign for the restrooms. "You two." He pointed at his watch. "We've pushed it too close. Go."

"What is he talking about?" Sorcha pulled me up the stairs and into the ladies' room. She checked the stalls, verifying they were empty.

"Sorcha! Has something happened? Are we using the mirror?"

She shook her head. "No. Our drops. We got caught up and nearly forgot. Twelve hours, remember?"

"Oh, right." I dug in my purse. "Two on the tongue." I untwisted the dropper top, letting two peppermint flavored drops hit their target. "Done and dusted." I put my vial away, watching Sorcha do the same. "I get we cut it close, but why were Cian and Daire so edgy all of a sudden."

The door to the bathroom swung open. Two women stood in the doorway. One was drunker than me, and the other had cropped purple hair and pale skin to the point of being ashen. The drunk one staggered toward the mirrors. She was dressed in a low midriff and leather miniskirt, and her makeup was smeared around her eyes.

"Do you girls have any lipstick to spare? I know we're not supposed to share, but this one sucked the gloss right off my face." The girl laughed, tossing her head back.

I went to say something, but Sorcha yanked me toward the door. "Uh, no. Sorry, we don't."

My sister pushed me through the bathroom threshold. I stumbled past the pale woman, but not before I caught the stark blue veins at her throat, or the way her nostrils flared as I passed.

The guys were waiting by the revolving doors, and Sorcha deposited me beside Daire. "That was a little too close for comfort," she said, jerking her head toward the bathroom.

"Did you see that smeared makeup? She could use a few pointers from you, Sissy."

"No, Edie." Sorcha gestured harshly. "The girl in the bathroom is hooking up with a vampire! Couldn't you tell?"

I had read about vampires, and I had seen them depicted in movies and television, but I had never seen one in the undead flesh. "Are you sure?"

Daire nodded. "We watched them come in from the street. I'm

surprised the vampire didn't conceal her presence. We're immune to undead glamour, but the hotel staff and CCTV surveillance aren't. That chill you felt on the street had nothing to do with temperature. That was your body's natural alarm against a predator. Cian's right. We took an unnecessary risk, letting our protections slip tonight."

"If we had crossed this intersection a few minutes later..." Cian let the weight of that near miss land, before glancing around the lobby. "This place is clear except for the bloodsucker in the bathroom. I think maybe we should call it a night and take a taxi back to the hotel."

I wasn't drunk anymore. That poor woman at the mercy of that opportunistic leech had sobered me cold. "We can't leave yet. First, we need to help that woman."

Daire shook his head. "I don't think that's wise, Edie. Even with the four of us together, we can't go up against a vampire. Besides the inherent danger to us as Fae, there are too many of them in the city to have this fight be one and done. This is their home turf."

"He's right," Cian agreed. "It's not just their fangs. Their fingernails are razor sharp, and they have preternatural speed. If one of us bleeds even a drop, it's game over."

I wasn't buying it. "We have weapons. Inherent weapons." I held my palm up, but my sister pushed it down.

"Eden, what did Merlin and the queen warn us about? No magic. No glamour. Did you get a look at us in the restroom mirror? Do you think I'd let my hair frizz like that if there was another choice? No matter how small the amount, using magic leaves a trail that can lead back to us."

"Sorcha, this is different," I argued. "That woman's life could be circling the drain as we speak. I know what you think, but this isn't the martinis talking. I'm stone sober. I understand the risk. The vampire's nostrils flared when you pushed me through the restroom door."

Cian motioned us away from the lobby doors to a set of parallel loveseats situated by a gas fireplace. "Eden, that nostril flare tells you everything you need to know. That vampire sensed something about you and Sorcha, and that's not good. The undead are cunning and very clever."

"Great." I lifted my hand before letting it fall to my lap. "Because of me, the vampire population of New Orleans knows there's a Fae foursome walking around."

Daire covered my hand. He had been uncharacteristically quiet. "Not necessarily," he offered. "Fresh drops. Higher potency."

I nodded, letting the feel of his hand on mine calm me. A breeze whooshed by us, and the hair on my arms went up. I don't know what caught my attention, but I glance out the lobby's main floor windows. The restroom vampire was on the sidewalk outside talking to someone.

"Sorcha, look." A surreptitious gesture past the revolving doors did the trick. "It's her."

The vampire was emphatic about something, and I didn't think it was over her recent kill. She craned her neck, peering through the glass windows. She was looking for us, but mostly me. Thankfully our seats by the fireplace were blocked by wide rectangular columns, and lobby windows were tinted for privacy and insulation.

"They sense us, but they can't place us," Cian stated. "That said, I wonder if there's another way out of the hotel. I'd rather not cross paths with the undead if we can help it."

"Let the leeches move off first," Daire argued. "It's after midnight during Mardi Gras. There's plenty of prey in the street and in the clubs to keep them occupied."

I went to get up, but Daire stopped me. "Where are you going?"

"Where do you think? I have to see if there's anything we can do for that woman. If she's alive, we can get her to an infirmary. If she's dead, we need to call the police."

"Let me go instead," Daire said. "You don't need to see that kind of brutality."

I appreciated his concern, but it wasn't necessary. I wasn't a stranger to carnage. I'd seen it up close and personal and at my own hand. In that respect, I now had the experience, and he, Sorcha, and Cian were the virgins.

"Whoever wants to come, do so. I won't stop you, but I need to check on that poor woman."

Cian and Sorcha shared a look, and then Cian nodded. "We'll watch the door. The one exception to the no magic rule is self-defense. My power is fire, and Sorcha's is wind. Forget daylight, the leeches will roast like they landed on the surface of the sun if they try anything."

Daire and I went up the stairs together. The front desk clerk's gaze followed us up, and Daire nodded to him in acknowledgement. "Think he's in on it? I bet he looks the other way, and the vampires compensate him."

"Compensate him with what?"

Daire was matter of fact. "His life."

He had a point. Still, there were plenty of dark corners in the French Quarter for vampires to do their nasty deeds. It was more likely the clerk had a fetish, or an addiction the vampires fed, or maybe they promised to make him immortal. Anything was possible. Or maybe he was just a clueless human and had no idea.

The ladies' room door was ajar, and I motioned for him to stay in the threshold while I checked inside. "Hello?" I called, pushing the door the rest of the way open. "I found some lipstick in my purse if you still want it."

A soft groan answered. The woman was half naked and laying with her legs sticking out from one of the stalls. The wall was smeared with blood, and there was evidence of a struggle. Drunk or not, she had fought for her life. Maybe that was why she still had a pulse.

I rushed to her side. Her throat was torn between her clavicle and her ear, and there was a bloody palm print on her cheekbone and smears in her hair where the vampire must've jerked the woman's head back.

"Daire! She's alive, but barely! Get help!"

By the time human help arrived, the poor woman would be dead. I had to do something. Gathering her onto my lap, I lifted my hand for a small crackle of energy. The light ball formed in my palm, swirling with my power. I'd only used it for defense, and had no idea if the energy could heal, but I had to try.

"Edie! No!" Sorcha rushed into the bathroom with Cian behind her. "As much as you want to, you can't help her that way."

Sorcha closed my fingers into my palm and the crackling light went out. Frustration, anger, and powerlessness warred in my chest, and my shoulders slumped. "What good are our gifts if we can't help other living beings?"

"We can help." Sorcha knelt beside me, wrapping her arm around my shoulders. "Broken bits of nature. Plants. Trees. The natural world. You know that. But we can't heal humankind. They possess their own spark of divinity. A soul." She kissed the side of my head. "Didn't Merlin teach you that?"

I nodded. "In the abstract."

"Books." Sorcha's cynical chuckle made me wince. "I'll take real life any day."

Daire hurried through the door with the hotel manager. "Holy shit!" The manager's knees buckled, and Daire grabbed the man under his arms.

"Easy, guy. You called an ambulance, right?"

The man nodded, swallowing hard. "There's always one on standby in the French Quarter. Especially at Mardi Gras. They'll be here any minute."

"Good," I said, and the woman groaned, again. "It's okay, honey. Help is on the way."

Her lids fluttered open, and for a moment terror ruled her eyes until she realized I wasn't the vampire. They closed again, and her body seemed to relax a notch.

"EMTs! Clear the entrance!" Heavy footsteps rushed up the stairs, hurrying toward the bathroom. The manager stepped out of the way along with Cian, Daire, and Sorcha.

The first EMT rushed through the doorway. His eyes flashed from brown to yellow, and his nostrils flared wide. He scanned me and the woman with his gaze, and I swear a growl left his throat.

"Can you tell me what happened?" he asked, kneeling with his kit as his partner joined him.

I got up to give them room to work but stayed to answer their questions. "I came in to use the restroom, and I found her on the floor. She'd been attacked."

His yellow eyes found mine, and his nostrils flared again, only less obviously. "Are you sure that's all?"

I knew then he was a supernatural, and if the shift in eye color and hairy knuckles weren't enough of a giveaway, that growl sealed the deal. He was a werewolf or at the very least, a shifter. Still, my friends and I were incognito. I didn't need to confirm our supernatural status with anyone.

"I told you what I know. I can tell you what I guess, though. If supernatural creatures are real, then I'd say she was attacked by a vampire. A female vampire with a blue veined throat and cropped purple hair."

I saw him exchange a look with his partner at my hypothetical. "Sounds like you hit the Bourbon Street bar scene a little hard tonight. Do you need us to check you out as well?"

I had faced real terror, and I wasn't about to flinch because an overgrown mutt flexed his muscles at me. He knew I was otherworldly, even if he couldn't pinpoint what or how, and he knew I was right about the vampire.

"Make of it what you will. I saw the woman leave. Was she a vampire?" I shrugged. "New Orleans is known for worse. I do know the woman I described came down those stairs, and when she passed me in the lobby, there was blood on her clothing."

I must've sounded convincing because he nodded. "Good. The police are on their way. They're going to want a statement."

I shrugged again. "I'm staying at the Hôtel Plaisir Royale. Tell them to ask for Daisy Buchanan. As in *The Great Gatsby*. I'll tell them all I know."

Daire waited for me outside the restroom door. When I walked out, I was shaking. He gathered me in his arms, kissing my forehead. "You handled that amazingly well."

"I need to use the other restroom. I have blood on my hands and arms, and I don't want to walk out into the street a calling card to every bloodsucker in the city."

"No problem." He guided me to the men's restroom, staying with me while I washed up as best I could. "I sent Cian and Sorcha to get coffee and beignets," he said. "They're bringing them back to our hotel. I also called for a taxi. I thought you might not want to walk."

"I'm sober, Daire. Completely and utterly," I replied, drying my hands and forearms with a paper towel.

"I know." He slipped his arm around my shoulders. "It's just a treat. We've all had enough excitement for one night."

I exhaled, annoyed with myself. "Excitement, huh. More like Eden strikes again."

"How do you mean?"

"If I hadn't gotten tipsy—"

He laughed, cutting me off. "Oh, love. You were *way* past tipsy."

I shot him a look as we headed down the stairs to the lobby. "If I hadn't gotten drunk, we wouldn't have been going to that café for coffee. It seems every decision I make causes something bloody to happen. It's like I'm cursed."

"That's ridiculous. People make their own choices. Like that woman in the restroom."

The taxi was waiting for us outside the revolving doors. I slid into the back seat from the curbside and waited for him to climb in and close the door.

"That woman was most likely glamoured," I said, thinking out loud.

Daire looked at me. "And how is that your doing? She and her undead playmate walked in on you and Sorcha, and we were only there because we needed to see to our own precautions. You are not to blame if others don't take the same care."

"Why do you sound angry?" His body language had stiffened, and his arms were crossed at his chest.

"I'm not."

"You certainly seem it."

"Well, I'm not."

"Good."

"Grand."

I burst out laughing at how stupid we were being, and he stared at me across his shoulder. "What's so funny?"

"We are, you big Winter jerk! You're annoyed with me, but you won't admit it. Even though I'm annoyed with myself, and I own it."

"That makes no sense."

I tickled his sides until he dropped his stroppy crossed arm vise grip to grab me in a hug.

"See?" I made the case. "It's okay to be upset with each other. It's normal."

"I wasn't upset with you for something you did. I was upset with you for taking the blame for everything bad in the world. You are not responsible for other people and their bad choices. We have a hard enough time with our own, thank you very much."

"You seem very tense."

He shrugged.

"I think we need to do something about that." I walked my fingers over his thigh. "Can you think of anything that might be a good stress reliever?"

His eyes found mine, and his hand slipped to my thigh as well. "They say beignets are good for de-stressing. The sugar and all."

"Maybe. What if we were to eat them in bed?

CHAPTER
Twenty-Six

DAIRE KEPT me at his side from the minute we walked through the lobby doors. Could he sense my butterflies the rest of the taxi ride to the hotel? Could he smell my need and my nerves? This was a weekend of firsts. And it was go time for the one thing I had wanted from the start.

The adrenaline from that awful vampire encounter hadn't ebbed. It had simply morphed into a different kind of rush. One that was impatient and tense. One whose outlet was both visceral and demanding. The sparks of which ignited in the back of that taxi.

Neither of us spoke, not that I could if I tried. My body already hummed with desire, even though Daire barely touched me. Anticipation was an aphrodisiac, and my heart hammered against my ribs. I was surprised Daire didn't hear it pound.

The elevator door slid open to an empty car, and the look he gave me traded butterfly flutters for a buzzing swarm. "Excellent." His mouth curved to a seductive, crooked smile. "I've been waiting to get you alone all night, and it might as well start now."

The lift slid closed, and Daire walked me backward to the wood and brass wall. His tongue traced the seam of my lips. "Push the stop button, Eden," he murmured.

I stretched for the operating panel but couldn't reach it. "I can't quite

—" He silenced me with a kiss, lifting me against the cold wall. My legs went around his hips, and I gasped at the fact we were doing this here... now. A breath from all kinds of exposure.

Daire pushed the stop button without breaking our kiss. The elevator jerked to a stop. "Eden, I dream about the feel of your body, the idea of mine buried deep inside you." He gathered my skirt, hiking it to my upper thighs.

My head shouted, "You're in public, stupid!" but my body yelled back, "So what!"

With one hand Daire pushed the black fabric over my hips, leaving a pair of lace panties the only thing separating me from the bulge at the front of his jeans. He had me surrounded, both captive and captivated.

"Daire." I unzipped his fly, delving my fingers into the open front vee. A gasp left my mouth again, and I froze at the nest of dark hair in my palm and the corded member straining to be freed. The man had been commando all night.

A sexy grin slid across his lips as he slipped his pants over his hips, giving me full access to his hard bar. "Surprises come in all sizes, Eden, and this one is all yours."

There wasn't an ounce of self-deprecation in that statement. His shaft was long and thick, with a ridged velvet head that jerked in my palm. I closed my fingers around the hard length and Daire sucked in a breath.

"Careful. I'm still pent from the grotto."

The memory of his hands on my body made my lower belly jump, and I tightened my grip on his shaft making his thighs and ass tense.

"Are you very attached to these?" he growled, hooking one finger into the side seam of my underwear.

"No...why?"

With a single tug he tore the lace in two at my hip, leaving me very open, wet, and hungry for him like never before. I let go of his hard bar to grip his hips, urging his full, corded length to the edge of my sex.

"Are you ready for this?" he asked, holding back. "Do you want this, Eden? Do you want me?"

I moaned when the tip of his swollen head feather-stroked my slippery cleft. "I want this, Daire. I want every inch of you."

With a guttural release, he drove himself between my soft, slick folds. I froze for a millisecond as he broke through my barrier, but electric jolts fanned through my core, replacing an instant of pain with sheer pleasure. I gasped as waves vibrated every nerve ending to a delicious tension. My fingers kneaded his hard ass beneath his denim, urging him harder, deeper, rocking the elevator until the alarm bells blared.

"This is the maintenance department. We received an automated alert...," a disembodied voice cut short, only to blurt, "Gerry... you gotta see this! Two people are at like rabbits in car two!"

Daire flung a hand toward the spherical surveillance camera on the lift's ceiling, shattering it completely. "Fecking humans."

I stifled a giggle, even as exposed wires crackled and snapped above us, but I couldn't stifle the embarrassed, yet secretly delighted grin on my face.

"We should probably continue this in our room," I whispered, hiding my face in the crook of his neck.

"You think?" With a frustrated chuckle, Daire helped me unwrap my legs from his hips and then his still hard member from my body. I shimmied my skirt into place, and we both tucked and zipped until we were semi-presentable.

I pressed the button, and the elevator jerked upward. "What about maintenance? I bet they have this on CCTV."

He shook his head, a satisfied smirk on his face. "If I had to break the no-magic rule, I was breaking it good."

The elevator door opened onto the penthouse floor, and we walked side by side to our room. Heat burned my face at what Sorcha would call a walk of shame, but Daire opened the door to an empty suite.

"Well, well," he teased. "It looks like Cian and Sorcha left the beignets and coffee and then headed off to have their own fun."

We were alone again. Only the ill-timed interruption had stilted our crescendo, landing it flat with neither of us satisfied. I stood with my arms loosely crossed, looking out at the lights from the city and how they cast a magical glow across the river. Interrupted or not, there was nothing I wanted more than to be here with Daire.

"It really is beautiful," I murmured, inclining my chin toward the view.

"It sure is," he said.

I caught his reflection in the window, and he wasn't talking about the city. Not with the way his eyes took in every inch of me.

There was nothing about Daire that was halfway. Everything, from the way he looked and smelled, to his clever mind and hard body, to the sound of his voice and the feel of his touch on my skin. Everything left me wanting more.

"C'mon. I think we could both use a freshen up." He held out his hand, and I followed him into the bathroom.

I turned on the tap, sparing a glance at the free-standing tub. Afterward. I smirked to myself. Soaking and luxuriating with Daire. Unhurried and very, very spent.

The water was hot, sending curls of steam toward the double vanity mirror. Daire was still in the bedroom. What was taking so long? I bit my lip. Nope. Patience. All good things come to those who wait, and those who wait *come* good... and hard.

I grinned at my own pun in the mirror. For the first time in my life there were no decisions to weigh. No one to tell me no, and I was enjoying every naughty second.

Stripping out of my clothes, I tossed my ruined undies in the corner and ignored the blood on my blouse. Though it was harder to ignore the crimson streaks on my arms where it seeped through the lace. Naked, I dipped my hands into the running water, rinsing my arms and then the sink.

Two thick terry robes hung in the linen closet beside the vanity. I slipped my arms into one, leaving the other for Daire.

"You're even hotter than that steaming water," he said, coming up behind me as quiet as a cat. His hands circled my waist to untie my robe.

"What took you so long?"

He smiled, turning me so my ass pressed against the marble. With one fluid move, he lifted me to the pink-veined granite. "You're blushing, Eden. As if your whole body is pulsing...waiting."

"Daire..."

I went to pull him closer to unzip his pants, but he stopped my hands. "This is what took me so long." He showed me a blue silk tie, fashioned into a blindfold.

"Daire." I tried again, only to be silenced with a kiss.

"Edie, you are so sexy and so fearless. I can't get enough of you. Close your eyes and let me love you properly this time."

He slipped the blindfold over my eyes and then separated the front of my robe. Running his hands from my shoulders to my thighs, he grazed the taut peaks of my breasts. "Just a scooch closer, love." He pulled me forward from my hips, and my soft, fuzzy mound brushed the cotton of his jeans.

"Can you smell me on you, Eden?" He pushed my knees apart and then slicked his thumb between my folds. "Taste."

I moaned at his words, and when he rubbed his thumb over my bottom lip, I thought I'd burst. His taste. My taste. Together.

Leaning back, I gripped the edge of both sinks and spread my knees wider. I wanted to grind myself against him for release, but he held me off.

"Soon, love," he murmured.

I heard the water change volume, and the sound of him rummaging for something. "I want you wet. Like this." He dripped warm water over my lower belly, so it trickled between my legs. "Like you were in the grotto, and in the elevator. Hot. Wet. Sweet."

I fumbled for his hand. Daire held a wet washcloth over my sex, letting the hot water mix with my slickness. Lowering his hand, he let me grip his hand as he teased me with the rough cotton seam. Tickling and grazing my nub until I squirmed at the slow sexy torture.

"Please," I uttered between gasps.

"We were interrupted. I want you overflowing with need like you were in the elevator and in the grotto. His free hand teased my nipples, rolling and caressing in time with the rough cloth.

"Almost, love...but not yet."

He stepped back from me, and I nearly fell off the vanity reaching for him. I ripped the blindfold from my eyes. Daire had shrugged out of his clothes, and he stood glorious and naked not two feet from where I sat licking my lips. I took in every inch of his body, especially his long, corded member, thick and waiting.

Stepping between my legs again, he dipped his lips to mine. Our tongues sparred as his hand teased my body, finally dropping his mouth to my nipples.

Daire tickled his fingers down my stomach, his thumb finding my erect nub. Sliding two fingers around my taut core, he tugged and teased, earning a whimper before gliding the same two fingers inside my slick entrance.

"Daire!"

He pulled his fingers away, licking them clean. "Come closer, Eden. You're too far away."

I wiggled to the end of the vanity and then wrapped my legs around his waist. He let a slow, sexy smirk take his lips. His swollen tip of hard bar was close, teasingly close.

"Daire, please!"

Without warning, he grabbed my hips and drove his thick, rigid member deep with a single violent thrust. A gasp ripped from my mouth, and I clung to him. He picked me up impaled on his sex, driving up and deep, hard and fast. My arms clung to his neck, and I thought he'd press my back against the bathroom wall, but he didn't. He carried me to the edge of the bed.

He filled me again and again, tension cresting us toward the precipice. This was primal. Wild. Feral, even. I cried out, my inner walls convulsing around his swollen shaft. Spasms radiated in waves through my core and up my thighs. My legs shook as tension exploded into bliss.

"Eden!" He roared my name as if the word had been yanked from his balls as he came, hard.

He held me as aftershocks quaked and then ebbed with our bodies still entwined. Finally, he freed his body from mine, but he didn't walk into the bathroom or reach for his pants. Instead, he scooted back onto the pillows and opened his arms where I snuggled warm and spent.

"A weekend of firsts," I mumbled.

His fingers twined in my ratty mess of curls. "So many firsts. First martini, first lava cake…"

I pulled the hairs on his chest.

"Hey! Ow!"

"There are more important firsts to list…well, *first*."

He dipped his chin down to look at me. "First dance club. First vampire scare."

"Daire."

"How about first love." He kissed me. "The most important and potent first of all."

"You forgot perfect. Most important, most potent, and most perfect." I yawned, stretching.

"Are you tired? Do you want to watch a movie?"

"Nuh uh. I thought I wanted to soak with you in that huge tub, but I think I'd rather lie here. Filthy, but sated. We can do the tub thing later, while we plan our morning."

"Anything in particular you want to do?"

I leaned up on my elbow. "Well, there is something I've heard about, but I'll need you to show me."

"What's that?"

I cocked my head to the side, thinking. "Well, it's called a sixty-nine."

CHAPTER
Twenty~Seven

I WOKE to the sound of running water. Daire was in the bathroom, so I stretched out starfish style across the mattress. His side of the bed was still warm. I rolled over smothering myself in his scent. If I didn't have sore bits proving my time with Daire was real, I would've thought I dreamed it.

Nope, it was as real as my delicious, tender, hurt-so-good, morning-after glow.

My burner phone dinged. I twisted around to my side of the bed to grab it from the nightstand. It was a text notification. Plumping two pillows behind my head, I snuggled against the headboard to read the message.

> Are you up?

"Barely."

> Are u solo today?

"Don't know yet."

> Going to breakfast. Txt me later.

"Who are you texting?"

I glanced up from my phone to see Daire in the bathroom doorway. "Sorcha. She and Cian are going for breakfast. She wanted to know our plans for the day."

"What did you say?"

"That we just got up and haven't talked about it yet."

He walked to the edge of the bed. "Good. Because what I've got planned would be considered T.M.I."

"Too much information, how?" I scooted over to let him help me up off the mattress.

"Nope," he said. "You have to close your eyes first."

"I don't know if you're being sneaky or romantic." I giggled, following behind him. When my feet hit cold tile, I stopped. "Why are we in the bathroom?"

"Open your eyes."

Daire had filled the large, freestanding tub with hot water and silky bubbles, and on the vanity were fresh-cut flowers, and a breakfast tray with a pot of brewed tea, croissants, and jam.

"Daire! When did you do this?"

He smiled, folding his arms. "You, my love, are a very deep sleeper. It was either surprise you with a bubble bath and romantic breakfast or go for a run. I decided to opt for a better, more satisfying workout."

"With croissants."

Laughing, he nodded. "Feed the beast."

Daire wore the bathrobe I left for him in the closet next to the vanity. I was in his T-shirt. Even rumpled he looked gorgeous, while I hadn't looked in the mirror since Sorcha pushed me past that vampire in the hotel restroom. I was a mess, and I knew it.

"Nibble, nibble, little mouse. You're chewing on your lip again, and you only do that when you're rooting around in your head or worried about something you shouldn't worry about."

"It's no big deal. I'm fine."

"If it's the continental breakfast, we can order something else if you want. If it's the bath, we can nix the whole idea and shower instead. Together or separately. Your choice."

He was rambling, which meant he was a little nervous as well. I don't know why, but it made me feel better and a small smirk tugged at my mouth. "Are you finished?"

"Are you going to tell me why you're suddenly in a mood?"

"I'm not in a mood. I'm thinking."

"Ah. So, full rooting mode."

I exhaled, tugging at a handful of tangled auburn curls. "I'm a mess, Daire. You've done this amazingly romantic gesture, and I look like the Badlands Banshee on her worst day."

"The Badlands Banshee. Hmmm, let's see. Wild hair..." He put a finger to his chin, debating. "You get full marks for a classically disheveled mane, but your scream?" He clicked his cheek. "Sorry, a poor show for a banshee, yet an impressive win in mastering multiple orgasms in one night."

I burst out laughing. That was exactly the kind of silly thing I needed to dispel my stupid insecurities. Daire scooped me up, whirling me around before setting me on my feet in the tub.

"Your choice, mademoiselle. Jets or no jets." He paused with his finger on the whirlpool button.

"The more bubbles the merrier." I yanked Daire's soft tee over my head and tossed it onto the vanity. Air jets churned foamy suds around my legs, growing the soap bubbles higher and higher. "Uhm. I may have spoken too soon. You better get in here, or you might not find me in this froth."

He turned off the bubbler and then shrugged out of his robe. "Note for next time. Bubble bath *or* whirlpool jets. Not both." He climbed into the tub and then eased into the steaming, fragrant water with me.

Daire sat with his back against the end of the tub, and I straddled his hips. Soft whipped cream bubbles tickled my breasts, and I scooped a handful, smoothing them over Daire's chest.

"What do you want to do today?" he asked, trailing his fingers over my hips. "We could take a riverboat cruise or just wander around the French Quarter. There's a guided walking tour of Lafayette Cemetery No.1. I know how you love spooky things."

I leaned back on my hands, my breasts jutting through the bubbles. "Maybe." Daire shifted beneath my weight, his storm blue eyes darkening with a more pressing suggestion. Pressing as in the hard bar of his member against my ass.

"So, what do *you* want to do today?" I asked, kneeling up, so my nipples were mouth height with Daire's lips.

A soft groan of want and anticipation left his mouth. "I said it at the grotto, and I meant it. You are a tease, and it's not bravado, anymore. You know exactly what you're doing."

"Do I?" I reached down to slide my fingers over his shaft. "I'm not sure."

With a sharp intake, Daire's body went taut in the water. "Gods, I've created a monster. An insatiable demon, and I can't get enough!" He bucked his hips, and I let go of his member, the fluid moves in perfect concert for a slick plunge, deep and delicious.

I rode Daire's thick length, rolling my hips in slow, tantalizing strokes. This wasn't the frenzied passion fest from last night. We made love, our hands exploring every inch of flesh with intent. Teaching each other. Learning each other's body. Loving each other. While last night was savage, this was savor. Breathing in time, our bodies meshed. A perfect fit.

Closing my eyes, I recalled every hard edge and supple cut of Daire's body. When I opened my eyes again, the water on his skin seemed to shimmer, except it wasn't the droplets that glittered. It was him. It was me. Our bodies were one, and so were our auras. Golden and swirling in soft coils around us. Magic poured from one to the other, and when Daire kissed me, I didn't know where I ended and he began.

The beauty and passion of the moment held us suspended, and the world fell away. Tension rose in color and bursts of dazzling light, replacing languid with urgent need. We met each crest thrust for thrust, burst for burst, hips rolling and driving deep, plunge after plunge.

The water in the tub swashed against the fiberglass sides, mirroring the tremors quaking my core. Flesh quivered, every muscle stretched and taut. With a ragged shriek, I gripped Daire's shoulders. Our bodies clung, hanging on every clenched spasm until grand release shattered us both. Panting, I slumped against his chest with the water bobbing around us like our aftershocks.

"If that's how you intend to say good morning every day, I don't think either of us will get much done." He chuckled, kissing my wet neck.

"It was the Badlands Banshee's fault. She made me do it."

"Ha! I thought I recognized that shriek. And here I thought it was *me* making you climax."

I nipped Daire's earlobe and then climbed off his lap. Scootching around, I laid against his chest, happy and relaxed, while he drew circles in the bubbles over my breasts and belly.

"A florin for your thoughts," he asked. "And don't tell me they're not worth that much because that's not true."

I played with his fingers as they swirled over my skin. "This has been the most wonderfully intense experience of my life. I don't know how I'll go home to my daily routine knowing I won't wake up and see you or be able to reach out and touch you just because."

"Same," he replied. "That's why I'm savoring every second of this weekend." He hesitated. "Things aren't great at home right now."

The way he paused told me whatever happened at the Winter Court weighed on his mind. I hated that he was burdened, especially since I understood the feeling well. Between a rock and a hard place.

Daire kissed the side of my head and then leaned his back against the edge of the tub. The move sent tiny waves through the bath water, and it lapped against our bodies.

"It's not great in Seelie either," I admitted, and I filled him in on what happened with Rylan. On Orin Fullore, and on Merlin's take of the whole situation.

"They did what?" Daire sat up at that, forcing me to turn around in the tub to face him.

"You can't be that surprised, Daire. I'm sure courtiers at the Winter Court gather snippets of intelligence and gossip and try to use them to better their ends."

"Yes, but for Orin to try and set his son up as your consort? Did he send Rylan into the Eventide after you? He must've had you under surveillance or how else would he have known. Has Merlin said anything else?" Daire shook his head. "There's ambition, and then there's insanity. What father would risk their child's life for political gain?"

I shrugged, pulling my knees into my chest. "Has Morgana ever talked to you about prophecies?"

"Why? Has Merlin spoken to you about such things?"

I nodded.

"What did he say?"

At the grotto, I held back and didn't share everything I knew with Daire. Things were different now. We were together. A team. Though it was a week and a half since that night.

I straightened, sitting tall in the cooling water. "Unlike Morgana, Merlin has the sight. He's as old as the ancients we Sidhe have forgotten, like Aerith. Yet, he's not of our ilk." I smiled. "Ilk is one of Merlin's words. Like kindred spirits. That's another favorite phrase of his, especially when he's talking about us."

"I thought you said you weren't sure what Merlin meant when he said we were kindred spirits."

"I didn't. Or not entirely, anyway. With Orin dipping his oar in and stirring things the wrong way, Merlin was forced to tell me more. It seems you were right when you guessed the old Druid meant we were fated. According to a hazy vision, you and I are connected in ways that go beyond chance. Beyond simple love and attraction. We," I gestured between us, "were inevitable."

"Inevitable in what way?" he asked. "How? Why?"

I shrugged again. "That, he hasn't told me yet. Perhaps he doesn't know. Like I said, the vision was fogged, but I promise you, I will tell you as soon as I know. I'm not in this alone anymore."

"You were never in this alone, Edie. I'm here. Whatever he says, if it affects you, it affects me, and we will deal with it together."

I scooted closer, and he put his hands on my shoulders, caressing my arms. "There's something else. I can see it in your face, love. What is it?"

"I told you I sensed a presence while we were on the island. I'm not saying it was Rylan, but my gut tells me its related, and..." I hesitated, unsure.

"Tell me."

"I'm scared, Daire." The words came out in a blurt. My, I-fought-a-Redcap-and-won bravado exposing its soft white underbelly.

"I don't blame you for being apprehensive. Not when bad actors are scheming, and you don't know all the players. I'm here, though."

"What about when we leave here tomorrow? There's Merlin's prophecy, and the references he's made over the years. About me. About the Sidhe. About the realms and how they were fractured. I'm scared it's all related and somehow it involves me...and now you. That we're being pushed and pulled by forces we can't see and don't know how to fight."

"Whatever those forces, they brought us together, right? Maybe instead of gearing up for a fight, we wait and see what happens. Either way, we have each other, and you have Merlin." He kissed me, his lips a gentle reassuring brush. "We'll worry when we have something to worry about."

I nodded, settling back against his chest with his arms around my waist. "Daire, have you ever thought about our respective courts, and how similar they are, despite being separated?"

"Of course," he replied. "Especially since knowing you."

"The Badlands, the Eventide. They both bear scars from the Western Rim War, so long ago. The same war that fractured Avalon. Sometimes I think if each court with their spies spent less time worrying about the other, then maybe we could reach a meeting of the minds and unify the realms once more."

He laughed, and his chest rumbled under my back. "That is an amazing thought, love, but you're forgetting one thing. The courts would have to give up sovereignty to one chosen person, and that will never happen. The only creatures greedier and more selfish than humans are the Sidhe." He kissed the side of my head. "You and me excepted."

"I know, but in the meantime, other courts, shadow courts, are forming. Outcast Fae everyone underestimates. Like Taltos and his Sluagh, and his newly formed Dusk Court."

Daire sighed. "I know. That's the problem I mentioned back home."

"My mother knew about Taltos's shadow court from her spies, so that tells me your father and his privy council had to know as well. Don't you ever wonder why they never do anything about it? Maybe talk to each other for the greater good of both courts? Isn't Taltos a threat to Unseelie as well as Seelie?"

He didn't answer right away, which told me he weighed his answer. Not because he didn't trust me, but because this was the underlying worry bothering him the whole time. "Yes, Taltos is a threat to Unseelie. Though technically he's an ally of the Winter Court. After the attack on the night of the gala, my father realized he was duped. The situation frayed the Privy

Council. There are factions now. Some pushing to solidify our treaty with the Sluagh, others pushing my father to sever it completely."

Now it was my turn to sigh. "I wish your father and my mother would talk, maybe form a qualified truce that could lead to a more permanent understanding. With Seelie and Unseelie allied, Taltos wouldn't have the same position of strength."

"That would be remarkable. Then you and I wouldn't have to sneak around and wait for stolen moments to be together."

I shivered, even in his arms. Was my tremble from the cooling water or because this conversation struck too close to what my gut said was the truth? I heard Merlin's words, *You need to be ready for changes you might not want to make.* Right now, the only change I wanted was a swap from a brewery tour to a ghost tour tonight.

CHAPTER
Twenty~Eight

"I'LL CHECK with the concierge about changing our tours and then get us a couple of coffees to go," Daire said, walking out of the elevator with me. "We can head to the beignet place for a fresh batch since the ones your sister left last night are a greasy mess."

"That's because we spent the day eating junk and binge-watching movies in our very large bed."

He nuzzled my neck. "That's not the only thing we spent the day doing in that bed."

"Go. Use glamour if you have to but organize that ghost tour."

I waited for Daire on a plush lobby sofa, playing on my phone, when I caught snippets of a conversation behind me. I didn't eavesdrop on purpose. They were just loud.

"What's wrong with the elevators today? I hate having to wait."

"There's only one working, Heather. Have some patience."

"Why haven't they fixed it yet? It's been all day and it's really annoying."

"The front desk said something about the surveillance system malfunctioning last night. Video feed. Audio. Everything."

"Typical. Probably vandalism. Some drunk off Bourbon Street."

"Nah, they said it was an ordinary night. No shenanigans."

My cheeks burned at bit, both for eavesdropping and for knowing it was definitely not an ordinary night. Still, I had to give Daire props. No one was hurt, and our identities were protected. Not to mention my dignity.

"Daisy..."

I looked up from my phone to see my sister walking towards me. "Hey. Where's your other half?" I couldn't remember Cian's incognito name.

"With Jay." She winked. "They're with the concierge and are having a little trouble convincing him to open up a ghost tour. It seems they're booked solid. I've been tasked with asking if you'd rather do a bayou-swamp-fan-boat thing or drive out to a plantation."

"Why would I want to see a plantation?"

"Because it's where they filmed parts of that movie you love."

"To be honest, I think I've had enough of the undead for one weekend, so no on the plantation."

"That's a no on vampires, and a yes for the alligators." She looked over at the guys and smiled, making a cut gesture across her throat which told me they both just lost a bet.

A sudden melancholy settled on my shoulders thinking about vampires and that poor woman in the lobby restroom. I wished there was a way to know if she pulled through or succumbed to her injuries.

"Are you okay?" Sorcha asked.

"Fine. Or I will be." I paused, glancing toward the guys. "Can you ask Jay to try one more time to find a ghost tour? I have my heart set, and I'm not up for a twilight fan boat ride in the swamp."

She nodded. "Ghosts, check. Gators, hard pass."

Astonishingly, the concierge managed four last-minute tickets for a guided ghost tour. I knew cash had changed hands under the table with the tiniest glamoured push. Daire did the honors since Cian refused, but it worked out. I couldn't blame Cian. He was bending the rules enough, giving Daire the benefit of the doubt.

The tour met outside and most everyone was in costume, making me feel like an out-of-place tourist. "Welcome!" Our guide flourished a bow. Dressed in full Victorian regalia, he sported a cape, top hat, and cane. "I am your host, Fabien, and tonight I will share with you the horrors and history of this city's mysterious and mystical past." He tossed up his cane, catching it with the same hand. "If you'll follow me, our first stop awaits."

The group walked in a cluster behind Fabien, talking amongst themselves. Daire and I paired off, with Cian and Sorcha ahead of us. So far, so good. No tingles.

"This is the famed House of Voodoo. Marie Laveau and her history have been surrounded by legend and lore for centuries," Fabien began at our first stop. "This Voodoo Queen held New Orleans spellbound, staging ceremonies in which participants became possessed by spirits. She dispensed charms and potions, told fortunes, and healed the sick. Some scholars believe that Laveau's feared magical powers of divination were actually based on her network of informants, developed while working as a hairdresser in households of the prominent. That she listened closely to their gossip, *but* that is the explanation for non-believers. Those of us who know magic and the preternatural exist, know better."

We walked past the Lalaurie Mansion, where grisly facts were spun together with myth and local folklore, leaving most of the group shivering. From there we walked to the New Orleans Pharmacy Museum, all the while listening to Fabien's stories of the paranormal and beyond.

"What would they do if I conjured an energy ball, just for fun?" I grinned, opening and closing my hand. Not that I would.

Sorcha laughed, looking at me over her shoulder. "If I wasn't afraid Cian would call this weekend quits, I'd dare you to do it."

Holding hands with Daire, the group crossed over to Bourbon Street, heading back to our starting point. "Wait." I tugged him to a stop.

"What?"

"There." I gestured at the entrance to the club on the corner. "I just saw the EMT from last night. He went inside."

"What's going on now?" Cian seemed reluctant to ask. "Edie, I swear. If you've done something else..."

Sorcha punched him for me.

"I haven't done anything, but remember the EMT that took care of the woman in the restroom? He just went into that club."

There were no lights around the windows or name on the awning. Just the letter X. "I don't know, Edie. I'm not getting a good vibe from this place," Daire replied.

"The place is probably a dive, but a bad vibe with no tingles attached isn't such a bad vibe." I tugged on his hand again. "Five minutes. That's all I need to ask him about that woman. I have to know if she made it or not."

Cian looked at Daire and then they both looked at me. "Five minutes," Daire agreed. "Not a second more. If any of us get any kind of feeling the place isn't safe, we're out."

I went up on tip toe, giving him a quick kiss. "Five minutes. Who knows, maybe this place is some kind of haven for paranormals. I told you I thought that EMT was a werewolf or shifter."

"You mean the hottie that came in with the medical kit?" Sorcha's eyebrows went up. "You did not share that juicy tidbit."

"What difference does it make?" Cian complained. "We've got enough smelly, fur-covered fae back home. We don't need to gawk here."

"We're not gawking. We're comparing." She took Cian's hand, tugging him across the street. "Besides, Edie is concerned for that poor woman, and I support her one hundred percent."

Cian rolled his eyes, but he followed her anyway.

"Your sister just wants to see that hot EMT for herself. Up close this time." Daire smirked.

"Pretty much." I laughed, watching Sorcha double-time it into the club with Cian. "At least she and Cian are well suited. He likes to window shop as well."

Club X wasn't exactly a club. It was more of a bar with a small stage. Just inside the entrance on opposite walls were cork boards, highlighting the bands scheduled to play over the next few weeks. Most were cover bands like the one we saw at the Cat's Paw, only these had names like: Wolfsbane, Crimson Sisters, and Purple Hex.

"I think Edie's right," Sorcha said, scanning the locale. "Definitely a sanctuary vibe."

Cian grumbled. "Or maybe it's a place for wannabe witches and vampires. There are humans who fetishize the lifestyles."

"I don't care what this place is, as long as I can talk to that EMT." I dismissed the naysaying and searched for the man. He sat at the bar, alone. From the way he was dressed, it didn't look as though he expected company, but he was about to get some, like it or not.

"I want to talk to him by myself. You guys weren't in that restroom while he worked to stabilize that woman. He might feel ganged up on if we surround him in his happy place."

Cian rolled his eyes again. "How do you know this is his happy place? It looks pretty sad to me."

"C'mon, Sunshine. Float your black cloud over to that table with me and let's order a drink." Sorcha walked with Cian to a corner table, leaving Daire to talk with me alone.

"If you want to talk with that guy, that's fine, but if he is what you sensed, then I'm not comfortable with you approaching him by yourself. This place is pretty crowded, and the natives are already getting restless trying to place us." I opened my mouth to protest, but Daire held a finger to my lips. "I'm not arguing this, Edie. It's dangerous, and you know it."

"I was only planning to talk with him, not invite him back to our room for a threesome."

Daire didn't budge.

"I'm a big girl, Daire. If you want to stand at the bar and keep an eye out, fine. I won't argue. I am going to talk with him, and I'm going to do so alone."

I turned on my heel and headed toward the bar. Daire was behind me, but he gave me my space. As much as this was a weekend of firsts for me, it was just as high a learning curve for him when it came to what made me tick.

I stopped at the barstool next to the EMT and sat. The man didn't look up from nursing his whiskey. Daire was on the opposite side of me, but two barstools down.

"Hello," I said, trying to get the man's attention.

"If you're looking for company, move on. I'm not it."

"I'm not looking for company. I'm looking for information." That got his attention, and he slid his eyes toward mine. "Remember me? Hotel bathroom. Vampire attack?"

Recognition dawned, and he straightened on his barstool, inhaling a breath through his nose. "Nope. Still can't place you."

"I'm not surprised. Look, I'm not stalking you, in fact, I don't want more than five minutes of your time. I just wanted to ask how that woman fared. Is she okay?"

He nodded, and a small smile curved on his lips. "She's hurt bad, but she'll pull through. They had to transfuse her, and she took more stitches than I care to count, internal and external, to close up the vampire's handiwork, but she'll heal. In body, anyway. I wish I could say the same for her mind. Trauma of that kind of attack runs deep, and there's no running from it. Even if you want to. It can make your life unbearable, and even make you do things against your nature."

"I know," I replied, noticing a shadow of something in his eyes. Was it guilt? Gods knew I had pangs of the same in the taxi afterward.

"Do you?" he asked, turning his eyes to me.

He must've thought I was one of those who tried to commiserate when I had no idea. "I don't mean from personal experience, but because I saw the terror in the woman's eyes when she came to, right before you and your partner arrived."

His eyes darkened at that.

"I'm sorry. Did I say something wrong?"

The EMT's grip on his whiskey tightened, and the glass spider-webbed in his hand. Daire slipped to my side, his hand already on my elbow.

"I didn't mean to upset you. I only wanted to know about the girl and to thank you for what you did for her."

He turned, and his mouth was a slash. "It's not your fault. You told us the truth without knowing who we were or if we'd think you were crazy, though something tells me you already knew Savio and I were more than we seemed." He growled low, the same way he did when he scanned the restroom that night. "Or we were, anyway."

"What do you mean, were?"

Anger and sadness warred in the man's eyes when he looked at me to answer. "After we got that girl to the hospital, we went looking for that purple haired vampire. You see, Savio and I knew exactly who you meant. She goes by Izzy Slash, but her real name is Isadora Cox. She landed in New Orleans about thirty years ago from somewhere across the pond. She's not nice. Especially when it comes to humankind."

"Is that surprising?"

He nodded. "More and more, yeah. The undead are split when it comes to how they view their number one food source. Some see them as just that. A herd. Other see them as a lesser branch of the vampiric family since they were all once human." He shook his head. "It doesn't matter. Nothing does, now."

The same melancholy took him, but he shook it off. "We found Izzy and confronted her about her violence. New Orleans takes care of its own, and that woman was one of ours. A teacher. Did she make a bad choice drinking so much last night? Yes. She was still one of ours, though, and Izzy knew it. She didn't like what Savio and I had to say, but she didn't make her move then. No. She waited for us to leave, then she and her friends ambushed us outside the bar."

"This bar."

He nodded. "Sav didn't make it. He wasn't a wolf, like me. He was a fox shifter. Too small to fight off a vampire. I tried to help him, but we were outnumbered. They snapped his neck." He gestured toward a memorial picture with two candles burning on the other side of the bar.

"What's your name?" I asked.

"Gil," he replied.

"I'm so sorry for your loss, Gil. Savio was brave to do what he did."

He nodded. "Brave, and a little stupid. I should've stopped him, but he'd have gone alone anyway."

Looking at Daire and I, Gil inhaled again. "Any chance you want to tell me what you two are? I've never scented the likes of you before, but I know you're not human."

"Sorry," Daire answered for us. "It's against the rules."

"I get that. This bar..." He gave a chin pop to the shabby tables and scuffed floor. "It's the one place in town safe for us to be ourselves. If you were human, you wouldn't have spotted the door, let alone been able to enter. It's warded, courtesy of the house band, Purple Hex."

I smiled at that. "Very cool."

Gil went to drain the rest of his whiskey, but the spider-webbed glass broke in his hand. "Shit." He grabbed a wad of napkins to mop up the spill. "Sorry about that. One of the drawbacks of being a Were."

"Let me help." I picked up one of the shards, underestimating its sharp edge. "Ow!" I jerked back my hand as blood welled on the pad of my thumb. "Stupid."

"Edie." Daire lock-gripped my elbow. My attempt at being kind had just outed me as Fae. "We have to leave. Now."

I shoved the throbbing digit in my mouth, but a susurrated hiss came at me from the other side of the bar. Three vampires circled me and Daire, their eyes fully dilated and black as hell.

Cian and Sorcha blurred across the bar to flank Daire, fanning out with me in the middle. "Okay, hive mind. What now?" Sorcha asked.

The vampires didn't attack, which was odd. It was as though they waited for permission, and that's when Izzy Slash walked in like the queen of the vampires.

"You know, I knew there was something familiar about you, little girl." Her high platform heels clacked along the floor as she walked. Her words were slurred through her fangs, sending a shiver through my gut.

"Daire," I whispered.

"I got you, babe."

"I don't think so, children. You see, I've been chasing your sloppy magic all over the city, but it wasn't until you and your boyfriend saturated your scent all over a certain elevator that I knew I had you."

I cringed inside. Me and my bad choices struck again, only this time I was taking my sister and the heir to the Winter Court down with me.

"You and your randy boy should've been more careful," Izzy taunted. "A little bird told me a High Sidhe was coming to town, but I didn't believe it. Then, you walk into my sight." Her laugh was evil, and my skin crawled with more than just prickles.

"Leave off, Izzy." Gil knocked his chair back, meeting her square. "You're gonna cause all kinds of problems for us, I can feel it. You got what you wanted, now leave!"

She laughed again, waving him off. "Heel, you mutt. You did your job and got her here. Why else do you think I let you live?"

My mouth fell open. How could I be so stupid?

"That's right, honey. This was a set-up, complete with a big, bad wolf."

The EMT slumped into a chair and dropped his head to his forearm, sobbing. If he expected sympathy or even understanding, he could forget it. I was having a hard enough time forgiving myself.

"What do you want, Isadora?" I raised my chin. I was not about to fall apart. Not here. Not now. We still had power, not to mention an escape plan. Now all we needed was an opening.

She paced in a slow back and forth, her finger tapping her chin. "What do I want. Hmmm. That's a good question. Oh, I'd keep you for myself if I could, but you're worth far too much in this deal. I couldn't say no."

Pausing, the vampire eyed Sorcha and the guys. "Then again, it's a fair bet your friends share your profitable blood type. Maybe I'll keep them instead." Her eyes flashed. "Keep some, sell some. Win-win."

A familiar hum sounded, and Izzy whirled with a clap. "Incoming, and right on time."

A shimmer formed on the opposite side of the room. The same kind of shimmer we'd seen just two days ago. It was a portal. A *Fae* portal.

A squad of guards in Unseelie uniforms rushed through the gateway with about a half dozen Sluagh. Longswords, spiked flails, and pikes, slashed and smashed with indiscriminate aim, sending bar patrons running for their lives. Screams reverberated from the walls, and blood slicked the club's floor in seconds. Furniture shattered, and bodies piled up.

"Get behind us!" Cian yelled to me and Sorcha, before he moved to flank Daire.

"Screw that!" Sorcha lifted both hands and crackling energy formed in her palms. I did the same, and the fab foursome became a wall of current.

The vampires shrieked at the bite of hot jolts. They jerked away, sending Izzy into a fury. "Don't let them escape!"

Cian and Daire hurled spinning balls of hot current across the room. They exploded in fireballs, sending what was left of the décor into an instant inferno. Flames burned, blistering and wild, engulfing the whole bar.

The heat was nearly too much, and I threw my arm up covering my face. "Sorcha! We need to leave!"

"I'm right behind you!"

"Not so fast, you Fae bitch!" The vampires fled, leaving Izzy on her own. "I'm not walking away with nothing!" The leech grabbed Sorcha's arm, only to jerk it back with a shriek. A current radiated around Sorcha's body like a high voltage forcefield. The vampire cradled her arm, but it was too late. It smoldered black, crumbling to ash against her chest.

"The Seelie heir! You fools!" The Unseelie captain rushed from the back. "Grab her before she gets away!"

Daire's arm dropped in disbelief, fizzling the energy in his palm. "Leto?" He stared at the squad leader, aghast. "What in Orcs Hell are you doing? Who sent you? Did my father sanction this carnage?"

The captain's shock gave us the opening we needed. "Medallions! Now!" Cian yelled.

I grabbed Daire's hand and whirled for the bar's mirror. "Home!" The word left my mouth without stopping to think *my* home wasn't Daire's home. It didn't matter at this point, regardless of what waited on the other side.

CHAPTER
Twenty~Nine

THE QUEEN'S portal opened and the four of us rushed out, sealing it before anyone could follow. Stunned, I didn't know how to react. Cian was another story. He seethed, pacing back and forth with residual fear and anger.

"What the actual hell, Daire? Those were Unseelie guards! And Sluagh! Ugh! Did you know your father and his animals were watching us? Tracking us all over the human realm?"

Daire's face was stunned. "Of course not! Do you think I would've let Eden or any of us in that bar if I knew? Cian, I'm gobsmacked! My father didn't even know I was gone from the palace. He's too busy with his latest mistress to pay attention to my comings and goings."

That was a familiar scenario. Except my mother put her spies and Caxton to work keeping tabs on me so she could practice being an absentee parent without the guilt.

The two Sidhe men stood glaring at each other. We didn't have much time. The portal opened a full day ahead of schedule, and Caxton would be here any moment with his men to investigate.

"Cian, you can't think Daire had anything to do with this!" I argued. "He and I are together. As in fated. I can't explain it now, but it's still the truth." I squeezed my way between them, looking to Sorcha for help, but she shook her head.

"Edie, I love you. I want you to have this with Daire. I want it to be all it *should* be. All you *want* it to be. I'm just not sure. This whole scenario is too convenient. It's too easy to believe it was all a set up."

"That's what we've been taught to think, Sorcha. Seelie good. Unseelie bad. Whoever is behind this is manipulating our ingrained suspicions to their own ends. Can't you both see we're all the same? We're Sidhe. It shouldn't be one court or another. We should be one people." I wiggled out from between the men to grab my sister's arms. "Change is coming, Sorcha. Can't you feel it? You play your frivolous court role well, but you are not shallow. You are just as clever and concerned as I am, so why not admit it? Avalon needs to change."

"That's very noble of you, Eden."

I whirled at the sound of my mother's voice. Her tone was polite yet biting. The same tone she used when she was about to ruin a courtier's life.

"Mother...you misunderstood what I said."

She put up a hand, shutting me down. "Imagine my pride, hearing my heir apparent ready and willing to destroy my throne for some radical idea of one republic." The queen shook her finger at me, but there was no humor in her eyes. "Methinks you've been spending too much of your time buried in books, and not enough time learning what it means to be a leader."

Sorcha didn't meet my pleading gaze. She kept her chin high, waiting for our mother to either bring the pain as an accessory to my treason, or dismiss her involvement as folly.

"Sorcha, you may go. I will speak to you about these shenanigans later." Her gaze turned to Cian who looked like he'd swallowed his tongue. "You were sent to keep my daughters safe. In case of trouble, activating the portal with medallion magic was exactly what you should have done, Cian Bannerol. For that you are to be commended. What I don't understand is how you could allow the Unseelie heir to wheedle his way into my daughter's affections! Was he under a confounding spell? Had you no idea of his true identity?"

I cringed inside, even though I knew my mother was simply trying to wrap her head around the situation.

"No, your majesty. Daire was uncloaked, though I did administer a dose of revelation power to the truth about his intentions."

"And?"

"Daire wasn't immune to the powder. He blurted his truth without hesitation. Bald-faced and very embarrassing. He was there for Eden, but not in any sort of nefarious way. He came to New Orleans to be with her. As simple as that." Cian shrugged. "A hook up based on mutual attraction. Girl wanted boy. Boy wanted girl. Close doors. Fade to black. Boom."

The queen's jaw tightened, and her eyes were more like steel than I'd ever seen before. I couldn't let Cian take the blame. He and his family would never recover.

"It was me! I did it. All me. I invited Daire to come to New Orleans. We spent every moment together, and it was wonderful. Cian and Sorcha couldn't dissuade me. They tried, but when I refused to budge, they shadowed us nearly everywhere."

The queen's eyebrow hiked. "Nearly."

"If you're insinuating Daire had me dodge my sister and Cian, the answer is no. Except for private moments, we were a foursome."

The queen's lip twitched. "Are you saying you accomplished everything I intended for you this weekend? That you practiced the arts we discussed before you left with the Unseelie prince?"

"Mother, please." My eyes darted to Caxton and his men, and from the burn in my cheeks I knew I was as red as a tomato. "I will tell you everything you wish to know. Just not here."

My mother actually seemed amused at my discomfort. I didn't care. Maybe I could resurrect my old spin plan, so she believed my rendezvous was a one up on Lachlan.

"Very well, Eden. If what I assume is the case, then why did you come home early? If your attraction to this boy is as strong as you've led me to believe, why would you sacrifice a third of your time to be with him for no reason?"

Daire and I shared a look. There was no dodging this situation. "Your Majesty," Daire began quietly. "We came back because a trap had been sprung to try and kidnap Eden. My being here in Seelie was not what Eden nor I expected. We had to move quickly, and portal jump when we had the chance." He kept his eyes level and his tone cool, but respectful.

"A trap." Caxton stepped forward, his gaze narrow. "Where? Set by whom?"

"We don't know," I blurted before Daire could incriminate his father before we knew the truth. "There were vampires involved."

"Vampires?" My mother seemed genuinely horrified. "Are you hurt? Did they bleed you?"

I shook my head. "Daire and Cian protected me and Sorcha. Someone purposely gave the vampires information about me. They knew I would be in New Orleans this weekend."

"But your drops." My mother was at a loss.

"The four of us were diligent, Mother. Our scent was not the reason the undead knew where to find us."

She seemed unable to fathom any more. "This is too much to discuss standing in front of a portal with you looking disheveled and pained. I want you to go to your chambers, get cleaned up, and then we can discuss what happened and try to piece together evidence to garner answers."

The queen snapped her fingers. "Caxton. Escort the Lady Eden to her chamber. Post a guard outside her door until I send for her." Her gaze turned to Daire next, who hadn't flinched. "As for our unexpected guest, he will be afforded accommodation equal to his rank. He is the heir apparent to the Winter Court, and as such the equal and opposite of my daughter. I will not be accused of treating him like the animals his father allows into his court."

"Mother!"

"Quiet!" she snapped. "I can smell him on you, Eden, and while your choice of lover doesn't offend, I also smell a distinct odor of Sluagh. You are going to have to account for that, young lady, or this will not bode well for you, or your Unseelie lover!"

"If Daire is to be at the palace while facts are being uncovered, may we see each other?" The request sounded pitiful, but I didn't care. The thought of Daire being so close, yet so far was crushing me.

My mother didn't say no, but her cold sniff told me everything. "Take Prince Daire to the south wing of the palace. He is to be accommodated in all things, except contact with either of my daughters. I will contact King Lachlan to see what he has to say about this encounter."

Four of Caxton's guards formed a quad around Daire, but he didn't budge. "For the record, Your Majesty..." Daire made them wait, and I held my breath. Not that I thought Daire would be suicidal enough to insult my mother, but he was also not about to be led away like an animal with a ring through his nose.

"You have something to say, Prince Daire?" My mother crossed her arms over her chest.

"I do. Like you, my father had no idea about Eden and me, nor what we planned. In fact, like you, he had no idea we had even met in the first place."

"Take him! Now."

My heart broke, crying out for him even as I stood planted in disbelief. He mouthed the words, "I love you," as he passed me on the path, and my hand gripped my chest. "I love you, too," I whispered back, hoping he heard me.

"Go!" my mother ordered. She put a hand on my shoulder and squeezed. It wasn't for comfort. It was to ensure I didn't chase after him and make a scene. I would never. Not because of her, but because Daire had been so brave in holding his own and upholding us. Why would I diminish that with a puerile scene?

The guards walked with him toward the south wing, leaving my mother speechless for once. It wouldn't last, of course. One look at me told me this was just the beginning of hell. I watched them crest the top of the hill, and then he was gone from sight. My knees faltered, but I refused to show that weakness in front of my mother. Not when Daire had been so strong.

"Eden..." She waited until the guards had gone before releasing her hold on my shoulder. "I have one question before Caxton takes you to your chambers. Did Merlin have anything to do with this assignation with the Winter prince?"

How could I answer without condemning my old friend? Myself? Daire? I needed to think, and I needed to speak with Merlin before my mother got the chance. If I told her the truth, Merlin would be banished before I could blink. He didn't deserve that. None of the people embroiled in this mess deserved the trouble they now faced. This began and ended with me. The Winter gala. The Eventide. Daire's island. Rylan. And now this. Me.

Reflex took over, and I shook my head. "No, Your Majesty. Merlin only supplied what you required of him. The rest was all my doing." Acknowledging my mother by her formal title put my statement on record.

She inclined her head, but I didn't trust she believed me for a second. Still, my mother was nothing if not an advocate of due process. Something contrary to her lust for power and her bottomless ambition. She'd get at the truth, even if it meant torture, but she'd never condemn Merlin, of all people, without proof. That bought me some time. Something my gut told me there wasn't much of.

I walked with Caxton to my rooms, feeling his hard gaze on me the entire time. If left up to him, he'd send Daire back to his father in pieces. At least my mother knew the value of keeping Daire at the palace and treating him well while she unraveled the truth of my near kidnapping. It would set precedent in case the situation was ever reversed.

Caxton opened my door and then waited for me to walk into my bedroom before closing and locking it shut. I slumped against the heavy wood already missing Daire. How were we to get through this? If Lachlan hadn't ordered me kidnapped, then who did? I really needed to speak with Merlin.

I had no choice. I was stuck until I wasn't anymore. Body and heart sagging with grief, I went to take a shower and do as my mother asked.

CHAPTER
Thirty

MINUTES WERE MY ENEMY, as were the hours that dragged the sun and moon across the sky marking time. It had been days since Daire's eyes last met mine, though it felt like years.

I knew in my gut he was no longer in the palace, nor in Seelie. I don't know how, but I sensed it. My mother must've put a gag order on the palace as there wasn't a whisper of gossip. I knew the court, though. They were whispering. Just not in earshot of me or the queen. I also knew, without trying, they were all hedging their bets on whether to back Sorcha as the new heir apparent. My position as heir meant nothing to me. The only thing that mattered was protecting the ones I loved.

Sorcha had been my only company since the whole thing blew up in my face. Whatever demeanor she held in front of the queen, she was still my sister, and she held me as I sobbed. She told me Caxton had grilled her with my mother present, and I knew without asking they had done the same with Cian. Whether they questioned Daire? No one said. Or maybe they couldn't.

Loving me, and wanting what I wanted, for me, was one thing. Falling on their proverbial sword was another, and I'd never ask that. The question begged, could a rival court interrogate a member of a rival royal family without repercussions? I didn't think so. It was more likely the queen sent Daire home, knowing he'd have to face his father's infamous wrath.

Now it was my turn in the hot seat. I sat with my mother in the Privy Council room. Everyone's hard stare hit me like a rock. At this point there was no benefit in finessing the truth, so I answered their questions, but didn't volunteer anything extra.

"Your Highness, you do know this could be construed as treason." Aldric Bannerol stood from his seat. Technically, Cian's father wasn't a member of the Privy Council but being a ranking member of the queen's spy network, I knew his skills were vital to my mother in these proceedings. At least that's what the council called this scheduled discussion. I wasn't on trial, but it certainly felt that way.

"Yes, Aldric, I am well aware of how my actions could be perceived."

"Is that all you have to say for yourself?"

"No, I have plenty to say." He had undoubtedly gotten the full New Orleans story from Cian and now wanted me to corroborate what he already knew.

I looked at him, and every other council member sitting so smug. "Not that it would mean a flying fig to any of you, but my mother, the queen, instructed me to go to the human realm for educational purposes. You all know what that entailed."

I paused for effect. Some members wore half-hidden smirks, others were expressionless, but they all knew it was to inspire me to mother's weapon of choice. Sex. "That said, the queen gave me leave to enlist a partner of my choosing, and I chose Prince Daire Dannean."

The collective hum was annoying, so I put up my hand very much like my mother. "Why are you shocked? Have you seen the Unseelie prince? He's handsome. He's well built. More importantly, he's skilled in the ways I needed. He's not an alien species. He's High Sidhe, same as me. Same as you. And like me, he's of royal blood."

Every eye was riveted, and I thought I saw a flicker of pride on my mother's face. "As to the incident involving my attempted kidnapping. How am I to blame for that? How is my sister...or Cian Bannerol?" Aldric didn't blink. Eyes slipped to him, and he wasn't about to let them see him sweat. I had to give him props for that.

"No one is casting blame on you, Princess. Neither are they casting blame on your sister or my son," Aldric replied.

"I see. Then who's left? It's very clear this esteemed body is here to cast blame on the heir apparent of the Winter Court. Namely, Daire Dannean." Grumblings went around the room, but no one had the balls to confirm or deny the fact.

"I was there. I was the one the kidnappers came for, but it was Cian, Sorcha, and Daire who were in mortal danger. If the kidnapping had succeeded, those vampires would have taken my sister, your son, and the Unseelie prince and either sold them as sex slaves, ransomed them on their own, or used them as non-stop drinking fountains for Fae blood."

My graphic depiction shocked most at the table even more than the idea of Daire and I bumping nasties. "None of you want to acknowledge the seedier side to this situation, or the fact that whoever is the puppet master had no problem partnering with human realm vampires. Who has that much to gain? That should be your first question. Who craves that much power they would willingly play let's-make-a-deal with the undead?"

My words must have struck a chord because the tenor of council murmurs changed. "Those who came through that portal were dressed in Unseelie uniforms. Were they truly members of the Winter Guard? Prince Daire only recognized one man. A guard named Leto."

There were more murmurs, and this time the queen quieted the room. I explained Daire's utter shock. How he questioned who was behind the blood bath. Aldric nodded as I spoke. Perhaps he did so unaware, but it told me Cian's story and mine were enough alike to give my version of events validity.

"I know I am unschooled when it comes to political dealing, but I know enough about political scheming to know the King of the Winter Court would never send his own personal guard, let alone use his own son, his heir, to kidnap the heir to the throne of his rival. He'd have someone else do the dirty deed for him." I looked directly at my mother. "Plausible deniability."

The doors to the Privy Council chamber opened, and Merlin walked in with a swirl of robes. He stood rather than take the chair offered but acknowledged my mother with a differential head dip before recognizing me. I always knew Merlin's mood by the glint or twinkle in his eyes, and even sometimes what he thought. Today his eyes were veiled, and even a little sad.

"Merlin," my mother began, waving Aldric back to his seat. "I believe there are things you wish to say to this council."

He shook his head, much to my mother's surprise. "I have nothing to say to your council, Your Majesty. What I have to say is for Eden's ears, though you have ordered I say it here and now. Yet, I do have some context that might shed light on what happened in New Orleans."

"Very well. Say what you must," she replied, but her face was not happy. My mother was the center of the Seelie universe, or that's what she liked to think. The fact Merlin, in effect, rejected her in favor of me, did not bode well.

"Firstly, the events in the human realm did not begin in New Orleans. They began the night of the Winter Court gala..."

Afraid to breathe, I listened as Merlin recounted the facts of that first night and his role in its planning. My mother's face was impassive, but there was a slight twitch in one eye, which spoke volumes about what seethed beneath her politic exterior.

"Also, I facilitated Eden in meeting Daire in Unseelie after that first encounter." I cringed inwardly as he revealed the events of what happened in the Eventide. All of it. Including the fact Rylan followed me, and how he came to be injured.

My mother stood from her seat. "Are you telling me my daughter, the princess Eden, was directly involved in the Sluagh seizure of the Eventide Forest?" I had never seen the queen so stunned, and the twitch in her eye was now a tick.

"Yes, my queen. Though Lady Eden was not responsible. She, like many others, was inadvertently involved. An innocent used in a larger, far-reaching conspiracy."

"Are you quite finished, magician?" The queen gripped the edge of the council table. Was it in anger or because her knees faltered? The notion of my mother with her knees cut out from under her wasn't pleasant. I didn't wish that at all. I wanted my mother to see beyond the borders of Seelie. Beyond her own selfishness. Perhaps gripping that table was the first glimmer of that.

"I'm finished with the backstory as it pertains to this council meeting, and with your permission, I'd like to continue."

My mother exhaled, and with a curt wave, she took her seat. Outwardly, she seemed composed, but I knew better. With her eyes on the old Druid, she curved slender fingers over the edge of each chair arm.

Merlin inclined his head again, eyes finding mine. From the shadow in his gaze, I knew this would be the last time I saw him for a very long while, if not forever.

"Eden, you have been through so much in the past month. Much of which is not your fault. Everything I taught you. All the lessons we debated over the years are bearing fruit. I told you of the hazy visions plaguing me. Of the threads unraveling faster than the fates could mend. Today, the fates have reached a crossroads.

"Everything you've been through since the night of the Winter gala has brought you to this point in your life. You are here for a reason, and not because Tianna, or her Privy Council, demand it. You are here because your destiny is finally clear. My sight is no longer hazy, and the prophecy is nigh."

"Prophecy?" The queen stood, incredulously. "What prophecy? If there was ever such a thing, especially one involving my daughter, I should've been informed."

Merlin inclined his head. "And so you were, Your Majesty. On the day of the twins' birth. I told you then, if the Sidhe gave birth to one with power over all twelve elements, the child would herald an end and a new beginning for the Fae."

"That's not a prophecy. That's musing." The queen flourished a dismissive wave.

The old Druid steadied his unblinking gaze on my mother, and she actually crossed her legs to stop from squirming. "The prophecy is nigh, Tianna. Whether you choose to acknowledge it or not. The realms as you know them, as Lachlan knows them, are changing."

She pointed at the sorcerer. "Changing. Not ending." She tossed another glib wave. "I don't give a flying fig if they change. I am queen, and the only thing that's *nigh* is my decision whether or not this particular child of mine remains my heir!"

"As you wish, Your Majesty." Merlin inclined his head once more, but then did the unthinkable. He turned from my mother to continue to address me.

"Eden, after you discovered Rylan was in the infirmary, you came to see me. You were unsettled. As always, you looked to take the blame on yourself. I've often wondered where you learned the capacity for such compassion and accountability." It was a couched dig at the queen, and it was clear then Merlin had no more fucks to give. The idea scared me because it meant my gut was right, yet again. My old friend would soon be gone.

"You questioned why Rylan Fullore would follow you into the Eventide," he continued, "and how he knew you'd be there. You also wondered who followed him into the forest and then chose to leave him for dead." Merlin touched the side of his nose. His signal I was clever and asking the right questions.

"That's all true, and I still have no idea."

He walked toward me, but only to better his vantage point in the room. "Darling girl, haven't you realized there are multiple layers to this plot?"

Moving to his place where everyone's eyes were on him and me, and not on my mother, was strategy of the highest art.

"I do now," I replied, "but what has Rylan and his father's misguided ambition have to do with what happened in New Orleans?"

"Like almost everything in this tangled, politic web, it's all connected. With you at the center. The ones who followed your friend into the Eventide are the ones who retrieved your dagger from the Sluagh and gave it to Rylan."

"The Sluagh had the dagger I used to kill that Fachan?" I asked, confused. "How would they know I was headed to Druitia's temple? That I had planned to use the portal there with Aerith's permission?"

The sharp collective breath at my familiarity with the ancient Leanan Sidhe brought the room to riveted silence. That's right, boys and girls. Suck it. It paid to be respectful and genuine.

"The same goes for Rylan. For Orin," I continued, "and the Sluagh and their Horde. If you were the only one privy to my plans, how did they know I'd be in the Eventide that night and use that fact in setting their mischief in motion?"

He lifted a finger. "Ah. That's the crux of it, right there. The moment my magic transported you to the Eventide, the Nocturna knew. It was all arranged so Rylan would have motive for entering the forest, thus setting the puppet master's wheels in motion. Ambition. The question now begs, whose ambition?"

"Orin. We know that?"

Merlin shook his head. "No, little dove. Orin is a cretin, but he is nonetheless a pawn. Same as his son. The only other player duped in this plot was Lachlan."

The room erupted in a frenzy of shouts, but my mother banged a fist on the council table, shutting them down. The sorcerer had gotten her attention. Finally.

"Think, Eden. Put the puzzle pieces together."

It was as if we were in the sorcerer's tower, and this was another lesson. Another conundrum for me to solve. My eyes took in the knowing look on the old Druid's face. There truly was a method to his madness, and that method was teaching me to think. Critically. Decisively. And most importantly, without judgement.

Merlin wasn't mincing words, but there was double meaning in his tone. Rylan Fullore was a courtier, like his father, and all courtiers were ambitious. Yet neither were far-reaching enough to be the puppet master. I took it apart and examined each event from all ends. The Fullore family crest was a serpent coiled around the base of a five-pointed crown. Five points represented the five main courts of Avalon: Summer, Spring, Winter, Autumn, and Shadow.

I looked at Merlin. "The Fullore crest. The coiled serpent. It has to do with rank."

"And?"

"Their ambition in keeping that rank at all costs."

"Yes?"

"Even if it means selling their loyalty to the highest bidder while hedging their bets."

"Are you saying they are the one's pulling he string in this mischief?"

I shook my head. "No. Absolutely not. They are blinded by their own shallow, selfish wants. The one controlling the strings is much more strategic, with a far reach."

"Very good." The old sorcerer gave me a close-lipped smile. "And who is it that has no real alliances within the established courts? The one whose hunger for power is growing? The one who walks with outcasts?"

I blinked. It's what I'd said earlier. Everyone underestimated outcast Fae. My eyes flew to my mother and then to Merlin. "It's Taltos. He's the puppet master."

Merlin angled his head, his eyes urging me to continue my thought. I kept going. "Taltos is gaining in ground and growing in power. You said it yourself, Mother. He seized the Eventide. Yet you, and the other courts, did nothing to stop him. You have refused to acknowledge him as an equal, and now he is beating you at your own games. Taltos is the hedged bet, and it's not implausible to think Orin Fullore and his son are not the only courtiers who have done so."

Merlin's mustached beard twitched. "So, to answer your questions as to who would have lured Rylan to the Eventide and then leave him for dead? Taltos. Who stands to benefit if Tianna and Lachlan refuse to join forces? Taltos. Who has a deep enough stake in using you and Daire to further their ends? The new King of the Dusk Court. Who hasn't taken history for granted, and knows an alliance between the Seelie and the Unseelie, even a grudging one, would hinder every chance at complete rule?"

"Taltos," I answered for him.

He inclined his head.

My mind spun.

The council room exploded with ministers arguing left and right. The queen sat silent, her fingers drumming the arm of her chair. Taltos. Everything Merlin said made sense. The puzzle pieces fit. An innocent night out. An innocent flirtation that blossomed into more. Both providing Taltos the means for a bigger plan.

"Merlin..." The queen stopped drumming her fingers, and the council hushed. "I have no issue with Taltos manipulating a situation to his ends. Ambition is Sidhe lifeblood."

"Mother, you forget. Taltos is not Sidhe. He's Sluagh. They have a very different view on lifeblood. I should know. I spilled some of theirs in the Eventide."

The queen's nostril flared at my impudence, yet every word I said rang true.

"Yes," she continued, her eyes flinty with me. "I will, of course, discuss the matter further with my council. What I don't quite see is this prophecy. The one Merlin claims is nigh. Taltos has certainly attempted to bring change to the realms, but he can't possibly be the one about whom this prophecy speaks." She turned cold eyes to me. "As my daughter so succinctly pointed out, he is not Sidhe."

"He's not."

"Not Sidhe or not one the prophesied one?"

"He's neither."

"Then whom is this so-called foretelling about?" Tianna asked.

"Eden," Merlin replied without hesitation. "Though, she is but one part."

"One? Then who is the other?"

CHAPTER
Thirty-One

"I'M SORRY, Your Majesty, that part of my vision is still hazy." Merlin rubbed what looked to be a silver ducat in his palm. To anyone else, the fidgeting would seem innocuous. I knew better. Nothing Merlin did was simple, or without purpose.

His fidgeting made him seem nervous. Perhaps that's what he wanted the council to think. I knew it was to call my attention to the coin and make me question why it was in his hand at this precise moment.

"Fine," the queen acquiesced. "If your vision is hazy, then at least give me an idea as to who and where the portends point?"

"I'm afraid I can't do that."

My mother stood from her chair, and the move was more an uncoiling than simply getting to her feet. "Can't—or won't?"

"It's a matter of semantics, Your Majesty. Either way, I have no predictions to share at the moment."

Tianna was quiet. A halcyon veil had fallen over her face, giving the appearance of calm. It was at her most serene that my mother was her most dangerous. "Merlin, I have a proposition," she replied, slowly. "You will return to your chambers to rethink your hesitation in this matter. If you choose to tell me what I want to hear, then all is well with the world. However, if you remain steadfast in your obstinance, you will be exiled to the Badlands and your birds killed." She spread her hands. "The choice is yours."

If you choose to tell me what I want to hear. Those words spoke volumes, and Merlin was no fool. "I see," he countered.

"So, you understand my full meaning?" She arched one perfect brow.

"Let's see what the fates have to say, hmmm?" He lifted his fidget coin for all to see. "Heads, I do. Tails, I don't." The coin flipped in the air, somersaulting before landing in his palm. He turned it over on top of his opposite hand and everyone craned to see.

"Alas...tails."

No one said a word, but many troubled eyes exchanged glances. Merlin's presence at the Summer Court had always been a reassurance. A secret arsenal, just in case. Tianna had drawn a line in the sand, and not to everyone's benefit.

"The fates never toy in matters such as these." Merlin tossed the coin to me, and I caught it. "It seems I have to decline your kind invitation, milady, as I'm needed elsewhere on more pressing matters."

Tianna banged a fist on the council table, but Merlin was gone in a puff of blue smoke. The council was in a confused uproar. No one was happy with my mother. I knew what most thought. If Merlin was no longer obligated to the Seelie queen, then what stopped him from allying with the Unseelie king.

I stared at the coin in my hand, only it wasn't a coin. It was a tricolored stone, no bigger than a silver ducat. I closed my fingers into my palm. Was I seeing things? I moved away from the arguing council and put the coin on an extra chair against the wall. Sure enough, the stone appeared as a coin once more. Merlin had spelled the stone to appear as something harmless, except when in my hand. The old Druid had my back, even in the end. I slipped the coin into my pocket.

"Everyone! Please!" Aldric Bannerol pounded the council table. "Shouting will get us nowhere. We all know the magician is as wily as he is gifted. He hasn't gone anywhere."

"How do you know, Aldric? You heard the queen. She gave him an ultimatum, and he thumbed his nose at her."

I didn't know the name of the councilor pointing the finger at my mother, but the queen's serene mask slipped a bit, and it was frightening.

To say the man's sphincter puckered was an understatement, even though every word he said was true.

"Enough!" Tianna's fingers pressed into the table. "I will deal with Merlin as I have from the beginning. I know him. I know his strengths, and I know his weaknesses." Her gaze slid to me as if she knew I was one of the latter. "Escort Lady Eden back to her chambers. It's time she put these shenanigans with the Unseelie prince aside and took up her role as my heir in the traditional sense, and what better way to uphold that tradition than for me to choose her a consort."

My heart dropped to my stomach. She wouldn't do that to me just to get back at Merlin. "Mother, please don't. I love Daire. With everything I am!"

"All the more reason to nip this in the bud. You will wed a consort of my choosing from the Spring Court, and you will do so in one month's time. Long enough to send invitations and arrange your bridal party. Our pleasure gardens will make the perfect venue now that everything is in bloom." She inhaled, straightening. "In fact, we should throw a ball announcing your betrothal."

"Mother, please!"

Tianna ignored me. "The more I think of it, the more I like the idea. A betrothal ball. Two weeks from today. Since this is a royal affair, perhaps I should invite the heads of all the main courts, including the Unseelie."

Her eyes were ice cold when they met mine. This wasn't just to punish Merlin. This was to hurt me. All the reasoning, all the critical thinking in exposing Taltos and his real threat was for naught. The queen had learned nothing.

I stood on the small round platform being poked and pinned for hours. Dresses for my trousseau had been ordered, along with every conceivable accessory. Not just for me, but for Sorcha too. She was to be my maid of honor, though my groom had yet to be chosen.

"I heard Mother has narrowed her list down to two candidates."

Sorcha sat on a plush chair watching me like a gilded bird. Funny, really. That's how I described myself to Merlin all those weeks ago. A royal dove in a gilded cage.

Little dove. My chest squeezed thinking about Merlin. I missed my friend, and I missed Daire so much it hurt. I still had Sorcha, but she was as resigned as me these days, and that made me sadder than I was for myself. Her wings had been clipped. Another of Tianna's serene tantrums to hurt me.

"Edie, are you listening to me?"

I exhaled a tired breath. "I heard you, Sissy. I don't care how many courtiers Mother parades in front of her throne, or how many dresses she orders. I refuse to get married."

The dressmakers froze with pins in their mouths. I glanced down at them, not caring who they told. "You heard me. Spread the word. Princess Eden said no. N.O."

Knock. Knock.

Sorcha got up from her chair to open the door to the queen's informal anteroom. My mother wanted me where she could see me, so all my fittings and wedding planning was done front and center. She'd tolerate no mistakes.

A footman carried in a tray with food. I had refused to eat, but that didn't stop the trays from coming. I allowed myself just enough, so I didn't keel over, but if the queen was trying to sell a plump partridge, whoever brokered this deal would get skin and bones for a bride.

"This pseudo-hunger strike is getting annoying, Edie. What good will you be to yourself or to me if you're too weak to fight back?" Sorcha took a sandwich and munched in her chair.

"I'm done fighting. If Mother wants me married, she'll have to prop me up like a mannequin."

"This isn't you, Edie. You sound like a dummy."

"Well, if the mannequin fits..."

She threw a grape at me, and it bounced off the hard-boned corset dress and down the front of the modiste's blouse.

"Ha! Two points." Sorcha mugged a self-satisfied grin.

The dressmaker was not as amused, and she and the other modiste put down their pin cushions and left for lunch.

"Ugh. Help me out of this before I stick myself with their pins, bleed all over the fabric, and they have to start again." I lifted my arms chest height, wiggling my fingers at my sister.

Sorcha unbuttoned the entire back, helping me step free of the iridescent white gown. "It's too bad. The gown is already stunning, and it's not even finished. Imagine how gorgeous it'll be when it's done."

"You wear it, then. Tell Mother you want to marry Cian. She'll be thrilled." My sister smiled, but her eyes wouldn't meet mine. "Sissy? What is it?"

"I am marrying Cian. It's been arranged. Six months after you're settled. Mother and Aldric already agreed."

My eyes went wide, and I gripped her shoulders from the small platform. "Are you happy about this? I can't tell. When we were in New Orleans, I swore you were head over heels for Cian. Daire thought so, too. Was I wrong?"

"You're not wrong." Sorcha's eyes met mine, and they were wet.

"What then? Is Mother sending Cian away right after your wedding? Are you both being sent somewhere awful?"

She laughed at that, probably because none of it was unthinkable. Not when it came to our mother. "No, nothing's wrong. In fact, I'm so happy I could bust and shoot glitter all over the room."

"As opposed to vomiting glitter all over Bourbon Street." I winked, and Sorcha threw her arms around my neck pulling me down off the platform.

"It'll be okay, Edie. I promise. I'll help make it okay."

Hugging her back, I choked down my own sadness. Sorcha was happy, and that made me happy. "At least one of us got their happily ever after with a man they actually love."

"Gods, Edie. What are we going to do?"

I pulled free from Sorcha, and I wiped her cheeks with both my thumbs. "Like you said. We'll make it okay." I took her hand, tugging her toward the anteroom door. "I couldn't care less about that dress or anything else Mother ordered for this charade. Let's go watch a movie and stuff ourselves with candy."

"What about your hunger strike?"

I glanced over my shoulder at the dress crumpled on the platform.

"I've switched strategies. Why should I make myself suffer any more than I already am?"

"I thought you wanted to give them a bony bride?"

"Not anymore. To market, to market to buy a fat piggie..."

She laughed, hugging me to her side. "Home again, home again, jiggety jig."

Four hours and an entire bowl of peanut M&M's later, Sorcha was in a sugar coma on the couch in my bedroom. The credits rolled on the second movie we watched, and I got up to snap off the video. "What humans lack in magic, they make up for in technology." I murmured those words the night I fought my way through the Eventide so I could see Daire. I lied to Sorcha. I wasn't done fighting. I was just tired.

I dug in my nightstand drawer for the burner phone from New Orleans. It was in my back pocket when we portal jumped from Club X, and Caxton hadn't confiscated it. Yet. Probably because he didn't know I still had it.

I sat on the bed and scrolled through the pictures. Me and Daire. Happy. Very much in love. Laughing together, and with Cian and Sorcha. These pics would have to last me a lifetime if my mother had her way. I could resist all I wanted, but in Seelie, a marriage only required a contract, and that would be signed two and a half weeks from now. My mother would choose one of the two courtiers still in the running and it would be game over. My only chance at happiness would be escaping to the human realm and disappearing into the throng of humanity.

Actually, that wasn't such a bad idea. Except all portals were guarded to the point of pain. Even Sorcha couldn't bribe her way out of Seelie. More specifically, the palace.

I needed Merlin. He'd find a way.

The tricolor stone was still on my dresser. I had tried stepping on it. But it wouldn't crush. I tried putting it in running water like the sprites said to do with their summoning wish. Nothing. The stupid thing wouldn't soften in my palm, nor did it change in sunlight or moonlight. What was Merlin's plan in giving me the stone if there was no aim?

His words went round and round in my head. "Sometimes the smallest detail will show you all you need to solve a dilemma." What was I missing? I picked up the smooth stone from my dresser and held it in my palm. "Dammit, Merlin! Talk to me!"

The slate blue strip at the center of the stone shimmered. "Smallest detail, right." I tossed the stone onto my bed, not sure if it would explode or send me whirling somewhere.

An azure cloud rose from the shimmering blue strip, and I heard Merlin's chuckle. "Clever you, little dove. You figured out the secret of the stone."

"Merlin?"

A shifting image of my old friend appeared in the blue cloud, similarly to the way he appeared in the bonfire. He inclined his head.

"Are you real or is this a spelled message?"

He laughed, and his blue eyes twinkled. "You're getting very good at asking the right questions." He tapped the side of his nose. "I am real, just no longer in your time and space continuum."

"The queen has picked a consort for me, Merlin. She's forcing me to marry."

"I expected as much. My hopes for your mother having an epiphany have long died, little dove. The future of your realm lies with you, and with Sorcha. She will have to lead in your stead, for I fear you will be hunted worse than you were before."

"Why?"

"It is not for me to say. It is only for me to help when the time comes."

"You're doing your cryptic thing again. I thought we put that behind us."

His eyes crinkled. "Whatever made you think that?"

"Mother is hosting a betrothal ball this weekend. Every royal house is represented. She even invited Lachlan, which means she hoped he'd bring Daire. She's hurting me at every turn, Merlin. Salt in my wounds."

"If he comes, then you make the night your own. Your mother would never have Daire removed if formal invitations went out. She'd lose face in front of the other royals."

"Lachlan already refused his invitation."

"Then you invite Daire yourself. Send the invitation. There is so much correspondence going back and forth, I guarantee you can slip the invitation in unawares."

"I'm watched day and night. It's impossible."

"Use the fire, little dove. Remember the bonfire?"

I scoffed. "I haven't the skill, Merlin. You never taught me those kinds of scrying spells."

"Oh, but I did, my darling girl. Think back to the poem I made you recite as a child."

"Fire comes with warmth and glow,
a thing you can ignite.
In flames I see what I would know,
It carries me through the night.
My voice, my face, a message now,
deliver straight tonight."

Merlin nodded. "It's a spell. Like a deprogrammed, unsanctioned portal, all you have to do is say the destination, and in this case it's with whom you wish to speak."

"Are you saying I could talk to Daire right now? Tonight?"

"Yes, but heed me, Eden. You must instruct the flames for his eyes only. Simply add a line of rhyme to the spell. It's easy once you try. If you don't, the scrying spell will become corrupted and there's no time to teach you another."

"I wish you had told me this sooner. It could've saved me some heartache."

"I'm sorry, little dove. Everything in its own time. Which is the other warning. Fire scrying is limited in scope and time, so be succinct. Use it sparingly and only for important instructions."

I smiled wryly. "So, it's more text than phone call."

"Eden..."

"Give me this one, Merlin, I haven't smiled in almost a week."

"The time is nigh, daughter of my heart. I will see you again."

"Wait! How will I reach you? What are these other colors on the stone?"

"The silver is a cross key to the Middle Course. Use it only as a last resort. The black strip is not to be used. Not unless I give you leave. It is to the Forbidden Realm. If you try to use it, it could kill you and anyone with you. Promise, Eden. Do not attempt it without my go ahead."

I nodded. "Of course, Merlin. Is it the same as the cold portal on Daire's island?"

"Yes. The same rule goes for that gateway. Not without leave."

"Will the fire spell reach you if I need you?"

I had never seen Merlin shrug, but he did with a small laugh. "I've never tried from here, so who knows." His face softened in the blue shimmer. "Take care, my darling girl. I will see you again."

The stone went flat again. The shimmer reabsorbing into the gray rock. The blue strip was gone, leaving only the silver and black. The Middle Course. Daire could get to the in between from the portal on the island. Or at least he used to. Fire, fire burning bright. My love and I will speak tonight...I hoped.

CHAPTER
Thirty~Two

FIRE SCRYING WAS an epic failure two nights in a row. I hadn't been able to reach Daire, which sent my anxiety through the roof. Was he hurt? Was he dead? Had Lachlan banished him the way my mother threatened Merlin? Or worse. Had he been married off to a consort from the Autumn Court?

The betrothal ball was beginning, and I was to meet the man who would be my consort. For such an advanced race, the Sidhe were backward when it came to marriage. Then again, when was marriage touted as something you did for love? It was a pact. A contract. Something to be signed, sealed, and delivered. Convenient. Political. And definitely for gain.

My ballgown held no mystique. It was sheer down my sides, leaving me commando underneath. *Commando.* The word conjured all kinds of memories. Happy. Wanton. And now, sad. Did Daire remember? Or had he moved on by force same as me? What I wouldn't give to see him again. Talk to him again. Even if it was for one night.

Gold trimmed the shimmering green fabric and spun gold mesh formed the sheer illusion down my sides. The dress was so tight I couldn't breathe, and I expected tiny x marks in my skin from the mesh, from my armpits to my thighs. It wasn't this tight at the beginning of the week, but I had been gorging myself after giving up my half-hearted hunger strike.

I felt ridiculous in this gown, and I wondered if this was a last dig courtesy of the queen before she handed me to the highest bidder.

The door to my bedroom cracked open, and Sorcha poked her head in. "Are you ready?" She pushed the door the rest of the way open, and I grinned at her. She looked beautiful.

"Sissy, if you intended to leave Cian breathless tonight, you succeeded. You're stunning."

She smiled. "I wish I could say the same about you, but that dress is a horror." She clapped her hands. "C'mon. You are *not* wearing that, and I don't care what Mother says."

Sorcha took over, and with a single fingernail, tore the gold mesh straight down one side. "Oops. Too much candy."

I laughed so hard I snorted. It felt good, like the old Edie and Sorcha.

"Too much candy is an understatement. I thought the modiste would burst a blood vessel with how she struggled dressing me. Plus, everything hurts. My boobs, especially. They're swollen and tender. And I think my pseudo hunger strike messed up my stomach. I can't keep anything down unless its sugar."

"Are you sick?"

"Lately, yeah. It's weird."

Sorcha stared at me. "Edie, I think lately is the operative word. Or more likely, *late* is the key. When's the last time you bled?"

"What do you mean?"

"Your moon time. When was the last time?"

I did a quick calculation. "The week before the Winter gala, why?"

"That party was a month ago. Edie, I think you might be pregnant."

Her words swept my knees out from under me, and I had to reach for the end of my bed. "No. I can't be. It's too soon." I shook my head. "Besides, Daire and I were only together a handful of times in New Orleans."

"Yeah, and that was a little over two weeks ago. When were you due for your moon time?"

I sunk to my mattress, counting the days in my head. "Oh, my gods." I had never been late for my moon time. Ever. And now I was a week late. My gaze jerked to my sister. "What am I going to do?"

"Right now? Nothing. You are going to get dressed and go downstairs with me. We'll figure this out together."

My head spun. I couldn't focus. "I can't, Sissy. I can't pretend like nothing's wrong. This whole arranged marriage is a mistake, and now I'm pregnant with Daire's child?" I jerked to my feet, panicked. "I am *not* passing this baby off as someone else's. No way. No how."

"No one is suggesting that. Take a minute and breathe. First things first. We need a pregnancy test. If you *are* pregnant, then Daire needs to be told. I'm not sure how or when, but we'll figure it out. At present, you need to keep your cool. Let's not throw the baby out with the bathwater."

"That's a horrible saying."

Sorcha laughed, smoothing my curls. "Yes, it is, but it's funny as hell."

"If I am pregnant, then Daire needs to be told *now*. Not after Tianna forces this marriage on me. I want him to know so we can decide what to do, together. Before it's too late."

"C'mon. Let's get you dressed and down those stairs. I've got money on you, so let's go."

"Money on me, how? That I give Tianna a fat lip?"

"Something like that."

My sister helped me pick a different gown, one of deep midnight blue. Storm blue. The same color as Daire's eyes. It was the color of the Winter Court, and I picked it for just that reason. If I was carrying Daire's child, I wanted to feel close to him tonight.

"Change that gold jewelry for silver, or better yet, diamonds, and let's go." Sorcha clapped. "Chop, chop. We have an entrance to make, and I want to make it memorable."

Maybe she and Cian were planning to whisk me away, and the three of us would get drunk on lemon drop martinis and dance in the sand. Could pregnant Fae drink? I knew from movies the answer was no for human women, but Sidhe? I was so out of my element.

I walked to the top of the stairs above the grand hall. I linked my elbow with Sorcha's, and she squeezed my arm. "From womb to tomb, Twinly."

"From womb to tomb." It was what Sorcha and I told each other as children when we had no one else. We started life together, and whatever happened in between, we would be there for each other in the end. Knowing there might be a little life inside me now gave that old comfort a whole new meaning.

Music played in the grand hall. Courtiers from every realm mingled and laughed, drank, and waited. Each assessed the other, taking mental notes. I spotted my mother at the center of it all. She was impeccable. As beautiful and regal as always, and tonight she was all smiles and gaiety. This was her moment, and I merely her pawn. It was how she'd planned it from the beginning, and silly me thought I could change things.

"Carpe Noctem, Edie. Seize the night."

The music changed, and that was our cue to descend the grand staircase. The queen would be at the first landing with my intended and his mother and father. I had no idea who it was, and I didn't care. I wasn't about to give an inch, especially not now. If that embarrassed Tianna, too bad.

Sorcha and I headed down the steps. We made the turn toward the first landing and the great reveal. My heart sank. Rylan stood with Orin Fullore and his second wife. Sorcha exchanged a look with me, and I balked.

"Oh, hell no." I turned on my heel and headed back up the stairs.

"Edie, wait!"

Sorcha caught me at the top step. "Don't do this. Please."

"Why do you care? Did you know about this stunt?"

Her chin went up, and a pang of guilt bit me at the hurt look in my sister's eyes.

"I'm sorry, Sissy. I know you didn't. You're just trying to protect me, and I love you for it, but I cannot stand beside Rylan and his two-faced father with a smile on my face."

"Please. It's important. Cian and I will keep the old man away from you. Maybe talk to Rylan. See what he has to say about this. Remember, he was a pawn too."

I stamped my foot. "Mother knows Orin sold his soul to Taltos! How could she do this? Do we need a vote of no confidence because I'm starting to think she's dropped her basket."

"The music is still playing. We can fix this. Cian and I will not let you down."

I inhaled, steeling myself. "Keep that grasping cretin away from me, or I don't know what I'll do."

"I will. I promise. Just get to the entrance hall. I promise it will be better."

We walked the stairs again, and I glared at my mother as I took my place on the landing.

"What was that little snit about," she whispered through a saccharin smile, doing her royal wave from on high.

"Fuck you, Tianna. Fuck you with a Redcap's pike, hard and sideways until you bleed from every conceivable orifice and die." I said it loud enough for everyone on the landing to hear and then let my own halcyon veil fall into place hiding my fury.

"You'll pay for that."

"I already have, so shut up. You wanted a windup toy for your charade tonight, you got it, but without my signature, there is no marriage contract, and I refuse. N. Fucking. O. NO!"

"You'll sign, or I'll take everything you love from you. Your life will be a misery."

"There's nothing left for you to take. Unless you mean Sorcha, and she's your spare, so there goes that plan."

Tianna would never know about this baby. I couldn't risk it. I had to escape from here, but how? Merlin said the Middle Course, but only as a last resort. Well, old friend, this was it. I needed to disappear into the human realm, and I knew just the people in the Middle Course to help. I checked my pocket for Merlin's stone. I wasn't taking any chances, even if it meant going with the clothes on my back.

"Enough. We will discuss this later. Our guests are waiting."

"No, Mother. *Your* guests are waiting."

Orin cleared his throat. "Shouldn't we be descending, Your Majesty? Rylan, take Eden's hand."

"Yes, Rylan. Do." I snorted. "I'm surprised your father let you have your balls tonight. I hear he keeps them in his back pocket, but you certainly upped your cred from when he left you in the Eventide to die. Oh, but that was because he sold you to Taltos. Didn't you know?"

"Eden."

I ignored my mother. "Probably not, because all these secret deals were changing hands. It's no wonder dear ol' Dad had no way to rescue you when all hell broke loose in the forest, and Taltos broke his end of the bargain. You remember what happened in the forest, right, Rylan? The Dearg Due attacked you, ripping your body with its fangs to get to your blood. I had a run in with bloodsuckers too, only mine were of the undead variety. Another of Taltos's futile attempts.

"Have you asked why you had to suffer that fate? I'll tell you. It's because Taltos didn't get me the way your father promised. So, I can only assume this farce of a marriage is Plan B. To deliver me to the Lord of the Sluagh, so he can rule the Summer Court, with me as his puppet. Probably the way he's doing with my mother." I laughed. "Hedging bets, right?"

"Shut your mouth! You have no idea what's at stake." Orin's face turned purple.

"Aw, nice to be validated. You know, you are as much a whore as my mother. Not because she enjoys sex, but because she sold herself in this deal, like every other common, grasping, courtier in this room."

"Common?" Tianna balked.

Out of everything I said, that was what irked my mother most? I shook my head. "Yes, Tianna. Common. Ordinary. Boring. Unremarkable." I raised an eyebrow. "Get the picture, or should I open a thesaurus and explain further?"

So much for my halcyon veil of serenity. I walked down the stairs with Sorcha, leaving that farce of a wedding party behind.

"Wow. I should've bet on verbal sparring instead of a right hook. I owe Cian ten silver ducats, but damn, that was worth it."

I laughed. "I'll pay Cian. There's more to come if they get anywhere near me tonight."

The night was soft, and I spent most of my time outside with my sister and my future brother-in-law. I loved the sound of that, and I couldn't be happier for them. Still, I didn't want them embroiled in this. I had already made up my mind. I was leaving. Which meant Sorcha's eyes would change to emerald and the mantel would fall to her to keep our batshit, treasonous mother in check.

"Look, I want you two to get married immediately. Don't wait." I grabbed both Cian and Sorcha's hands. "If there's one thing this past month, or so, has taught me, it's take whatever happiness is offered. Don't wait."

Cian eyed me. He had gotten to know me so well while we were in the human realm, and I wanted to tell him about the change in my circumstances, but I didn't. Same as I wasn't planning on telling them about heading to the Middle Course tonight. Plausible deniability. It was more important now than ever.

As for me, there was no reason to stick around. I knew how to contact Merlin if I needed, and I'm sure Aerith would find a way to get word to Daire. I only hoped he wasn't facing a marriage coup on his end.

"Sorcha, is something going on with your sister I should know about?"

I nodded. "Sorcha already knows, and I'm sure she'll tell you as soon as it's safe to do so. I only ask that you both keep my secret."

"What secret?"

Sorcha pulled him down to the low marble bench where we sat at the edge of the veranda. The party had spilled into the pleasure gardens, and I longed to walk by myself. Maybe even head to the beach. Whatever was about to happen, this was still my home, and I wanted to say goodbye.

"You two find some time to be alone. I meant what I said. Don't wait to get married. Even if it means you do it on the sly. Once the contracts are signed, it's too late. Don't let Tianna pull a fast one on you." I nodded. "Because she will if it suits her." I got up from the bench to walk toward the wide steps leading to the lawn.

"Wait!" Sorcha grabbed my hand. "You can't go yet."

I angled my head, doubting her sudden need to keep me on the veranda. "What's going on? You know I'm a sitting duck out here for uncomfortable questions I'm not about to answer."

"I know, but—"

"What Sorcha means is if you leave, you'll ruin my entrance."

I whirled around to peer over the edge of the railing. Daire stood in the shadows with his wonderful, crooked smile. "I thought your father declined the invitation."

Daire shrugged. "He couldn't have declined, because we were never invited."

"She lied." Anger warred with bliss, but I had to laugh. "Why am I surprised? Everything that comes out of that woman's mouth is a lie."

Sorcha hugged me. "I didn't tell him, but you should. Tonight. Whatever you decide, I support you. Both."

Her words were quiet and for my ears only. I squeezed her harder. "I love you too. Even if that means it's from far away."

She froze for a millisecond but then stepped back with a nod. "I understand. I also get why you're telling me not to wait to get married."

"Tag, you're it, green eyes."

"I hate this, Edie. You've got to know that."

I nodded. "I do, but it can't be helped. If I stay, it's not just *my* life I put in danger." I hugged her quickly again and then raced down the stairs and into Daire's arms.

CHAPTER
Thirty-Three

HIS ARMS WERE around me in an instant, and it was like we'd never been apart. "If no invitation came, then how are you here? The portals are locked."

"Your old friend." He stepped back to reach into his pocket. When he pulled out his hand, there was a smooth stone in his palm. The same kind of stone Merlin had given me the night of the Winter gala. "Don't ask me how, but it came in a pouch attached to an owl."

I laughed, and the sound was a relief. Altair and Lyrae had gotten out with their master. "You have no idea how much we owe that bird. How long do we have?"

"That's just it. There's no time limit on the stone. He said to use it in case of emergency. To everyone except you, Sorcha, and Cian, I look very different." He stepped back in a courtly bow, spreading his arms. "Same me. Different wrapper."

I threw my arms around him again. "Let's go. I know some place quiet where we can talk. There's something I need to tell you."

We raced along the shadows for the abandoned shed I'd shown the sprites. The key was exactly where I'd left it, and we headed for the stone stairs to the beach. The waves were soft, the sound calming my nerves.

Not that I was worried about what Daire would say. I just didn't know how to start.

"What is it, love? You look like you need to pace."

I pulled him to sit beside me on a fallen branch, keeping his hands in mine. "Daire. We've known each other a little over a month."

"Five weeks, and two days, to be exact," he replied.

I nodded. "Yes, well. In that time, we've gotten close. Closer than close..."

"Eden, are you trying to propose to me?"

Breath left my lungs in a sort of gurgled grunt. "What? No. I mean, I'd love to marry you, but no. That's not what I'm struggling to tell you."

"Good, because I came here planning to propose to you." He knelt in the sand and then reached into a different pocket for a ring., a beautiful ring. A large sapphire the color of his eyes. "Eden Aossi, will you be my wife?"

I nodded, not trusting my voice.

"I'm going to need to hear an actual yes." He laughed. "Just to be sure."

"Yes, you Winter jerk! A thousand times yes!"

With a grin, he slipped the ring on my hand and then gathered me in his arms. "We'll need to leave here. Tonight. Together. I can get us to the island and then from there we can use the portal to the Middle Course. I've used that portal before to get to the human realm. I think we'll be safe there."

"Funny you should say that." I pulled back so I could see his eyes. "We need some place safe because...we're going to have a baby."

His mouth dropped, and he blinked.

"I know it's a shock. It was to me too. I haven't even taken a pregnancy test, but I have all the early signs. I wasn't sure how I would get word to you, but then you were here, and now you've asked me to marry you, and we have to leave. It's all a huge clusterfuck."

"Wow. Did you rehearse that ramble?"

I punched his shoulder. "That's all you have to say, Daire Dannean? I'm having your baby, probably...most likely...and you're upset I'm rambling?"

"You're doing it again."

"Daire!"

He gathered me close, kissing the side of my head by my ear. "A marriage, a baby, a new life. I couldn't be happier."

"Are you sure?" I pulled away from him again, watching his face. "We're both giving up what we know for what we don't."

"Is that so." His mouth went from smiling to a thin slash. "Let me tell you what I'm giving up. I'm giving up being my father's pawn. His puppet. I'm giving up being forced to choose a wife from the most insipid, vacuous group of girls known to the universe. Simply because they have the right pedigree."

I laughed. "At least Lachlan was letting you choose. Do you know who my mother settled on for me? Rylan Fullore. There's something underhanded with her agreement with his father. I can feel it. I think my mother sold her throne to Taltos, as long as she can stay the realm figurehead." I shook my head, clearing the noise. "I don't care anymore. Sorcha knows the heir apparency is now hers, and she's okay with it, I guess. I think it would be different if I wasn't pregnant."

"Bain has no idea he's it, and I don't care. If Lachlan gave a flying fig, he'd have trained my brother as well, instead of letting him be a forever frat boy."

A twig snap had me whirling to my feet. Daire pushed me behind his hip and we both held our breath. It could've been anyone. A couple looking for a tryst in the dunes or a midnight swim.

"I watched her come this way, sir," a male voice called. "She wasn't alone."

I motioned for Daire to follow me down the beach. We hurried, rushing hand in hand but keeping to the shadows. "There's a cave near the curve of the peninsula, and we can wait there until the coast is clear."

"You hate caves."

"Not so much anymore. Your grotto changed my perspective."

"There! It's her! On the beach!"

"One of you tell the queen! They won't get far now!"

It was Caxton and a squad of his men. "Shit," I mumbled under my breath. "It's the captain of my mother's personal guard. He must've had people watching me." I scanned the shadows for a safe place for us to use

Merlin's stone. "We have to go now, Daire. Crush underfoot and boom. Easy peasy."

"We'll have nothing, Edie. Just the clothes on our backs."

I went up on tip toe to kiss him quickly. "We'll have each other. Once we get to the Middle Course, Aerith will help."

With a nod, he dropped the stone on a flat rock in the sand and then wrapped his arm around my waist. "Ready?"

I nodded.

"There! They're getting ready to jump!"

"The portals are closed! They can't!"

"Go! Stop her!"

Daire crushed the stone under his heel, but the cross key spewed a sliver of a shimmer and then nothing. "Shit!"

"What happened? Why didn't it work?"

"I don't know, but we don't have time to figure it out." Caxton's men raced toward us in the sand. Daire grabbed my hand pulling me toward the dunes. "We'll have to run for it."

"No, we won't. I'm not sure if, or how this will work, but I've got a backup plan." I took Merlin's tricolor stone from my pocket and rubbed the silver strip with my thumb. "Middle Course!"

I made sure to say the destination clearly, and in an instant, a silver mist rose from the stone's surface. "This should be fast. I hope." The cross-key mist enveloped us, and whoosh! The next thing I knew, Daire and I stumbled into a dimly lit tunnel.

The stone was still in my hand, so I stowed it in my pocket. For the time being, its magic was spent. Still, Merlin was in the Forbidden Realm, so I needed to keep the stone just in case. The old Druid never said he was with Arthur and Guinevere for sure, but my gut told me that's where he'd escaped, knowing my mother couldn't follow.

Merlin's directive warned "not until I give you leave," when it came to the stone's Forbidden Realm portal. That told me that going there was a possibility at some point in the future and maybe meeting the fabled once and future king and his queen. When? Who knew? Daire and I had bigger problems. Like getting away from my mother and her jackals.

"Have any idea where we are?" I asked, glancing down a corridor that looked as though it had been carved with pickaxes and chisels.

He nodded. "We're in the dwarves' passage. It's relatively safe, or at least it was the last time I was here." Daire felt along the walls, both hands hunting for something.

"What are you doing?"

"I stowed a portal key in a crevice somewhere along this stretch of rock on my last visit."

I watched him, chewing my lip. Something didn't feel right. The cross-key Merlin had supposedly sent had failed. If Merlin had truly sent that cross key, that wouldn't have been the case. Merlin didn't make novice mistakes.

"Daire, can you describe the owl that brought you the cross key?" I asked, trying not to sound accusatory.

His fingers trailed a long crevice. "He was mostly gray with black feathers and a white underbelly. Why?"

"I think we just escaped another set up. Merlin's owl is the color of wet sand with brown feathers. It wasn't Altair that delivered that stone, and the note wasn't from my sorcerer. I think perhaps Morgana may be involved with Taltos or whoever is currently in bed with the Sluagh lord."

"Like your mother?"

The real possibility hit like a brick. "I'm ashamed to say, it might be. She banished Merlin, or more accurately, he left before she could banish him, leaving her without magical backup. It makes sense she would try and entice Morgana away from the Winter Court. You said Lachlan clipped her wings. My mother undoubtedly dangled a carrot if Morgana proved herself in this small task."

"If my cross key had worked, do you think it would've taken us to the island?"

I shook my head. "No, I don't. I think it was meant to detain us somewhere we couldn't escape."

"You're still chewing on your lip. What else is racing through that clever mind?"

A pleased smirk touched my mouth. Daire still had his back to me, hunting for his key. I loved that he thought I was clever as well as beautiful.

"Tell me. I don't need to turn around to see your wheels spinning."

"Fine. We're in the Dwarves Passage. A part of the Middle Course you're familiar with, yet I didn't tell the cross key to take us here. The in between has hundreds of tunnels leading to caverns and subterranean towns. How did we end up here? And don't say coincidence."

"When we were just about to jump, this part of the Middle Course popped into my head. I didn't utter a word because I didn't want to screw up our last chance at escape." He grunted, reaching toward the higher crevices. "Damn. I thought the key was here."

I looked both ways down the tunnel and then listened. "Do you hear dripping water?"

"Of course. There are a bunch of underground springs that feed the in between. How else would the lesser Fae and other inhabitants survive?"

I grinned, reaching inside my pocket for both my dragon pendant and the sprites' summoning wish. "I think my good luck charms are about to pay off."

"You wear those all the time. You never said they were good luck charms."

"I should've told you what they are, or more precisely what they represent. This one is a pendant Merlin gave me when he first told me you and I were connected. A dragon for you, and one for me. One green eyed. One blue eyed. It was supposed to act as a portal key when I got to Druitia's temple in the Eventide, but Merlin didn't trust me not to lose it. So, he made me a living portal key instead."

"Wait. What?"

I told him the story, and he lifted the pendant from my hand to kiss the heart shape before slipping the necklace over my head.

"And this?" He dangled the coin shaped pendant from his fingers.

"It's called a Toghairm Mian. Or a summoning wish. Kip and York gave it to me before they had to escape to the Middle Course with Aerith." I told him the story as well, this time in more detail. "All we need is running water, and they said they would do the rest."

"What does that mean? Do the rest."

"I have no idea, but I trust the sprites. Why don't we see if my presence opens the portal first? If it doesn't, we can try and summon Kip and York."

Daire looked up and down the rock corridor as well. "Portal first, right."

"You do remember where it is, yes?"

He exhaled, raking a hand through his hair. "I'm sorry, Eden. I thought I'd remember but I haven't been here the last few years."

I saw frustration building, and we didn't need that. So far, so good, that no one from either court followed us. It was still a possibility they might, so we needed to move on. The last thing I wanted was our presence to bring trouble here, the same way my presence had in the Eventide.

"It's okay, Daire. We'll find it, but it's important we stay calm. There's always another way. Let's find some running water."

We followed the echoes, listening, and the trickling grew louder. Muffled voices pierced the relative silence, and I looked at Daire. "Do you remember who lives down this way?"

"I think it might be a small band of Hobgoblins, but I'm not sure. If memory serves, the village they served was razed when a manmade lake was installed. All the houses were abandoned and the families relocated, so with no one to serve, the Hobgoblins moved to the in between."

"They're kissing cousins to Brownies, right?"

"In that they are house Fae and do simple chores in exchange for food while the family they serve sleeps, then yes. Like Brownies, Hobgoblins are peaceful but easily annoyed."

I snorted. "Sounds like Sorcha, sometimes. Peaceful, yet easily annoyed."

The narrow passage branched in two directions, one dark with no sound or signs of life, and the other leading toward a carved archway.

"Okay. Which way?"

He pointed toward the archway. "I know where I am, now. Ahead is Rawenril; it was an encampment that became a town. We can find whatever we need there, including running water."

The path swung toward the left, and we walked through the curved archway. The sound of voices blurred amid telltales sounds of village life, and I smiled. "Maybe we can stay here for a bit. At least until we find our feet."

"I'm not sure about that. Everyone in Rawenril has to pull their weight. I don't think there's much call for ex-Sidhe royalty."

"You seem to forget I'm pretty handy with a sword." I pursed my lips, waiting for his retort.

"That's very true. You are good with a sword, but you don't have your weapon with you." He smirked, but he took my hand and kissed the tops of my knuckles. "Your jewelry, on the other hand, might fetch us something. Lodging. Food. Maybe even more appropriate clothes."

"We've been betrothed for all of an hour or so, I am not bartering my ring. Nor am I trading my pendants. The rest of my jewelry, fine."

He shook his head. "The diamonds we keep. When we get to the human realm, there are plenty of places willing to pay for gold and gemstones."

The path through the arch overlooked the town below. The place was vibrant. Alive with everyday comings and goings. The rhythm of real life, instead of the banal, repetitive existence at court.

Winding our way down, the path spilled into the main street. There were market stalls and vendors selling every kind of ware. Food stuff, not so much. "Is food scarce in the Middle Course?" I asked.

"It didn't used to be."

We walked through the center of town, taking in the sights and smells, until Daire spotted a familiar locale. "The hammer and anvil," he said, pointing to the sign swinging from a post. "If memory serves, this is a pretty good inn. We can get a room and decide what to do next."

"I thought we already decided. Find the portal."

I must've spoke a little too loudly because the people working at the surrounding stalls went silent, as did their customers. "Oi! There's no portal here. Not anymore. So, you best be on your way."

The deep voice belonged to a rather large, hairy hybrid creature. I couldn't tell the mix, but if I had to venture a guess, I'd say a cross between a Halfling and a Boggart. Which would account for his semi-human-like features.

"What happened to the portal?" Daire asked. "I haven't visited Rawenril in a few years, but it hasn't changed that much."

The half-Boggart sized us up and down. "You look like you've been to a party. A fancy dress one at that. What be the occasion?"

I watched the interaction. The creature didn't answer Daire's question. Was that intentional, or was he just easily distracted?

"We've come from our betrothal," Daire replied, taking my hand. "We are to be wed."

For some reason, that seemed to pacify the creature's irascibility for a moment, and he nodded. "Well, congrats to you both. That's lovely." He even smiled, and I was surprised he had a full complement of blunt white teeth. I don't know why, but I expected them to be sharp and yellow.

"I had an acquaintance who lived here years ago, but we lost touch. Perhaps you know him." Daire inquired. "Trord Zagtaal. He's a—"

"Silver Dwarf," the half-Boggart chimed in with another smile, so I guessed it was okay we asked. "Old Trord retired to Sliwendon, on the other side of the in between. He was a lovely neighbor. We were sorry to see him go."

He angled his head, eyeing us differently now. "What did you say your name was?"

"Jay." Daire inclined his head. "And this is Daisy, my betrothed."

"Pleased to meet you both. I go by the name Loll. If I told you my full name, you'd never be able to pronounce it, so it's just Loll."

He turned his big head toward me. "That's a mighty pretty necklace you're wearing. I've only seen one double dragon pendant like that. It belonged to someone I knew, too many years ago to count. Sorcerer, he was."

"Was his name Merlin?" I asked, and Loll's bulgy eyes went wider than I thought possible.

"That's right." His eyes fixed a little too intently on me. "How did you know?"

Did his scrutiny mean something or was it just his way? "He was a friend of my father's," I replied with the first tap dance that came to mind. "Unfortunately, he's gone now."

The half-Boggart's frown made his face crumble in on itself. "Merlin is immortal. You lie." His last word left his mouth like a hiss.

"No, you misunderstood! I didn't mean Merlin died. I meant my father had passed on. I don't know anything about the magician. I haven't seen him since I was a child, but heard he lives in another realm."

Loll blinked, as if trying to figure out if we were genuine or not. "So says you. Is that why you're looking for a portal?"

Before I could answer, Daire shook his head. "No. I just remember there being one in Rawenril."

"There was." Loll circled around to the back of his stall again. "The

King of the Dusk Court closed it. Said the Middle Course was his now. Of course, none of us here have laid eyes on the man, though we hear he's really Sluagh." He glanced up at us from his work, and it was clear he was gauging our reaction.

"I'm sorry to hear that," I replied. "I don't know this court. Is it new?" The conversation was getting sticky, so it was best to plead ignorance.

He shrugged his hunchbacked shoulders. "Could be."

"Okay, well, thanks for your help." Daire slipped his arm around my shoulder. It wasn't just an outward show of affection; it was to steer us clear of a likely spy.

"Ugh! Note to self, Daisy. Don't volunteer information!"

"It's okay. We didn't use our real names."

I inhaled. "I suppose, and no one knows about my pendent but you and Merlin. Not even Sorcha." I fidgeted with Daire's hand on my shoulder. "I can't believe that cretin's reach made it to the in between. What's next? The Rugged Peaks and the dwarf realm?"

"I don't think he'll stop until he controls all of Avalon. After that, what's to stop him from moving into the human realm?"

The thought was sobering, but I didn't press.

"Let's find that running water and get your sprite friends to help us out of here." Daire glanced over his shoulder. "I'm starting to feel like the walls are closing in."

Melancholy tapped on my shoulder, and I wanted to curl up under the covers with Daire and never come out. "The walls *are* closing. Not just on us, but on all these innocents. I hope this prophecy Merlin spoke about happens sooner than later."

"Listen." Daire lifted his head. "Do you hear that? It's like a dull roar."

"It sounds a little like a waterfall, but it couldn't be. We're underground."

He tugged my hand, steering us through the crowded thoroughfare until we got to the edge of the main street. It wasn't a waterfall we heard. It was a waterwheel.

"Will that do?" he asked.

"Kip and York didn't specify naturally running or not, so running water is running water." We rushed around to the overflow where the water churned in white bubbles. I took the summoning wish off my neck and then detached the coin from the chain. "Here goes nothing."

I tossed the wish into the bubbling water, and in seconds, the water parted, and Kip and York climbed out from the muddy bottom. "Milady! We told ya we'd take care of the rest!"

Besides seeing Daire standing beneath the veranda balustrade, I was never so happy to see two friendly faces. I embraced them both, and we laughed like children. When I finally let go, they both looked at me, their heads angled in the exact same way.

"So, who's this?" Kip asked, elbowing York. "I bet tis' himself."

Daire looked as though he didn't know how to reply.

"Yes, Kip. This is *himself.*" I caught myself before I used Daire's real name. "I'm Daisy, and this is Jay."

The sprite stared at me as if I'd gone round the bend. "But I thought..."

"Ach, Kip. You really are thick." York shut him up. "I'll explain later. In the meantime, we need to get our friends to safety. You know Rawenril isn't what it used to be."

Kip nodded. "Very well. As long as you explain it." He dug in his pocket for another coin, and he tossed it into the water as well. This time the water didn't part. It dried up completely. Instead of a muddy bottom, there was a shimmering void.

"Is that what I think it is?" I asked.

"A portal, Aye. Now jump, before the feckin' thing closes on us. We only brought one coin for the toll." The four of us held hands and jumped. There was no vortex. No gateway. We simply landed in a different part of the Middle Course.

I blinked once and then squeezed my eyes shut, allowing my senses to equalize, but when I opened my eyes again, Aerith was waiting for us.

"Eden of the Summer Court. What brings you to us?" Before I could answer, her gaze moved to Daire. "Ah, I see."

The Leanan Sidhe was as lovely as I remembered. Only now, instead of trees and the beauty of the forest surrounding her, there were rock walls studded with natural gems that glowed in low jewel tones. An underground waterfall cascaded into a wide pool, with soft carpets of green and white moss climbing the cavern walls like tapestries. The effect was a subterranean palace fit for this ancient queen.

"Daire, this is Aerith, Forest Mistress and Guardian of the Oaks." I couldn't remember her actual title, but it sounded close.

"I'm much more than that, Eden, but I know your heart meant no disrespect." She circled us both, her eyes noting everything. "Son of the Winter Court. What brings you here?"

"Eden. She is my betrothed."

Her green gaze softened. She inhaled, touching my shoulder as she circled my side. "I think there's another reason. A tiny, but very, very important reason you chose to risk such a treacherous jump from the surface realms."

Dealing with Aerith was like dealing with Merlin. There was no getting away from them knowing the truth of a situation, so it didn't pay to try. I told her our entire story so fast, I thought I'd run out of breath. "It was either a jump to the in between, and from there, passage to the human realm, or live as prisoners or worse. We chose exile in the human realm."

"Is that all?"

I told her about Sorcha and Cian, and about my suspicions about Taltos, but she already knew. "...and I think I may be pregnant," I blurted at the end.

"Darling girl..." Aerith smiled, and the cavernous palace brightened. "There is nothing to think. You are with child. A baby that belongs both to the Seelie and the Unseelie. One who will carry the hopes of all Avalon."

No. The ancient had to be mistaken. "Aerith, with all due respect, I think Merlin would've mentioned something this monumental, and he didn't. I think the fates may have woven a wrong thread."

"The fates aren't wrong, Eden. The prophecy was very clear: A child of winter and summer, ruled by moon and sun, elemental born with powers twelve to fell the bonds of Avalon. Merlin knew from long ago, but his hands were tied. He was forbidden to interfere."

The old Druid's words echoed in my head again. If the Sidhe ever gave birth to one who pulled power from all twelve elements, the event would herald an end and a new beginning for the Fae.

My head spun. "But Merlin *did* interfere! He was the one who made it possible for Daire and me to be together. He facilitated everything, and he admitted as much to my mother."

"Ah, yes." Aerith's face was both wistful and resigned. "Merlin does tend to bend the rules at times. He only did so because he loves you, and he knew you and Daire were destined to be together and be the parents to this foretold child. He also knew you'd both do whatever was necessary to ensure your child would live."

Daire scoffed. "Ensure the child would live, only to be a sacrificial lamb later? I don't think so. We'll live as mortals before I allow that to happen. I'll have our powers, our natures, bound. Stripped. I know it can be done."

"That is a choice, true," Aerith replied. "One of many you will face in both the near future, and the far."

"No." I shook my head again. "I won't have it, either. Our child will live in peace, to grow in love and encouragement. Not war."

Daire and I didn't bolt for our lives and our future, only to be sucked back to sacrifice the child we ran to save. I shook my head, but Aerith took my hand and joined it together with Daire's. She covered our laced fingers with her own hand—and a vision hit. A girl, with Daire's raven hair and eyes that were a perfect blend of emerald and storm blue. She brandished a sword. Was it my sword? I couldn't tell. Only that it swirled with glyphs and runes glowing with iridescence and power.

Excalibur? No way.

"You cannot change what the fates have put in motion, Eden." Aerith's smile wasn't sad, just knowing. "Your child and her destiny were written into the threads of fate long before the compact fractured between the realms."

"She's just a baby! She's not even born yet!" My entire body quaked, and a scared sob left my mouth. Daire wrapped his arms around my shoulders, rubbing warmth back into my shivering form.

"A baby that won't be born unless you take care to keep her safe. Factions already gather, hunting you. I don't have to tell you whom. You already know. Word of the prophecy has leaked, and avarice and mendacity rule more than ever. When the time comes, the child of winter and summer will have the option to either take up her mantle, or not. The fates cannot interfere in free will."

I perked up at that. "Our daughter will have a choice?"

Aerith inclined her head. "As did you. Merlin warned about choices and their consequences. He warned change was coming, and now it's here. He also knew his time with you in this incarnation was over the moment your mother questioned him about the prophecy. He cannot be with you now, but he will be again. When needed."

Daire kissed the top of my head, holding me closer. "What do we do now, Aerith?" he asked. "It seems we are at your mercy."

"I would have you stay here, but even the in between is no longer safe. Your intuition was correct, which tells me the fates are guiding you. You must vanish into the human realm." Aerith turned, taking two vials from one of her ladies. "One is a serum to mask your Sidhe nature. The other to reveal it. One drop is all you will need of either." I opened my mouth to question, but she shook her head. "No, neither serum will hurt the baby."

With a wave of her hand, four satchels appeared. "Identification. Money, and clothes. Kip and York will accompany you, for now, as safeguards and intermediaries with me, here." She touched the side of her nose the way Merlin did. "It seems my old friend has rubbed off on me when it comes to bending the rules for those we love."

Kip tossed a coin into the cavern pool, and it opened the same as it did at the waterwheel. "Ready when you are, milady." He rubbed his hands together. "I've always wanted to see the human realm."

York cuffed him again. "Quiet, you dolt. Can't ye see they're having a moment?"

Daire grinned. "Are they always like that?"

"Pretty much."

He turned, and the humor in his eyes sobered a bit. Not shadowed, and not sad. Just real. "Forever and a day, love. Say the word. It's our leap of fate."

"Forever and a day, but it's much more than a leap of fate. It's a leap of Fae."

Epilogue

DAIRE HELD OUT HIS HAND. "This washed up from the Faewyn Sea years ago. I found it amid the rocks along the shore where we first parted. I don't know why I picked it up then, or why I shoved it in my pocket the night we escaped the Summer Court, but I'm happy I did. As far as I can tell, the carvings on it show it's a piece of something dedicated to Danú many eons ago. Something in its aura tells me the stone possesses a spark of creation that led to the birth of our realm."

"Our realm. As in Avalon as a whole?" I reached out a hand to touch the sea worn stone. Its carvings were barely visible, but when either of us ran a finger over the flat surface, they glowed with a faint blue sheen making the markings a little easier to read.

Daire put the stone back into a black velvet pouch pulled from his pocket. "I think it might be perfect for our needs, but we need to talk to Aerith. Merlin would be the better choice, but since he's not available, she's our next bet."

"Our needs?"

"Eden, we're exiles now, and not by choice. If our baby holds the future of Avalon in her hands, then we need the odds stacked in her favor. Even with Aerith on our side, we can only teach her so much from a distance. For our daughter to fulfill whatever fate has planned, she needs to know where she comes from firsthand. She needs to know the realms, and they her. What do you think?"

I moved away from him to sit on the living room couch in the cozy cottage York and Kip found for us. We'd been in the human realm for a few weeks. Everything was strange and new. Even the smell of the air and the taste of the water. I had no idea how much time had passed in Avalon in comparison. Aerith never said, and I didn't ask. I suppose I didn't want to know. Not that Sorcha, Cian, or even my mother would change much. The Fae didn't age the same way as humans. Not that it mattered. We were here, and they were there.

"No." My hand went to my belly, protective and defiant.

"No, you don't agree, or no, you don't want to discuss it?"

I wasn't about to argue either point. By now Sorcha's eyes were the emerald green of the heir apparent, telling the entire Summer Court I was no longer part of the plan. Would they think me dead? Who knew? Did they care? Probably not. My mother would spin my sudden disappearance to whatever suited her political needs best.

The thought of Sorcha carrying the burden of being Tianna's heir apparent without the benefit of Merlin for a mentor made my heart ache. At least Cian was her chosen consort. That my sister had someone of her own in her corner helped me breathe a little easier. If only.

Life as we knew it was over the moment Sorcha snuck Daire into my mother's farce of a forced engagement party. Still, the truth of just how much our life had changed didn't hit until Aerith allowed me to say goodbye. I didn't know how the ancient facilitated our ethereal contact without tipping her hand to Taltos, but she did. She found a way through that unspoken, almost extrasensory way twins communicate, and the memory was bittersweet.

A soft wind off an illusory beach mimicked the shoreline beneath the Summer Palace. The breeze teased Sorcha's wispy blonde hair the way it had so many times before. It wasn't real, of course. None of it was, despite how warm and strong my sister's hands felt in mine.

"I can forgive you and Daire for choosing to bolt, but that you left without a single word of warning?" An all too familiar huff left her mouth. "You have no idea the chaos you left behind."

She was right, no matter how good my guess. "I'm sorry, Sorcha. We had no choice. It was jump or be jumped. Mother sent Caxton to the beach. Either someone saw me with Daire, or they saw me with someone, and she wasn't going to take a chance on my ruining her plans any more than I already had."

She humphed, but there was neither dismissal nor annoyance in the sound. "I guess you have me to thank, then. If I hadn't snuck Daire into Mother's farce of a forced engagement party, you might be a prisoner of the court by now. So good on me."

"That's very true, even if none of us realized it at the time."

"Mother is practiced at political maneuvering. We should've guessed."

I shook my head. "It's not our fault there's no warmth in the woman who is supposed to love and protect, not only us, but her realm. You have to be vigilant now. She's vicious on a regular basis. She'll be worse now that she feels cornered and outmaneuvered."

"Don't remind me." The shadow crossing her face spoke volumes about the questioning she went through, and Goddess knows what other measures Caxton employed to get her to talk.

"Sorcha, I—"

She stopped me cold. "I don't know what you and Daire have planned, and I don't want to know. Just promise me you won't leave me alone for good."

"You have Cian, Sorcha. Hold onto that for all it's worth." I paused, matching her vise grip on my hands with my own. "Please, please, heed what I said the last time I saw you. Don't wait to marry Cian or it might be too late. Trust no one but each other. It's not safe."

For all my sister's free-spirited bravado, dread shadowed her still olive-green eyes. The fact her eyes hadn't changed color yet told me the Summer Court and its queen hadn't given up the search for me as the heir apparent. I was the key to holding up their end of whatever bargain they struck with the self-proclaimed King of the Dusk Court. It was only a matter of time, though. For Sorcha. For me. For my baby.

Sorcha opened her mouth to argue or question, but then she closed it again. Plausible deniability. It was a permanent state of affairs for us when it came to our mother and her court. It's the only reason she survived the interrogation that followed after Daire and I jumped.

Emotions warred on my sister's face, but she finally nodded and then kissed my cheek. The illusory feeling was part tingle and spark, part feathery soft, but all Sorcha, nonetheless.

"I hate not having a choice, Edie, but I understand." Tears glistened unshed in her eyes. "Just find a way to let me know you're okay, or I swear I'll burn your favorite hoodie and matching sweats."

I half-laughed at that. "Keep them as collateral until I come back. I don't know when or how, but I will...someday." Aerith warned me not to reveal too much, so I didn't go into detail about where we were or why.

"Good." Sorcha exhaled at that. "Because I do not want to be queen."

I almost didn't reply, but I couldn't leave my sister with false hope. Not when practically everything and everyone around her was two-faced. "I'm not coming back to be queen, Sorcha." I moved her hand to my belly, and I didn't need to say anymore. The prophecy about my baby uniting the fractured realms would be common knowledge soon enough, and the stuff of legend shortly thereafter.

"What about Bain?" she asked. "Him too?"

I shrugged. Daire's brother wasn't my concern, and the less I said, the better for everyone. "Just worry about you and Cian. Bain is his father's son. He'll wheel and deal and revel in the power that comes with being the heir to the Winter Court, once they realize Daire is as gone as I am. Hell, it might be a commiserating moment for Lachlan and Tianna, bonding over their treacherous and disloyal children." I broke off my grin, meeting her eyes. "I'm sorry, Sorcha. I never wanted to put you in this position."

Rock. Hard place.

"Cian and I will figure it out. Thought, I think it's kind of cool Aerith was able to tap into our twin powers so we could say goodbye" Sorcha was trying to be cheerful, and I appreciated it. "I never told you, but I was jealous of everything you learned in Merlin's Keep when it came to your power and the rigors of court. Mother never allowed me the same training, so I guess the joke's on her now." Her smile paled, and she squeezed my hand unable to say more.

"On the bright side, maybe Aerith will let us use this twin connection again. It's certainly better than human realm methods."

"Fact."

The bittersweet moment ebbed with the ice-cold weight that Sorcha wouldn't be in the next room or just down the hall. She wouldn't plop onto *my bed for a good gossip or slam into my room to bicker. Daire was my other half, but she was my sister. Warts and all.*

I pulled her into a bear hug, holding on for as long as I could. Sorcha faded in my arms, leaving me alone on the illusory beach. In that moment, the once soft breeze turned cold and eerie, as though someone watched, and the import set the hair on the nape of my neck on end...

"Eden, are you listening?" Daire's voice brought me out of my revery. Aerith's twin gift was weeks ago, and this was now. "We eventually need to go home, and this stone might be the answer." He sat beside me on the sofa. "Of course, Aerith will need to see it. Merlin too, if he wasn't gone."

My hand was still on my belly. We jumped to a safety that was fragile at best. That cold, knowing wind on that illusory beach showed me the truth of our tenuous state as much as it showed me it would be years, if not decades, before I spoke with my sister again. Still, Daire's life had been thrown into the upside down as much as mine and he deserved an answer.

"Eden..."

I turned to meet his eyes. "You're right. Eventually we will need to go back, but not until the prophecy calls. Until then, not a moment sooner. The rivals of sea and sky can wait..."

Thank you for reading! Did you enjoy? Please add your review because nothing helps an author more and encourages readers to take a chance on a book than a review.

And don't miss more of the *The Avalon Courts* series coming soon. Be sure to sign up for her newsletter at mariannemorea.com

Until then, discover MIST AND DIVIDE, by City Owl author, M.E. Shotwell. Turn the page for a sneak peek!

You can also sign up for the City Owl Press newsletter to receive notice of all book releases!

Sneak Peek of Mist and Divide

BY M.E. SHOTWELL

Cold.

Just how far it ebbed its way into my chest, I wasn't sure.

I blinked it away. Heard it through numb ears. Tasted it on frozen lips.

The rows of alabaster trees in Ashwan Forest didn't seem to care about the cold or the blood that had shunted to my vital organs. Two hours now and my hands and feet suffered for it.

That was the thing about the cold. It betrayed the body, no matter the amount of fabric and hides and furs. It seeped into the thinnest cracks in my armor—a snagged sleeve over my wrist, a tear in my cloak, a pinhole in my boot.

I tightened the collar of fur around my neck in aching slowness, my hair tucked between my ears and cloak. My hood lay on my shoulders, out of the way of my peripheral vision.

I had tracked the otari when the sun hit low, the time it abandoned the sea to forage for nocturnal critters as they awakened. Its tracks were easy enough to locate. Two front flipper arches, like boomerangs, etched into the snow, along with the rear hoof. The telltale signs of a mature otari, the only animal left on Corallon whose fat was dense enough to provide fuel. The meat it provided was a bonus, albeit a slightly chewy and bitter one.

Actually killing it took skill and most of all, patience. They were skittish creatures, jumping to alertness at a foot's crunch of snow, a muted cough, or sometimes what seemed like nothing audible.

Now was the hardest part. I waited for the next breeze for noise cover, then reached beneath my cloak to the pouch tied around my waist. I secured a pellet, a smooth rock amongst my collection of ammunition. In my other hand was my sling, a bit of rope with a pocket along the middle for the projectile. I secured the end's loop around my forefinger and pinched the other end's knot. I'd only get one shot.

The sling worked best by spinning it across my body, in a figure eight, then releasing. But here I had to make my best single swing and release.

I moved my hands out of the cloak's opening on my right. It made no sense to have it open in the middle, down my torso, when hunting. That was an archer's preference.

Evella, the sideways hunter, Reil would say. Then I'd tease him about his dwindling arrow supply and knock out our dinner with one try of the sling.

But he wasn't here now. He couldn't block the otari from fleeing. He couldn't share in the spoils. He couldn't comfort me, or make me laugh, or reassure me that there was still goodness to be had in this world.

There was only me.

With the rope's ends in my left hand and pellet secured in the right, I froze.

The otari perked up its tiny triangular ears for a moment, then slapped them back down.

Now.

In one fluid movement, I swung the rock pellet in an arch, releasing the rope at the right moment to fling it directly toward the animal's head.

A crack of a branch behind me snapped the animal out of its calm, my pellet nipping its hind hoof as it raced away.

Now I had two problems. The otari got away.

And someone else was near.

I wrapped my sling back into my hip satchel and unsheathed my blade from its holster. The metal was barely longer than my hand, wrist to fingertips, but it did the job well enough. These days it was hard to find metal, let alone someone who could work it into weaponry. At least on Corallon.

I crouched low and snuck right to get behind the intruder. The snow reached over my sorry excuse for boots to my calves. If it was a hunter, keeping low was the safest option, despite my frozen legs. It wasn't uncommon to have an arrow fly by from unskilled hunters who didn't see me, or the occasional one who did.

A grunt came from ahead. The breeze whirred in my face as I stood downwind, and I smelled the newness of him. No otari oil on his fingers, or ale on his breath, or wood smoke in his hair, or dirtied animal fur on his body.

He sat between two alabaster trees, like a plump flea amidst the white teeth of a comb. The summer forest, though short lived, provided tall grass between the skinny, white-barked trees, filling in the floor and offering plenty of shelter for woodland creatures. But in the winter, the grass lay dormant. The forest was spikes of white that branched into full webs of limbs and twigs in the canopy, as if stretching and searching for their long-lost leaves.

We were near the northern edge of the forest, right before the trees gave way to acres of field. If I ran out to him from behind, he could run for it in that direction. Beyond that stood my family's home. The snow-covered field in winter minimized unwanted visitors, animal, or human. I wasn't about to let him be one.

His other option would be to run west, where he'd have ten or twelve paces before reaching the cliff to the sea.

I took a final quiet step to better make out my adversary, a man on his knees catching his breath.

In a leap I wrapped one arm around him, my blade in the other at his neck.

"Don't move."

He remained still, his body thin but solid under the thick cloak. I wasn't sure if I could've overtaken him if he had snuck up on me.

"You could very well slice me," he whispered. "I do realize that. But not before I'd yell and attract those Raiders."

His breath smelled fresh, like a sprig of mint with a rich spice.

"What are you talking about?"

He turned and looked at me, his face light brown with the start of dark stubble, a contrast stark against my white skin and the barely whiter snow. He tipped his head to the bush. "Down there."

"Don't try anything." I kept the sharp end of my blade aimed at him as I released my grip and crept along the ground. He could easily run. To be honest I wasn't sure if I'd go after him. I simply wanted to make sure *he* wasn't after *me*. Running would only alleviate that concern.

The sun had long gone over the horizon, but as I reached the land's edge, I could make out a clunk of rusted metal in the moonlight. Four figures carried it through the surf, onto the sand in organized heaves. Two of them collapsed on the beach by the structure while the other two caught their breath. Their clothes were dark in color and clung to their bodies, unlike the amalgam of my pelts and furs and cloak. Every now and then someone moved just right for the moonlight to shine off something on their clothing—a clasp or buckle. Or maybe it was some strange armor.

"What are they doing here, so far north?" I whispered to the man who remained ten paces behind. It wasn't entirely surprising to see Raiders. The town reported more frequent sightings in the last several days. It was hard to know which rumors emanating from the townsfolk were true. They used gossip and conjecture as their main form of entertainment, each tale taller than the last. Apparently at least one of them was based in truth.

The stranger crept closer to me, crunching and panting.

"Are you trying to attract attention?" I whispered.

He caught my glare. "Apologies."

I pictured throwing him off the side—for the noise, for invasion of the space he occupied around me. And for making me lose the otari.

The four on the beach chatted. I looked at the young man and placed my finger over my lips, then inched as close to the edge of the cliff without hurling over, my stomach to the ground. Whatever they were doing here, it couldn't be good. If there was some plan to attack Corallon, or take more of its young inhabitants, I could warn everyone. It would give them time to collect their weapons and defenses, come up with a plan. I needed to know how many more there were, if this was their targeted landing point, anything that could help. Perhaps if I did something good for the town, for Corallon, then my past would be forgotten...

One of the Raiders looked up, and I pulled back, knocking over the man who had barely balanced himself squatting.

"Someone is up there." A voice echoed from below.

I rolled over and planted myself on top of the man, the tip of the blade near his eye. "Don't. Move." I mouthed the words, and he nodded with the smallest of movement.

The voices below continued. "It might be—"

"If we've been discovered already, our mission is compromised. We must leave."

"But what about—"

"Not tonight, son."

The other two whined, then grunting commenced as they pushed their metal ship into the sea. I waited for the splashing to cease before braving another glance.

"I think they're gone." I released the stranger entirely from my body weight. But not from my suspicion.

I dared a peek at the shore. The beach had cleared, their metal ship nowhere on the water. I stood, scanning the ripples of the water. It was rumored Raiders used enchanted steel to make underwater ships. Other hearsay highly doubtful proved true. How would steel float? What made it enchanted? It was nonsense.

But now I wasn't so sure. The moon gave up no objects floating on the sea's surface. In one moment the ship and its crew were on land, and the next, gone.

"They should call them Invisible Raiders, shouldn't they?"

I turned to my new neighbor. "What are you doing here? Who are you?"

"I could ask the very same of you." He brushed snow off his black cloak. It cried its age, that of a fresh, newer cloak. Older clothing, like what remained available in Corallon, was faded, tattered, and mended many times over. No stitch looked out of place, though the lighting was poor. As for his trousers, well, he'd get along better in the desert of Yobrol than the Corallon winter.

His indignation waned as I sized him up. "I was looking for food, if you must know."

"By the looks of it, you were sightseeing for food."

"What's that supposed to mean?"

I shook my head. Although he might get away with it more at this hour of night, a black cloak might as well have announced his arrival. Not to mention it didn't look like he had weapons on him. At least I didn't feel any when I pressed him to the ground.

"Are you traveling alone? With family?" I briefly scanned behind him, half afraid the whole ordeal was a trap laid out by a group of men.

He continued brushing off snow, having made it down to his knees. "I have no family."

I looked him in the eyes; they were deep brown, nearly black in the night. "You're a Displaced?"

He nodded once.

"From where?"

He sighed, seeming annoyed with my interrogation. I could very well just stab him instead. It wouldn't be hard seeing as I was still irritated he chased away the otari. Others out here wouldn't have hesitated to kill a stranger that chased away their prey.

"From the south."

"And how did you get here?"

"By heading north."

I drew my blade, aiming it at his chest. "I don't have the time or patience for games. I spent the better part of the evening tracking down the otari that you scared off, so I don't have much sympathy for you, either. In fact, I should ask you to pay for the loss."

He put up both hands. "Please. I apologize. I really don't have family, or shelter for tonight. I've had very little to eat besides...well, whatever it was that lady gave me yesterday morning that felt like leather and tasted worse."

There was only one food that could be described so distastefully and accurately. *Dried gunnel skin.* It wasn't animal skin at all, but a filet of gunnel smoked until it curled. They only lived along rocky shorelines and were a major food source when the waters were too cold for red sardines. Which meant he had traveled from the southern shore of Corallon to here in two days.

Which meant he was lying or, for what he lacked in survival skills, he made up for in quick feet.

"It's getting dark. I suggest we go our separate ways and try not to ever encounter each other again." I sheathed my blade and traipsed out of the forest edge into the blanketed field.

"Wait."

I stopped. *Don't turn around, Evella. You'll regret it.*

I pivoted back. Funny how my body didn't listen to my head.

"Can you at least point me in the right direction? May I walk with you until we reach a town?"

"I'm not going to town."

"Not going to town?" He nervously chuckled. "What, do you live out here in the open?"

"No, I live in a house. You may have heard of it. Walls made of stone. A roof."

"Sounds lovely."

I turned around and marched northward. This man had taken enough of my attention. And my fuel and meat. Mother and Father would be wondering about me. I wasn't to venture long past dusk. Mother would say it was because of the predatory animals and occasionally dangerous people, but I knew better. Most of the big game, save for the occasional boar or snowcat, had been hunted to extinction years ago, and as far as dangerous people, well, danger was relative.

No, I knew what she thought amid those words.

She didn't trust me. Despite being seen as too old to be living with my parents. Despite what I provided for them.

It wouldn't help my cause if I didn't show up home soon. My knees ached from all the standing, and the cold pierced my joints as I got into a steady pace. I tried ignoring the loud footsteps behind me, the stranger fighting the snow as if it took his feet hostage.

"You know I did kind of save your life back there."

I paused, foot mid-air waiting to grasp my next step.

"With the Raiders and all."

I considered his point. At least for the time it took my words to form. "Never mind that when they discovered us, they fled." I dabbed my nose on the back of my hand, the walk stirring circulation from both physical exertion and mental annoyance. "But, who knows? Maybe they would've chopped me to bits." The sarcasm oozed out my lips. That wasn't what Raiders did. At least not on land. While they had a reputation for pilfering towns and travelers for their food and supplies, Raiders preferred the more confusing crime of kidnapping, stealing away young men and women. I did fit the profile of those taken, being nineteen. But did anyone know what else they were looking for in their victims? Or what they did to those poor people?

"They could've taken you." Apparently wherever he was from, he'd heard the same.

"Then I wouldn't have to listen to you."

"That hurts."

I broke a smile, despite my efforts. He wasn't going to leave me alone unless I did kill him. Which, with the increased talking, didn't seem that implausible. I'm sure the town would love that. *Trapper Girl Murders Man Who Saved her Life*. Rolls off the gossip tongue.

However, if he was a Displaced, I couldn't leave him out for the night. A Displaced had no say, no choice in what happened. He couldn't help where or when the quakes struck. Or the why or how or who. No one knew the truth behind them.

All anyone could do was survive. To not help a Displaced was to let another person or family die.

It was Father's spoken policy—a Displaced was family. Unfortunately, not everyone felt the same.

"What's your name?"

He caught up to me through the snow, looking like a newborn deer grasping the concept of walking. "Arek. Uh, why do you ask?" His apprehension was almost endearing, half-cowered, ready to recoil as if I were a snake about to strike. I nearly felt sorry for him.

"Because I like to know the names of everyone who stays in my family's home."

"Really? You mean it?"

I sighed. "I can't let a Displaced stay out here for the night, especially not one looking as unprepared as you."

I winced despite myself. *You don't have to make the truth sound mean,* Mother had said.

Truth doesn't depend on feelings, Mother.

"Anyway, I'm Evella Trapper." I kept my hands within my cloak, hesitant to expose them to the cold and saving myself the formality of greeting customs. Elbow to elbow was too friendly, a hand to his shoulder and his on mine too formal not to mention awkward with the touching and closeness of it.

"Evella. Very well."

"Have you heard of it? My name?"

He swallowed slowly. "No. Should I have?"

I grinned, biting the inside of my cheek. "No. That's actually for the best." I began walking again, and he continued by my side.

"Why's that?"

I peeked at his oval face, his profile plain but strangely handsome in the moonlight. "Less explaining to do."

Don't stop now. Keep reading with your copy of MIST AND DIVIDE

Don't miss more of the *The Avalon Courts* series coming soon, and sign-up for Marianne Morea's newsletter at mariannemorea.com

Until then discover MIST AND DIVIDE, by City Owl author, M.E. Shotwell.

Ten Lands Divided. One Shattered Past. A Forbidden Magic on the Brink of Awakening.

In a world torn apart by the catastrophic Quake, Evella Trapper has lived a life of isolation on the northern banks of Corallon. For generations, her family has struggled to survive, relying on hunting and trapping to sustain them—but no matter how much time passes, the sins of her past still haunt her.

Everything changes when Evella meets Arek, a stranger displaced by the quakes, who reveals a shocking truth: the king has sent him to recruit her for a secret army, one that wields a powerful, forbidden magic —*Soulmagic.*

As the quakes grow stronger and threaten to tear the world apart, Evella embarks on a journey to master her powers. But her Soulmagic only emerges in her sleep, leaving her unable to fight back in the waking world. With the fate of her family, her homeland, and her own future at stake, she must confront her darkest fears—both the ones buried in her past and those that threaten the fragile peace of the present.

Joined by a team of *Soulmagi*, Evella faces the ghosts of her past, uncovers the deadly truth behind the quakes, and must make an impossible choice. Will she harness her power in time to protect the people she loves and secure the future she desperately wants?

Acknowledgments

When an author publishes a book, whether it's their first or their five hundredth, it's nothing less than a defining moment in their life. Since I began this writer's journey, I've run the gamut in terms of emotion...from *no excuses, do the work*...to *what was I thinking? To be careful what you ask for because you just might get it*!

Though I've been writing for the past decade, *Rivals of Sea and Sky* is my debut Romantasy and I'm thrilled! So many people have helped and encouraged me, even when the writing dragon had me spewing fire and belching smoke at every turn.

My unbelievably patient husband, Bill, for putting up with the insanity and verbal barrages that accompany being glued to my laptop for hours. Our three kids for knowing enough to leave Mom alone when she's writing.

My amazing team at City Owl Press, be it a developmental edit, a line edit, a proofread, or if I just need to bounce an idea, you guys rock!

And last but certainly not least, I want to thank God for all his blessings. The longer I live, the more I learn to appreciate what could very easily be taken for granted.

Enjoy the book!

About the Author

MARIANNE MOREA has always been a scribbler. From the time she could write her name, she has been making up stories, writing characters and dialogue in the corners of notebooks.

She has been married for 28 years, has three beautiful kids, three dogs, and a cat. She is a 2nd degree black belt in traditional Japanese karate and loves to travel. Her romantic and spontaneous husband shares that passion with her, so her stories get plenty of inspiration!

She is also a founding member and previous President of The Paranormal Romance Guild, a not-for-profit organization for readers and authors of the genre.

mariannemorea.com

facebook.com/mariannemoreaauthor

instagram.com/marianne_morea

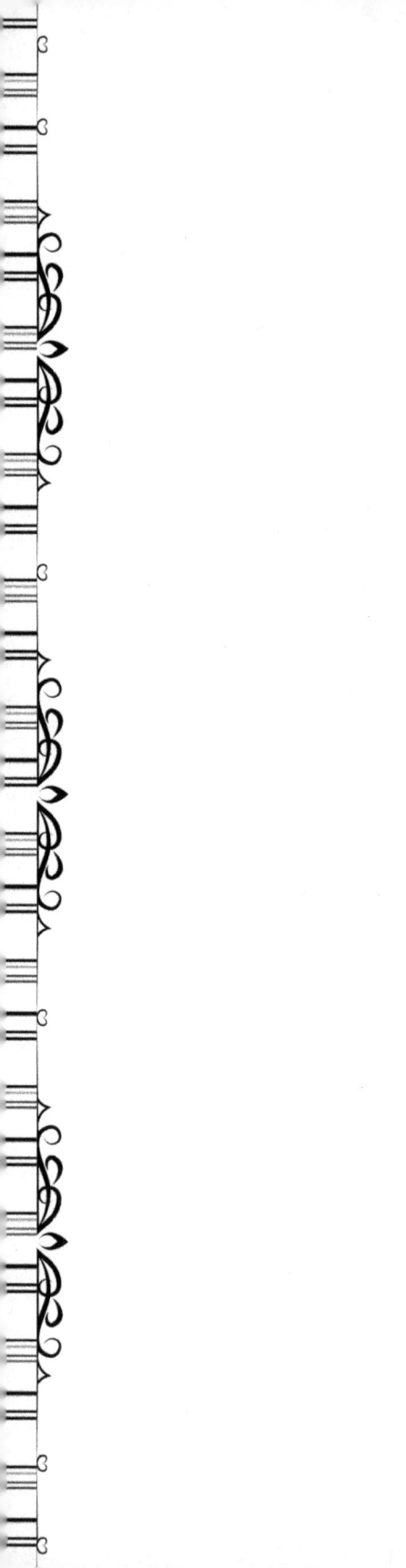

About the Publisher

City Owl Press is a cutting edge indie publishing company, bringing the world of romance and speculative fiction to discerning readers.

Escape Your World. Get Lost in Ours!

www.cityowlpress.com

facebook.com/CityOwlPress

x.com/cityowlpress

instagram.com/cityowlbooks

pinterest.com/cityowlpress

tiktok.com/@cityowlpress

www.ingramcontent.com/pod-product-compliance
Lightning Source LLC
Jackson TN
JSHW081857100825
88919JS00001B/1